Also by R.F. Ryan

FINNEGAN GILHOOLEY

Between Greed and Manhood

Of a Different Stamp

Scorn to be Guilty

As the Crucible Closed

As the Crucible Closed

Finnegan Gilhooley
Book 4

R.F. Ryan

As the Crucible Closed
Paperback Edition

Wolfpack Publishing
1707 E. Diana Street
Tampa, Florida 33610

www.wolfpackpublishing.com

Paperback ISBN 979-8-89567-586-1
eBook ISBN 979-8-89567-585-4

The frontier promoted the formation of a composite nationality for the American people. In the crucible of the frontier, the immigrants were Americanized, liberated and fused into a mixed race, English in neither nationality nor characteristics.

—Fredrick Jackson Turner, 1893

I can still see the butchered women and children lying heaped and scattered all along the crooked gulch as plain as when I saw them with eyes still young. And I can see that something else died there in the bloody mud, and was buried in the blizzard. A people's dream died there. It was a beautiful dream.

—Nicholas Black Elk, 1932

As the Crucible Closed

Chapter 1

FORT SMITH, ARKANSAS

December 24th, 1889

A FEW LANGUID SNOWFLAKES COULD BE SEEN FALLING outside the leaded window of the judge's home. Finnegan, as requested, hefted a large piece of oak and placed it on the blaze inside the fireplace. With his chore seen to, he returned to his chair just in time to receive his coffee from the lady of the house. With a warm drink to complete the cozy surroundings, there was little more a man might wish to possess, other than an after-dinner cigar.

He nodded to the Judge's wife. "Thank you, Mary."

She shook one motherly finger at him. "Do not partake of too much; it will keep you up all night."

"I will make a best effort to be abstentious." He withdrew his preferred brand of smoke from a jacket pocket and then produced two more.

The lady nodded to the assembled Christmas Eve revelers. "I am off to bed, gentlemen." She pointed to her husband, the Honorable Judge Isaac Parker. "Do not stay up too late. We have much to do in the morning to make ready for the grandchildren."

The judge nodded solemnly "Even on the birthday of our Lord and savior there is no rest for a grandfather."

"Good night, gentlemen." Mary nodded all around and left to the chorus of goodnight wishes returned to her.

Finnegan passed his two spare cigars to his host and the other guest. "I took the liberty of procuring you a Daniel Webster, Charles. As I recall, you have found my locally procured stock to be too harsh for your taste.

Charles Maledon, the country's best known and longest serving hangman, nodded in approval of the gift. "I am terribly fond of Websters, Finnegan, but seldom can justify the expense." He smiled down at the cigar. "Many thanks."

"It is Christmas, Charles. Some extra expense is warranted." Finnegan lit his cigar and let out a plume of smoke as he stared out the window toward the town's cemetery.

The judge moved toward the window as he sparked his own cigar. "It seems strange, does it not, gentlemen, that Belle should be lying out there as we sit here enjoying our after-dinner coffee?" He chuckled. "Not that I ever felt the need to invite the woman to Christmas dinner, but still, it seems rather off around here since she departed. I believe if she appeared at the door this night, I would readily invite her in."

Finnegan looked over to his friend. "I should think the requests levied by specters should be honored regardless of the date, Isaac."

The judge nodded. "Quite right. Quite right."

"Ah, Hell's bells." Maledon bit the tip from his cigar and carefully deposited the removed potion in an ashtray. "Foolish damn talk if I have ever heard it. If specters existed I would have them flitting about my brow so constantly I would never get anything done. Gentlemen, I would not dare to postulate as to whether Belle Starr currently resides above or below, but I know to a certainty that she will not be ascending your front stair this evening, Isaac."

The judge shook his head. "No, I suppose she will not." He puffed his cigar. "I suppose my true lament on that score is our continued inability to discover the identity of her murderer so that the three of us might conspire to send him to face Belle, or whatever justice resides on the other side."

Finnegan gave the aged judge a considered look. "Isaac, if you do not mind my saying so, you seem particularly fixated on the late Belle Starr this evening. Not that I would speak ill of the dead, but I was under the impression that you did not much care for the lady while she lived."

"It is not precisely that I miss her, Finnegan." The judge smiled. "Her demeanor was never to my liking. It would be more accurate to say that I miss what she represented, and I dislike the change her passing and the passing of those like her promotes. These are a time of great flux, gentlemen."

Finnegan puffed his cigar and gave the declaration some thought. In February of that year Finnegan had been out attempting to track down one of the many miscreants he had been bringing to the Judge in return for bounties the last few years. Instead of the miscreant, he had found the body of a woman lying in the road, clearly murdered and left to molder. Finnegan had loaded the corpse on his pack mule and returned to Fort Smith, where the woman was readily identified as Belle Starr, a lady of renown to, apparently, everyone other than Finnegan Gilhooley. Since February, the Judge had suggested several suspects for the killing and the various suggestions had been looked into by Finnegan and the other marshals in the court's employ. As far as Finnegan was concerned, any of the men he had spoken with regarding the crime would have richly deserved a bullet or the rope, but there was no factual proof that they deserved either specifically for the crime of killing Belle Starr. Such petty nuances were of great importance to the Judge, so the crime remained unsolved and the perpetrator unpunished. So far during his time in Arkansas and Oklahoma, Finnegan had found rather few men who, in his opinion, did not warrant shooting, but the Judge held to a higher standard and Finnegan was obliged to follow the set precepts while he was ostensibly in the court's employ.

The gunman knocked ash into a nearby tray. "It cannot be that the poor woman's demise came as a surprise to you, Isaac. She was, all told, famous for keeping company with ruffians, rustlers, robbers, and the like. While I am loath to quote such a scurrilous periodical, as I recall, the *Police Gazette* referred to her as no less than the bandit queen of Oklahoma."

The judge smiled and shook his head at the memory of Miss Belle's infamy. "She was unique in that regard." He peered out the window a moment longer. "No, my friend, it is not that the woman's passing surprised me in any way. It would be more apt to say that I find the current lack of surprises worrisome these days."

Maledon arched one eyebrow. "The lack of surprises, Isaac?"

The aging adjudicator slowly nodded. "Yes, Charles. Just once during my tenure in this wilderness I would have liked to have been surprised, but a departure from the predictable would have been especially welcome these last few months." He sighed. "The word has come down that what remains of the Indian Territory will be opened to settlers when the spring thaw arrives. What little remains since the land rush of the previous April is to go up for grabs, as well. Less fanfare will attend it, but the end result will be the same.

They have not made a formal announcement as of yet, but it shall occur, sure as sunset."

Finnegan rubbed his chin. "Well, I suppose it was somewhat naïve to believe that such a wide swath of arable ground would be left to the ownership of the Indians."

The judge's eyes narrowed. "Naïve? It was promised to them in perpetuity."

Finnegan smiled. "The promises of Congressmen are capricious at best, and fabrications at worst, Isaac. No sane man places much stock in them."

"Hmmm. Yes." The old man returned to his chair. "If Congressmen are to be trusted so little, how much weight would you give to the whimsies of Supreme Court justices?"

Maledon groaned and sat forward a bit in his chair. "Say it ain't so, Isaac."

"If only I could, Charles."

Finnegan knocked more ash into the tray. He did not understand the reference. "Something troubles you regarding the Supreme Court, Isaac?"

"It troubles me that they have seen fit to worm their way into my business." The judge stared at the gunman for a moment, seeing he did not understand. "For more than a score of years, Finnegan, there has been no appeal from my court involving capital punishment. I was the court of last resort and Mr. Maledon was the mechanism by which justice was delivered. Now..." He clutched one fist open and shut a few times before laying the hand on his leg. "Now, the collection of lawyers that have settled in this town, not unlike the scum at the bottom of a fetid pond, have seen fit to pester and prod Washington city to the point that they have broken to the pressure and allowed Supreme Court oversight regarding my decisions. I fear we have seen the last of that rare animal known as justice in this far-flung land, my friends."

Finnegan shook his head. "I must admit, I have never been completely comfortable with the practice of hanging. It may seem a meaningless distinction, but I greatly prefer to shoot those evil men I encounter rather than turning them over to other men to sort out. Having admitted as much to you fellows, I thoroughly understand the necessity of a court such as yours, Isaac, and an apparatus such as yours, Charles. Men such as yourselves are required if one wishes to bring civilization to a wild land, as this once was."

The judge nodded. "Yes, well, that was not the opinion of those in Washington. It was not their opinion when they continued to diminish my jurisdiction. It was not their opinion when they chose to continually break their word to the tribes. It is not their opinion now that my very purpose has been called into question. After all, what is the purpose of a judge if he must have his rulings forsworn by other men in other courts? From this point on, I will be little better than a clerk."

Maledon sneered and spit down into a nearby cuspidor. "Them lawbookers back east might be slipshod when it comes to handing out their edicts, but there's one thing they ain't taken into consideration. I never lost a wink of sleep hanging men for you, Isaac. I trust your good judgement, but I'll be damned if I'll hang a man on the word of some dandy who ain't never even met the man in question, and sure as hell won't be there to see the bastard swing. A real man ain't afraid to gaze on what he sowed. I won't hang nobody for men who would declare such business by the damned mail."

Parker smiled at his old friend. "I appreciate the sentiment, Charles, but I doubt the issue will amount to much. The entire purpose of giving the higher court oversight regarding my rulings is to prevent all future hangings. These men aim to take the teeth out of our good justice." He pointed across the room. "In some manner, they agree with the esteemed Mr. Gilhooley."

Finnegan held up one hand. "I did not say anything explicitly, Isaac."

"No, perhaps only implied a bit, eh?" The judge shook his cigar at the gunman.

"Implied what?" Maledon did not enjoy obfuscation.

Parker cleared his throat. "As my Pinkerton friend described it, mechanisms such as the Fort Smith court were necessary to settle this wild land. Of course, an idea is implied in the statement. Mr. Gilhooley would suggest, if only subtly, that once the wilderness has passed away, it would be best to let the court and the scaffold pass with it."

Finnegan cast a rather sorrowful look on the old man. "I do not know if I would say it is for the best, but it is surely the way of the world, Isaac. All things come to an end in their own good time. Fighting the progression rarely profits a man."

The judge grimaced. "Ah, yes, but it is our nature, is it not, Finnegan? You use a gun, I make use of legal doctrine, Charles has his rope. We fight. We are fighters; it is in our character to lay siege against what offends or attacks us. Even if the cause is hopeless, we still feel compelled."

The gunman slowly nodded. "I have always felt compelled, my friend. Although, as I age, I find making peace with the lack of victory to be more a formality than a harsh disillusionment. I might go so far as to say I have come to expect it."

Maledon slowly raised his scarecrow-like frame up out of his chair and stood before the fireplace. "Gentlemen, while I enjoy a good bit of speculation into philosophy as much as the next man, I feel I really must turn this conversation toward more practical matters."

Finnegan cocked his head to one side. “Such as, Charles?”

“Such as, what the hell any of us are to be doing with ourselves come the spring? Isaac has more or less said they’re to shrink his court down to the size of a thimble. As you said, them Washington city pencil pushers ain’t going to allow no more hangings.” The greyed executioner motioned to Finnegan. “And what with the dissolution of Indian Territory, I guess your bandit hunting won’t be too damned profitable anymore. Not much reason for bad men to hide out around here if there’s going to be a Methodist revival every night and a milk cow tethered to every tree.”

Finnegan scowled and recoiled a bit. “By God, Charles, you do paint a bleak picture. If that comes to fruition, I cannot say as I would prefer to stay in the vicinity.”

The hangman stuck his cigar between his lips. “Nor I, Finnegan.”

Parker enjoyed a short chuckle. “Perhaps the three of us should open a mercantile near the graveyard. The citizens might enjoy receiving their produce from three solid citizens such as ourselves.”

Maledon offered a quizzical stare. “Isaac, I cannot say as I would care for that. Truth be told, I would not care to stay in this area at all if we are to no longer be engaged in our current business. I ardently believe that the fear of the rope is all that keeps most of these miscreants in line. They may come to lynch us when they learn we can no longer act in our official capacity.”

Finnegan rubbed his chin. “While I assume you were jesting, Isaac, our friend Charles raises an excellent point. I do not believe life will be very pleasant for me around here once it is known that I no longer enjoy the protection of the hanging judge. I rather pride myself on being quick, but a man must sleep sometime."

Parker shrugged. "Sadly, I would concur, gentlemen. To put it bluntly: once my teeth are officially removed, I think it would be best if you both got the hell out of here. I would imagine the deputies will be able to operate free from reprisals, but the hangman and the killer will be better off removing themselves."

Finnegan sighed and lifted his coffee cup. "Well, then, gentlemen, to the end of an era." The other men lifted their cups, as well. "I must say, it was jolly good fun while it lasted."

Maledon took a swig of coffee and lowered his cup. "Eh, these last few years were nothing. You should have been here at the start when we did a considerably more brisk business. Should have come down in '76 or '77 instead of hanging all those coal miners up north."

Finnegan shook his head. "I have told you many times that I had nothing to do with those men swinging."

Maledon smoothed his beard. "Sorry, I guess I just assumed you was lying."

Finnegan shrugged. "A fair enough assumption." He turned to the judge. "What is next for you, Isaac, now that your wilderness is to be forcibly settled?"

The old man sighed. "Oh, perhaps Mary and I will light back to Missouri for a spell. We can visit some of our old chums from our school days and see what has become of the place."

Finnegan arched one eyebrow. "It is a seething caldron of malcontent former rebels and other assorted scum."

Parker shook his head. "Finnegan, is there any place on earth that suits you?"

"A small portion of Montana once found favor with me."

"You may wish to return there at the end of my tenure."

Finnegan gave the notion some thought. "I am not certain circumstances promote that notion. In the employ of the Cattleman's Association, I earned a percentage of ownership in the stock of several ranches that were, at the time, quite prosperous. In keeping with my usual luck regarding financial matters, the territory was assailed with a winter that caused destruction on a level not seen since the great flood."

Maledon nodded. "Read about that. They'd been saying for years that Montana country was a cattleman's paradise. Nothing but grass and water and land aplenty. "Was it '86 that horrid winter came on 'em?"

"It was." Finnegan contemplated his cigar. "Whole herds were laid low, not to be seen again until the spring thaw. Those coyotes that survived were quite well fed on my beef when the sun eventually warmed the earth." The gunman shrugged. "At any rate, I am still owed my percentage, but, as any man acquainted with arithmetic will tell you, it is best to allow for an increase in numbers before calling in a debt. Given a few seasons and some mercy from the elements, my investment may yet still bear fruit. In the meantime, I believe it would be best to keep my distance and allow the cattlemen time to recover their own finances. After all, a prosperous man is proud to pay what he owes, while the pauper's only option is truthfulness and default."

"So, then, you need only find something to amuse you during the slump between the disappearance of this wild land and the fruition of your ranching investment." Ever the optimist, the judge offered a comforting smile.

"This development does place me in something of a pickle, gentlemen. Fort Smith and the surrounding Indian Territory were somewhat of a last bastion for a man such as myself. I have no idea where I might find a steady supply of evildoers from which to draw steady wages."

Maledon rolled his cigar between his fingers. "Can you not simply return to Chicago and resume your duties with the Pinkerton Agency?"

Finnegan groaned. "I suppose I might, although it would be a frightfully dreary sort of work. They would surely place me on a picket line, breaking union worker heads for a few dollars a day. The thought of it wearies me."

Parker waved one hand dismissively. "You are too good of a man for such dirty business, Finnegan. Perhaps you should go west. There is surely some place remaining in need of a man with your level of skill. Despite your protestations and predilections, you did a fine bit of work here rounding up heathens and delivering them to the dungeon. I believe that in this last year you have even begun delivering more than you shot. Could it be you are growing lenient in your dotage?"

The gunman shook his head. "It is only that I am becoming a poorer marksman, I assure you."

Maledon pursed his lips and puffed his cigar. "Now that I think of it, it does seem as though you shoot damn few men lately. When you first arrived here, it was hard to say if you ever passed on shooting a man and, now, I cannot recall the last you felled. I agree with the esteemed judge, you are growing lenient."

Finnegan let out a long plume of smoke. "If it will cause this prattling to cease, I will promise to shoot no less than three men on my way home this evening. Will that assuage your worries as to my fortitude." Both men nodded, grinning. "Very well, then. If either of you truly wish to offer assistance, you might be so kind as to suggest a future port of call for a man such as myself. Even before the good judge's announcement, I have given the matter consideration and found few options presented to me."

Parker motioned with his cigar. "Now that I think of it, Finnegan, I have been hearing no end of rumors regarding that ridiculous Russian possession we purchased near the northern pole. Men keep mumbling that there is gold there along with the bordering British possessions. Where there is a gold rush, men such as you are always required to keep the peace. Who knows, you may conjure a method to come into possession of a gold mine while you are about your usual work."

Finnegan shook his head. "No, I have lost the will to go searching for gold mines. I also have it on good account that the northern reaches you speak of are positively infested with bears. I will have no part of that."

Maledon rubbed his weathered face. "Bears? You must have killed two score of men just since I have known you. How is it that a few bears could trouble you? To my knowledge, they do not even possess guns."

"A man's whimsies are a fascinating thing." Parker sipped his coffee. "Might I make another suggestion that is broader in scope, Finnegan?"

"Your counsel is always welcome, Isaac."

"Perhaps instead of casting about for a new place to practice your old trade, you should consider both a new place and a new trade. A man ought to consider an alternate path every now and then, especially if he finds his current path blocked with hourglass sand."

"Rather poetic, Isaac."

"Thank you."

"So, you would suggest the time of the hired shootist is at an end?"

"I should surely say the time of the well-compensated

shootist is at an end." Parker assumed a coy look. "Can you honestly claim that you are so well paid now, between your stipend from the Pinkerton Agency and your bounties, as you were during your glory days?"

"Ugh," Finnegan sneered. "I shudder to think what you might be referring to as glory days. Although, I must admit, my purse is somewhat lighter than it once was in that regard." He thought on it a moment. "On the other hand, if my race does in fact pass from the earth, I doubt too many will mourn us. Who can say, perhaps this is the final motivation I require to finally try my hand at farming."

Both Maledon and Parker stared blankly at Finnegan, but it was the hangman who spoke. "I would rather swing from my own damn rope than farm."

Parker nodded. "I would prefer to share the loop."

"Yes, well, I suppose you are correct." The gunman sighed and noticed that his cigar was burning low. "Nothing lasts forever, gentlemen. And the good days seem to pass all the quicker for it." He raised his coffee cup once more. "To the end of an era. They will miss us when we are gone."

Chapter 2

FORT SMITH, ARKANSAS

December 25th, 1889

Finnegan awoke to a dusting of snow on the ground, which he took note of as he made his way out the backdoor of his boarding house and over to the neighbor's smokehouse. He entered the small structure, located the item he searched for, and exited the tiny building with all due haste. He was crossing the snow-covered yard that separated the two pieces of property with a linen-wrapped bundle in his arms when he noticed a young man running toward him.

Finnegan stopped, recognizing the young fellow as the local telegram runner. "Malcolm Fitzgerald, what are you doing up and about working? Are you not aware it is Christmas day?"

The boy stopped and caught his breath. "I am afraid it makes little difference to me, Mr. Gilhooley. I live with my uncle in the telegraph office and, as bachelors, we do not much indulge in Christmas celebrations."

"I have been a bachelor my entire life, Malcolm, and have rarely missed an opportunity to insinuate myself into a Christmas dinner somewhere. This year you and your uncle may join us here at the boarding house. My landlady, Mrs. Covington, puts on a fine spread and, as the man providing the main course..." He held up the linen-wrapped bundle, "I believe I am allowed one or two guests."

"That is very Christian of you, sir. I will pass the invitation along to my uncle. Will there be pie?"

"I should certainly hope so."

"In that case, whether my uncle wishes to attend or not, I will surely be there." He extended a telegram to Finnegan.

The gunman transferred his bundle to one arm and took the missive. "Very sensible of you, Malcolm." He felt about his person. "My apologies, young man, I did not think to put a coin in my pocket before leaving the house."

"Think nothing of it, Mr. Gilhooley. Merry Christmas." The boy ran off toward the snowy town, wearing a broad grin.

Finnegan stuffed the telegram into his coat pocket and continued on his way into the boarding house. Once inside, he made his way to the kitchen where Mrs. Covington was already about her morning chores. She glanced up from the dough she was kneading and offered her most regularly paying boarder a smile commensurate with his finances. "Mr. Gilhooley, what brings you about so early on this frosty morning?" She wiped her forehead with the back of one hand and left some flour behind.

Finnegan set his bundle on the kitchen table and pulled the linen from around it. I have come to deliver the household's Christmas gift, Mrs. Covington."

The lady surveyed the offering. "Mr. Gilhooley, that is a very fine piglet. Wherever did you get it?"

"I came across the beast in my travels. I believe it was running wild. At any rate, there was not a farm in sight, and no one present to lay claim, so I dispatched the animal and then put Mr. Stewart across the way to work smoking it for this occasion."

"It is a grand beast, sir." She approached and gave the fair-sized young pig a more thorough inspection. "It would fairly feed an army."

"Well, it should serve to feed the house." Finnegan held up one hand. "Oh, I hope you do not mind, I have invited both young Mr. Fitzgerald and his uncle the telegraph clerk for dinner this evening."

The lady smiled even wider. "Oh, yes, Mr. Gilhooley, that is a fine Christian invitation to extend. They are more than welcome."

"Thank you, ma'am." A recollection struck the gunman, and he pulled the telegram from his pocket. "I had almost forgotten that young Malcolm gave this to me." He unfolded the flap of the envelope and drew the document from within. As he read, his eyes narrowed and a slight frown formed on his brow.

The landlady took note of the change in his countenance. "The news does not suit you, sir?"

Finnegan ran one hand over his face. "It is not so much that, ma'am, as that I am not certain how to take it." He placed the missive back in the envelope and placed the two items back in his coat pocket. "Please excuse me, ma'am. I believe it would be best if I visited the judge for a short time. I will be back in ample time for dinner."

Judge Parker read over the telegram and placed it on the end table next to him. "Rather clipped and cryptic, is it not?"

"I should say so, yes." Finnegan nodded and lit a cigar.

"I take it you are acquainted with this Melinda Meagher?"

"Very well acquainted. At one time I intended to marry the woman."

The judge blinked at his friend a few times, allowing the statement to sink in. "Truly?"

"Yes." Finnegan shifted in his seat. "Is it so odd that I should have once entertained the notion of marriage? All men surely do at some juncture."

"I suppose so...it is only...well, never mind that for the moment. Can you conjure a reason this woman would wish for you to travel to such a place as Nevada on a moment's notice with all due haste?"

"I cannot. When last I corresponded with her, she made her home in Montana and made no mention of leaving. I cannot imagine what might have possessed her that she would wish to travel to Nevada, of all places, or a town I have no knowledge of. Until receiving that telegram I had never heard her so much as speak the name Nevada, much less whatever small outpost Greenfield might be."

The judge licked his lips and sipped a cup of tea. "And yet she requests you come running." He smoothed his beard and raised his eyebrows. "Are you on friendly terms with the woman?"

"Yes, as far as I know."

"And she is a comely young lass?"

"I always considered her so."

"Then, if I found myself in your position, Finnegan, I believe I would purchase a train ticket and proceed to Nevada with all due haste."

Finnegan laughed. "That is damned impulsive advice from a man such as you, Isaac."

"Oh, when it comes to the pursuit of women, cold

contemplation cannot enter into it, my friend. If I had shown the slightest hesitation in courting Mary, I would not be awaiting the arrival of my grandchildren today. You said yourself that you once wished to marry this woman. Well, go to Nevada, rescue her from whatever peril she finds herself in, and marry her. Is it truly all so complicated that I must explain matters to you further?"

Finnegan laughed again. "Thanks to your careful explanation, I now see it is only a simple matter, quickly seen to."

"Only last night you, I, and Maledon came to the conclusion that we must all pull up stakes and be away from this place sooner rather than later." Parker shrugged. "From what I read in the papers, Nevada is not currently enjoying the best of times, but one place is generally as good as another when a fellow is casting about for a new start. If the object of your desires is there, more the better."

"So, I should, in your opinion, board the morning train west?"

Parker smiled. "The evening train might be preferable. A man, O'Dell by name, has let it be known that someone has made off with the piglet of his prize sow and he intends to kill the pig thief on sight if the law does not bring him justice. Such heady crimes as pig theft can rend a community apart in short order."

Finnegan scowled. "Hell's bells. I should have known that animal was too fine a specimen not to have an owner somewhere."

Parker shrugged. "If you do not get to chasing that woman, Finnegan, Maledon and I may be forced to hang you."

"It would be a pity to have a falling out over something so trivial. Even more of a shame be forced to cheat you out of your fun by appealing to the Supreme Court in Washington."

Parker shook his head, looking solemn. "A scornful fact to bring up. Unfortunately for you, the High Court has a strict policy of never interceding in cases of pig theft."

"I will miss you, Isaac. You and Charles, both."

The old judge stared down into his tea cup. "I will miss a great many things, Finnegan."

Chapter 3

DODGE CITY, KANSAS

December 31st, 1889

There had been so many wrecks, breakdowns, fires, and other conflagrations on the rail line in the last few days that there were no Pullman cars available. This unfortunate occurrence had forced Finnegan into a common passenger car. He was not happy with the development, but he had grown somewhat inured to it over the years. Rail travel was always an adventure, and Finnegan knew he should count his blessings. He could have been hideously killed in one of the wrecks instead of simply finding himself herded into a vessel little better than a cattle car. Simple survival was often all one could ask of the rail system.

The Pinkerton placed his various pieces of luggage on the far end of the wooden, unpadded bench seat and settled into the space that remained. He rubbed his face and rearranged his belongings a bit when the train jostled to a start. When he looked up again, there was a young Indian man in a fine tweed traveling suit sitting on the bench opposite him. In many parts of the country, it might have been unusual to see an Indian riding in the same car with white people, but in

Kansas it was quite common. On the outskirts of Indian territory, functionality trumped any bias. Finnegan nodded to the young man, and he nodded back.

Finnegan withdrew a cigar from his vest pocket. "A fine warm day for winter, is it not?"

The Indian glanced out the window and smiled. "It is, sir." He cocked his head from one side to the other. "If it would not be impertinent, might I ask your name, sir."

Finnegan raised his eyebrows. "Impertinent?"

"Yes, sir. It means impolite."

Finnegan nodded slowly. "I am aware of the word's meaning, young man. I have simply not heard it uttered in quite some time."

"My instructors at Carlisle often cautioned me regarding impertinence."

"Carlisle? The Indian academy?"

"The very same."

Finnegan placed the cigar between his lips and found a match. "Yes, well, they instructed you quite well in the use of English. You practice the art far better than some I have met who would claim it as a native tongue."

"Thank you, sir."

The Pinkerton extended his hand. "Finnegan Xavier Gilhooley."

The young man shook. "Jock Bull Bear. I thought you might be Finnegan Gilhooley."

Finnegan puffed his cigar. "Have we met before, young man?"

"Not formally. I recognize you from having seen you in Arapaho country some years previous, when you shot and killed Peter Counts-His-Horses."

The Pinkerton nodded. "Ah, yes, I do recall the incident. Was Peter a friend of yours?"

"If that man had friends, I was never made aware of them. As I recall, the general consensus was that you dispatching him was quite a boon to the community. Afterward, the small store was able to keep both vanilla and kerosene on hand without fear of Peter stealing it to drink."

Finnegan shrugged. "In that case, you are welcome."

"It was an impressive exploit, Mr. Gilhooley. Most of the men were too frightened to confront Counts-His-Horses regarding his wickedness. You approached and made short work of the fellow as though he were no more than an errant piglet."

Finnegan gave the boy a sideways glance, trying to determine how much he might know regarding past crimes. "It is always difficult to say what man will give you trouble and what man will be handled without labor. Although, even the piglet you referenced can lead to trouble." He reached over and opened the window a crack to allow the cigar smoke out. "There is little purpose dithering over what may transpire before it is upon you. It is all only conjecture, after all."

"That is an impressive philosophy, sir. I am not certain I would have the courage to make use of it for myself."

"If you are wise enough to avoid gunfighting as a profession, it should be a moot issue." Finnegan puffed toward the window. "What profession do you follow, Mr. Bull Bear?"

"I am a teacher by trade and have taken to searching for methods that will allow my people to assimilate into the society of civilized men."

Finnegan smiled. "If you ever encounter civilized men, please make me aware of it with all due haste."

"Very humorous, sir." Bull Bear appeared to enjoy having someone to talk with. "Have you elected to leave Indian Territory, Mr. Gilhooley? The law-abiding people of the area will miss you greatly."

Finnegan rubbed his chin. "I would not go so far as to say I am leaving Fort Smith behind permanently. I travel west to visit an old friend who tells me she is in need of assistance. For the time being, it is only an errand." He shrugged. "Although, who can say? My destination may appeal to me. What prompts your trip, Mr. Bull Bear?"

"I travel west to investigate the possibility of a new messiah."

Finnegan arched one eyebrow. "Beg pardon?"

"I travel to Nevada to investigate the rumors which are currently circulating amongst my people. We have been told that a new Christ is risen in the west. Naturally, I am eager to discover the truth of the matter."

"Naturally." Finnegan tapped the ash from his cigar. "Mr. Bull Bear, pray tell, what part of Nevada do you travel to?"

"Specifically, the town of Greenfield, sir."

Finnegan nodded. "Yes, naturally." He licked his lips and stared out the window for a long moment. "So, then, an Indian Jesus has presented himself in the town of Greenfield, Nevada, and you are currently traveling there to visit with the fellow?"

"Yes, sir."

"Is the existence of this messiah a well-known fact, Mr. Bull Bear?"

"It has become a much-repeated rumor among the Arapaho, sir. As I said, no one has, as yet, traveled to Nevada to authenticate the facts. That is my stated goal, sir."

Finnegan nodded again and rubbed his tired face. "Mr. Bull Bear, it would appear that we are to be traveling companions for quite some distance. I am pleased that you seem to be such an affable fellow. One does so detest traveling long distances with grumps, or that most damnable type who constantly whistles a tune that cannot be identified."

"I rarely whistle, sir."

"In that case, we should be able to determine the location of your messiah without a harsh word passing between us, which will be grand. It is my understanding that messiahs tend to frown upon ill will between men."

Chapter 4

DENVER, COLORADO

January 2nd, 1890

Descending from the train car, Finnegan was greeted by the grinning faces of two young men he knew well. He set his carpet bag down on the roughhewn planks and extended his hand to his friends. "Abijah, it is fine to see you again."

The fresh-faced Pinkerton grinned at his mentor. "I must say, it was something of a shock to receive your telegram. I thought you might have found a perfect home in the court of that Arkansas hanging judge. From the awful items presented in the papers, I would have thought you two would make a fine and lasting pair."

"No paradise lasts forever." Finnegan turned to the other, fairly new-minted Pinkerton agent. "Mr. Horn, it is fine to see you again, as well."

The young man from the southern desert tipped his wide-brimmed hat back and shook Finnegan's hand. "I reckon by now you ought to call me Tom. Since you got me my current position and meal ticket and all."

Finnegan chuckled. "I cannot say as I stretched the truth

any in your recommendation, Tom. It is hard to conceive of a fellow who could be of more use to the agency. If anything, you may regret asking for my reference someday, once the boredom inevitably sets in."

Horn shrugged. "Sorry to report that happened mighty quick after signing on, but it is a fine thing to have regular pay, so I ought not complain. Any man in his right head ought to prefer boredom to hunger."

"It is best for a man to count his blessings and leave the rest unsaid." Finnegan glanced over his shoulder and noticed his fellow adventurer sidling up next to him. "Ah, gentlemen, let me present Jock Bull Bear, quite possibly the finest traveling companion I have had the luck to make the acquaintance of yet. He is well read in the classics, which makes for excellent conversation, and he in no way partakes of tobacco, which has saved me a great deal of money these last few days. Jock, this first fellow is Abijah Smith, whom I have known since he was a boy, and the fellow with the very fine hat is Tom Horn, formerly the prince of the Mexican border and now only a lowly Pinkerton agent like the rest of us."

Abijah put out his hand. "Pleased to make your acquaintance, Mr. Bull Bear."

Horn shook Jock's hand, as well. "What kind of Indian are you, Mr. Bull Bear?"

"Southern Arapaho." The young man smiled at Horn's lack of formality.

"Huh, can't say as I've tangled with an Arapaho that I know of. You old boys anything like Apaches or Comanches?"

Jock grinned. "Considerably more manly and generally more beautiful in form."

Horn laughed. "Well, I'll give you that for sure. Old Geronimo was uglier than a mud fence." Horn clapped the young man on one shoulder and pulled him forward. "Come on, me and Abijah mean to buy this haggard old killer Gilhooley a meal while he's in town and you had best come along. Might be the only time you meet someone who ain't trying to kill him while you're traveling together."

The four men meandered down one of Denver's rather rancorous streets, past the piles of refuse and various stacks of bottles that resided outside the taverns. Building codes had been adopted after the great blaze, but they went unenforced and remained largely unknown. Some quarter-mile from the train station they located a passably decent looking café and made their way inside. Taking seats at the nearest available table, they settled in, and Finnegan took a moment to review Abijah Smith.

"Well, my young friend, you appear happy and healthy, even if you have been forced to take up your old profession. I must admit, I was somewhat disheartened to hear you did not discover the motherlode at your mine."

Abijah laughed. "Ah, yes, about that venture..." He glanced over to Horn. "All things considered, we may have found something preferable to a motherlode. Searching out and finding that rare animal, the New York speculator, is far less dirty and more profitable, at least in our case." Abijah reached inside his jacket and withdrew an envelope. "I am quite pleased to say that I am currently able to repay you the money you advanced me."

Finnegan slowly reached out and received the envelope. "Well, perhaps now I have truly seen it all. A hole in the earth that actually pays dividends."

Horn laughed. "Them three dandies was in the nicest pressed suits you ever did see..." He pointed to Jock. "Even nicer than this fella's. Them city boys forked over no less than eight thousand proper Yankee dollars for that pit we was sweating in, Finnegan. Did it with straight faces acting like we gave 'em a right fine deal, too." He slapped one hand down on the table. "Hard to credit. Wouldn't credit it myself if I didn't have Abijah here to swear my word on it. Saw it sober, so I can't claim delusion."

"That is an impressive bit of hornswoggling, Tom." Finnegan shook his head.

"Made me wish I'd picked older men for partners when I got started so some of them would have passed on when them Yankees came along." Horn winked at Abijah. "But a man can't predict every little thing in business."

Jock laboriously adjusted his suit and settled into his chair. He did not appear altogether comfortable inside the confines of the café. "What sort of mine did you operate, Mr. Horn?"

Horn rubbed his chin. "Well, now that you mention it, I guess we never did quite settle on what we were looking for. As I recall, we started out swearing to the Lord Almighty and any other fella that came along that there was gold in that hole and I think it would be best, now that we've shuffled it off onto someone else, we ought to keep saying it. Lest them New York dandies cry foul and come looking for us."

Finnegan waved one hand dismissively. "If they truly press the issue, simply take an infiltration placement and change your name. That modest debilitant has saved many a Pinkerton many a dollar over the course of the agency."

Horn waggled one finger. "Now that is a bit of brilliance, Finnegan."

Finnegan smiled and sat back in his chair. "I have not made it this far in life by allowing opportunities to pass by, Tom."

A heavy-set man wrapped in a white apron approached the table with his lips knotted into a sneer. The fellow took a moment to adjust the rolled-up sleeves of his food-stained shirt and ran one hand over his beard before speaking. "I don't know if any of you is aware of the fact that we don't serve this one's kind in here, but that's how it is."

Finnegan slowly craned his neck to stare up at the man. He left his smile in place as he pointed across the table at Abijah. "I assure you, sir, despite this young man hailing from Pennsylvania, he is quite capable of behaving in a civilized manner."

The proprietor glanced between the two Pinkertons. "It ain't him I mean."

Finnegan laughed. "Well, sir, if you are informing me that you do not serve Irishmen, I must inform you that I have shot the last two or three gentlemen who have proved vexatious in that regard. I realize that most of my countrymen are not fit table companions, but do not feel I should be lumped in with the other Hibernians out of hand."

The proprietor took a half-step back. "I...I mean the damn Indian. We don't allow darkies, Chinamen, nor Indians in here. No matter what kind of Baptist meetin' suit you put on 'em."

Finnegan looked to Jock. "The man does make a point, Mr. Bull Bear. That is, indeed, the suit of a Baptist revivalist." He looked back to the proprietor. "Be gone, you insufferable jackass."

"Mister, this is my place, and I got a right to serve who I please, when I please, and there ain't a damn thing you can do about it, neither." The proprietor seemed quite adamant.

A playful glint passed through Finnegan's eye. "Sir, you are correct in saying that it is not my place to tell another man his business or preferences in his own establishment. What I will say, is that you had best look to your own interest before engendering the ill will of another man."

The proprietor puffed up. "And who the hell are you that I ought to have a care regarding your ill will? You ain't gonna shoot me in front of other folks."

"Oh, it is not myself to whom I was referring. I am only a simple Irishman, Finnegan Gilhooley by name." The proprietor did his best to keep his lips from quivering. "Do not fret, my friend, I am not your direct concern. Ask this gentleman, if you do not believe I speak the truth." Finnegan pointed across the table again. "This fellow is the framed scout and interpreter, Tom Horn. You may recall hearing of his exploits during the recent Indian uprising war in the southern desert."

Horn glared at the café owner and tipped his hat. "Pleased to make your acquaintance, sir." The proprietor's Adam's apple bobbed up and down.

"Yes, Mr. Horn is well known for his predilections toward making war on the red man and has killed several dozens of them in pitched battle. Given that fact, you may be wondering why it is that Mr. Horn would deign to take his mid-day meal in the company of one such savage." Finnegan grinned. "The answer is very simple: Mr. Horn fears this savage greatly."

Horn nodded, looking somber and just a bit frightened. "That is the gospel truth there, my friend." He stared wide-eyed up at the proprietor. "Ain't you never heard of Jock Bull Bear?" The proprietor slowly shook his head. "This red devil setting here before you is the most bloodthirsty, coldhearted, murderous, vicious, and cruel hell spawn I have ever had the misfortune to cross paths with. I have it on good account that he's old Geronimo's bastard son come back for revenge on the white man, and no less a personage than Sitting Bull himself has begged him not to visit it upon us out of sheer damn pity."

Finnegan chimed in when he noticed Horn was slowing. "This infidel has scalped ten score of men. Ravaged who can say how many maidens, and made countless orphans. I have personally witnessed him in league with witches and seen him make use of black magics supplied by the heathen gods he gives homage to." He pointed one stern finger at the proprietor. "If you do not give this man a meal, and promptly I might add, you endanger yourself, your children, and your children's children. It is not enough for a man like this to simply take vengeance upon the poor fools that offend him. He will wipe your seed from the earth, sir. Take heed, and be about your work."

The proprietor slowly took a few steps backward. "Well, mayhaps, just this once, since he's here with you fellas."

Horn shook his head. "I ain't even certain I can eat, now that you got me thinking back on the last café owner that got sideways of Jock here. Can't hardly sleep no more since I seen that. Awful way to die. Right there on his own griddle like that."

Finnegan shook his head. "Even the war did not produce such an atrocity."

"I'll get you boys some steaks and a pot of coffee." The proprietor began his retreat into the kitchen.

Finnegan removed two cigars from his pocket and handed one to Horn. "Dreadfully slow service in this place, is it not?"

Horn nodded. "Colorado won't be out much when Jock here murders that fella and all his offspring and cousins and such."

Abijah rubbed his face and sat back in his chair. "Oh, why stop there? Should it not be necessary to hang the man's horse while Jock is about his rampaging?"

Finnegan lit his cigar. "How about it, Jock? Does the man's mount require punishment in kind? Mr. Horn and I are willing to provide any sort of assistance you might ask of us to avoid becoming the target of your wrath."

The young man in the tweed traveling suit cleared his throat. "Mr. Gilhooley, I have never done anything even remotely resembling the deeds you suggested to that man."

Horn laughed. "Ah, heck, Jock, we know that. Finnegan here is just glad to have someone turn pale for once that ain't specifically terrified of him."

Abijah chuckled and shook his head. "I had nearly forgotten the glib entertainment you offer, Finnegan." He stared at his mentor for a moment. "What is it that brings you west? I would have thought you would be quite content in Fort Smith, far from the home office with a seemingly endless supply of miscreants to keep you amused. What could possibly dislodge you from an earthbound Eden?"

Finnegan puffed his cigar. "Ah, poor Abijah, look to your bible and you will be informed that even Eden does not last forever. Although, that sad fact is only a contributing factor to my journey. While I have it on good account that Fort Smith will soon not be what it once was, I have, in fact, been set in motion by no less a personage than the redoubtable Molly Meagher."

Abijah sat back in his chair and stared in wonder at his old friend. "Molly Meagher? The woman from Minnesota?"

"Yes, she has contacted me by telegram and asks that I make haste to the barren wastes of Nevada."

Abijah rubbed his face for a moment and then resumed staring. "Molly Meagher? The same woman you met so very long ago in the north woods?"

Finnegan nodded. "The very same."

Abijah sat forward a bit. "The same woman you traveled to Montana for? The woman who rejected your proposal?"

"Yes." The gunman nodded once more.

"Finnegan, you are quite mad." The young man shook his head again. "Do you realize that you are mad?"

"The insane tend to look at the world from a skewed perspective, my friend." Finnegan grinned.

Horn somewhat laboriously set his borrowed cigar between his lips. "Finnegan, is it true what he says about you chasing the same woman all this time?"

"It is."

"How long since you met this gal?" Horn moved the cigar back and forth between his teeth.

"Oh, well, Molly and I were first acquainted in '76, the night I traded gunfire with the James brothers at a picket in Minnesota. That was the night I obtained my Remington, as well. All things considered, it was a fine evening, excluding the wound I received, of course."

"Uh, huh." Horn nodded. "And you chased her all the way to Montana once? That is a goodly distance."

"I had some other business in the territory, but, essentially, yes."

"And now you've picked up and are running to the desert to see her again?" Horn seemed equally befuddled.

"I am indeed."

Horn struck a match and puffed his cigar. "But, she ain't your woman? I mean, you ain't been churched?"

Finnegan chuckled. "No, we are not wed, Tom."

Horn waved smoke away from his face. "And you don't...I mean you don't act like you was?" He glanced furtively toward Bull Bear, hoping the young man was too naive to understand the topic under discussion.

Finnegan raised one eyebrow. "I assure you, Tom, she is not that type of woman."

"I'm certain she ain't." Horn rubbed his chin. "There

ain't a doubt in my mind that this Molly is the very picture of a proper Christian lady, it's just..."

Finnegan knocked the ash from his cigar. "Something confuses you, Tom?"

"Well, it's just... if she's a proper Christian lady, what the hell do you keep running after her for? It might doom me to perdition, but I got to say, I greatly prefer the company of improper ladies to proper ones, and no small amount of experience has taught me that the less proper they are the more preferable their company is. I would go so far as to state that a man's time would be better spent chasing a damned improper woman than a wholly proper one."

Finnegan laughed. "Ah, poor Tom. Perhaps someday you will have lived long enough to understand. I cannot imagine living in a world where Molly does not have a place. If she had sent a telegram from the North Pole, I would make the same haste. Some matters are simply fated to be so, and it gladdens my heart that I have been called to action once again. She always offers entertainment, though I imagine it is not the sort you so eloquently described."

"Uh huh." Horn nodded. "Well, I got to say, I think Abijah might have a point about you being crazed. Maybe you spent too much time in that wet Arkansas air. I've heard it can do things to a fella's head."

Finnegan grinned. "If you think my journey stems from madness, you need only inquire of my friend here to determine a proper perspective for measurement. Jock, would you be so kind as to inform my friend as to the purpose of *your* journey?"

Bull Bear brightened a bit at the change of subject and straightened in his chair. "Oh, certainly." He smiled at Horn and Abijah, glad to add to the discourse. "I travel west to meet the new messiah."

Abijah cocked his head to one side. "I am sorry, perhaps you could say that again?"

"I travel west to assess the validity of a messiah who is said to have risen in the town of Greenfield, Nevada." Bull Bear was quite happy to repeat the statement.

Horn sat back in his chair and crossed his arms. "I suppose it's a bit hard to believe that Jesus might have come back up in the Sierras, but, then again, it's sorta hard to believe America's most famous assassin has been loping after a woman who won't take to his bed for about twenty years. Many a miracle has been discussed in a short time at this table. I feel fairly honored to have been witness to all this. Greenfield is fairly far up north, ain't it?"

Jock nodded. "It is, sir."

Abijah chuckled. "Mr. Bull Bear, does Greenfield, Nevada not strike you as a rather out-of-the-way place for a savior to rise?"

Bull Bear nodded. "It does. Although, I am told Bethlehem is an out-of-the-way place even now."

Abijah shrugged. "Yes, I have never been there, but I am told the same." He cocked his head the other way. "Uh, Mr. Bull Bear, how is it you have been charged with determining the credentials of a messiah?"

"I was given the duty by the elders of my tribe."

Abijah nodded. "I see. Why is it your tribe has an interest?"

Jock sat back as the proprietor placed a plate of quite good-looking food in front of him. "They are interested because the new messiah is said to be a Paiute Indian."

The proprietor crossed himself. "Saints preserve us."

Finnegan waved a hand at the man. "Be gone, it is not polite to eavesdrop." The man walked back to the kitchen. "Now, Jock, continue expounding on the Indian Jesus."

Jock continued as though it were a perfectly normal subject for discussion. "I cannot offer any certainty as to what is fact and what is fancy, my friends. The man I search for is known as Wovoka. I am told he is also called Jack Wilson by the white men of his town. He is a Paiute. I am told he has visited Heaven. There, he was shown a ritual that will allow the tribes to see the dead and speak with them so that we may all make ready before the end comes."

Finnegan puffed his cigar. "The end?"

Jock shrugged and looked over his food. "Wilson has prophesied that the end times are approaching. He has predicted the time of the end and claims that all the white people will be removed from the earth. This land will be returned to the Indians. The buffalo will return. The world will be as it was for our grandfathers." Jock forked a potato off his plate. "Well, perhaps our great, great grandfathers."

Finnegan nodded. "He has provided a date?"

Jock chewed a potato. "Supposedly. It is difficult to find specifics when all one may do is strain tales from varied letters. Some claim Wilson is a prophet of the Lord, some claim he is the messiah in the flesh. Those more hardhearted say he is a simple fraud."

Abijah sat forward. "What do you believe, sir?"

Jock started in on his steak. "I have no idea what to believe, Mr. Smith. That is why I am traveling to Nevada. My people wish to know what is fact and what is fancy before we make any claims or adopt any practices."

Abijah appeared perplexed. "What practices do you contemplate?"

Jock looked up from his plate and smiled. "Mr. Smith, surely there is someone no longer with us you would like to see once more?"

Abijah looked over the assembled gunmen. "I should imagine any man would."

Jock sliced off more steak. "My people wish to know what Mr. Wilson purports to know and what claims he may make. They wish to know specifics regarding the ritual so that they may speak with those they have lost." He paused in his eating. "We have lost many to disease in the last few years. The pox and illness from bad water. There is not one among us who has not lost...much. Many children."

Horn rubbed his chin. "This ritual you're talking about, it's a dance, huh?" Jock nodded. "It's one of them things like the sun dance, ain't it?" Jock nodded again.

Finnegan eyed the newly-minted Pinkerton. "What, pray tell, might the sun dance be, Tom?"

Horn rubbed his chin a bit more. "Well, as I was told, it's one of these things the Indians do to see visions of what's to come or heaven or whatnot. They don't eat, don't sleep, don't drink water for as long as they can take it. They dance in the sun until they more or less lose their senses and start to see things. I'm told they pierce themselves and hang themselves, too."

Finnegan shook his head. "Tom, I would venture to say that if they hung themselves a man would have a hard time ever doing that particular dance twice."

Horn grimaced. "Not like a white man hangs hisself, Finnegan. They poke a hole in their hide, string raw hide or hemp rope from it and hang off a branch or something until they...hell I don't know...I guess until they see heaven or that Indian Jesus fella."

Finnegan appeared skeptical. "Mr. Bull Bear, is what Tom tells me the product of frontier yarning?"

Jock popped the last hunk of steak in his mouth. "It would not be how I would describe the sun dance, but it is not far from an accurate assessment, either. I have never participated in a sun dance, but I am told all of that can occur. Most sun dances occurred before I was born."

Finnegan knocked more ash from his cigar. "I suppose it is not much different from the Christians I have heard of who handle snakes to prove their faith."

Jock pushed his plate away. "We are all Christians where I live. I am told Jack Wilson is a Christian."

Horn grinned. "I suppose that would explain how the fella got to be the new Jesus."

Finnegan grinned at the former scout. "Perhaps you should come along with us and meet the man, Tom. You and a recently roused savior would have much to discuss. Where better to obtain salvation than directly from the tap, as the barmen say."

Horn shrugged. "Truth be told, I'd like nothing better, Finnegan. This work for the Pinkertons is a boring sort of drivel most days. The last bunch me and Abijah chased after, there wasn't nothing to it other than trailing after them until we was damn near back in Mexico. When we finally got to them, they was worn out and practically asked to go to prison. They'd even spent all the money from the train." He sullenly shook his head. "I'd much rather go look at the second coming, but I doubt they'd let us loose. Regular pay don't come for nothing."

Abijah waggled a finger at Finnegan. "Naturally, you suspect this Wilson fellow is the cause for your Molly's call to service?"

Finnegan stubbed out his smoke. "I would hesitate to attempt any predictions regarding what Miss Meagher might require. She has proved far too unpredictable in the past for any such attempts." He took a deep breath. "Though, it is difficult to imagine what else might prompt the invitation. It is highly suspicious that a savior should rise at the same time Molly would opt to begin teaching the children of Greenfield their letters. To imagine the two are unrelated begs credulity."

Abijah sat back in his chair, looking perplexed. "Finnegan, I would agree that, from what you have told me of the woman, Molly would take great interest in the coming of an Indian messiah. What I cannot keen is what the woman might need your assistance for. I hope I do not offer any offense when I say you have never struck me as the type to become an apostle."

Finnegan took a moment to contemplate the comment. "I cannot disagree with you on that point, Abijah. I suppose I cannot say what she might want of me, either." He smiled at his old friend. "Perhaps she merely wishes to bid me farewell before the end of the world is upon us."

Chapter 5

GREENFIELD, NEVADA

January 5th, 1890

Finnegan stepped down from the coach and stretched out his back. He looked around the small town spread out before him. "Ugh." He twisted his neck back and forth. "It has been some time since I have been forced to travel in such a conveyance." He looked down the road that led to the town. Someone had apparently taken the time to shovel a path through the snowdrifts, allowing the coach to pass. As Finnegan stood in the town square, more snow was falling. From the rate of accumulation, it would not be overly long before the coach ceased to be a workable option.

Jock pulled his traveling suit coat close around him. "I am not accustomed to such a mode of travel, either, and I am certainly not accustomed to such a depth of snow. It does not build up so in our country." He grimaced, looking at the high-piled snow. "The engineer claimed the train would not be able to pass if much more came down, and now it is snowing once more, Finnegan."

The gunman nodded. "Yes, Jock. I believe we may be

staying in this hamlet whether we prefer it or not. At these elevations, some matters are out of our control. We should be glad that we have been lucky enough to make it to what passes for civilization. If we had been marooned at the Walker River Reservation, we may have found ourselves bartering for a place to sleep and a share of the government beef ration."

Jock chuckled. "If you barter for a part of government beef ration you may find yourself owning a portion of that which only exists in a bureaucrat's ledger. It is often an ephemeral commodity."

"As a man who has formerly owned railroad stock, I am inured to possessing the invisible or ethereal." Finnegan took his bags from the rear of the coach and looked over their options once more. "The general store is commonly a proper starting point for a search. If fortune is with us, we should be able to locate my friend and your messiah with a minimum of effort."

Jock shivered and took up his own luggage. "Any warm building will do. I am beginning to wonder if it might not have been preferable to come in search of Wilson in the summer months."

"You may debate the wisdom of your journey all you like, Jock. I have long since ceased to contemplate such matters in regard to Molly Meagher. There is little purpose to considering what a man has no choice in." The two men slogged through the ever-increasing snow and eventually made it to the boardwalk and the relative safety of the awning in front of the general mercantile. They spent a brief moment stomping their feet and knocking the snow from their shoulders out of politeness before entering the building. Inside, they found a potbellied stove with the grate in the front open.

Flames could be seen licking within. Finnegan set his luggage to one side of the door and approached the stove to warm his hands. "Ah, that is fine." He removed his gloves and rubbed his hands together briskly.

A greying man with broad shoulders and a rather dirty apron approached, toting a pair of coffee cups in his hands. "Something warm on the inside helps greatly." He motioned to the coffee pot on the stove and handed Jock and Finnegan the cups. "Help yourselves, men."

Finnegan took the cup and nodded. "Many thanks, friend."

"Ed Dyer, owner and proprietor." He pointed to Jock. "I reckon I can guess why this gentleman is here, but..." He looked Finnegan over with a quizzical eye. "I would hesitate to guess what has brought a man such as you to this quiet little town. We rather pride ourselves on being dull around here."

Finnegan poured himself a cup of coffee and sipped it, enjoying the warmth. He nodded toward Jock. "And what would you assume is that young man's purpose?"

"That young fella is here to see Jack Wilson. I would bet my last dollar on it." The store owner rubbed his chin. "You, on the other hand, well, you've got a look about you that makes me think you're of a mind to use them guns you're carrying."

Finnegan glanced down at his guns. "I present the appearance of a man in a foul mood?"

"You do."

Finnegan sipped his coffee again. "I have been beckoned here, from quite far afield, by a woman who may have based the request on nothing more than whimsy."

Dyer nodded. "Yeah, that would go a long way in

explaining that scowl. Got to imagine it's got some portion of whimsy to it, as well. What woman called on you?"

"The lady's name is Melinda Meagher. She is a school teacher by trade." Finnegan continued sipping his coffee.

"Meagher?"

"Yes."

"Yellowed haired, a bit younger than you?"

"Indeed."

"I do know that lady." Dyer motioned toward Jock. "Just lately you two will have a good chance of finding what you're looking for in the same spot."

Finnegan rubbed the back of his neck. "Meaning what, sir?"

"Your lady friend has been spending a good deal of time with Jack Wilson. Been kind of keeping an eye on him, you might say, and acting in a clerical capacity." Dyer produced a coffee cup of his own.

Finnegan groaned and poured out some coffee for Dyer. "The newly risen Jesus has need of a schoolteacher to guard him?"

Dyer stared at Finnegan for a long moment. "Mister, I don't know who might have told you what, but Jack Wilson sure as hell ain't Jesus. Far as I can recall, he's the third of about five kids his old mama begot. Maybe it ain't my place to say, but that don't suggest virgin birth to my way of thinking."

Finnegan looked from Dyer to Jock and then back again. "In truth, sir, I could not care less if Mr. Wilson is the messiah or a saloon piano player. My only concern is the location of the lady so that I may inquire as to the purpose of my visit."

Dyer shook his head. "Women. I wouldn't doubt that it might be easier for a fella to find a newly risen savior than to calculate what might be going through the mind of a woman at any given time. You ought to count yourself lucky you were able to make it here at all. Your lady's request might have been for nothing if you hadn't been prompt in traveling. Old Jack is overdoing it a bit these days, if you ask me."

Finnegan stared at the man over his coffee cup. "Mr. Dyer, perhaps I misheard you. Are you insinuating that Mr. Wilson has something to do with the amount of snow this town is receiving?"

Dyer nodded. "I'll tell you right now, it ain't Jack's fault and a man ought not to lay the blame on him, neither. Jack warned 'em. I was standing right there when he told 'em how it would be."

Jock took a hesitant step forward. "Mr. Dyer, hello. My name is Jock Bull Bear. I am pleased to make your acquaintance. Are you referring to Jack Wilson's abilities as a rainmaker?"

"Damn right I am. Although rainmaker don't hardly cover it." Dyer chuckled.

Finnegan licked his lips. "Sir, you would claim that Mr. Wilson is the cause of this blizzard?"

Dyer scratched the back of his head. "Well, I guess it ain't my place to say one way or the other what makes it snow, but I will tell you this: John Josephus, the Indian Police captain, comes in here and says to Wilson that he'll give him a horse, twelve dollars cash money, and a damn fine axe if he'll come out by Josephus's place and make it rain. Wilson tells Josephus that he was aiming to make it rain like the damn great flood anyhow, so there ain't no reason for trading horseflesh or cash money. Says he'll do it for a picnic lunch what with it having been his intention to start with, but Josephus'll have to wait. A week later, Jack comes to me and wants a ride in the wagon over to Josephus's place. We go over and Jack tells all them folks that's gathered up out there that he's gonna make it rain and rain and rain some more, cause he ain't gonna be able to stop it once he gets it started and then, to top it off, it's gonna snow all damn winter so a man can't hardly get in and out of this valley." Dyer paused to chuckle again. "Well, he asks all them folks if they're apt to handle that much rain and, of course, they all cheer and declare they'll take all he's got. I guess it's just man's nature to overindulge."

Finnegan handed Jock a coffee cup and filled it. "I suppose at that point, Mr. Wilson made the heavens open?"

"Old Jack says a prayer, stomps around a bit and, God strike me dead if I'm lying, it started to rain inside of that hour." Dyer laughed. "Rained pretty damn regular all that summer, which is something I sure as hell never seen since I been here, and it's been snowing like this ever since the rain stopped. If Jack ain't careful, we'll all get snowed in and the whole damn town'll be swamped." Dyer shook his head and sipped more coffee. "There is such a thing as too much of a good thing, don't you know."

Finnegan rubbed his eyes. "Mr. Dyer, you are truly certain that the current predicament may not be simply an ongoing bout of precipitation and coincidence?"

"Might could be." Dyer cocked his head to one side. "What's the trouble, sir? You don't believe in magic or miracles?"

Finnegan smiled. "Quite the contrary. I spent many years in the employ of one of the world's great magicians. A man by the name of Allen Pinkerton."

Dyer rubbed his chin. "I have heard of the fella, but was unaware he was a magician. What sort of tricks could he do?"

"He could conjure money out of thin air along with criminals and conspiracies." Finnegan grinned. "The fellow could do it quite consistently, as well. I daresay he had more than one increasingly wet winter to his credit."

Dyer nodded again, considering the matter. "Well, give Jack a bit of time. It's my understanding that his abilities in regard to such matters as making it rain and predicting the future are a sort of new development. If they ain't, he sure ain't mentioned them before now. Time was, he was mostly just of use for digging post holes."

Finnegan finished his coffee and set the cup on a nearby table. "I suppose it would be best to see to the verification of these matters in person." He motioned to Jock. "My young friend here is charged by his tribe with the important duty of determining the status of Mr. Wilson, as regards his being the messiah or a saint or a rainmaker. I am charged with locating Miss Meagher, which will inevitably lead to my suffering to atone for my many past sins and discretions. Truth be told, I may find myself glad to have a savior close at hand for both confession and forgiveness."

Dyer simply stared at the gunman for a long moment. "Mister, I don't know what all that means, but I can try and get you out to Wilson's place if you like. I ought to make my way out there with some salt, coffee, and other fixings sometime soon here, else their bellies will be rubbin' on their backbones."

Finnegan turned to Jock. "Well, there you have it, my friend. Your savior and my...well, shall we call her the one who shall test me in the wilderness? My Molly is billeted with your man Wilson. It would appear fate has brought us together and we shall remain that way for the foreseeable future."

Jock drank a bit of coffee, holding the cup with two hands for the warmth. "It may be fate that has brought us together. It may be something else entirely."

Finnegan nodded. "I suppose it is possible that we have met so that you could be converted and become the proper catholic I never was."

THE DEEP SNOW made for difficult travel. The horses Dyer had provided were large animals in good condition, but even the greatest of beasts cannot run a steeplechase for miles on end. In some areas, the snow had drifted and formed a hard surface that the horses could tentatively walk upon. Unfortunately, the majority of the snow fields were not well frozen, and the horses burst through the top layer and sank to their bellies, where they impotently wallowed. This required the riders, not the horses, to do most of the work.

Finnegan stomped forward, breaking through snowdrifts that were up to the buckle on his gun belt. He did not so much step ahead as leap, allowing his body weight to crush the snow some, then tug on the reins of his horse. This trail breaking procedure had taken them roughly half a mile before Finnegan could finally see the other side of the open snow field, trees, and what he prayed was a lessening of the snow depth. He turned back to Dyer and Jock. "I believe we are about through the worst of it, men."

Dyer paused in tugging on his horse's reins some twenty or thirty yards behind Finnegan. The trail breaking helped, but it did not increase the willingness of the horses much. "That is good to hear. I am just about ready to shoot this damn nag and fashion it into snowshoes."

Finnegan hung his head before leaping forward once more. "By God, I wish you had mentioned that notion earlier." Finnegan gazed across the featureless snowfield, which was bathed in moonlight. The trees in the distance were only black shapes with muddled outlines. "Mr. Dyer, you are quite certain we are progressing in the correct direction? I would not care to cross this opening more than once."

Dyer stopped his tugging and wiped sweat from his brow. "I was damn sure when we started. Fair sure, around the time the sun set. Now, I more or less figure if we don't find Jack's place, we'll know we made it to California by the sunny weather and the gold layin' around."

Finnegan paused to huff, puff, and leap once again. "My only worry is that there are only three horses and two spare men to eat if I am forced to wait out the winter up here." Finnegan grinned back at Dyer. "I can only assume you would suggest we eat poor Jock first. He is the youngest and should be quite tender compared to two such ragged old men as us."

Dyer shrugged. "I can't be sure of that as yet, hold steady." He turned back toward Jock who brought up the rear of the small party. "Jock! Can you hear what we're sayin' over here?" The young man held his hand to one ear and shook his head while trying to slog forward in case the matter at hand was important. "Naw, he can't hear us." Dyer nodded. "Yup, we'll eat him first."

When they finally made it to the tree line, the party received some relief. The horses could be led from tree well to tree well, with only minimal trail breaking being required. Weaving from low spot to low spot, the party made its way through the trees and boulders until they came to a small collection of dwellings. The structures appeared, in design, between huts and shacks. Lumber frames poked out of the brush that was piled and strung over them. In spite of the crude design, the dwellings were, in fact, keeping the snow out and had not collapsed from the weight of it. They were roughly ten feet in width and about eight feet tall, with smoke drifting up and out of the holes in the center of their roofs.

Finnegan stumbled into a path that had been beaten down and jerked his horse forward into it. He knocked the snow from his hat and placed it back on his head. "Molly, you surely never fail to surprise."

"What's that, now?" Dyer came up behind him.

"Oh, nothing. I was just lamenting my current predicament." Finnegan knocked snow from his shoulders.

"Well, you picked a fine time to bother with that. We're here now. Won't have to eat the young Indian nor these old horses."

Finnegan nodded. "Yes, I realize we will not be forced to such an extremity, and it makes me a bit regretful. I have never tasted a stew formed from an Arapaho scholar and a mercantilist old swayback. Now, I fear I never will."

Dyer shrugged. "We got to get back to town someday. Mayhaps you'll get to try it on the return trip." He pointed forward and to the right. "It looked fairly different the last time I was up here. Jack and the boys was just putting these up and, course, there wasn't five damn feet of snow on the ground, but I think that shanty there is the one old Jack is livin' in." Dyer chuckled. "I know it don't look like much, but it's pretty damn cozy on a night like this."

Finnegan wiped sweat and snow from his face. "It is a far finer house than I have ever owned." He looked back to see Jock entering the trail. "Well, since we have all made it out of the wilderness and there appears to be no reason for cannibalism, I would suggest we knock on one of these doors and determine where the local messiah and my wayward school mistress are hiding."

"Uh." Dyer made his way up next to Finnegan in the trail. "Mr. Gilhooley, when I said that your lady friend was up here with Jack, I didn't mean to suggest they was up here... well, together like, if you get my meaning."

Finnegan sighed. "Mr. Dyer, I would hope that after our many years of acquaintance, Miss Meagher would have more regard for me than to request my traveling over most of this great nation, in the winter, so that she could personally announce her engagement to the coming savior to me." The dry good salesman only stared. "Mr. Dyer, I would never suspect Miss Meagher of immoral activity."

Dyer rubbed his face. "Yeah, well, just so you don't get to thinking I suggested it. That's the important thing. You seem like the kind of fella might get in a snit over that, and I don't imagine you carry them guns in anticipation of snakes."

"I am far too tired to duel anyone in defense of honor, currently, Mr. Dyer. Let us investigate these huts." Finnegan stomped through the snow to the closest domicile and thumped upon the thatched door. After a moment, the door was brought open a small amount until the snow piling up stopped its progress. Finnegan craned his head around toward the crack. "Good evening. We come in search of Miss Melinda Meagher."

A boy of about ten looked sideways at the gunman and the snowy world. "The white lady?"

Finnegan grinned. "She is, indeed." The boy pointed toward one of the larger huts off to the right. "Many thanks, young man." Finnegan turned to the others. "This way, gentlemen." In their hopping and sliding manner, the three men made their way to the large hut and Finnegan beat on the door once again. When it opened, the woman he had not seen in many years was the one who opened it. "Hello, Molly. I hope I am not interrupting your dinner."

The woman stood in the hut doorway, only capable of staring for a long moment. When she finally found her wits, her face broadened into a smile, and she leapt forward, throwing her arms around the gunman before her. "Finnegan! You are here!"

Finnegan turned a bright shade of red and gave her back a very light tap as she squeezed him around his snowy neck. "I have never been one to turn down an invitation."

She released him and stood in the doorway again. "I can barely believe what I am seeing. You are here, standing in the snow, so very far from Fort Smith. I can hardly credit it."

Finnegan shrugged. "It is not so much of an imposition as you may imagine." He looked back to the men with him. "Although, I believe we would all greatly appreciate it if you were to invite us inside so that we were not standing in the snow you mentioned."

"Oh, my goodness, yes, of course." She moved to the side.

Finnegan ducked and entered the dwelling. As his associates entered, he motioned to them. "I believe you already know Mr. Dyer, and this other gentleman is Jock Bull Bear, who has been kind enough to remain in my company for very nearly the entirety of my journey and has proved to be a fine companion."

Molly extended her hand to the young man. "It is a pleasure to meet you, Mr. Bull Bear." She smiled. "I feel rather certain that you have not traveled all this way to make my acquaintance."

The young man smiled back. "It is lovely to meet you, ma'am, but you are correct. I have come in search of someone else."

She nodded. "In that case, allow me to introduce you to the owner of this house, Jack Wilson." A man who had been hunched over near the fire in the center of the hut let the blanket that had been up around his head fall to his shoulders. He stood and pulled the blanket around him with one hand while putting his other hand out. Molly motioned between the two. "Jack Wilson, Jock Bull Bear."

Wilson looked nothing like the mythical medicine man Finnegan had been expecting. The fellow wore faded and patched trousers, a tattered and much-mended work shirt, and boots that had seen better days. He had the appearance of a working hand who was fit enough to handle most any labor. It was obvious that he had spent far more of his life with a shovel in his hands than he had in religious contemplation or trances. Jock shook the man's hand. If he was disappointed by Wilson's appearance, he did not show a glint of it. "Mr. Wilson, I have come a long way to meet you, sir."

Wilson offered a fatherly smile to the young man. "Yes, all the way from Oklahoma. It is an honor to meet an emissary of the Arapaho."

Jock stared at the man, awestruck. "Sir, that is...that is incredible. You know all that simply by looking at me?"

Wilson chuckled. "I know because your uncle sent a telegram asking after you three days past. It is not so hard to recall a name such as Bull Bear."

Finnegan laughed. "A telegram. Very droll, sir."

Wilson extended his hand to the gunman. "And you, sir, must be Finnegan Gilhooley."

Finnegan grinned. "Did my name come to you in a vision, as well?"

"Molly has told me a great deal about you. She was very proud to tell us that you shot Jesse James once. We were more impressed when she explained who that was." He smiled at the lady. "Although, I must say, I find it far more impressive that you would travel so very far to help a friend. Anyone can go about shooting people; hardly anyone takes the time to aid their friends."

Finnegan shrugged and knocked some of the remaining

snow from his shoulders. "Every ten years or so Molly and I like to have a bit of a visit. Whatever dire straits she finds herself in here is likely only an excuse to facilitate a reunion."

"I should hope so, Mr. Gilhooley." Wilson motioned to the fire. "Please, come by the fire. Warm yourselves and we will get some food warmed, as well. It is a terrible long journey from town to here in this weather." Wilson shook a finger at Dyer. "You should have insisted they wait until the morning, Ed."

"The young buck was in a fit to meet you Jack, and this here assassin was intent on seeing the lady." Dyer squatted by the fire.

"Mr. Gilhooley is not an assassin, Mr. Dyer." Molly shot a stern look toward the dry goods salesman. "In fact, he is a detective and Deputy U.S. Marshall."

Finnegan chuckled. "I can excuse Mr. Dyer's mistake. I would hardly be the first assassin Judge Parker has seen fit to affix a badge to." He motioned around the hut. "Miss Meagher, if you would be so kind as to aid me with the horses, I believe Mr. Bull Bear would like to make a few formal requests to Mr. Wilson, and would prefer not to wait in line."

Dyer moved to get up. "I can aid you with that."

Finnegan waved one hand while Molly got into her coat. "I assure you, Miss Meagher is more than capable in the handling of stock. Warm yourself, sir." The two moved out of the hut and into the snow to where the horses were tied to a small set of trees on the edge of the camp. The fluffy snow made little noise as they trudged through it. Finnegan took the reins of the two closest horses and pulled them into the broken trail. "It is fine to see you again, Molly." He offered a shy smile. "In truth, I had begun to wonder if we would ever see each other again."

She shook her head and took up the last horse. "If I had not seen fit to call upon you, I had been nursing the notion of visiting you in Arkansas."

Finnegan laughed. "Oh, Molly, this is preferable. Even with the waist-deep snow, this place is better. Arkansas and Oklahoma offer fine sport for a man such as myself, but they are not proper places for your sort." Finnegan followed as Molly led a horse toward a lean-to that contained several other animals. Once inside, they began removing the saddles from their respective animals. Finnegan set the first saddle on a pole mounted on one side of the structure for that purpose. "Well then, shall we continue to muse, or are you prepared to explain my purpose here? I would like to flatter myself that you wired solely out of yearning to see my handsome face once more, but I suspect a more practical motivation."

Molly set another saddle on the pole. "I must say, I rather like the added character the years have given your face. It would not be saying too much to call you distinguished, Mr. Gilhooley."

"Is distinguished the word educated schoolteachers use in place of scarred, Miss Meagher?" He pulled the saddle from the second horse. "What is my purpose here, dear Molly? We may as well bear the matter out."

Molly grew oddly serious. "Finnegan, I have asked you here to do no less than to offer a chance to facilitate the eventual peace of the nation."

Finnegan nodded slowly. "Naturally, that would be your request." He smiled. "Molly, in what manner could a man such as myself possibly contribute to peace?" He would have appeared shocked, but had been rather expecting the incredible.

She grinned and began combing down the nearest horse with a handful of hay. "I can understand your confusion,

Finnegan. I must confess that you are not the first vision I bring to mind when contemplating peace, either. In this particular instance, though, I feel you are the acme of perfection."

"She offers flattery. A bizarre request is bound to follow."

"Finnegan, you must protect Wilson at all costs. It may be difficult to credit, but if this country is to find safe harbor in the next century, Jack Wilson will be the man to guide it there."

The gunman did his best to not sound overly skeptical. "Jack Wilson, the man in the hut built of sticks?"

Molly placed a hand on her hip. "Yes, Finnegan."

"The man dressed to resemble a well-mannered ditch digger?"

"Yes, Finnegan." There was an edge to the confirmation.

"Very well, then." Finnegan took a moment to choose his next statement. He cleared his throat. "Let us assume, for the moment, that Jack Wilson will someday receive the thanks of a grateful nation. If the fellow is, in fact, our savior in some respect, why would he require my protection? Who could possibly wish to harm a savior?"

Molly licked her lips. "Finnegan, a short review of the Bible will show that the world is not kind to saviors, prophets, or any man who conceivably communes with a higher power."

"Molly, I find it doubtful that anyone will wish to nail that Indian farmer to a cross any time soon. It would be a touch uncivilized, even in this howling wilderness."

"Finnegan, you cannot yet appreciate what this man has brought about amongst the Indians. You cannot conceive of what this man intends to accomplish, what he will accomplish."

"Accomplish?" Finnegan slowly shook his head and

pulled a cigar from his pocket. "Molly, I have spent many a long day on the train coming here. All those days were in the company of the young Mr. Bull Bear, and he has given me a quite thorough description of Mr. Wilson's proclamations, intentions, and the various miracles he claims to be capable of conjuring." He paused to light his cigar. "I would readily admit that the fellow's talents appear quite impressive. Although, even if his magical abilities are shown to be genuine, I fail to understand how he is meant to bring about peace on earth and goodwill toward all men. Such a thing requires more than snowfall and parlor tricks, lass."

She grinned. "Finnegan, I assure you, the man is capable of far more than any of that." She took a step closer to him in the dark stable. "Finnegan, this man, through sheer power of faith, is uniting the Indian tribes."

"Uniting them?"

"Yes, he is bringing them together so that they will soon function as one people, one race. A race that could very well be the equal of the European race on this continent."

Finnegan puffed his cigar. "The equal, dear Molly? In what possible respect?" He raised one eyebrow. "You surely cannot be suggesting that the Indians could...could collectivize, rise up and win back the lands they previously inhabited and had charge of."

"And why not? I would never suggest something as vicious as a violent uprising, but their mere joining together would give them the position required to negotiate for proper terms from the government. Faced with an adversary on equal terms, the government would have no choice but to barter a settlement and return a good deal of land to them. Certainly, a more proper share than what they have currently been cheated and threatened into accepting."

Finnegan puffed contemplatively. "Molly, if this man

Wilson were to convince every Indian brave in this nation to join together into one army, and then utilized his god-granted chicanery to transform loaves into Winchesters with which to arm them, the force could still be handily defeated by any given state militia or the troopers from one or two forts. There are very few Indians left on this earth, Molly, and even fewer who are of military age or condition. As a race, they sicken and wither."

Molly assumed a most serious visage. "If what Wilson promises truly comes to fruition, the number of troops on the field will be of little consequence."

Finnegan knocked ash to the ground and stepped on it. "Such a battle would certainly be of note. It has been my experience that little other than numbers carry weight when it comes to battles. What sort of prophesy is Mr. Wilson proposing, specifically?"

"He..." Molly appeared slightly apprehensive. "He has suggested that there will be an upheaval."

"An upheaval?" Finnegan puffed, yet again. "Of what nature, lass? Of men or earth?"

"The visions he receives are not perfectly clear, Finnegan."

"Visions so rarely are."

"Finnegan, he has seen a... a rapture of sorts. The white men may be forced from the continent. The Indian will assume control. The dead may rise. The buffalo will return."

Finnegan sighed. "Dear Molly, it is difficult to say which prediction is the more fantastic in that list." He set a sly smile on his lips. "Sadly, when the white race is exterminated or flung back across the ocean, I shall no longer be able to guard Mr. Wilson."

"This is no matter for jesting, Finnegan. That man is the lynchpin in a mechanism to bring about a new world, in one form or another, and he requires protection. If you are truly my friend, you will provide it."

The gunman held up his hands. "From your lips to God's ear, Molly. I shall guard the fellow with my life and be pleased to be of use." He lowered his hands. "You must know by now that I am always ready to serve." He stared at the schoolmistress a long moment. "I am proud to call you friend and proud to be well enough thought of that you would call for assistance. That being stated, I must ask you, dear Molly, is it not possible that you have been, in some manner... deceived here, lass? If it is so, you are in good company."

Her eyes grew wide. "You would suggest I am the victim of a scheme of some sort here?" She laughed. "To what end, Finnegan? I have no millions for Wilson to make off with. I have no political or governmental connections for the man to make use of. I am nothing more than a roving schoolteacher with a small collection of coins in her purse for room and board. What purpose can be served by my being hoodwinked?"

Finnegan paused to contemplate the query. "Molly, oftentimes a charlatan's true motives are not easily discerned. I cannot say why this fellow may wish to convince school-marms and a horde of red savages that he is a magician descended from on high." He paused to puff the cigar. "What I can assure you of, dear lass, is that the fellow cannot travel to the next world, speak with God, see the future, or produce rain on demand. These things are not within the purview of mere men, and you would do well to keep such truths in mind as we discuss this matter."

She pulled her hair back from her face and pushed her fur lined hat down more firmly to her head. "Were Moses and Jesus not mere men, or appeared as such? Why is it that people the world over believe there were prophets who once walked the earth, but it is no longer a possibility? There are thousands of men, women, and children to the south that believe their prophet walked amongst them not more than a generation ago. All this is readily accepted, but an Indian such as Jack Wilson is greeted with nothing but invective and suspicion?"

Finnegan sighed. "Molly, I know more than a few who call the Mormons a pack of fools and madmen. I know more than a few who say the same of Catholics. I very well might reach the same conclusion if I took the time to contemplate the matter regarding my own beliefs. I do not know if one man's religion is any more sane than another's. What I can inform you of, unequivocally, is that the man in that hut is not the son of God. He is not a prophet of the Lord. He is not an associate of the Almighty or the understudy to an angel. He is a man who clearly aspires to owning some sheep and a house with a window."

"If that is the case, how would you explain the adulation of such a vast array of Indian tribes? Emissaries from all over the continent have come here to learn from Wilson and pay homage to him."

Finnegan rubbed his eyes. "I seem to recall a tale where one of those tribes you mentioned swapped Manhattan Island for a handful of beads and baubles. I am not certain we should trust the red man's scrutiny. Were they not praying to various rocks and trees not so long ago?"

"What of the Mormon delegations sent to investigate?"

Finnegan chuckled. "I know to a certainty I should never trust the sagacity of white men."

"Regardless of what you believe, Finnegan, there are a great many who do believe this man is possessed of insight, wisdom, and knowledge far afield from that of a mere Indian, and that puts him in danger."

Feeling there could be little purpose in continuing the current debate, Finnegan decided to simply concede the point and move on. He took a seat on the hitching post. "Very well, Jack Wilson is the second coming and must be watched over. Who, pray tell, would wish to do the man harm?"

Molly appeared pleased to have somewhat subjugated the gunman. "As time passes, Mr. Wilson may face many enemies. For the moment, there is only one fellow that is of particular concern. There is a man in Greenfield named Tom Mitchell, the Paiutes call him Hummingbird. It is said that he holds a deep grudge against Wilson and may seek his vengeance any time now."

Finnegan nodded, feeling a bit better to be back on ground he was familiar with. "Ah, well, even saints have someone who might wish to place them on a pyre. Who is the fellow?"

"I suppose you could characterize Mitchell as something of a rival to Wilson or, rather, was formerly a rival to Wilson's father for the position of medicine man within the tribe. Although the Paiutes do not make use of the same structure as other tribes, some of the features are shared. The position of chief, as an example, would not be..."

Finnegan held up one hand. "Molly, perhaps we could discuss the vagaries of their tribe someplace warmer, someday. For the moment, I would simply like to know what sort of fellow this Mitchell is, to better understand how much of a danger he poses."

"He is quite dangerous. It is commonly held that he is responsible for the tribe losing their most powerful shaman, Wodziwob." Molly glanced about the small structure and took a step closer to Finnegan. "There is no telling what some of these men are capable of when they become jealous of another medicine man."

Finnegan nodded and knocked ash down to the snow. "I see. In what manner did this fellow Mitchell kill Wobbly-knobby?"

"Wodziwob."

"Yes, that chap."

"Well, Mitchell did not kill Wodziwob. It is said he stripped him of his booha."

Finnegan cleared his throat. "Would that be some sort of crippling?"

"It could be looked on in that manner. It is the worst possible fate for a shaman, at any rate."

Finnegan stared at the woman. "Molly, what precisely is involved when one is stripped of their booba?"

"Boo-ha." Molly sneered. "Are your mispronunciations intentional?"

"No. It is a bit chilly, dear. May we continue?"

"Yes, certainly." She paused to collect her thoughts. "When one loses their booha among the Paiutes, they lose their mystical powers, so to speak. In Wilson's case, he would no longer be able to visit the world of the dead or cause the weather to change."

Finnegan could not quite conceal his shock. "Molly, have you brought me here, the distance of half a continent, so that I might keep one magician from stealing the magic beans of another?"

"There is no need to be impudent."

"I am merely attempting to understand my purpose here."

"Very well, then. Yes, Wilson is in danger from Tom Mitchell. The man may merely attempt to... corrupt Wilson's abilities in some manner. If he becomes frustrated in that attempt, he may elect to simply pick up a rifle and shoot Wilson down in the street."

Finnegan rubbed his face. "An act I would almost welcome for its tangible aspects."

Molly pointed one finger at her oldest friend. "Finnegan, you may scoff now, but mark my words: once you have spent a few days in the company of Wilson and witnessed what he is capable of, even you may come to believe."

Finnegan tossed his cigar out into the nearest snowdrift. "Molly, do not misunderstand my...hesitancy to embrace all this. Of all the souls I have known, I would say you are the least likely to be accused of foolhardiness or engaged in a lark. I have no doubt that you have been, in some manner, convinced this man Wilson is possessed of some sort of... specialty. Truly though, lass, I must confess to you, I have not been able to muster much belief in any form of divinity since the Battle of Gettysburg, and I doubt I ever will. You honestly expect I will end up on my knees praying with that digger Indian before all this is finished?"

Molly smiled and shook her head. "I would never seek a conversion for you, Finnegan." She grinned. "If for no other reason than I am quite fond of you just as you are. All I would ask is that you stay here, keep watch as I have requested, and do not disregard any possibilities out of hand. Who knows, you may view the world differently before this visit is at an end."

"Oh, after a few weeks of guarding the new messiah from assassins I imagine I will consider many things in a different light." He shivered and pulled his coat around him. "May we venture inside, dear Molly? If we remain out here much longer, I fear your friend Wilson will have to venture to the land of the dead to converse with us both."

"You make a fine point." She patted him on the shoulder. "Thank you for coming, Finnegan. There are few men as loyal to a friend as you in this world."

He chuckled. "Yes, well, you are the only person I have ever known who has invited me for a visit. I daresay, it would have been foolish to turn down the offer." He looked around at the dark snow fields. "Though, I must confess, I would enjoy this outing a great deal more if you had discovered your messiah in Mexico. Perhaps on a sandy beach."

"Oh, if this sort of thing were not sporting you would have no interest in it, Finnegan."

Chapter 6

GREENFIELD, NEVADA

January 6th, 1890

The Silver Spur Café was the only eatery in the small town of Greenfield or, rather, it was the only eatery Finnegan had seen protruding above the snowdrifts. He had trudged to the small café through the knee-deep drifts that surrounded his boarding house. As he came through the door, just before the noon hour, he found Bull Bear and Wilson seated at a table toward the back of the establishment. They were the only two people in the place. The proprietor stood in the kitchen, smoking a cigar with a book opened before him on the table he clearly used for preparing meals.

Finnegan shook the snow from himself and dragged an extra chair over to the table were the two men already sat. The gunman slowly removed his coat, hung it over the back of his chair and lowered himself to sit. "Hello, gentlemen."

Wilson smiled. "Good day, Mr. Gilhooley."

Bull Bear motioned for the cook. "You should have some coffee, Finnegan. You look chilled to the bone."

Finnegan removed his hat and shook it. "Yes, well, I believe I would be warmer if my landlady was of a mind to heat the better part of the house. Since I am her only boarder, she feels the need to close up portions of the dwelling at night. It would seem her labors separate my room from the stove." He shivered and glanced toward the café cook stove. "Sir, I would be more than happy to pay double for a meal if you will stoke up that device well to prepare it." The proprietor shrugged and began shoving wood in the stove. "At least there is one man in this town who is willing to prevent my impending death." He shivered again. "Mr. Wilson, would you care to enlighten me as to why there are no other boarders at my lodgings in a town of this size?"

Wilson frowned slightly. "The people have been leaving this place for some time now. They do not find as much silver in the mines as they once did. Now there are fewer mines and fewer miners." He sipped the coffee in front of him. "It may be good for the farmers and the Indians. They will not take the water from the river to work the mines. They will not cut the trees so we can gather pine nuts once again."

Finnegan nodded somberly. "Perhaps you will someday be able to dig down through the snow and reach either a tree or a river and all will be well." He turned toward the kitchen. "Coffee, sir, for pity's sake."

"You are not enjoying your visit to our land, Mr. Gilhooley?" Wilson appeared more concerned than insulted by Finnegan's foul mood.

"Not as yet, sir." He rubbed his eyes. "Did you gentlemen bring Miss Meagher to town with you this morning?" Finnegan had returned to Greenfield with Dyer the night before, but Molly had elected to remain among the Indians.

Wilson shook his head. "Miss Meagher is teaching the children of the camp to read and write. I cannot write the white man's letters. Miss Meagher has been very good to us.

She has written many letters for me. Given time, she has told me she will teach me to read and write."

The proprietor set a cup of coffee before Finnegan, and he placed his hands around it. "Thank you, sir." He took a long sip. "I am certain Molly will educate you, Mr. Wilson. It has been my experience that Molly tends to educate those around her whether they wish it or not." He took another sip. "Are there bears in this country?"

Wilson cocked his head to one side. "Bears, sir?"

"Yes, Mr. Wilson, bears. Large furry creatures that eat men and other soft delectable beasts." Finnegan sounded more than a bit perturbed. "Miss Meagher should not be inhabiting one of those huts if there are bears in this area."

Wilson sipped his coffee again. "Sir, I have not seen a bear in these parts for quite some time."

Jock sipped his coffee. "Finnegan, I believe the bears are asleep this time of year."

Finnegan sneered. "Well, I suppose if an animal can fall asleep, he can bloody well wake up again, can he not?" He looked between his two friends, but they clearly took the question to be rhetorical. "Yes, well, it is good we have settled that question." He drank more coffee and felt himself beginning to warm. "My apologies, gentlemen, the weather and the state of my boarding house has placed me in a foul mood. I shall do my best to become better company." He took out a cigar. "Are you learning all you had hoped to learn from Mr. Wilson, Jock?"

The young man held up a small leatherbound book he used for notetaking. "I have already learned much, but I am not yet certain if I have learned enough to report to my elders. I would very much like to witness one of the dances from which Mr. Wilson receives visions."

Finnegan lit his cigar. "Would that be the dance that

allows you to converse with departed relatives?" Jock nodded. "If you attempt too much outdoor dancing presently, you may all join the dearly departed."

Wilson nodded. "Mr. Gilhooley may be correct, Jock."

Finnegan began puffing his cigar and the small vice seemed to cheer him. "Well, then, Mr. Wilson, Miss Meagher has informed me that you fear you may be ensorcelled by a fellow named Tom Mitchell. Is that correct?"

Wilson stared at the gunman. "Ensorcelled, sir?"

"Yes, ensorcelled." Finnegan turned to Jock. "Surely you are familiar with the term."

Jock shook his head. "I am sorry, Finnegan. I am not."

"When one is hexed by a sorcerer they are said to be, quite naturally, ensorcelled." He looked from one man to the other. "Does that not follow?"

"I suppose it does." Jock seemed a bit confused.

Wilson leaned forward. "Is it bad to be ensorcelled, sir?"

"I would imagine so." Finnegan knocked ash to the café floor, where it disappeared into the puddle of water that was forming at his feet from the snowmelt. "Now that I ponder the matter, though, it occurs to me that I have heard the occasional tale regarding a man being spellbound for his own good." Finnegan puffed his cigar. "A witch, wizard, ogre, or pagan god may curse a fellow so that he falls into romance with a woman he might not otherwise give suit to or tricks him into pursuing some quest he would otherwise not attempt."

Wilson raised his eyebrows. "What is an ogre, Mr. Gilhooley?"

"An ogre is a man of gigantic stature, such as Goliath from the Bible." Finnegan smiled at the shaman.

"Ah..." Wilson nodded. "And you have seen such men, they are common in the east?"

Finnegan shook his head. "No, Mr. Wilson. What would make you imagine that?"

"You mentioned you had heard tales of their doings." Wilson appeared perplexed.

"Yes." Finnegan nodded. "But those tales are a fiction, Mr. Wilson. Stories made up in order to entertain or fables told to teach a lesson."

"I see." Wilson rubbed his chin. "So then, you would say that the story of David and Goliath is a fiction, as well?"

Finnegan laughed. "Surely, or a gross exaggeration, at best."

"Do you believe other stories in the Bible to be a fiction?" Wilson appeared somewhat worried.

"I...I cannot say what might be fact or might be fiction in that particular tome, Mr. Wilson. I suppose determining what to take from the Bible or leave between its pages is the work of any given man who reads it." Finnegan tapped more ash from his cigar. "You mentioned you cannot read English, as yet; how is it you have come to possess a knowledge of the Bible?"

"A great part of it has been read to me by the Wilson family who own the ranch where I labor. I have worked for them since I was very young and have performed a great deal of work around their home. They considered it their Christian duty to educate me in the teachings of the Bible."

"The Wilson family? Is not your family the Wilson family?" Finnegan blew out smoke.

"The Wilsons have been kind enough to allow me the use of their name. It is common among the Paiutes to have both an Indian name and a name given by the white man." Wilson sipped his coffee. "You white men seem to have a terrible time understanding who you are discussing if you do not use white man names."

Finnegan turned to his traveling companion. "Is your name not truly Jock Bull Bear?"

"It is." Jock shrugged. "My people do things differently."

"Yes, well, I suppose men must make their own customs according to their needs." Finnegan tapped ash down to the wet floor where it sizzled. "Mr. Wilson, it is quite fascinating to discuss biblical giants with you and the nature of the naming scheme in these parts, but I would be remiss if I did not bring us back to the original topic I wished to discuss. My friend Miss Meagher did not bring me here so that I might debate the validity of the Old Testament with you."

"Oh, yes." Wilson smiled. "She believes I am to be encircled."

Finnegan scowled. "Ensorcelled."

"En-sore-elled?" Wilson attempted.

"Ensorcelled." Finnegan scowled again. "Hexed, damn it. Hexed will do for our purposes."

Wilson sat back, still smiling. "Very well, hexed. Does that mean the man Miss Meagher warned you of will wish to take my booha?"

Finnegan motioned with his cigar. "Yes, booha is the word Miss Meagher used."

Wilson sipped his coffee. "Mr. Gilhooley, it is very nice of Miss Meagher to show such concern regarding Tom Mitchell, but there are many things Miss Meagher cannot understand, as yet. She has not lived among the people of these hills long enough. If she was to stay here, she would learn enough to understand, but she will not be here long enough for that."

Finnegan raised an eyebrow. "She will not?"

"No. She will be leaving a year hence, no more." He frowned. "I will be sad to see her go, but I have been assured she will stay no longer."

Finnegan tapped ash again. "Who has assured you of this, Mr. Wilson?"

"I have received word. Some knowledge is given very plainly, Mr. Gilhooley." He reached out and patted Finnegan's hand that lay on the table. "That is the same way I know that you have not been brought here to save me from being...hexed by Tom Mitchell. You have come here to save Miss Meagher and to gain forgiveness from a man you have greatly wronged." He slowly shook his head. "I am sorry, Mr. Gilhooley, but you could not help me in the matter of Tom Mitchell even if you wished to. You are not one of the people. You cannot intervene in matters of booha. Tom Mitchell will do what he believes he must, and you will do the same. I will be thankful for what little assistance you may render, but it may not be adequate."

Finnegan looked from Wilson to Jock and back again. "Mr. Wilson, if I wished to intervene between you and Mr. Mitchell, all that would be required would be for me to draw my pistol and shoot the man down. I assure you, it is a very uncomplicated practice and has proved quite reliable over the course of my professional endeavors."

Wilson drank what remained of his coffee. "I am certain it is a very simple matter, Mr. Gilhooley. I myself have killed a great many rabbits. In this case, it does not matter much, though. You will not kill Tom Mitchell. Tom Mitchell will outlive both of us by many years."

Finnegan smiled. "Mr. Wilson, I fail to understand how you could know such a thing."

"Of course, Mr. Gilhooley." Wilson motioned for the proprietor to bring him more coffee. "All men who have not been given the knowledge fail to understand. That is why so many take an interest in men who have the knowledge.

Perhaps you should dance with the people, when we dance, so that you might understand."

"I have never been much of a dancer, Mr. Wilson." Finnegan turned and gazed out the window for a moment. "What was that you said regarding the payment of penance?"

"Penance?" Wilson squinted.

"You mentioned that I have been shepherded to this darling hamlet so that I might be forgiven by someone I have harmed or who holds a vendetta against me." Finnegan continued to stare out the window.

"Hmm." Wilson rubbed his smoothly shaved chin. "I am not certain you understand, sir. I do not mean that you must be given forgiveness, the way a priest gives forgiveness. I am not certain anyone other than God can grant forgiveness." He rubbed the back of his neck, contemplating the matter. "Mr. Gilhooley, when men fight, the earth is not right. Fighting injures the balance of the earth and the sky, and even the snows as they fall. You fight too much, more than a man ought to. You must make right that which has been unbalanced by your fighting. One of the men you have fought with will come here so that you might find steadiness. So that you might find peace amongst the fighting. I believe another may come so that you can know true mercy."

Finnegan rubbed his eyes and sipped his coffee. "Mr. Wilson, on the rare occasion when I am forced to reunite with old acquaintances, those I have had business with in the past, I am often forced to act quickly and have no opportunity for making amends."

"Oh, there will be trouble, sir." Wilson nodded somberly. "There is trouble wherever you go, but you should not think only of the bad. Think of the good that will eventually come of all this, and you will be a happier man as you travel through life."

"I suppose I may at that." Finnegan watched as a coach came through the slop and snow that covered the declivity that was formerly the town's Main Street. "And what gives you solace as you travel through life, Mr. Wilson? Do you presume to lead your people to the promised land? I have been told that you do."

Wilson stared down into his coffee. "I have written the President. I have informed him that it would be best if he were to appoint me Governor of the west. I have told him that I would be glad to work for him and make the land a good place for the whites and the Indians. There will be plenty for all; there is no need for us to fight. The Indians can work as the whites do and the whites can learn our ways, as well. There is no need for us to hurt each other by turns."

"Governor of the west?" Finnegan turned to Jock. "It is an ambitious appointment he seeks."

Jock shrugged. "I suppose it cannot hurt to ask. I have been told as much by many of my instructors."

Finnegan smiled. "What sort of compensation did you request? It has been my experience that it is best to ask for a large sum in advance when bargaining with government representatives. The preferred method is to ask for roughly four or five times what will be required for costs and a small profit, so that you may be swindled down to half of what you requested and, of course, you can be assured of only ever receiving half of what was promised. The remaining stipend obtained using this method is just enough to survive, but it is the only method I know of that will keep a man from starving in government service."

Wilson rubbed his chin again. "I asked for a small stipend and a one-hundred-and-sixty-acre farm."

Finnegan grimaced. "In that case, upon your appointment, you can be assured of receiving two nickels to rub together and a plot of ground just large enough for a privy to stand on." He shook his head. "It will hardly be an allotment properly suited to a Governor, much less a Governor who presides over such an expanse." Finnegan drained the remainder of his coffee and motioned to the proprietor for more. "How long have you possessed clairvoyance, Mr. Wilson?"

"Clairvoyance?"

"The ability to see that which has not yet transpired." Finnegan shook his head. "For a man given charge of so very many magical inclinations, you have learned terribly little of the proper terminology. If you are to be Governor of the west, you must learn your terms, from ensorcelled to clairvoyance, and certainly gratuity, if you wish to enter the fray of politics, sir."

Wilson nodded and took his coffee from the owner by turn. "I will try, Mr. Gilhooley." He sipped the fresh coffee. "I began to see that which has not yet occurred about two years ago. I went into the canyons to speak with the spirits and speak with God. While I was there, I traveled to heaven. Since then, I am often given word of what is to be. Although, I am not always certain how to explain what is to be or not to be."

Finnegan grinned. "Ah, yes, that is the question." Both men stared at him blank faced. "If we are to be spending an extended period of time together, I will have to insist that you both learn the works of William Shakespeare, at least to some degree, so that you may better appreciate how humorous I am."

Wilson frowned. "I am trying very hard to learn my letters, sir. I am sad to say you will not be here long enough for me to finish learning them."

Finnegan waved one hand. "In that case, you may disregard the suggestion. Learning the works of the bard has profited me very little and I doubt you would gain much of anything from it, either." He sipped his new cup of coffee. "Might you have any thought of the name of the fellow I will be having a donnybrook with in this town? It would be both helpful and impressive if you could name the man for me." Finnegan thought on it a bit more. "A date for his arrival would not be disregarded, either."

Wilson sighed. "Mr. Gilhooley, are you hoping that I will inform you as to the man's identity so that you will be forewarned and thus able to fire upon the gentleman before he can fire upon you?"

"Given my druthers, I prefer to have first right of refusal when it comes to gunplay." Finnegan looked from Wilson to Jock and back again. "Is that not a reasonable preference?"

Wilson sighed again. "I suppose it is, and I suppose it has served you well in the past, sir. It will not aid you in this instance, sir. You will know the gentleman by sight and neither of you will kill the other."

Finnegan nodded. "I have always been more than willing to draw the line at crippling if crippling is all that is called for. Oftentimes, it is more effective. A broken fellow can serve as an excellent example to others who would consider attack in the future."

Wilson chuckled. "Mr. Gilhooley, I believe you will simply have to wait and see how matters unfold for yourself in the coming days."

Finnegan sneered. "Mr. Wilson, I can only hope you are not too offended when I observe that there is damn little purpose to having a seer around if the fellow refuses to fully relate his prophesies. You may wish to avoid gaining the literacy Miss Meagher has offered to you. If you are able to write all of this down, your followers will inevitably demand more specificity and you will never have a moment's peace."

Chapter 7

GREENFIELD, NEVADA

January 7th, 1890

As the day had gone on, the leather straps of the snowshoes had elongated a bit and required readjustment. Other than that, Finnegan had no complaints regarding the implements. They were far preferable to crashing through the drifts and leaping from step to step as he had the previous night in search of Wilson's camp.

Pausing to move the buckle of one snowshoe another hole forward on the strap, Finnegan grinned at Dyer. "These are fine accoutrements, sir. Did you make them yourself?"

Dyer chuckled. "They come from Chicago, same as canned ham and Pinkertons. I don't know any more about stringing sinew and bending wood than the next dry goods salesman, but I guess somebody in one of them slaughterhouses over there does. Been told the Indians around here once produced these items, but I reckon they've lost the knack or prefer the Chicago-made implements, as I do."

"Have you ever visited Chicago?" Finnegan stood, finished with the adjustment.

"I have not."

"You are surely a better man for it. It has been my constant labor the last handful of years to conceive of methods for avoiding that town, and I am proud to say I have managed it consistently."

"Don't care for the place?"

"It is corrosive to both character and peace of mind."

"Huh." Dyer grinned. "Sounds like a damn fine place to visit."

Finnegan smiled back. "It is well known to only be truly poisonous in large doses. Unfortunately, I have had more than my share of doses heaped upon me already." Finnegan looked over the high desert country they were slowly making their way through in search of an elk herd. "I greatly prefer a location such as this."

Dyer wiped sweat from his brow. "Yeah, it is nice up here. Even better since the miners all cleared out. There was about a ten-year stretch when you couldn't hardly hear yourself think up here, but now that the silver's played out, and it ain't worth what it used to be, a fella can sneak in a quiet bit of hunting again." He shrugged. "Or I could, if I could shoot worth a damn. Handy, you showing up when you did. I guess what with you being a nickel book assassin and all, you're probably a fair hand at shooting dinner, huh?"

Finnegan considered taking the time to explain the nuances of his profession to the dry goods salesman, but thought better of it. "I have some experience with hunting animals, yes." He began plodding forward across the snowfield with Dyer by his side. The snowshoes alleviated the need for one man to break trail and the going was far more pleasant. Finnegan hefted his rifle in one hand and turned to his companion. "Mr. Dyer, spending many years in the capacity of a detective has made me somewhat curious. Might I inquire: if Mr. Wilson intended to make the voyage into town the other morning, why was it so necessary for us to travel to his camp last evening?"

Dyer shrugged. "Your pal Bull Bear seemed awful eager to get a look at Jack, and..." He shrugged again. "There's an Indian gal up there who's company I rather enjoy. Ever kept company with an Indian gal?"

"I cannot say as I have."

"Well, in my experience it's a damn sight nicer than keeping company with white women. An Indian gal will make you dinner, hand you your jug, and not once make mention of a damn wedding chapel."

"I suppose each man must search out the solace he prefers." Finnegan pointed forward. "You believe the elk are concealed somewhere on the other side of those trees?"

"Uh huh." They continued to march forward. "I seen them in there in bad winters before. There's a kind of deep, broad sort of gully on the other side. The snow blows over one part of it and the grass ain't covered much, even in a year like this. Them elk need that grass, and they'll go for it where it's easier to get at. Likely a bunch of them piled in there."

Finnegan nodded. "In this annum they should be rather desperate, I should think."

Dyer pointed to Finnegan's rifle. "I'm not sure what kind of hunting you done before, but elk are on the large side for critters. Is that funny gun gonna have enough oomph to put one down? It looks like a shotgun or something."

Finnegan smiled down at the Purdey. "It only resembles a shotgun, sir. It is the common choice for men who hunt large African game such as elephants and the like. I assure you, it is more than ample for a large deer." They approached the trees. "I have used it in a variety of capacities, and it has always proven to be effective. My only real difficulty with it has been locating a sufficient supply of ammunition. Fortunately, the ball is of a common size. I can normally locate a gunsmith capable of reloading the cases. Purchasing the ammunition from a British manufacturer is quite punitive."

"You certainly take an avid interest in your equipment, Mr. Gilhooley. Although, I suppose such things are your business." Dyer glanced over at the Pinkerton. "Speaking of which, how is it you are available for this outing? I would have thought your Miss Molly would have insisted on you staying close to Jack, or bringing him along, at the least. Ain't you here solely to guard him? Least ways that's how it was explained to me."

Finnegan chuckled. "I inquired of Mr. Wilson whether or not he would be in need of protection today, and he assured me that it was not necessary. Miss Meagher could hardly argue the point. Such protestations might corrupt her confidence in Mr. Wilson's supernatural abilities."

Dyer chuckled back. "I guess a fella has a right to be skeptical when he first encounters a different kind of critter such as Jack Wilson, but I'll guarantee you, sir, you will eventually find yourself either awed or baffled when it comes to old Jack."

"Detectives do not care to be baffled, Mr. Dyer, and I believe my capacity for awe dissipated many years ago."

"Might be time to dust both of 'em off here in a while. Jack's got a certain way about him. When you first meet the man, you get to thinking he ain't quite right in the head. Then, once you get to know him a bit, well...you get to thinking there's a method to his particular madness. Next thing, one day, before you really even notice it happened, you catch yourself believing."

Finnegan glanced over at the dry good salesman. "Believing what, precisely?"

"Just believing in...Jack, I guess. It's damned odd. You get to thinking there's no way in hell a man could do what he..." Dyer stopped in his tracks, crouched, and motioned forward. "I think I saw something move up there in the trees. Got to be an elk; I don't know what the hell else would be wandering around here." He glanced down at the corroded Henry rifle he held in one hand. "I reckon you ought to move along first."

Finnegan nodded and whispered to his companion. "This should be an interesting test of Mr. Wilson's abilities. He assured me we would return with meat." Finnegan checked the wind to make certain it still blew into his face, and then began to slowly plod forward in a low crouch. He could only hope that whatever animal dwelt within the trees would not catch sight of him, and would thus allow him to approach within range for a shot. As he moved forward, he was able to slip into a trough of sorts in the snowdrifts. The depression allowed him to proceed with very little of himself exposed. The drift ran tangential to the trees, but it did allow him to gain ground in the basic direction of the sighted animal. When they made it to the tree line, both men paused and peeked over the edge of the drifted snow.

Finnegan brought his head just barely above the ice crystals and then brought it back down quickly in concert with Dyer. The older fellow grinned at the Pinkerton. "Like I told you, they congregate here in the cold."

"One of those two closest will do nicely."

Dyer scowled. "Them are cows, the female of the species."

"And far better dinner fare, in my experience."

"That I will stipulate to. Them horns taste awful." Dyer rubbed his frosted beard. "They're a goodly distance, yet."

Finnegan nodded. "This rifle has an adjustable sight for such shooting." He glanced to the right. "I will crawl up that small declivity and use the pack board to steady the shot." He slung the rigid, rudimentary pack frame from his shoulders.

Dyer shrugged. "Very well. I'll stay here so as not to spook them."

Finnegan made his way to the small gully that split upward from the drift. He crawled to the apex of it and then jammed the pack board down into the snow so that it was at the correct height for him to be seated behind it. The elk in the distance took no notice of him as he placed the Purdey over the board and reached forward to flip up the second leaf on the weapon's rear sight. The front sight settled onto the shape of the larger cow some two hundred yards away. As the front sight settled into the bottom of the notch on the rear, Finnegan drew in half a breath and squeezed the trigger. The recoil rocked him back, knocking the pack board loose. As Finnegan brought the rifle back down, he could see one elk running off into another stand of timber and the dark shape of the other lying where it had formerly stood.

Dyer came trudging up the small gully. "I'll be damned, Finnegan. That big gun near knocked that old girl right over. I ain't never even seen a buffalo gun do a job like that."

"It is effective for large game." Finnegan stood and began knocking the snow from his clothing. "We have much work ahead of us and it will be a tiring journey back to town, but well worth it to have fresh meat this evening."

"Fresh liver."

"Ah, there are few things finer than elk liver. It will be far preferable to the fare that comes out of your canned goods."

Dyer's eyes narrowed. "You don't care for my canned goods?"

"Not compared to fresh victuals. Who would?"

Dyer shook his head. "Oh, no, I imagine anyone would prefer the newly minted stuff. It's only that I got most of that stuff I been feeding you and Mrs. Culbertson from a rather shady fellow at a well-reduced cost, and I was wondering if you'd suffered any ill effects."

Finnegan scowled back at the dry goods salesman. "Mr. Dyer, such an admission would be far more endearing if it had been made previous to my ingesting the aforementioned canned goods."

"Yeah, I suppose it might, but then who'd eat all that stuff?"

FINNEGAN PULLED the length of leather strap looped around the shoulder straps of the pack board tight. With the load somewhat adjusted, he took his rifle back from Dyer and they proceeded further down the steep slope they were descending. Each man carried a shoulder and ham from the deceased elk, along with a collection of finer cuts contained in burlap sacks. Dyer had the liver in a sack positioned on the very back of his pack board and the organ continued to leave an impressive blood trail even after they had traveled several miles.

The two hunters had been taking turns in the lead as they made their overloaded way down toward the valley the town of Greenfield lay in. The man in the lead had to first push his boot down into the snow and loose earth, compact it, then bring his other foot forward. The maddeningly slow dance needed to be repeated over and over again so that the men would not fall, roll, and likely be maimed by the pack boards and their loads.

Dyer jammed his boot down and spurted out a plume of frosty air. Steam was rising from the man's coat collar. "How many elk you shot, Finnegan?"

"I believe this is my third. I shot two some years back in Montana."

He chuckled as best he could, given his level of exertion. "What the hell was you doin' up in Montana?"

"Visiting Miss Meagher and seeing to a few other duties."

"That Molly is a damn fine woman. You ought to quit visiting with her and marry the gal. Settle down and get her to quit her damn foolishness. Don't know what that gal is doin' here pondering over Wilson and writing letters for him, but if you ask me it can't lead to nothing but trouble. You ought to make her an honest woman and make her behave. Be best thing for her in the long run."

"If there is a method to make Miss Meagher behave, I am not aware of it." Finnegan paused. "What makes you say nothing good can come of Miss Meagher's presence here?"

Dyer paused and looked up at the gunman. "Well, what the hell good could possibly come of any of this? Jack's got half the damn country riled up what with all them other Indians coming and going. That woman of yours ain't helping matters by penning letters to every fool who hasn't heard of Jack, as yet. Now we got Finnegan Gilhooley staying at the boarding house." Dyer wiped his brow. "No offense meant, you seem like a nice enough fellow, but from what I heard from folks in the last few days, there ain't much difference between you and the pox coming to town."

Finnegan shook his head. "Mr. Dyer, while I have participated in a great many unfortunate and uncivilized events over the years, I assure you: I have not precipitated any of them."

"I'll keep that in mind when..." Dyer looked past Finnegan toward the top of the ridge they were slowly dropping from. "Now what the hell would somebody be doing up there?"

"Up there?" Finnegan was just beginning to contemplate a method for turning to look uphill when a loud thwock sound emanated from the pack board and he was forced forward into Dyer. The dry goods salesman managed to catch the gunman for a brief instant as the sound of a gunshot filled the air.

"Finn, I believe someone shot you." Dyer stared up at the Pinkerton with eyes more tired than frightened.

"I believe you are correct." Another thwock came from the rear of the pack and the two men were forced to give in to gravity. They became a knotted ball of snow, wool clothing, guns, and bloody meat as they began their roll down the shale-strewn precipice. Linked at first, they were separated when they contacted a rather large pine tree. The pine broke their union, and both men made their own trail for a few moments before being tossed into the same small gully near the bottom of the incline. They came to settle only a few feet apart with a single elk ham coming to rest between them. Neither man possessed a rifle any longer.

Several minutes passed before the snow ceased cascading down the hill and Dyer lifted his face a bear inch up out of the snow. A hoarse whisper was all he could manage. "Finnegan, are you dead?"

A snow covered lump off to Dyer's left responded in an equally low whisper. "I still live. Do not move and do not speak up."

"I ain't entirely certain I can move, anyhow." Dyer let out a long breath. "Finnegan, I have suffered several good hits to my head in the last little bit, but I seem to recall you being shot."

"You are correct."

"Twice?"

"Yes."

"Then you fell down that same damn mountain that has likely killed me."

"Correct again."

"Mind explaining how exactly it is you ain't playing a harp, then?"

"I believe the extended range and the cargo of the pack board allowed me to survive the initial attack. As for falling down the mountain, it is only by God's good grace either of us still draws breath. I contacted the tree with great force."

"As did I." Dyer groaned softly. "Finnegan, would you mind terribly telling me why it is you wish to lie here in the snow? I do not believe it will be an enjoyable experience for either of us, but should we not at least attempt to make our way back to town so that we might die by the fire in my store?"

"Mr. Dyer, I will not obfuscate the fact that I am in a great deal of pain currently. I would like nothing better than to move about some and attempt to mitigate the throbbing in my various limbs, but I must insist that you remain still. A few minutes more is all I would ask."

"What in hell difference can a few minutes make?"

"I would estimate that to be the time required for the bastard who shot me in the back recently to descend the ridge with the intention of investigating our corpses."

"Finnegan, I do not believe freezing to death in this snow is a good use of the mercy God has shown me after rolling down that mountain."

"Mr. Dyer, I do not wish to sound gruff, but if you queer my ambush this day, I will gun you down in that bushwhacking bastard's stead."

Dyer let out a small groan, but remained perfectly still. "Mr. Gilhooley, you may not mean to sound gruff, but you damn well do. I will hold here."

"Many thanks."

Time passed at a grueling rate as the two men lay in repose, doing their best to hold their faces up out of the snow without being of notice to anyone who might approach. Somewhere in the distance a crow made its call and the occasional whisp of snow would come swishing down the mountain. Other than that, the world was quite still. Dyer was just beginning to think he might be forced into breaking his word to Finnegan to ease the throbbing in his legs when the sound of crunching snow reached his ears. As the footsteps drew closer and closer, Dyer was certain the approaching assassin could surely hear his heartbeat and breathing from yards distant. It sounded as if the fellow were about to step onto Dyer's back before something finally happened. When the bushwhacker was practically on top of Finnegan, the Pinkerton pulled a small revolver from the folds of his coat and fired four rounds into the chest of the attempted killer. The man fell backwards and landed in the snow in front of Dyer. The dry goods salesman watched as the light left the fellow's eyes.

Without adieu, Finnegan climbed up out of the snow and began reloading the small gun he had used to great effect. The gunman stared down at the dead man for a moment before returning the little gun to his vest pocket. "Dyer, pick yourself up."

The dry goods salesman pulled himself from the snow and stared at the expired man while he swept the snow from his clothes. "Gilhooley, that..." He glanced from the dead man to the Pinkerton and back again. "That took a good deal of dedication."

"It often does." Finnegan knocked snow from his jacket. "Do you recognize the man?"

"I..." he leaned forward and took a step closer. "I believe I do, Finnegan. I know I have seen him in my store. He was employed at one of the mines and...for the life of me, I cannot recall his name or if he ever gave it."

Finnegan gazed up the mountain at the trail the two men had left from their rapid descent. "A miner?"

"Yes, I am fair sure of it." Dyer looked to the Pinkerton. "Do you not know him?"

Finnegan chuckled. "Why should I know him?"

"He tried to murder you, Finnegan. Does that sort of thing not require at least a blushing acquaintance?"

"Oftentimes not." Finnegan pointed up the hill. "I can just make out what must be two of our elk quarters and what I believe is your rifle. I do not see mine, damn it." Finnegan motioned to the dead man. "You should help yourself to that fellow's. I daresay it is superior to that old pump handle of yours."

There was a click in Dyer's throat as he swallowed. "I am not certain I can take a dead man's rifle."

"It fires a much more reliable cartridge than your rifle and its owner will not be having need of it any longer." Finnegan swept the last of the snow from his pants. "Oh, very well, then. Allow me to ease your conflicted sentiments." Finnegan knelt and took the rifle from the dead man's grip. "There, now, I have taken possession of this poor departed soul's property, and I now pass it along to you. You certainly have earned it. I greatly appreciate your cooperation in laying my trap." Finnegan held out the Remington rolling-block. "Take it in good conscience, sir."

Dyer slowly took the weapon. "I will take it, but I make no claim to keeping it. The man may have heirs."

"The bastard may have a congregation. His behavior would be in keeping with that type." Finnegan sighed. "We should be about our work, Mr. Dyer. We must collect our meat and find my rifle. I pray it has not suffered damage. I am not certain I could live with the knowledge that I let it come to ruin."

Dyer stared at the gunman. "The rifle? That is what strains your good humor in all this?"

"I consider it to be one of my oldest and surest friends. I would mourn its loss greatly."

"Mr. Gilhooley, I feel I would be remiss if I did not tell you that some of your statements, and actions, have given me worry this day."

"My statements and actions give me worry many days, Mr. Dyer. I have simply learned to live with it. Is there a possibility that this gentleman fired on us believing us to be claim jumpers or the like?"

"I would not think so, given the slim returns in the area these days. I don't believe we passed over an active claim during the whole of our hunt."

"Are there many mines still operating in the area?"

Dyer limped over and took a seat on a fallen tree trunk. "Not near as many as there once were. Say maybe a half dozen. What makes you ask?"

"If this man was a miner, as you recall, and he resided in the area, it stands to reason that he would be employed at one of the mines still in operation. With any luck, I should be able to determine his identity, and from there I may be able to decern his motives for the attempt on my life." Finnegan shrugged. "Or your life. It is best not to assume anything in these situations."

"Well, that is all very neat, Mr. Gilhooley. Is that the sort of thing you detectives are trained in?"

"By Allen Pinkerton himself, sir. Now that I think on it, Mr. Pinkerton gifted me the gun I used to dispatch that fellow. My association with the old man never fails to serve me well."

Dyer shrugged. "Seems to be treating you well, aside from the occasional fella like this trying like hell to murder you."

"As I said, sir, the attempt may have been made on your life. After all, you recognize the man and I do not." Finnegan smiled and began limping uphill.

"Now, what would a man like me have done to earn killing from a fella like this?"

"Perhaps he is a frequent purchaser of your canned goods." Finnegan stopped short and lifted one boot from the snow. "Bloody hell, I believe I have just stepped on our elk liver."

Jack Wilson helped Dyer off with his coat and hung it near the wood stove that occupied the center of the dry goods store. "I seen many a strange bit of wonderment in my day, Jack, but I daresay I had not seen the like of this until today."

Wilson shrugged. "Mr. Gilhooley had no choice. The man was an assassin of low character, and his evil deeds could only end in one manner."

Finnegan removed his own coat and handed it to Wilson. He rubbed his blue hands together, eyeballing the Indian sage. "Mr. Wilson, would you have me believe that you witnessed the attack Mr. Dyer and I suffered in your mind's eye? If that is the case, I am sorely disappointed you did not take the time to warn us in advance."

Wilson cocked his head to one side. "Mr. Gilhooley, if you do not mind my saying so, you seem rather obsessed with prophecy and clairvoyance. Such obsession is not good for a man's humor. I am capable of such things and even I know that ruminating on them all the day long is not healthsome."

Finnegan licked his lips and did his best to not let his irritation show. "Very well then, Mr. Wilson, how is it then that you have knowledge of what occurred without Mr. Dyer or I offering up the details?"

Wilson pulled a coffee pot and a cup from the stove and offered the cup to Finnegan. "I was hauling a load of grain and a few marooned passengers from the train back to town when I heard shots at the bottom of the large shale slide. As I knew you and Mr. Dyer were out hunting in that direction and that you were unlikely to find game there, I could only assume that one of your many sundry enemies had found you and attempted to exact the vengeance men such as yourself are so very fond of."

Finnegan scowled and held up the cup for Wilson to fill. "And how is you know I have enemies in this area?"

Wilson laughed and filled the cup. "I have told many that you have come to town on Miss Meagher's bidding. They had told many others, and whenever they do, those told often swear curses upon you and pledge some truly foul intentions. How many men attacked you?"

Finnegan sipped the coffee. "Just one. I daresay if luck had been with him, he would have accomplished the deed, too."

Wilson set the coffee pot on the stove. "Ah, yes, but if luck were not with you, you would have never lived long enough to reach Greenfield. A man like you should not trifle over luck. Yours will hold. I have seen it."

"And there is the second sight we are not to spend too much rumination on." Finnegan shook his head. "I do not suppose you could be so helpful as to ask the spirits the name and associations of the would-be assassin here. We found a knife in his possession inscribed with the initials A.L., but that is all."

"I have traded rabbit pelts and pine nuts with a fellow by the name of Albert Larson, who was employed as a miner at the Mary Louise. He was a bit shorter than me, about the same age, and had red hair. Is that of assistance?" The soothsayer offered only a small smile that might have been sly if not for the glint in his eyes that bespoke innocence.

Finnegan sighed. "Yes, Mr. Wilson, that is of assistance. Thank you."

Wilson nodded. "I am always happy to help. I must say, Miss Meagher is considerably less nervous regarding my being assassinated since you arrived. Although, I am not sure the best method for preserving my life is to invite to visit a man who most people wish to kill. Do you suffer from this same form of persecution wherever you go, Mr. Gilhooley?"

"Oh, I suppose I had managed to convince the vast majority of the citizens of Fort Smith and the surrounding Indian territory that the possibly gained glory would never be worth the sting of the attempt. It is wearying to think I may have to begin teaching the lesson once more here."

"You will soldier through, as always." Wilson patted Finnegan on the shoulder. "Will I be able to reach the deceased fellow with a pack mule?"

Finnegan gave a confused stare. "Mr. Wilson, we are in possession of the man's rifle and the knife I mentioned. His pistol was a rotten old cap and ball piece. If you wish to own his boots, I will not argue the point, but that hardly requires a pack mule."

"Mr. Gilhooley, I go to retrieve the man's body so that he may be given a proper burial." Wilson took a step toward the door.

"Do you intend to blast the man a grave with dynamite?" Finnegan could barely credit what he was hearing.

"I intend to place him on the rear wall of Isaac McDonald's ice house until the thaw arrives and a proper hole can be dug." Wilson pulled his hat down to guard against the coming cold. "I would do the same for any man; the fact that he was an assassin does not enter into it." He looked to Finnegan. "Speaking of regarding all men equally, I believe you know one of the gentlemen I transported from the train today. I am certain you will meet later, as he is boarding at your residence."

Finnegan narrowed his eyes. "Who might you be referring to?"

"I did not catch the gentleman's name." Wilson turned to go.

"Then how is it you know I am acquainted with him?"

Wilson turned back and smiled. "I was told, Mr. Gilhooley. Unlike most men, I do not need to be told twice."

"Yes, I noticed you did not require an explanation of the word clairvoyance twice, either. I hope the word is of use to you, sir."

FINNEGAN LOOKED into the cracked mirror that adorned one side of his rented room and straightened the well-starched collar that was hooked into his most recently laundered shirt. He had heard a rumor that his landlady did a fair boiled wash, but had yet to receive an offer or, probably more importantly, a price quote regarding the service. Deciding that the collar looked well enough, he briefly considered adding a necktie. He knew there was likely one buried somewhere in the depths of his suitcase, but he elected to skip the notion.

Molly had accepted an invitation to dine at the boarding house that evening, and Finnegan wanted every aspect of the evening to go smoothly. He buttoned up his black vest over his fresh white shirt and then added the small Cloverleaf Colt to the vest's pocket. The small gun had treated him well earlier -- perhaps it would continue to offer good fortune. Over the vest, he hung his shoulder holster that kept a Colt Frontier hanging vertically at his side. Below those two guns, he strapped on the belt from which his 1875 Remington hung. Taking a moment to glance in the mirror, he took note of the fact that many might suggest he was overly well armed for a romantic dinner, but Wilson's premonition regarding the new boarder in the house had Finnegan oddly spooked. So far, the man had done little in Finnegan's presence to prove himself to be a legitimate magician, let alone a messiah, but still...the fellow had an odd way about him. Finnegan popped open his pocket watch and saw that he had no time for such woolgathering. He was on the verge of being late for supper.

Coming down the stairs, he was greeted with the sight of Molly sitting in the parlor with his landlady, Mrs. Culbertson. While the lady had always been exceptionally cool to Finnegan, he was pleased to discover the treatment did not extend to female visitors. The old crone had provided both tea and biscuits to the company. The aged widow even wore a smile and had taken the time to sit and chat a bit. Finnegan approached and offered a small bow. "Good evening, ladies. How does the evening find you?"

Mrs. Culbertson, who had never offered much in the way of warmth previously, looked up from her seat at Finnegan as though he were a long-lost son recently returned from war. "Very well, Mr. Gilhooley, and so pleased to see you this evening." She practically grinned. "I have been chatting with

Miss Meagher and she informs me that you were formerly a member of Stuart's Stranglers."

Finnegan blinked and licked his lips before answering. "We did not describe the group as such while I was in the employ of Mr. Stuart."

The old woman shook her head. "You ought to have, and been proud of it, as well. When Mr. Culbertson and I were first wed and tried our hand at ranching up by the Power River, those loathsome rustlers drove us to poverty and, if you ask me, poor Mr. Culbertson to an early grave. The more of them you swung from a tree, I say, the more likely you are to enter heaven, sir."

Finnegan shrugged, having long since grown weary of such discussions. "In that case, Stuart's Stranglers it is, and you may consider me a former captain in the brigade."

"God bless you, sir." The landlady climbed up and out of her parlor chair and smoothed her apron. "And here I thought you was nothing but Arkansas bounty hunter scum, and come to find out you're a hero to all them that ever suffered on the northern range." She took Finnegan's hand. "Dinner is half price this evening, sir."

"Well, then, I am obliged to you, madam." The landlady scuttled off and Finnegan lowered himself into the unoccupied chair. "It is good to know you sing my praises wherever you go, Miss Meagher."

She bowed a bit from her sitting position. "I am forever champion of the character and legacy of Finnegan Xavier Gilhooley."

"That is a lovely frock. I must admit, I am surprised you manage to keep yourself and your wardrobe is such good condition living in Wilson's makeshift village."

"Truth be told, I spend most nights with the Wilson family at their ranch house. As you know, I have great respect to the Indians and the way they glean what they can from the land, but a fourposter bed and a feather pillow are fine things when a lady can obtain them."

"Your secret is safe with me, Molly." Finnegan glanced over to the flames that burned in the fireplace. "I am told a new boarder has taken up residence today. I am somewhat ambivalent about the fellow, but at least it has motivated Mrs. Culbertson to begin heating the house in earnest. I was beginning to think I would have to light a fire in the cuspidor in my room to alert the woman to my discomfort."

Molly laughed. "What sort of fellow is the new guest?"

"I cannot say, I have not met him yet."

"Then why the ambivalence?"

"Your friend Mr. Wilson has made the dire prediction that I know the man. If I know the man, the odds favor him not being fond of me. It may create an awkward environment in the house. I don't suppose Wilson might have an extra hut available for a wayward Pinkerton?"

Molly waggled one finger at the gunman. "You should take Jack's predictions more seriously. So far, I have not known him to miss the mark. Just yesterday he told me you would be having need of a pack mule; did that prediction come true?"

Finnegan rubbed his chin. "Mr. Dyer and I did, in fact, collect some meat today."

"Well then, his prediction regarding the new guest will likely be spot on, as well." She reached out and patted his hand. "Perhaps it will be an old friend."

"The odds are not in favor of that, dear." A bell rang in the direction of the dining room. "Well, I suppose we shall discover the mystery guest's identity presently, if the gentleman deigns to join us for dinner." Finnegan stood and put out his hand to help Molly from her chair. The two moved to the dining room door where Finnegan breeched etiquette by opening the door and stepping through it before the lady. He stopped just inside the door and surveyed the empty room. He smiled and turned back toward Molly. "My apologies. I...well, I suppose I do not truly know what I expected. At any rate..." He held the door open. "We are alone." He motioned for her to enter with one hand and moved to the table to withdraw her chair for her. "I cannot help but wonder if Mr. Wilson's prophecy shall prove incorrect. If one vision can be proved askew, perhaps we may rest easy regarding the end times."

"Finnegan, you find mirth in the strangest places. I am never quite certain if you would prefer Mr. Wilson were the second coming or a shameless charlatan."

The gunman moved around the corner of the table and took a seat. "As a detective, I am constantly on the lookout for charlatans and other creatures of low character. That having been said, I would dearly hate to miss the end of the world. It breaks my heart to imagine it might occur long after my natural death. Participating in the rapture as a member of the deceased would strip the whole affair of its intrigue."

"Finnegan, the oddities that float through your mind, I swear." She shook her head and looked to the other end of the room where the door to the kitchen was opening. Finnegan glanced at the opening door. The color draining out of his face told Molly that it was not likely Mrs. Culbertson who was entering. Finnegan leapt to his feet, knocking the chair over behind him and drew the pistol from his hip holster. Molly slowly turned to look at the gentleman who stood, stock still and obviously shocked. She glanced slowly between Finnegan and the new arrival before speaking. "Finnegan, do you know this man?"

"I know him as well as I know any man on earth, by sight

and reputation." He cocked back the hammer on the Remington. "Miss Meagher, allow me to introduce Alexander Franklin James."

The slim, greying man at the door cleared his throat and let the door swing shut behind him. He was surely shocked, but let only a glimmer of it show. "Finnegan Xavier Gilhooley, if I am not mistaken."

Finnegan sneered. "You would have me believe you are here purely from happenstance, sir?"

The gentleman held open his coat. My lack of a sidearm should serve as ample proof..." He cocked his head to one side. "Is that my old pistol, you damn Irish cur?"

"Mr. James, I would remind you, there is a lady present."

The former rebel glanced to Molly. "My apologies, ma'am. I was overcome by passion for a moment." He scowled at Finnegan. "It has been some time since I have had the pleasure of Mr. Gilhooley's company and was not expecting to sit down to dinner with him any time soon." James pursed his lips. "Do you intend to shoot me down, unarmed, in the presence of this fine woman, before I have even been given my supper?"

Finnegan let his thumb stray up to the hammer of the revolver. "You are certain you are not armed?"

"I have not gone armed in many years. Some men change with the times, Finnegan."

"Some do not." Finnegan gently lowered the gun's hammer and slowly returned the gun to its holster. He smoothed his frock coat and took a step back to collect his chair. "I suppose there is no need for us to disrupt Miss Meagher's dinner. If we have business, it can always be seen to when we are without female company."

James swallowed, his Adam's apple bobbing, and took a step forward to the chair at the opposite end of the table from

Finnegan. He brought out the chair and slowly lowered himself into it. "Very gracious of you, sir."

"Let it never be said that I did not give my fellow man every opportunity for peace." Finnegan sat and shook out his napkin.

Molly slowly turned toward the new dinner guest. "Sir, I take it you are Mr. James, late of Missouri?"

"I am." James saw to his own napkin. "Have we previously been acquainted, ma'am?"

"No, sir." She glanced to Finnegan. "We did not meet when you were in Minnesota."

James formed a slight smile. "It has never been proven that I was ever in the state of Minnesota, ma'am. I only stand accused of visiting the place."

Finnegan showed a glint in his eye. "If you have never been to Minnesota, you must have mistaken the pistol on my side for another. I found the piece in the north woods. As I recall, it was misplaced by a loathsome criminal and bushwhacker."

James gave a cold stare. "Yes, I suppose I must have." James turned to Molly. "You are a northerner, ma'am?"

"Born and raised, sir."

"What brings you to this odd outpost? If you do not mind my asking, of course." James calmed a bit as Mrs. Culbertson entered, carrying a particularly familiar piece of meat.

"I take an interest in Indian affairs, sir. I have come here to assist Jack Wilson in his endeavors." Molly stared at the former bank robber with something approaching awe. "How is it you find yourself here, sir?"

"I am merely a victim of circumstance, ma'am. The train could go no farther due to the snow, and this was the only available place of sanctuary." He looked from Molly to the landlady. "Mrs. Culbertson was good enough to find room for me on short notice."

"Yes, Mrs. Culbertson." Finnegan eyed the evening meal. "Strange you did not feel the need to mention that such a famous personage as Mr. James had come to stay in the house."

The woman used her left hand to set a pot of potatoes on the table before looking to her new guest. "Famous? Was Mr. James an associate of yours with the Stranglers?"

James coughed. "Stranglers?" He grinned at Finnegan. "I cannot claim knowledge of what the lady describes, but the organization certainly sounds to be perfect for a man of your inclinations. Was the group based out of Pennsylvania or Chicago, ma'am? Those are the two places Mr. Gilhooley has performed most of his strangulations in the name of corporate profit."

Finnegan chuckled and shook his head. "I suppose I should not bother to take offense from the accusations of a man so well known for murdering in the name of personal profit." Finnegan looked to the landlady. "Have you truly never heard of Mr. James, madam?"

"Why would I have heard of any Alexander James? It is a common enough name to be sure, and to my knowledge the man has not been elected president." She motioned to the evening meal. "Best stop yapping and get to your half-price meal before it freezes solid."

Finnegan rubbed his chin. "Yes, about that, madam. Would this be elk roast I see here?"

"Purchased from Mr. Dyer this very day and prepared to perfection." The woman smiled, quite satisfied with herself.

"Ma'am, are you aware that I not only shot this particular elk, but freighted it many a weary mile to bring it to Mr. Dyer's door."

She shrugged. "What of it?"

Finnegan sighed. "I suppose it should not come as a shock to me to discover I am being served my own elk meat at only a slightly reduced price."

The landlady nodded emphatically. "Any good Christian ought to count their blessings and be glad to be still drawing breath so that they may do so." She turned to leave. "Knock on the kitchen door when you've finished. If you aid me with the crockery, I'll provide coffee."

James let out a laugh at as the woman disappeared. "I found no water in my room, so I entered the kitchen in search of a method for washing up before dinner. She provided me with hot water, in return for a penny."

Finnegan nodded to his nemesis. "I take some comfort in the knowledge that I am not the only man being extorted in this house." He took up the plate of elk meat and passed it toward Molly. "I would agree with the lady of the house in one regard: we should eat before it all spoils." Molly took some of the meat and passed the plate on to James. The food made a round about the table and the various occupants began dining. Finnegan popped a small bit of meat into his mouth and sipped the slightly suspect glass of water he had been provided with. "Do you truly find yourself here by chance, Alexander?"

"I do, Finnegan." The southern insurrectionist tried the potatoes and seemed to enjoy them. "How long has it been since we last visited?"

"Nearly ten years have passed since we last spoke at the Marshall's House in Independence. If you would take a compliment, I would say that you look to be in better health than previously." Finnegan offered a sardonic smile. "A change of pace would seem to agree with you."

"Life is much easier when a man can live and travel

without being hunted like an animal and harried wherever he treads. There is much to be said for being able to check into a boarding house under one's own name." He shrugged. "Although, obviously, a man cannot expect to go everywhere unnoticed. I am sure you often suffer the same difficulty. What is this talk of Stranglers?"

"Nothing more than the pandering of newspapers and the droning of fools." Finnegan turned to Molly. "It is nothing shy of incredible to me that you should find yourself dining here tonight after the many times we have discussed this very fellow. I would imagine Miss Meagher has kept nearly as close an eye on your career as anyone, Alexander."

"I would not consider my undertakings to be worth the trouble, but I am flattered, nonetheless." He cleared his throat. "How long have you known Mr. Gilhooley, miss?"

"Oh, well..." Molly wiped her mouth with her napkin. "It is rather ironic to note, but Finnegan and I were first acquainted the night you shot him in the Blue Earth Woods. I found him in the road and brought him home. It took some time for him to convalesce."

James only stared for a moment. "Fascinating, miss."

"She speaks the gospel truth, Alexander. She rescued me the night you did not shoot me and were not in Minnesota. I suppose then it would follow that was the same night I did not shoot your brother."

James assumed a very sly grin. "If it had not been for my brother inadvertently bumping my arm, I believe I would have killed you that night, Finnegan. Now there is a bit of irony, miss. Your fine friend here, and myself, may be the only two men on earth who can claim that Jesse James once saved our lives."

Finnegan grunted in shock. "Now there is a claim I would have never thought to make."

Molly sat forward a bit. "Mr. James, if it would not be impolite, might I ask you a question?"

The old killer shrugged again. "Have at it, miss."

"I am aware that your...public persona has changed a great deal in the last few years, but is it not imprudent for a man such as yourself to leave the state of Missouri? Do you not...worry?"

"You inquire as to whether or not I fear retributions for my past behavior?" He turned to Finnegan and smiled. "Both legal and personal?"

"Precisely." Molly tried the elk meat.

"Not many give care to the old grudges and vendettas anymore." James sounded almost mournful as he spoke. "The War, the years after. So much foolishness, so much sadness. So much loss that need not have occurred."

"Yes, if only certain men had been willing to embrace higher virtues instead of stooping to low vice." Finnegan grinned in disbelief. "Alexander, how can you, of all men, possibly claim to have been a victim or, at best, a bystander in the foolishness that flourished in the years after the War. I would go so far as to say you were no less than the pied piper of those who gave false hope that the south would rise again."

James lifted one eyebrow. "That is a harsh statement for a man to make over the dinner table, even for an Irishman with little breeding."

"Perhaps I only mean to test the validly of your statement regarding your being armed."

"If that is your wish, then a better subject would be your attempted bombing of both my mother and the young children in her keeping." James spit out the words with the first real anger he had shown that night.

"You bloody well know that was none of my doing, sir." Finnegan balled one hand into a fist.

"No, just the work of your peers and associates, then." James leveled an accusatory finger. "Someday, the good Lord may make mention of the fact to you that a man who does nothing to keep a bomb from being thrown is no better than the man who throws it."

"And what would the good Lord say regarding the practice of shooting innocent farm boys during bank robberies, or the trampling of girls as evil men flee justice?"

"Trampling! May the devil take you. Give me my old pistol -- I know you carry a spare -- and we will settle this outside." James leapt up, sending his chair clattering back.

Finnegan slowly stood and wiped his mouth with his napkin. After carefully setting the cloth on the table he motioned toward the door. "With your leave, sir."

"Oh, for the love of all that is holy." Molly tossed down her napkin and planted her palms on the table. "Do you two fools honestly intend to abandon this perfectly delectable meal for the opportunity to shoot each other out in the snow? Only two men of such storied reputation could possibly act so stupidly."

"The gentleman has made an offer much to my liking that I have anticipated with great expectation for many years, Molly. If this is stupidity, then stupidity has been the great pursuit of my life." Finnegan looked to James for a second opinion.

The outlaw stood, his scowl turned to a small smile. "Finnegan...I am not certain I have ever been privy to a more concise definition of the pursuits of men such as us." He turned to Molly. "Miss, if someone of your wisdom saw fit to dine with me every night, I imagine my life would have taken quite a different turn."

Molly shook her head. "One thing I can say for certain is

that Mrs. Culbertson's chairs can hardly run the hazard of much more of this."

Finnegan, perhaps for the first time in his life, appeared somewhat embarrassed. "Ah, yes, well then, I suppose if you withdraw the offer." Finnegan slowly lowered himself to sit once again.

"For the evening, at least." James collected his chair and sat, as well. "I suppose we owe Miss Meagher that much."

Finnegan sighed and looked to Molly. "I must confess, I never imagined I would be receiving advice regarding what you are owed from Frank James, my dear."

"If there is one thing I have learned in a long and strange life, Finnegan, it is that one never knows what may lie around the next bend in the road." James resumed sampling the meat. "You truly shot this animal?"

"This very morning." Finnegan resumed eating.

"I am a bit surprised you have embraced such activities." James sliced into his roast.

Finnegan raised an eyebrow. "How do you mean, Alexander?"

The outlaw shrugged. "I was under the impression you Irish loathed any pursuit that might be considered an endeavor for a gentleman."

Finnegan chuckled. "I assure you, there is a great difference between shooting pen-raised pheasants and the collection of a beast such as this." Finnegan stopped and stared at James. "You are certain you only arrived on the train this very day?"

"I give you my word, I did not walk here." James wiped his mouth. "This is quite delicate fare for an animal that roams in the mountains. One would be tempted to think living in a place such as this would render the meat tougher. The animal was difficult to bring down?"

"Securing the creature was without incident, but transporting the beast back to this village proved difficult. You are certain you have no acquaintances in the general area?" There was a slight edge to the question.

"How on earth would I know anyone in this benighted place? When I entered this room and saw you, I could have been knocked over with a feather. What would be the odds of another former associate lingering in this tiny hamlet?"

"Yes, I suppose the odds would be against such a thing." Finnegan had a potato and smiled at Molly. "Well, this will surely be reported to Mr. Wilson."

"I am duty bound, Mr. Gilhooley. Rest assured, he is far too humble a man to rub it in, overly much." Molly seemed quite satisfied.

James glanced between his two dinner mates. "A Mr. Wilson is to be made aware of my arrival? I can only pray he does not take note of my presence to the same degree Mr. Gilhooley has."

Finnegan shook his head. "He is already aware you are here. Mr. Wilson was the gentleman who transported you into town from the train."

"I recall the gentleman." James appeared perplexed. "If he brought me here, why would he wish to hear from Miss Meagher what he already knows?"

Finnegan sighed. "It is not that he would wish to know that you are here, since he is already aware. What he will wish to know is that you and I are previously acquainted, or rather that there has been a great deal of acrimony between us in the past."

James scratched his chin. "I have never been accused of learning quickly, but I cannot say as my understanding has been furthered."

"Oh, pity's sake." Finnegan set his fork down. "Wilson is

a savage, formerly clad in a loincloth, but recently recognized as the risen Jesus. If you find that difficult to credit, you may find it even more bizarre to be made aware that the son of God has little better to do with his days than prattling off predictions and holding his ever-expanding record of accuracy over my head."

James sipped his water. "I...I must say, I do find it hard to credit that our savior has returned and chooses to spend his days on earth in your company, Finnegan."

Finnegan shrugged. "You, no more than I." He resumed eating roast. "I am a bit surprised to learn you have taken to traveling by train, Alexander. Does the odd conductor not recognize you and raise an alarm?"

James laughed. "Oh, I am occasionally recognized, directly after a performance or such. Sadly, no alarms are raised. More often, autographs are requested. One poor sap recently asked me to sign the flap of the family bible. Mankind is a strange race."

Finnegan looked up from his plate. "Did you say performance?"

James offered a rather shocked look. "You are unaware of my current endeavors?" He wiped his mouth. "I would have thought you, of all men..."

"Would what, Alexander?"

"I suppose, I naturally assumed you would rather keep track of me and my general doings." The outlaw shrugged.

"I assure you, sir, there are more than enough barroom sweeps, chicken thieves, and ne'er-do-well shootists in this great nation to keep me busy. Most of them born far more recently than you." Finnegan sliced off a hunk of roast and devoured it.

"Yes, well, I suppose so." James turned toward Molly. "I have spent the last few years offering up what might be termed remembrances in a traveling show that features men of my generation who garnered some level of fame in their youth."

Molly's eyes grew a bit wide. "Mr. James, are you describing what some would refer to as a wild west show?"

"Yes, miss, you could call it such."

Finnegan rubbed his eyes. "Alexander, truly? You travel about bragging and boasting of your vile acts and low behavior? How is it some bank teller's son has not blown you off the stage in a hail of buckshot?"

James licked his lips. "I could just as easily ask you how it is that one of the millions of workingmen you labor daily to hold in bondage has not seen fit to shoot you down in the street for your misdeeds."

"I assure you it is not from a lack of attempts. My intelligence may grow duller with every passing year, but so far my quickness remains." Finnegan let a small smile play across his lips. "Do you don a war bonnet and pretend to be an Indian chief for the second act, Alexander?"

"Very humorous, Finnegan." James showed a sneer. "For the most part, I relate a few tales from the war of northern aggression and a collection of observations on how the world has changed in my time."

Finnegan nodded. "Yes, of course. I had nearly forgotten you were in the war, Alexander. Did Jefferson Davis ever give you brave boys medals for shooting negros in Kansas?"

James smiled. "I have never cared for medals. Did you by any chance receive one from the City of Chicago when you helped to hang all those newspapermen they labeled as insurrectionists after the Haymarket affair?"

"I did not. Although, now that you mention it, I may have to bring that to the mayor's attention the next time I find myself near the home office." Finnegan moved his neck about to work out a kink that had been there since falling down the mountain.

"Gentlemen." Molly smiled at both of them. "This is terribly gloomy talk for proper dinner conversation." She set a small piece of roast in her mouth. "Have you had the opportunity to meet any other famous personages while performing, Mr. James?"

James slowly turned to Molly. "A few, miss. A former President, several of the Indian chiefs, some of whom put up quite a fight before entering show business." James ate his last potato. "What is your vocation, ma'am?"

"I am a schoolteacher to earn my living and something of a student of the world to feed my soul." Molly grinned.

"Very well put, miss." James looked to Finnegan. "I am rather loath to offer a compliment, sir, but you have quite fine taste in dining companionship."

Finnegan shrugged. "That compliment I will readily accept. Miss Meagher's companionship is always an unrivaled pleasure." He finished his elk. "You are absolutely certain you only arrived this very afternoon?"

"I believe you have asked me that already, Finnegan. Why should you show so much interest in the time of my arrival?" He looked from Finnegan to Molly and back again. "I willingly confess that I had hoped to never find myself in your company again. Why on earth would I wish to show up early for the affair?"

"Yes, naturally." Finnegan ate his final potato. "Disregard the inquiry." He turned to Molly. "If you are quite finished, I will escort you home, Miss Meagher."

Molly smiled and nodded to the man who had formerly been the second most famous man in America. "It was...it was intriguing to make your acquaintance, Mr. James. I never, for a moment, contemplated that we should meet.

After all the...the comments I have heard regarding you over the years...well, it was intriguing."

James stood and offered a small bow. "It has been a pleasure, ma'am. As we find ourselves rather trapped in this same small town, perhaps we shall see each other again over the coming days."

Finnegan stood. "I am certain we shall see each other again, Alexander."

James gave the gunman a weary look. "Lodging together in this snowbound town, I should think so." He rubbed his tired eyes. "Perhaps it will be good to catch up."

The Wilson family ranch house was only a few miles out of town and Molly had elected to stay there for the night, as usual, instead of shifting for herself in Jack Wilson's improvised village. Finnegan could not help but smile, seeing Molly wrapped in a collection of furs and other cold weather implements. In terms of frosted furriness, she was only exceeded by the horse beneath her. As she rode, a plume of vapor would emerge from the small, uncovered slit formed between her hat and scarf, then another plume would come from the horse. In the moonlight, as they crossed a largely empty, snow-covered plain, it made for a pretty picture.

"The world is a strange and wonderous place, Miss Meagher."

She laughed and turned toward Finnegan in the saddle. "Wonderous? I should think you would consider the presence of Mr. James in town to be more of a cosmic prank than something to wonder at."

Finnegan groaned. "As God's chosen people, the Irish are often tested in this manner. Although, I must say, placing

Frank James in the room down the hall, after having spent so very many years hunting him, is a bit over much, even given the Almighty's superlative sense of humor."

"I am certain the Wilsons would be more than willing to offer you lodging for the night, Finnegan. They are quite a gregarious lot."

"Lodging?"

"Well, yes." Her eyes blinked at him in the moonlight. "You surely cannot be contemplating spending the night in a boarding house two doors down from your mortal enemy. The two of you very nearly began shooting over the dinner table. How can you hope to cohabitate?" She laughed again. "It is all very well and good to jest about prophecies and bygones, but actually living within arm's reach of your nemesis seems quite mad, even for you."

Finnegan arched one unseen eyebrow beneath the coyote fur hat he had purchased from Dyer. "Molly, I will not allow that man to force me from my lodgings. Not under any circumstances."

"Force you? Honestly, Finnegan, it is Mrs. Culbertson's boarding house, hardly the Battle of Hastings. It is little more than a drafty old shack that offers rather disappointing victuals. Stay at the Wilson place and have a decent rest. If it were not for silly pride, you would jump at the offer."

"It is a lovely offer, but not required. I have paid my bill into the next month and intend to make use of the room I have rented."

"For goodness sake, you know as well as I do that you will surely spend the whole night concealed in a gloomy corner awaiting the attack of the dreaded Mr. James."

Finnegan let out a chuckle. "He might have been dreaded by some, though I would not count myself among them. The man was more of an irritant than a real danger."

"An irritant?" The surprise in Molly's voice caused her horse to jump slightly. "That man has already shot you once, and you would refer to him as a mere irritant?"

Finnegan shrugged. "He shot me, I shot him and his brother. Thus is the desired end of men shooting at each other. It was the nature of our mutual business, my dear."

Molly snorted. "Well, if you can be so glib about the fellow putting a bullet into you, perhaps you should go room with him. Any normal man would see madness in the very proposition, but I frequently forget that you are no normal man."

"I will take that as a compliment." He turned to her, grinning. "Even if it is not meant to be one, dear Molly."

Chapter 8

GREENFIELD, NEVADA

January 8th, 1890

Finnegan lowered himself into the same chair he had occupied the previous evening. Frank James had assumed his previous position, as well. The only items that had changed were the lack of female companionship and the nature of the meal. Mrs. Culbertson was busily placing a sparse breakfast before her two boarders.

Finnegan cleared his throat and nodded to the lady of the house. "Good morning, Mrs. Culbertson. How does the morning find you?"

"Well enough, sir. Though I can see out the window that it is snowing once again, and we may yet all be buried if the good Lord does not send us some relief." She glanced between the two boarders. "You men will find the strength of character to behave as Christians toward one another, or civilized men of some sort, I should hope?"

James cocked his head to one side. "Why would you ask such a thing, Mrs. Culbertson? Have we not conformed to the rules of decent society thus far?"

"Aside from threatening to shoot each other in the street last evening, I should say that you have." She scowled a bit. "I suppose I should appreciate your willingness to take your scuffle outside. I surely do not wish to hire the Jacobson boy to come in here and mortar over bullet holes, much less remove corpses."

Finnegan tried the coffee before him and found it to be on the near side of palatable. "You will have no trouble of that stripe from us, madam." He smiled at James. "Least ways, not in the house. Both Mr. James and I were raised better than that. If the need arises, I assure you we will kill each other in the street like proper murderers."

"Thank the Lord for small mercies." Mrs. Culbertson disappeared into the kitchen and the two men were left alone to dine.

James procured some bacon and passed the plate to Finnegan. "Did you sleep well?"

"As quietly as a well-fed baby." Finnegan took the bacon and offered the plate holding eggs. "And you, my friend?"

"Oh, about as well as I ever do. I hold my pistol in my hand while I sleep. Always do, probably always will. You being in the vicinity makes no difference."

Finnegan licked his lips. "I thought you mentioned that you no longer went armed."

"I do not *carry* a pistol these days, but sleeping with one is a different matter." James tried the coffee and grimaced. "I find it hard to imagine you do not make a few...shall we call them, precautions, before turning in?"

"I do, at that." Finnegan forked eggs into his mouth. "Remaining safe while I sleep has always been something of a difficulty, given my line. The first method I employed was to simply sleep where I was not meant to be sleeping. I even went so far as to pass the nights in a church belfry, once upon a time."

James chuckled. "Novel, sir. I should think a church belfry might not be so bad. I have spent the night in many an improvised camp or hovel. Comparatively, the belfry would at least be free of vermin, or one would hope."

"It was surprisingly cozy." Finnegan shrugged and continued eating. "As time has gone by, I have come to find such hijinks wearisome. If nothing else, it vexes to pay rent on boarding that is not truly used for boarding. The last few years I have developed a debilitant that is quite simple and effective. So much so, that I employ it in every room I take my rest in, regardless of how many Missouri bushwhackers currently occupy the hotel."

James grinned. "I see. And what method is it, precisely?"

"I make use of one of my carrying cases and use it as a support for a shotgun. The gun has a rather short barrel and, when aimed in the general direction of the door, can be counted on to properly broadcast shot in the direction of an intruder. Naturally, a string is run from the door to the trigger on the gun. Simple, but highly effective."

James nodded, somewhat impressed. "And if the assailant should enter by way of the window?"

Finnegan shrugged again. "These days, as troubles seem to multiply, I have taken to carrying two shotguns. One is the sort of foreshortened Greener I am sure you are familiar with. The other is a repeater of the sliding action variety. Truly a mechanical marvel and quite reliable. I have it on good account that it will soon be produced by Winchester and supplant all other models."

James wiped his face. "I must admit to have some curiosity in that matter. I have heard of the new repeating shotguns, but have not had opportunity to try one out."

"Admittedly, I came by the thing through rather nefarious means, but a man can hardly be held to account for retaining such an item, even if his ownership of it did not come by the usual route. I have the intention of bringing the weapon with me today when we travel to the mines north of here. If you like, you may inspect it at some point." Finnegan popped a hunk of bacon in his mouth.

"What's this now?" James stared quizzically.

"Yesterday, while laboring to pack out the elk you had for your supper last night, I was ambushed by a jackass with a rolling block. If not for the padding of an already deceased animal, I would surely not be alive to ingest this rather mediocre breakfast."

James glanced to the kitchen door. "I should think Mrs. Culbertson's mentioning last night's unpleasantness would have informed you that she is in the habit of listening from her post."

"An increase in her knowledge can only help the state of our coffee." Finnegan took in the last of his eggs. "The fellow who ambushed me is said to have been employed by a mine to the north of here. I intend to travel there today with the intention of investigating both his motives and associates. The weather appears quite mild for the season; it should not be an overly arduous journey and we should return in plenty of time to receive another helping of my elk for our dinner."

James appeared more shocked than upset. "Finnegan, that is all quite interesting, and I daresay I would enjoy inspecting the shotgun, but why, precisely, would I wish to accompany you, or anyone, on an errand of that sort, which is none of my business? I am afraid I must decline the invitation."

Finnegan sighed and drank down the remainder of his coffee. "Alexander, do not make the mistake of considering it an invitation. One way or the other, I intend to have full knowledge of your whereabouts while you are in the vicinity. I am offering you the choice of lying dead in the street or accompanying me on my errand." Finnegan wiped his face with his napkin and set the cloth on his plate. "The decision is yours, sir. If it is to be the street, I would invite you to procure your pistol now, so my day is not wasted. I might also take a moment to remind you that while you have been larking about, recounting tales of Kansas massacres and playing cards, I have been dispatching ruffians, debauched soldiers, and even the occasional railroad baron, on a regular basis. Consider your current condition before making your decision."

James cleared his throat. "Upon consideration, I have rethought the matter, and would be glad to accompany you for an outing. Of course, I will be bringing the aforementioned pistol. Even you would not suggest that I should be forced to ride into an unknown camp unarmed."

"I would suggest no such thing." Finnegan smiled. "And if you should be struck by the urge to try your luck with me... well, at your pleasure, sir."

"You always were too damn proud, Finnegan. One day you will pay the price for your vanity."

"Perhaps today." Finnegan stood and pushed his chair under the table carefully. "I go to make ready. As I said, I will bring the shotgun so that you may have a look at it." He straightened his coat. "Do not forget your pistol, Alexander. I am not the newly risen savior, so I cannot say what the future might hold."

James put one hand up. "Finnegan, forgive my ignorance, but what is this talk of saviors and messiahs you continue to offer? I am still quite confused by what you and Miss Meagher were attempting to discuss last evening."

Finnegan sighed deeply. "Oh, Alexander, you are not the only man in this area who finds himself confused. This place seemed built to befuddle."

The horses leapt from the deep snow into a well-trod ditch of sorts that previous riders had stomped down into the drifts. Both men and animals were grunting and out of breath from the traversing of yet another snowfield. More flakes drifted down and there was no sign of relief from the skies above.

James pulled his borrowed fur hat from his head and knocked the snow from it. "I am sorry, Finnegan, but I am afraid I still do not quite fathom what you are claiming here."

The Pinkerton shook his head. "I claim nothing, sir. All assertions have been made by others. All declarations are the product of hearsay or obfuscation." Finnegan paused for a moment to consider all he had witnessed thus far. "I will say this: there is something damned odd about Mr. Wilson. If nothing else, it is highly irregular for a fellow to be questioned regarding his relations to a deity, and to not show much interest in the matter. At a minimum, I would imagine the fellow ought to make more of an effort to gain by the notion of being God's red son."

James replaced his hat. "Did you not say the man has contacted the Federals in search of both a salary and a position?"

Finnegan laughed. "Yes, I suppose he did, but that is more of an absurdity than an attempt at perfidy. I would think when put to the test, even you or I might conjure a confidence scheme superior to that."

"Perhaps the fellow is simply an ignorant savage, playing at some game he does not fully understand."

"Perhaps he is the second coming. I am not certain which I would find more disturbing, currently." Finnegan reined in his horse and James came to a stop next to him. "That is likely our destination, Alexander."

"It may be the mine you search for, or it may be a different outfit entirely." James shrugged. "At all events, I wish you luck."

Finnegan smiled at the retired Confederate. "Wish us both luck, Alexander. You are coming along. I did not drag you this far to let you approach from the rear, now."

"Finnegan, I daresay you are nervous unto hysteria on that topic. I have no more of a notion to revenge myself on you than I would any given Pinkerton or Federal. As I will not live long enough to murder even a tenth of your ilk, I reckon it is best to avoid the whole pursuit in total." He pulled a spindly cigar from the inside pocket of his coat. "In that same vein, I might also add that I have learned it is best to only be introduced to new people in public venues where rash action is certain to bring consequences. This frozen wilderness hardly qualifies. No, I believe it is best that I remain back a bit."

"Alexander, just the other evening you expounded at great length on how no one recalls your name or bears a grudge against you. Now, you are worrying over who may lurk in this backwater camp?" Finnegan shook his head. "I must ask: are you worried you will be recognized by an enemy or an associate?"

"Associate? Here?"

"Perhaps a remaining friend of the man who fired upon me yesterday? It may be that the man will wish to confess a conspiracy or two before he meets his maker."

James laughed. "Ah, so, it is not only that I wish you dead, I have now hired two or three assassins to see to the work. You do have a high opinion of yourself and the impression you leave on your fellow man, Finnegan, I will give you that. Truthfully, sir, until last night's dinner, you had not crossed my mind in years."

"You do not bear me a jot of ill will?"

"Not a bit."

Finnegan struck a match and held it out for James to light his cigar from it. "Very well, then, you should not take issue with accompanying me into this possibly hostile camp. Would it not be a shame if I were to die so recently after reconciling our differences?"

James puffed smoke. "You would wish for me to act in support of you, should trouble erupt?"

"We are the last of our kind, Alexander, regardless of our former allegiances. I would say that makes us brothers in arms, so to speak."

"Yes, I suppose you would say that. Over the years I have heard Pinkerton men say many things." James surveyed the general area around them. "Oh, to hell with it, I suppose I might as well go with you rather than remain here alone, anyway. Left here by myself a damn wolf pack may gnaw me to pieces."

"Ah, see, now you are coming around, Alexander. There is much to be said for cooperation." Finnegan motioned forward. "After you, sir."

James scowled slightly. "There is ample room to ride abreast. A fair share of the hazard should do."

"Excellent." Finnegan gave his horse a small kick and the two animals began moving forward. As they neared the camp, smoke could be seen rolling from the chimney of a small cabin and from another structure that may have been a larder of some sort. Trails had been dug from the two structures running to what was quite obviously a mineshaft. The shaft sported a crudely constructed shack of sorts in front, and a large pile of fresh earth could be seen resting on top of the freshly fallen snow. The men who worked this claim were not lazy. Amateurish assassins, perhaps, but not lazy. The two men rode up to within a few yards of the main cabin and Finnegan yelled out to whoever might be dwelling within. "Hello! Is there anyone inside there?"

The door of the cabin slowly creaked open and a grey-haired old black man in a pair of dirty overalls came out to stand in the ever-deepening snow. "What in blue blazes is this?" He gazed in wonder at the two mounted riders. "You two picked some damn weather to go visiting." He spit tobacco down into the snow.

"Our apologies, friend. I hope we are not interrupting your labors." Finnegan did his best to offer a kind smile.

"You ain't interrupting nothing but my making dinner for the five most ungrateful dregs the good Lord ever saw fit to saddle a poor old man with. It's mostly just that I can't rightly imagine what might possess two fellas to go galivanting around in damn blizzard. What you want up here?"

"We are in search of some diggings known as the Mary Louise. Is this the place?" Finnegan knocked snow from his coat sleeves.

"Hell no, this ain't the Mary Louise. This abominable hole in the earth is the Lola Montgomery, and while I never had the misfortune of meeting Miss Lola, she must have been a lowly whore to have a worthless claim like this named after her. You got more gold in your teeth than ever came out of this mine." He laughed, showing that he had precious few of the aforementioned teeth. Two more black men, both considerably younger, stuck their heads out the cabin door and a third appeared above them at the diggings. They all looked quite surprised to have visitors.

"Well, then, there you have it, Finnegan. We find ourselves at the wrong location." James tipped his hat to the elderly gentleman and moved to turn his horse.

The old man reached out and grabbed the horse's bridle. "Whoa there, mister." He pulled down the horse's head to get a better look at the rider. "I...I swear I know you from someplace. Say something more."

James scowled down at the old man. "Say something more? What is this? Unhand those reins."

It was a bit of a stretch. But the old fellow managed to leap up and snatch a hold of James's scarf. He tore the garment away and stood there staring up into the Confederate's aged face. "Jesus deliver me, I do know you."

James pulled the scarf from the old man's grip. "Not damn likely. I should think I would recall being acquainted with a man so rude as you."

"Like hell..." The old man took a step back and motioned for the two younger men in the doorway to take notice. "That right there...that man you see right here on our own good doorstep, that's none other than Frank James."

James pursed his lips. "I see, yes, well, perhaps we have met before. You will have to excuse me if I do not recall. At all events, good day, gentlemen."

The old man's eyes grew a bit wild. "I can tell you just where we met, mister. It was in Lawrence, Kansas. The day the place burned and nary an honest man can claim to have seen the sun come up the next day. I seen you there with that devil Bill Quantrill and that damned imp Bob Younger. I won't never forget your face, nor your voice."

James rubbed his chin. "Yes, well, I suppose every man has a few moments in his past he might regret." At the close of the surprisingly sullen statement, Finnegan burst out laughing. He laughed so much that he was forced to steady his horse. When the guffawing had somewhat subsided, James turned to the Pinkerton, obviously vexed. "Something about this conversation strikes you as humorous, Finnegan?"

The gunman brought himself under control as best he could. "My apologies, gentlemen. I do not mean to make light of anything the two of you are currently mulling over. I am certain it was quite sad when this man dragged your friends or family out into the street, murdered them, and burned the town. I only laugh to let the Almighty know I appreciate his jesting. After all, we climbed to this frozen mountain to discover how many men hereabouts might want to kill *me* and now, at the very first door we knock on, we find a former victim of one of your massacres who wishes to kill you. I say, Alexander, the whole thing is most poetic."

"You have an unsettling sense of the poetic, Gilhooley." James straightened in the saddle. "Well, as I said, in every man's life there are a few items of note that did not proceed as he might have wished or moments he might prefer to change, given the opportunity. I assure you, sir, given my druthers, I would change a great many details relating to the...the unfortunate incident at Lawrence."

"Incident?" Finnegan did his best to appear quizzical. "I have not often heard the matter referred to as such, Alexander. I have heard it called the Sack of Lawrence and, of course, the Lawrence Massacre, but never an incident. Where is it, precisely, you picked up that term?"

James licked his lips. "Finnegan, you may find it less amusing when these men come to the obvious conclusion that a man who travels with Frank James is surely a cohort of that same man. In all likelihood, whatever is about to be visited upon me is to be visited upon you, as well."

Finnegan chuckled. "Oh, I rather think not. First, I am quite proud to inform these fine, gentleman, that not only was I absent from this continent while they were indentured. When I did arrive, I served with distinction in the Grand Army of the Potomac." He sat forward in the saddle conspiratorially. "I also might add that I have, primarily, ventured here to assist in the raising of a new messiah, just a very few shades lighter than you gentlemen. Now, how is that for a letter of introduction, my friends?"

The old man glanced back and forth between Finnegan and James a few times. "You wore the Blue in the war?" Finnegan nodded. "And you come here with none other than Frank James for company?"

"Well..." Finnegan shrugged. "I essentially forced the man to accompany me on a few errands this day. I press-ganged him not because I enjoy his conversation, mind you, but because I feared he would get into mischief or possibly hire my murder. As you well know, it is hard to say what rebels may consider a good use of their time."

The old man slowly nodded. "Yes, sir, hard to say. What was that about a messiah?"

"It is not currently of consequence." Finnegan smiled at James and turned back to the old man. "Sir, if you do not mind my asking: what is it you have in mind for the illustrious Mr. James? I always intended to shoot the fellow, but I would venture a guess and say you would prefer a lynching."

The old man spit down into the snow. "He dragged my kin out of their own damn house, stood behind 'em and gunned them down. I don't reckon he deserves any better. Couldn't even look 'em in the eye when he done it."

James sneered. "Sir, I am not responsible for the death of your kin. I have committed many a sin in my time, but I am not guilty of that particular crime. I would refer you to

Captain Quantrill, but he has long since passed on and you would surely have to visit hell to contact him."

Finnegan gave James a skeptical look. "You killed no one at Lawrence?"

James swallowed. "I did not kill any negros."

"Damn you for a liar." The old man motioned to the wall of a nearby dugout used to hold some stock. "You get down off that horse, stick your face in that wall, and wait to meet your judgement."

James straightened up in the saddle. "I will do no such thing."

"Then we will damn well assist you." The old man was opening his mouth wider to yell to his associates, but Finnegan's Colt flashing out of the shoulder holster made him stop cold. "What the hell's this now?"

"I do apologize, sir." Finnegan kept the gun low so that none but the three men gathered near the door could see it. "Under different circumstances, I assure you, I would enjoy nothing more than watching Frank James get his just reward up against a wall. Unfortunately, I have given certain pledges to this despicable specimen, and while I do not find it completely believable, he does claim to be innocent of the particular charge leveled against him. As it stands, if you do not allow us to leave this place, unmolested, and refrain from following us after we have left, I will be forced to shoot down most, or all, of your family. Would it not be a shame to lose two families to this one scoundrel, sir?"

The old man's eyes burned. "You truly think you can shoot us all?"

"I can shoot you very easily. After that, the matter will not be your concern. Leave off of this, sir. Mr. James will be back in Missouri soon enough. You may take a break from your mining, locate him, and murder him with full relish. I will not make a move against you. I simply cannot allow you to kill him today. Do you understand?"

The old man looked from the muzzle of the Colt and then over to James. "I will be seeing you again. You may make your warrant on that, Mr. James."

James nodded. "I expect you are not the only man I will have to make an account to before my time is ended. Good day, sir." James wheeled his horse and began slowly riding away from the mine site.

Finnegan nodded to the old man and pulled back on the reins to turn his horse. "It was a pleasure meeting you, sir. I can certainly sympathize with your sentiments. Please, go back inside."

The old man spit again. "Might see you someday too, mister." He began backing inside.

"I too have much to answer for. I will keep a wary eye out for you." Finnegan turned his horse as the door closed and rode off, only glancing back once or twice to make certain they were not being followed. Soon enough, he met up with James, who was slowly making his way farther up the mountain. Finnegan let out a small laugh as he came up next to the outlaw. "I am somewhat surprised you wish to continue on to the next mine. Perhaps it will be revealed that Mary Todd Lincoln is the cook at the next place and then you will truly find yourself in a pickle."

James chuckled. "Mrs. Lincoln has no reason to bear me any ill will. You, like that fellow back there, have me confused with a different villain."

"Did he, truly?" Finnegan withdrew a cigar and bit the tip off.

"Gilhooley, you have always held that you had no part in the bombing of my family home in Missouri. You have always claimed that it was the work of your fellow Pinkertons, and not you personally."

Finnegan held up one hand. "I merely say I had no part in the matter. As for whether or not my fellow Pinkerton employees had anything to do with it...well, Alexander, the Pinkertons are not the only men who might have wished to throw a bomb into your house."

"Regardless of that, you say you did not bomb my mother, while others of your ilk may well have. Given that fact, is it really so hard for you to believe that while others may have done great evil in Lawrence, I might not have been one of their number?"

The Pinkerton eyed the outlaw suspiciously. "Ah, so now we are to discuss a matter of gradation, eh, Alexander?" He lit his cigar and tossed the match away into the snow. "Might that not be a bit petty by this time in our lives? Somehow, I doubt I could convince you that I am the one and only angel to have ever been in the employment of Allan Pinkerton. I can tell you now, you have little chance of convincing me you rode all those years with Bill Quantrill and managed to avoid staining your soul in some unrepairable way. In truth, I cannot say I much care what evils you perpetrated in Lawrence or any other place."

James laughed again. "You, of all men, do not care what crimes I have or have not committed?" He shook his head in disbelief. "I was under the impression the examination of my sins was your life's work."

Finnegan puffed his cigar in the cold air. "Oh, do not mistake me, Alexander. There was a time when I closely examined all facets of your behavior. Not that it ever did me much good." He shrugged and guided his horse over a fallen tree trunk. "But that was many years and many miles ago. Long before that kangaroo court in Missouri absolved you.

Long before your brother lay dead. I suppose I could lie and tell you that I have embraced peace over the years, or that I have matured and offer forgiveness to all men, but the truth of the matter is far more mundane."

"And what would that be?"

Finnegan smiled at his old nemesis. "The truth of the matter is that I am no longer being paid to consider your sins, Alexander, so I have lost interest. I certainly do not wish to spend my time larking about punishing antiquated villains from a long past war that was truly none of my business, anyway. If I should pursue and punish you free of charge, where would the foolishness end? Should I track down sad old Jefferson Davis and place a ball in his old carcass, as well?"

"I can readily see how that would be a long running chore for a fellow. You are likely right not to begin." James knocked some snow from his horse's mane. "Davis has passed. I was told...I believe it was this last Christmas."

"I cannot say as I ever had interest in the man beyond his accidentally bringing me into military service. More or less the same way you accidentally brought me into the business of chasing train robbers."

James sighed. "I tried to explain that very oddity to my brother, once, many years ago."

"Explain what, precisely?"

"Oh, well..." James offered a very mournful look. "As you well know, my brother Jesse was neither peaceful nor kind. Thinking back, even as a child he was given to the most terrible fits of rage. The war did nothing to allay them. At any rate, he was once expounding vigorously as to the manner in which he intended to dispose of all federals and Pinkerton scum. In response, I mentioned the staid fact that it was hardly Allan Pinkerton's prerogative to begin chasing us. If we had not chosen to rob banks and trains, the man would have likely allowed us to go about our business growing cotton at a loss and starving slowly."

Finnegan nodded, smiling. "Yes, well, much like myself, Mr. Pinkerton rarely indulged in activities that did not offer a profit. Or, at least, the chance of added publicity for the firm. I doubt he would have bothered to harass a set of innocuous sharecroppers."

James rubbed his eyes. "I have often paused to consider how much different life might have been if I had simply returned to the plow after the war."

Finnegan groaned. "From what I have seen of farming, I believe you chose correctly."

James chuckled. "Oh, it was not simple laziness, although, that did feature in the decision, I suppose. No, we began as we did...well, it was very difficult in the South after the war. The tyranny we suffered is hard to describe."

Finnegan grinned around his cigar. "Tyranny? By God, you Americans do have an awfully high regard for your damned immutable rights. I have never heard the like of some of what you blurt out from time to time."

"You would mock me? What the hell would you know of it? Do you know what it is like to live under the boot of a conqueror?"

"As only an Irishman bloody well can." Finnegan pulled his smoke from his mouth to allow for a belly laugh. "You damned Americans never know how well off you truly are. Every time the fools of my native country show the poor judgement to rise up against their oppressors, neither the foot soldiers nor the ring leaders are shown anywhere near the deference you daft buggers were offered. In Ireland, a rebel ends his days up against a wall, and a revolutionary leader dangles from a rope. They are certainly not allowed to return to their mansion like Lee or dodder about aimlessly like Davis for twenty-five years. With few exceptions, I have found the native-born sons of this continent to be quite a soft bunch, given to little more than complaining. Did it ever occur to you that you were blessed by God just to have guns to assist your asinine revolt?"

"They suspended our rights. They occupied our land. They billeted their pig soldiers in our very midst..."

"You rose in armed rebellion." Finnegan shook his head, once more. "Did you expect them to bring you tea and a plate of cookies after hostilities had ended?"

"We fought as gentlemen. They acted as savages." James held his head high.

"Was Lawrence the work of gentlemen?" Finnegan winked. "I think perhaps you are indulging in a bit of hypocrisy there, Alexander. It might be better if we could both admit that war is hell, and it has a tendency to turn us all into devils."

"Yes, well..." He rode on in silence for a long moment. "You may have stumbled upon something there. The war was not good for my character. It certainly did nothing to improve my brother's. How did it effect yours?"

"I rather think it formed it, more than changed it. I was quite young when I was placed in that bonny blue coat. Now that I contemplate it, I have had a gun in my possession ever since. Your brother was but a child in the war as well, as I recall."

"He was."

"Well, then, I suppose you could say the war formed both myself and your younger sibling."

James rubbed his eyes. "War raises many an unfortunate child." He reined in his horse and paused. A half mile in the distance, smoke curled up from the chimney of another cabin.

Above the cabin was yet another mining derrick. "I should think now you might give more consideration to my statement regarding my remaining well in the rear when you visit these camps."

Finnegan shook his head, obviously amused. "Dear Alexander, I am not about to allow the oddity of a lifetime to dictate my behavior in general. It is incredible that we ran across men with a grudge against you in the last place. More incredible yet that the fellow with an axe to grind was capable of recognizing you, but let us be practical: these mountains cannot be solely populated with men who have been wronged, been abused, or been witness to the sins of Frank James. You were not so profligate as all that."

"You are a damned pest, Finnegan Gilhooley."

"That is the path the good Lord has set for me. Now, get moving. I still do not trust you to my rear." The horses plodded through the snow until they reached the mine site. Half buried in snow sat a collection of dwellings not unlike the previous spot, the glaring difference being that several children were running about the place. The youngsters were clearly enjoying the snow and the respite from whatever constituted their normal duties. A boy of about ten came loping up to the riders. Finnegan smiled down at him. "Good day, child. It is good to see someone still finds amusement in this accumulation of ice and cold."

The boy wiped snow from his face and grinned. "You don't like the snow, mister?"

"I like it just fine, in small amounts at times of my choosing. It is good you can keep your chin up so, young man." Finnegan looked around the mine site. "We wish to chat with your parents or whoever is about that may have a few more years on them than you, my young friend."

The other children had stopped in their revelries and

stood watching the exchange with the visitors. The young gatekeeper stood up to his full height in the snow. "And who should I say is calling, sir?"

"One Finnegan Gilhooley and..." The gunman thought back to their recent experience at the mine farther down the mountain. "And his associate."

"Finnegan Gilhooley?"

"That is how it is pronounced. Now be a good lad and find us one of your kin to chat with." Finnegan watched as the boy scampered off to one of the low-built cabins. He turned to James, still smiling. "There now, does that satisfy? I daresay that young man should not recognize you from the picture his father keeps over the mantle, eh?"

"It is most appreciated, Finnegan. Although, I should think giving your name is hardly a safer option than giving mine."

"Oh, I am a bit better thought of than you, Alexander."

"Is not the purpose of this little lark to discover the friends of the man that tried to kill you yesterday morning?"

"That is part of it."

James gave the Pinkerton a quizzical stare. "If that is not our purpose, why in blue blazes are we here?"

"Perhaps I simply fancied a ride in the country. You need to learn to live in a more relaxed manner, Alexander. You will worry yourself to an early grave at this rate."

"And it is difficult to imagine how a man as lax in his figuring has lived so long as you...what's this now?" James pointed to the front door of the cabin the boy had disappeared into not a few moments earlier. The boy had returned and now held an old Kentucky rifle along with the assorted claptrap to make it fire. The two men sat on their mounts and watched as the child laboriously poured powder down the barrel from a horn, wrapped a ball in a cloth patch, and began slamming the whole works home down the barrel with a well-polished ramrod. "Does the youngster intend to go squirrel hunting this day with that old peashooter?" James chuckled. "I had much the same outfit when I was in short pants. What of you, Finnegan?"

"The first musket I received was a gift from the Union Army."

"That is not the makings for a happy childhood." James motioned again. "Ah, he has the cap on properly now... Finnegan does it appear as though he..." Flame and smoke belched from the gun and Finnegan fell from the saddle. James looked slowly from the youngster to Finnegan and back again. "I will be damned." He swung down to the ground and continued to glance between shooter and victim. "Finnegan, do you live?"

"I damn well do, although the confusion is vexing."

"Well, perhaps...oh, hell, wait a moment." James ran forward through the snow. The young man had begun an attempt to reload the old deer rifle. James snatched the gun from his hands and tossed it off into the snow. "What in hell are you about, you murderous scamp?"

The boy looked up at the Confederate as though it were the most normal thing in the world to shoot the last man who had ridden into the yard. "Mister, that man is Finnegan Gilhooley."

James blinked a few times. "How is it you have the faintest idea who Finnegan Gilhooley might be?"

"My own dear momma curses his name near every night, sir."

"As do I, but I have ample cause. What cause does your mother have?"

"She tells us quite frequently how an evil man named Finnegan Gilhooley killed her own good uncle up in

Montana and how, if the rascal hadn't done it, we'd all be living up there fat on the hog, running cattle and doing a prosperous business in steamboat traffic. Gets her right riled to discuss the loss of a prosperous business, don't you know." The boy leaned to look around James in the direction his gun had been flung. "You'd best be prepared to pay for any damages you've caused to my musket, sir. It's the only one I got and if it's been broken, I have a mind to put the law on you."

James let out a laugh. "The law on me? That's damned bold talk for a scamp who's just gunned down a visitor."

The boy shook a small finger at the old rebel. "My momma has told me for years now that if any member of our family slaps eyes on Finnegan Gilhooley, we're to start shooting and offer no quarter, just as bold as John Paul Jones in one of them books. Now, you can't hardly tell me that it's against the law to do like your momma tells you, but I damn well know it's against the law to damage another man's rifle." The boy glanced about furtively. "Don't tell my momma I cussed."

"Oh, your secret is safe with me." James turned back to see the Pinkerton was still lying in the snow. "How goes it with you, Finnegan?"

"How the hell should it go?" Finnegan rolled onto one side and began hunching up to regain his feet. "That wretched homunculus has placed a ball somewhere within." He stood and managed to get ahold of his horse's reins. Oddly, the animal had barely moved since losing its rider. "There does not seem to be much blood. The round may have collided with my Colt."

James arched an eyebrow. "Homunculus?"

"I will explain another time." Finnegan pointed to the mining derrick where several men now plodded toward the visitors. "The young man's kin approaches." Finnegan made an attempt at remounting his horse, but fell to the ground. "Bloody hell."

James gave the boy a shove back toward the cabin door. "Get inside to your mother boy."

"But, mister..."

"Just get." James gave the kid a small kick. "You have defended your family honor enough for one day, boy." James moved forward, getting between Finnegan and the approaching men. "Gentlemen, gentlemen, there seems to have been a bit of an accident. It is not a grave matter, but just the same, I believe my friend and I ought to be on our way with all haste." James pointed to a fellow near the front of the four-man troop. "Would you assist my friend in getting on his horse, please?"

The miners all took a moment to look around the camp and assess the situation. The man James had made the request of felt the need to ask a question. "I knowed I heard a shot. Who's shooting?"

James cleared his throat. "There is a boy about this place who was fussing with an old blunderbuss and accidentally sent a ball into my traveling companion. Now, we do not wish to make a fuss or involve the sheriff, but we must be on our way. I worry for my friend's condition."

The miner rubbed his dirty face. "Little Andy shot 'em?"

"I did not have the pleasure of learning the youth's Christian name. Now, if you will not be of assistance, I will help my friend myself." James moved toward Finnegan, but stopped about halfway when the miner queried again.

"Little Andy's a careful lad. I doubt he'd accidentally shoot a fella."

Hearing his name discussed, the young man with atrocious timing stuck his head out the cabin door he had formerly retreated into. "It weren't no accident, pa. That there man is Finnegan Gilhooley. Told me his name his own self and I reckon he got what's coming to him."

The miner's upper lip curled. "That man is Finnegan Gilhooley?"

James sighed and rubbed his eyes yet again. "It would appear there are few people in the vicinity of this mountain range that are not familiar with your labors, my Irish friend. Perhaps in the future you should give more consideration to the punishments you dole out. I believe you have overdone things somewhat."

Finnegan regained his feet again and grunted. "That would be a fine topic of conversation for the ride home, Alexander."

A murmur passed through the miners as they discussed the matter before them in low whispers. When they appeared to have reached a conclusion, the closest fellow made an announcement. "Mister, I don't know who the hell you are, or how low a man might have to sink to call that scoundrel friend, but you can go, and we'll be keeping that damned rascal for sure. If you know him, you damn well know we got cause."

James shook his head. "Well, how is that for hospitality. You say I must go but he can stay for dinner." James smiled at Finnegan. "Quite rude, wouldn't you say?"

"We ain't gonna feed that bastard, we aim to string him up." The lead miner took a step forward. "Just like he done to my wife's kin." The miner turned to Finnegan. "Don't even try and deny it, you coldhearted devil."

Finnegan leaned against his horse. "What was the name of your wife's relation?"

"William Downes, God rest him."

Finnegan hung his head, clearly mulling the matter over.

"I truly cannot say whether I killed the fellow or not. Just now, it does not ring a bell."

"Damn you." The miners all took a few steps forward.

James let out a long sigh and drew his pistol. "There now, that is enough of that." The miners froze. "You there..." James moved the muzzle of the revolver over to the youngest of the miners, a spry fellow who looked about sixteen. "Assist my friend in returning to the saddle."

The young miner looked to the older man in front. "Should I, pa?"

The older man looked from James to his son. "Well, Jedidiah, that man's got a pistol pointed at us and you got a worn out shovel. Probably best to do like he tells you."

The young man walked to Finnegan. The gunman motioned toward his saddle. "Take hold of that stirrup, if you would be so kind." The young man held the stirrup and helped Finnegan guide his foot into it. "Some small assistance rising, young man?"

The youth helped boost Finnegan up. He stared up at the gunman once he had him in the saddle. "Mister, you really hang my mother's uncle?"

Finnegan smiled down at the youth. "I do not hang men." He pulled his Colt and gave it a quick inspection to see if it had been damaged. The gun appeared in good order. "If I am your great uncle's killer, I shot the man and likely had ample reason. Move away and back with your kin, young man." Finnegan waited until the young miner had rejoined his family. "Alexander, get back on your horse."

James nodded and walked to his mount. He swung into the saddle but paused. "Finnegan, not that I wish to prolong this little encounter, but should we not at least inquire regarding your would-be assassin?"

Finnegan groaned, not particularly in the mood for

further palaver with the group. "Very well, we have come all this way, I suppose we may as well." He looked over the assembled men. "You gentlemen may have noticed that one of your number here at the Mary Louise is missing today. He is missing because he ventured into Greenfield and attempted to murder me one day past. I wish to know why he attempted this cowardly act and how it is that you were aware of my presence in Greenfield? Speak freely, we are well past the point I might be so petty as to visit some sort of retribution on you. I am willing to let bygones be bygones, if you will."

The pater familias apparent took a step forward. "Mister, we ain't missing nobody here, and this ain't the Mary Louise. This here is the Temperance Downes, named for the woman whose uncle you hanged."

Finnegan sighed. "This is a fine bit of luck we're having here today, eh, Alexander?"

"I would think it best for us both to avoid playing cards today." He looked to the miners. "Do not follow, gentlemen. There has been more than enough foolishness this day. I see no reason to add to it." The father of the group nodded, and James nodded back. He wheeled his horse. "Let us be on our way, Finnegan, if you are able."

"Very kind of you to inquire, Alexander. I believe I can continue."

After their experience at the Temperance Downes mine, the two bold adventurers came to the conclusion that it might be advisable to return to Greenfield. With no doctor residing in Greenfield, Mr. Dyer had been kind enough to inspect the wound and pronounced it interesting, but hardly fatal. The ball from the Kentucky rifle had likely been misloaded by the enthusiastic young man, and, in his haste, the youth had failed to add a sufficient amount of powder. Between Finnegan's many layers of heavy wool clothing and the ball encountering one of the leather straps of his shoulder holster, the projectile had just barely broken the skin. There was a large bruise and possibly a broken rib. The dry goods salesman proclaimed Finnegan was apt to live another score or two.

With no better option, Finnegan trudged through the snow back to his boarding house and arrived just as Mrs. Culbertson was placing what passed for dinner on the table. Finnegan took a chair opposite the elder James brother and stared at the man for a long moment. "Alexander, the situation we find ourselves in puts me in mind of some Greek myths I have read in years past." He sipped the landlady's substandard coffee. "I wonder if we will not be forced to share this boarding house and be likewise forced to associate for all eternity as punishment for our many and sundry sins."

James shrugged, quite unconcerned. "I imagine we will be stuck here so long as the snow continues to fall and the rail schedule is bungled." He looked up from his plate of ham. "For a man who almost certainly considers himself the protagonist of his biography, you are oddly obsessive regarding sin. Do not men such as you generally find justifications that comfort you when your conscience begins to prick?"

"My apologies if I seem melancholic. I suppose being shot by a small boy has put me in something of a mood."

James chuckled. "It did come as something of a shock. You did rather make a fine sitting duck of yourself. I am fairly kicking myself, thinking back on all the grand tales I have heard of you over the years and all the times I took to the saddle in the middle of the night having been informed the deadly and dreaded Finnegan Gilhooley was stalking close to my doorstep. If only I had known you would present such a still and stable target I would have remained in bed."

"Even you would not fire upon a ten-year-old child, Alexander."

"No, but I might at least chide the little fellow before he sent me to see Saint Peter." James broke out fully laughing, and Finnegan joined him. When they were done, James wiped a small tear from his eye. "It is good you can find humor in such things, Finnegan. Without that trait a man in our line often turns sullen."

"Yes, well, I might laugh more, but it pains me somewhat. That is a bit in line with Greek tragedy as well, now that I think of it."

"You are given to overthinking these matters, Finnegan." The old outlaw shook his head. "I might add that you are being somewhat ridiculously romantic. A man like you can hardly afford such a vice, sir."

Finnegan wiped his mouth with a napkin. "I have suffered many an accusation, Alexander, but I believe you are the first man to call me romantic."

"Oh, please, you had best save that bluster for those who fear you. The more I learn of your recent movements, the more I begin to think you have lost all reason. You begin by traipsing across most of this nation to aid a woman you have barely laid eyes on in a decade with a chore she had not bothered to describe. After arriving here, you immediately begot to training as a disciple of a red savage messiah who aims to wipe your kind from the earth..."

Finnegan held up one finger to make the outlaw pause. "I would not call myself a disciple, merely a bystander. I would also add that Mr. Wilson has not threatened to wipe our kind from the earth, he only intends to fling us back from whence we came."

"I came from Missouri, and would like nothing better than to return there, so perhaps Mr. Wilson will get his wish. Although it does beg the question as to what Mr. Wilson intends to do with us native born sons."

Finnegan chuckled. "It may be that he has not considered the matter much. There do appear to be a few glaring holes in his philosophy. I suppose we should not be too hard on the fellow. After all, it must take quite some time for a religion to develop answers for every eventuality. It is complicated labor, Alexander."

James shook his head. "You flirt with blasphemy there, Finnegan. Careful, lest your soul is endangered."

"Strange advice to receive from a man who has flirted with perdition most of his life."

"Do not jump to conclusions when it comes to what another man may hold sacred." James resumed nibbling at the ham. "Disregarding your other odd behavior, perhaps the greatest act to marvel over might be our trip this very day where both of us faced more than a little danger to absolutely no purpose. If I did not know better, I would say you wished to get us both killed."

Finnegan shrugged. "In hindsight, I would say that we make an unfortunate pair for touring."

"Yes, well, so long as you are ready to admit that I am satisfied."

Finnegan smiled. "Just so long as Frank James is satisfied. Goodness knows that is all I have ever wanted."

"It is fine to know you are willing to leave me to my own devices, Mr. Gilhooley. I would hope that if nothing else, our experiences today have proven I do not wish to play you false or end your life. If you would be willing to leave me be, and allow me to conduct myself as any other marooned traveler might, it would be much appreciated." James motioned to Finnegan's midsection. "Besides, I doubt you would welcome another adventure, at least not until you have had time to heal from the last one."

Finnegan took in a bit more coffee. "I would have thought you would gain no small amount of enjoyment from the day's events."

"I would confess to a small amount of glee when you were shot from the saddle."

"Posh, after so many long and undoubtedly weary nights recounting past glories to dull-eyed fools in the crowd, you must surely welcome a bit of an escapade. Nothing wears on a man such as boredom."

"You are mistaken." James swirled what appeared to be gravy into his potatoes. "I no more miss the years past than I miss an ailment or the pangs of an injury. Jackasses such as ourselves always recall the thrill of the chase, the glory of victory, the spending of the spoils. We so readily forget the surgeon digging out an errant ball or the feeling in the pit of the stomach when we learn of fallen comrades. I am not so foolish as to delude myself with fairy tales, Irishman. Look back on those old days with whimsy if you like -- I never will."

"First romance and now whimsy; what do you take me for, Alexander? I only meant that a man often finds boredom no less trying than hardship and toil."

"I suppose that is correct. Although, boredom is more troublesome to the young."

Finnegan forked a hunk of ham into his mouth. "So, if you no longer wish to accompany me on outings, what is it you intend to do with your time while you are stranded here?"

"There are several books I have always meant to read. I can imagine no better time to take care of the chore. I would wholeheartedly suggest you do the same."

At the suggestion Finnegan laughed, but cut his mirth short when his injured ribs spoke up. "You would recommend I hide here in this rather shoddy boarding house to avoid meeting any more of the type we were acquainted with today? Such an action does not seem like the best use of my time."

James shook a finger at Finnegan. "That may be the trouble right there, Pinkerton. You appear to be under the impression that your time must be put to some sort of use. Have you never noticed the rather large horde of men in this world who are content to do little more than to linger and watch the world pass by from their front porch?"

Finnegan smiled. "Yes, Alexander, I have taken note of the large number of malingerers in this world. You feel it would be better for men such as us to join their ranks?"

"It very well might be." James contemplated his coffee cup. "How many souls might be considerably better off today if you or I had elected to sell ladies undergarments or work our hands bloody farming cotton? Neither of us can claim sainthood. Neither of us live without regret. Obviously, we can barely leave the doorstep without encountering a fellow wielding a legitimate grudge. How could one argue otherwise?"

Finnegan sipped coffee and winced. "I might allow such contemplations to bother me, Alexander, if it were not for the fact that I have never considered it my duty to act solely in the interest of the general public. I suppose it is perfectly possible I may have created a few widows or even the occasional orphan, but that was not my primary intent, and I cannot help but notice the public offered little assistance when my father fell. You say we have not helped the world better itself. I might venture that the world was not deserving of our succor."

"Spoken just as a product of the corporations should speak, Finnegan. I might say that..." James snapped his jaw shut at the door as the dining room opened. Several men, all wet to the knees from sloshing through the snow, began filing in. They all nodded and moved to various chairs around the table. Of the four men, three of them were lean, sinewy fellows with deeply tanned faces. The fourth was fleshy and considerably more jolly in appearance. They all settled into their seats and slowly turned toward the original occupants of the room.

The oldest of the lean men cleared his throat. "Good evening, gentlemen. I hope we have not interrupted your meal too much. It has been a long journey, and we are thankful that we arrived in time to receive some sustenance." The outlaw and the gunman both nodded. "I am Elsmere Doubleday." He motioned to the two younger men to his right. "These are my sons, Johnathan and Michael." The two young men smiled and nodded. The older gentleman motioned across the table to the jolly fellow. "Our friend and neighbor, Vincent Heth."

The jolly fellow grinned and pulled the plate of beef toward him. "Two awfully well-dressed gentlemen." He speared some beef off the platter with the serving fork and nibbled it. "Didn't imagine we'd find two like you in this dingy little place. 'Course, I didn't necessarily think we'd find much of anything here, and trudging here from where the train dumped us has me even less expectant, but you'd never know it to hear these three talk." He shook his flabby head. The very soul of hope, these three."

The elder Doubleday cleared his throat again. "You will have to excuse Mr. Heth; travel does not agree with him."

"Starving don't agree with me, Elsmere." The man gobbled the forkful of beef. "I suppose a man need not bother with grace if he ain't got a plate, huh?"

Finnegan stared at the fellow for a long moment. "Well, I am certain Mrs. Culbertson will locate some crockery for you shortly."

"I would sure appreciate it." Heth gobbled a second helping. "And who might you two be, anyhow?"

Finnegan brought his hand nearer the Colt concealed under his frock coat and he noticed that James moved his hand nearer his pistol, as well. "Finnegan Gilhooley."

"Alexander James."

"You two got the look of men who either sell ladies undergarments or maybe cotton merchants. Which is it?" Heth grinned and chewed his beef.

Finnegan eased away from his pistol, since the declaration of their names had not evinced a reaction. "I have come to Greenfield to visit a friend and Mr. James is merely passing through, as they say."

James offered a warm smile. "I am quite marooned, gentlemen. I assume you have suffered the same fate?"

Doubleday shook his head. "No, sir, this is our destination. We have been dispatched here by Wilford Woodruff." Both the gunman and the outlaw stared blankly. "The leader of our church." Doubleday noticed no recognition. "We come from the Great Salt Lake...Zion."

"Ohh." James looked to Finnegan and let a small grin play over his face. "They are some of those strange fellows who passed through Missouri before the war." James's brow furrowed. "You attempted to settle there, but your prophet died or was killed, was he not?"

Doubleday slowly nodded. "My father joined the faithful in Missouri. He later joined the brigade and made the walk to California. Brigham himself helped my mother and I across the mountains." He could see neither man really followed what he was saying. "The leader of our church has given me the mission of traveling here to speak with Mr. Wilson. He is a local man who..."

Finnegan held up one hand. "I am aware of what the fellow purports."

James sampled his coffee. "You all have come here to visit with Finnegan's Indian Jesus, eh? He is an interesting fellow, from what little I have seen of him and been told."

Doubleday turned to Finnegan. "You are a friend of Mr. Wilson?"

Finnegan rubbed his eyes. "I am acquainted with the man." He sighed. "I was told that your...church had already sent a group of emissaries here to discuss matters pertaining to the afterlife and possible resurrection with Mr. Wilson."

"Yes." Doubleday took no notice of Finnegan's sarcasm. "I have come to discuss a few matters with the gentleman that are of interest to our new leader."

Heth let a deep laugh roll out of his fleshy head. When he was done, he sneered and looked to James. "I been hearing about this Indian fella all the way up here. I've been privy to a few folks claiming they can hear God talking over the years, but I hadn't met a single fella who believed them, until now, that is." He shook his head. "Damnedest thing I ever did hear of."

Finnegan arched one eyebrow. "I take it you are not of Mr. Doubleday's particular faith?"

"Can't say as I ever took much bother to choose a faith. Probably never would have paused to consider the matter if I hadn't ended up living amongst them that never cease to declare and refine their faith. Was a might bit quieter all over that Utah desert before all these desperate odd Bible thumpers moved in. They are good for business, though."

"Business?" James scratched the side of his head.

Heth motioned to his associates. "This lot almost always employs a fella like me when they go on the road. There's many a merchant or other fella that won't have nothing to do with these here Mormons. Other times, there's things that need to be seen to on the road that's beneath 'em. Either way, it behooves the faithful to keep a man like me on hand."

Doubleday delicately adjusted himself in his chair. "The members of our faith do often employ men such as Mr. Heth to assist us in varied matters. Contrary to what you may have been told, there are few... doings barred to us by our faith. We merely find our travels to be eased if we allow a man like Mr. Heth to make our arrangements and speak with certain parties." Doubleday offered what appeared to be a disappointed smile. "We chose Mr. Heth to accompany us on this particular journey because he is familiar with the Indians of this area and has had a long association with them."

Finnegan gave the man a matching scowl. "Association?"

Heth grunted "I mostly sold them liquor. Back when there was plenty of work in these parts, these here particular injuns was damned apt to take on wage labor. Made them somewhat unique." He chewed more beef. "A trader could sell them just about anything. Them having existed on little more than pine nuts and the salvation of God's grace to bring 'em rabbit meat made 'em keen interested in who-hit-John and other modern wonders such as canned ham."

James grimaced. "Very kind of you to bring these simple aboriginals into the civilized age."

"Well, that was how I always looked on it. Some didn't share the same view, of course. Bible beaters and other types moved into these mining camps same as everywhere else, and a man couldn't ply a decent trade anymore." Heth let loose a deep laugh. "I got run outta this country by...hell, I think it was Methodists, so I headed down south to try and make a dollar off this lot. Shows what a man like me often gets for scheming." He grinned. "Whiskey sales have fallen off something terrible."

Doubleday slowly nodded. "Thankfully, the lack of a steady liquor trade in Utah has made Mr. Heth available to accompany us."

Heth waggled a finger. "In all honesty, I was kinda, sorta interested to get another look at this here country again. I'd heard it was all dried up of silver and all the folks had moved off. Didn't particularly believe it, but here we are, and she sure does look empty. I expect there are a fair number of injuns still lingering about, eh?"

Finnegan wiped his mouth. "A fair population of Indians do reside in this area, sir. Although, I should warn you that many residents of this place will take a dim view of you selling them spirits."

Heth waved one hand. "That was not my intent. Even if I wanted to, I have failed to bring any wares with me. Was running a bit low, anyhow." He leaned across the table toward Finnegan conspiratorially, but failed to lower his voice much. "While I would not claim Utah to be the most profitable land for a man like me, I still do a tidy business when the sun sinks down and them who frown on spirits can't see them that indulge. Sad part is that a fella like me can't exactly purchase corn to replace the lost stock. Many a fella is thirsty in in the great desert of Zion, but can't find no relief due solely to the hypocrisy of corn farmers."

At the declaration, James broke out laughing. He brought himself under control, but turned a bit red from embarrassment. "My apologies, gentlemen. The man's statement struck me as humorous." He cleared his throat, pushed his plate away, and stood. "I believe the events of the day have overtaxed me and I am no longer fit company." He nodded to the assembly. "Good night, gentlemen. I am sure we will meet again in the morning." He turned and walked from the dining room.

Finnegan drained the remainder of his coffee. "Mr. Doubleday, would it be safe to assume that you will wish to visit with Mr. Wilson tomorrow?"

Doubleday nodded. "We have traveled far, sir. An audience with Mr. Wilson is our sole goal. To put it off would serve no purpose."

Finnegan nodded. "Very well. I have a mind to search the fellow out in the morning, as well. If you would not mind, perhaps it would be most efficient if we saw to the chore together."

Heth grunted again. "I think that's a dandy notion. Wouldn't mind having this bunch off my hands for a small while." He grinned again. "It'll give me a chance to wander a bit and refresh a few old acquaintances in these parts." Heth rubbed his chin, deep in contemplation. "Just how many folks have departed this place in recent times?"

"I have no way of knowing that, sir." Finnegan placed his napkin on his plate and stood from the table. "I have been told a great many men who formerly worked the mines have left, taking their various family members with them. As you surely saw on your way into town, there is many an abandoned building."

"Yes, sir." Heth continued rubbing his chin. "The thing I did not notice was a marshal's office or jail. What sort of law resides here presently?"

Finnegan gave the fellow a thin smile and produced the

badge issued to him by Judge Parker. "Mr. Heth, I am a deputy U.S. Marshal. I have no jail and have no need of one. I tend to simply shoot down miscreants and leave them for the snow to cover. Does that statement give you reason to change your future plans?"

Heth leaned back in his chair. "No, sir, I'm just a curious fella. Had nothing in particular in mind you or another badge packer might take umbrage with. Good evening, sir."

Chapter 9

GREENFIELD, NEVADA

January 9th, 1890

Mrs. Culbertson had grown more diligent about the heating of the boarding house as her number of boarders increased, but not to the point it felt all that comfortable. Rising in the morning, Finnegan could feel the various aches and pains the previous full day in the saddle had instigated, along with the pangs the boarding house bed seemed to cause on a nightly basis. Of course, the bed had been considerably more comfortable previous to Finnegan receiving a gunshot wound, but it seemed silly to quibble over such small changes. Some mornings it truly felt as if Finnegan might finally be approaching the day when he would be too old to continue being Finnegan Gilhooley.

After performing his ablutions with some exceedingly chilled water, Finnegan dressed and made his way down to the dining room to investigate the potential for breakfast. He discovered that there were still a few victuals left that had not been consumed by the seemingly bottomless pit that resided somewhere inside Vincent Heth. The Doubleday men and

James were both slowly finishing up their small portions while Heth continued to gobble what little remained.

Finnegan rapidly seized some bacon and a small portion of egg before the gentile guide to the Mormons could ravish it. The gunman stared down at his tiny repast and scowled before sitting. "Good morning, gentlemen." The assembled men nodded.

The senior Doubleday wiped his mouth and looked to Finnegan. The emissary appeared to be looking forward to his day. "'Round about what time would you like to begin our journey today, sir?"

Finnegan rolled his eyes. "Oh, as soon as I am able to ingest this massive feast, we can be on our way." He took up a fork and scooped up what appeared to be the first of two forkfuls. As he chewed the eggs, he heard the front door of the house clatter open and footfalls approaching through the hall that led to the dining room. As always, the gunman let his right hand stray down to the butt of the Remington on his side. He brought his hand back up when he saw a familiar face pass into the room. "Mr. Dyer, what brings you out on such a frigid morn? I would think you, of all men, would have the sense to remain close to the hearth on a day such as this."

Dyer knocked the snow from his hat and seemed to show little concern for messing Mrs. Culbertson's floor. "Mr. Gilhooley, if the decision were purely mine, I assure you I would be more than happy to remain by the fire, but my hand has been forced, so to speak. I've been sent here to bring you a message."

Finnegan gobbled his one and only shred of bacon. "You are a bit old to be delivering telegrams. What sort of news do you bring, Edward? Has the bold Mr. Wilson announced that Nevada wishes to leave the Union? If that is the case, tell him I will make common cause with him." Finnegan smiled over at James. "I wish to discover how the other half lives, this time around."

"Finnegan, this ain't got nothing to do with Jack Wilson, this is all regarding you." Dyer appeared somewhat upset. "There's these two fellas over at my store and they're...well, from the way they're acting and from what they're saying...I think they intend to kill you, Finnegan."

The gunman hung his head. "Sweet Mary, has every jackass I have had the poor fortune to anger or irritate taken it upon themselves to settle in this place?" He brought his head back up. "Did you happen to catch their names, Mr. Dyer?"

Dyer shrugged. "One of them is a fella named Carlisle. Only thing I know about him is that he works a mine called the Temperance Downes up on the mountain."

Finnegan nodded. "Yes, that man has ample reason to wish me dead. The other?"

"The other is a miserable damn cur by the name of Eli Sommers, and I have heard many a tale about him, Finnegan. He's said to have shot men all over and I heard of him shooting two at once down in Virginia City. I guess he must have run out of drunks to murder and been forced to come here for honest labor. I think he's been working at that same mine, off and on. He's a horrid sort of trash..." Dyer glanced over to Doubleday, who had his hand raised and wore an inscrutable look. "You in wonderment regarding something, partner?"

Doubleday looked to Finnegan. "Sir, am I to understand that there are two men just down the way, that wish to...well, wish to engage in some sort of gun battle with you?" Finnegan nodded and sipped his coffee. "Sir, is not a declaration such as that cause for slightly more...surprise on your part, or at least greater questioning?"

Finnegan grunted. "Hardly. It would seem this portion of Nevada is something of a dumping ground for fools."

James shook his head. "I would say it is more likely that you are simply so irascible that nary a day passes without you pushing one of your fellow men to a state where they consider murder. You have been at that very poor habit so long that you cannot now move from the doorstep without encountering someone you have wronged or enraged. Essentially, your chickens have come home to roost, Finnegan."

The gunman carefully set down his coffee cup. "Mr. James, am I mistaken, or did we not happen upon an entire family, just this day last, who wished to stand you up against a wall and execute you?"

James shrugged. "I am aware of my own shortcomings regarding my treatment of my fellow man, and they are mine to consider. This morning we are discussing yours."

"I do not feel particularly in the mood to discuss anything, other than interrogating Mrs. Culbertson as to where the remainder of my breakfast might be. Though, I suspect the answer lies buried in Mr. Heth." Finnegan slugged down what remained in his coffee cup. "Thank you for the message, Mr. Dyer. Please stay if you would like to attempt to find sustenance. If not, please do not let this foolishness keep you from your work."

"Keep me from my work!" Dyer chuckled. "I'd damn well say it will. I sure as hell don't want to be nowhere around when you go after that Sommers fella. Tell you honest, I'd appreciate it if you'd call him out in the street so you don't shoot up my store. If one of you hits that wood stove and breaks out the cast iron, it's gonna be a damn long winter."

Finnegan rubbed his eyes. "Call him out in the street? Mr. Dyer, you do form some odd notions." The gunman stood and set his napkin on the table. "Mr. Doubleday, I regret to inform you that I will not be accompanying you to meet Mr. Wilson this morning. After thorough contemplation, I have decided to stay in this cold morning."

Dyer's eyebrows rose nearly to his hairline. "Staying in? You ain't gonna do nothing about that rascal Sommers?"

"No," Finnegan stated, quite flatly. "I have grown weary of dealing with such fools. My mucking about with them must cease some time, why not this fine crisp morn? There is nothing to be found in this place other than madness. Since I have been here, I have been ambushed while packing meat and shot by a child. I refuse to continue in this manner. I intend to retire to my room. If Mr. Sommers, or his associate, wishes to speak with me, they may find me there. Good day." Finnegan turned and left the dining room.

James grinned at the dry goods salesman. "I suppose it does not get much more simplified than that, sir." He set his napkin on his plate and got up from the table. "Do you intend to pass Mr. Gilhooley's message along to the men who seek him?"

Dyer shrugged. "If it'll get them out of my store and on to causing trouble someplace else, I reckon I will." He looked furtively around. "If I do, I'm not certain Mrs. Culbertson's forgiveness will be forthcoming." He rubbed his chin. "On the other hand, I live in this town, so I don't imagine I'll be needing to stay at the boarding house, and the preservation of my stove is a damn sight more important than the preservation of her goodwill." He shrugged again. "Best expect them shortly."

James grinned. "I believe I will retire to the parlor to await them. It is always pleasant to have entertainment presented to you instead of being forced to search it out."

★★

The aging outlaw had not flipped through too many pages of an old Harper's Gazette before he heard the front door of the house swing open and two sets of snowy footfalls approaching. James adjusted himself in his chair and watched as two heads carefully peeked around the corner into the parlor. Two sets of eyes darted about the room and eventually became two bodies as the men slowly entered. James offered a small wave and smiled. "Good morning, gentlemen." His smile widened. "Do not mistake me. Born in the great state of Missouri. I am not the man you seek."

One man narrowed his eyes. "You was with Gilhooley at the mine yesterday."

"I surely was, and I hope neither of you bear me any ill will for that incident. Under most circumstances, I would have been more than happy to let that rather enthusiastic young man murder Gilhooley, and then bought the sprat a lemonade to celebrate his deed. Sadly, I was obliged to the blackguard at the time and my choices were severely limited."

The rather better dressed of the two, presumably Sommers, grinned at the old man's yarning. "Well, that is quite an honest declaration, sir. Would you, by any chance, be able to inform us where Mr. Gilhooley might be, presently?"

James nodded, looking somber. "He announced at the breakfast table, quite plainly, that he intended to retire to his room. Number eight, top of the stairs and just to the right." James winced and attempted to look fatherly. "Gentlemen, it is not my business, truly it is not, but I must advise you against having a visit with Mr. Gilhooley."

Sommers smiled. "And why might that be, sir?"

"Young man, many a fellow has attempted to give Mr. Gilhooley that which he richly deserves over the years, and many a fellow has come off the worse for it." James shrugged.

"In my younger years, even I once attempted it, and I barely survived the encounter. Would it not be preferable to simply forget all this nonsense and resume whatever it was you were doing the day before Gilhooley darkened your door?"

Sommers rubbed one side of his jaw and continued to smile. "Well, sir, I appreciate the advice, but I have dealt with several like that Irishman in my time. Largely reputation and very little grit. I doubt this one is any different. Top of the stairs and to the right?"

"That is correct." James resumed flipping through his magazine. "Do not say I did not warn you." James leaned over in his chair a bit so he could watch the two men ascend the staircase. Leaning a bit further allowed him to see the door to Finnegan's room.

Sommers stood in front of the door and rapped with one knuckle. "Gilhooley, we know you are in there."

An irritated Irish brogue came from the other side. "I should bloody well say I am. These are my quarters. Where else should I be?"

Sommers shook his head. "Gilhooley, this is not proper for a man such as yourself. Show some pride. Come out and face us like a man."

"I do not wish to have anything whatsoever to do with you gentlemen. Depart. Be on your way and Godspeed."

"Gilhooley, it does not do well for a man such as you to show yellow at the end like this. Come out."

"If you fools wish to have a conference with me you will have to enter. I have retired to my quarters and have no intention of leaving today. Be gone, damn you."

"Have it your way, Gilhooley." Sommers cocked back the hammer on the pistol in his right hand and threw the door open with his left.

James instinctively winced as he watched the two men

blown back from the door. One sprawled out on the second-floor landing, while the other, Sommers, was cast through the railing and landed in the small hallway below. With smoke still hanging in the air, James caught a glimpse of Finnegan. The Irishman called down to the outlaw. "Did that one round do for both of them?"

James slowly nodded. "I believe it did. The loudmouth lies down here if you wish to investigate."

Finnegan emerged from his room holding the bizarre shotgun he had acquired. "I believe I will take your word for it." He set the shotgun back inside the door. "A full load of shot does make a Godawful mess, does it not?"

"Yes, well..." James stood and set his magazine on a nearby end table. "I do not think our landlady will be pleased with this, Finnegan." He slowly approached Sommers. "Although, I suppose this sort of thing is to be expected when one willfully gives board to a former member of Steven's Stranglers."

"*Stuart's* Stranglers."

"Beg pardon." James gave the corpse a small kick. "He is surely done for." He scratched his chin. "I cannot help but wonder where they will store these fools until the thaw comes."

"That is hardly my concern."

James gazed up at Finnegan. "Then who should concern themselves with it? Did you not state just the previous evening that you are the one and only custodian of justice lurking about this place? In that capacity, I would think you should, at least, take responsibility for the corpses you personally create."

"Custodian of justice?" Finnegan shook his head. "For a former bank robber, you are surprisingly concerned with the civil government of this town. You should inquire as to whether or not the citizens here might elect you mayor. Then you could be in charge of throwing this riffraff in a snowdrift." Finnegan heard a door creak just down the hall and saw the flabby head of Heth extend out from the jamb. "My apologies if you were woken, sir." Finnegan placed a cigar between his lips.

"It is about time I roused myself and found activity for the day, at any rate." Heth stared at the body and the broken railing behind it. "There was some trouble, I take it?"

"There was, but it has been seen to." Finnegan sparked a match and lit his cigar. "Perhaps it is for the best that you were roused. If you could locate your heavier clothing for outdoor use and give me some assistance disposing of the eternal remains of these gentlemen, it would be much appreciated. Somewhere, I forget precisely, there is an icehouse made use of for this sort of difficulty. I would ask Mr. James to assist me, but I grow weary of his constant commentary." Finnegan pulled his watch from his pocket. "Alexander, what has become of Doubleday?"

James motioned to the front door. "He left in the company of Dyer and said he meant to acquire mounts and directions to go visit that Indian Jesus you're all so fond of."

"Ah, very well, perhaps I can still catch him and guide him to the camp."

James shook his head. "Well, if you think I am dragging along with you again, you have another thing coming. I abandoned foolishness of this type many years ago and do not appreciate being reintroduced to it. You may retire to your room to lay traps for ne'er-do-well trash, but I intend to retire to mine to get some peace. Two dead men is enough to satisfy me for one day. Good day, sirs."

Finnegan shook his head. "You always were something of a lay-about."

The horses floundered in the snow and Finnegan yanked on the reins in one last attempt to get them forward and into the well-beaten path that surely led to Wilson's impromptu village. A stiff pull and a few unkind words convinced the horse to launch itself up over the last drift. Seeing that some other beast had been convinced of the plan's intelligence, the remaining horses followed suit rather rapidly.

Finnegan swung up into the saddle and looked back at the elder Doubleday. "When my business in this mountain paradise is completed, I believe I will inquire as to the possibility of being posted at the company office in San Francisco. It is my understanding that it rarely, if ever, snows in that city."

"I have heard that town is rarely troubled with snow." Doubleday shrugged. "Although, I have also been told that they never have summer, the ground often quakes, and they burn the place down every six months just to kill off the stench."

Finnegan considered the review. "By the time this little adventure is over I might consider all that a small price to pay for a life without snow." He got his horse moving down the narrow path. "Mr. Doubleday, I hesitate to ask, as the topic is rather none of my concern, but your arrival and your intentions have aroused my curiosity. Might I ask you a question regarding your duties here?"

"Certainly. What I intend to do here is in no way secret."

"Very well, then. It is my understanding that you have come here to rather assess Mr. Wilson's standing as a prophet, or messiah, or something of that sort. Would you say that is correct?"

Doubleday nodded. "As I understand the matter, that is what I was sent here to accomplish, yes."

Finnegan turned in the saddle to get a better look at his traveling companion. "I can readily see how a fellow such as Wilson would be of interest to your church and of personal interest to you. I can also appreciate your wanting to assess his...credibility. What I have yet to grasp is what methods you intend to employ."

Doubleday squinted, looking confused. "Methods, sir?"

"Well, yes. How does one go about proving the validity of a prophet? I have given the matter no little consideration since arriving here, and have yet to arrive at a conclusion. I would be much obliged if you could instruct me as to what method you intend to make use of."

Doubleday pulled his hat from his head and knocked the snow from it. "It is strange to say, sir, but until you brought the matter up this very moment, I had not given the specifics of my commission much thought." He turned in the saddle to glance back at his two boys. He seemed a bit uneasy to discuss Wilson in their presence. "Since you have broached the subject, I suppose some contemplation could not hurt." He replaced his hat. "I suppose if the man is legitimate...in his claims, whatever those prove to be, then God will give me a sign. If the man is a charlatan, God will surely wish to make his chosen people in Zion aware of it. As their representative, I would assume the sign will be provided to me."

Finnegan chuckled. "It is a very orderly deity you find yourself serving, Mr. Doubleday. Will you require full revelation, or will the occasional burning bush suffice?"

"Look around you, Mr. Gilhooley. Is there not a correct amount of grass for each deer, a correct number of deer for each cougar? The world is quite orderly and balanced. Why should man's relationship with God be any different? If it is God's will, it shall be done."

Finnegan shrugged. "If you take a number of dumb animals eating each other as proof of divine revelation, I believe you and Mr. Wilson should have no end of topics for discussion."

Doubleday gave his horse a small kick and moved up closer to the gunman. "What of you, Mr. Gilhooley? From what you say, your lady friend is a believer in Wilson. You have met the man, and you continue on in this area. Do you believe he is...blessed in some way? Has he been chosen?"

Finnegan chuckled. "Mr. Doubleday, this business with Mr. Wilson is hardly the first ridiculous cause Miss Meagher has chosen to take up. She even took the time to nurse my miserable carcass back to life once. I would venture to say that Miss Meagher is primarily interested in Mr. Wilson's possible leadership of..." Finnegan paused to find the correct phrase. "As a possible leader of some sort of Indian tribe coalition, to enhance the bargaining abilities of the savages. When Miss Meagher was young, an incident involving the hanging of many Indians occurred near her home, and the memory of it somewhat haunts the poor girl. She has long wished to assist the race of red men in some way. Her presence here is yet another attempt." He shrugged. "As for my remaining here, I serve at the pleasure of the aforementioned lady. My belief in Mr. Wilson's divinity has nothing to do with the matter. I might also add that if I had any tangible proof to offer you, I would likely not have inquired as to whether or not you had a method for testing prophets."

Doubleday offered a downtrodden smirk. "Well, then, Mr. Gilhooley, I would say we find ourselves in something of a pickle. Perhaps in matters of faith it is best not to search for proof too eagerly."

Finnegan laughed. "It is not the first conundrum I have faced. I take solace in the fact that I now at least have you to commiserate with. Perhaps if we cooperate in search of a solution, we will have better success." Finnegan brought his horse to a stop in a wide portion of the trail. Doubleday managed to bring his horse up even with him. The gunman motioned ahead. "There is the village Mr. Wilson has founded. The huts are cozier than they appear."

Doubleday eyed the collection of odd huts. "Wilson chooses to live here?"

"I am not certain he has been given a large number of other options, but yes, to some extent this is his preferred living arrangement. That is my understanding, at any rate."

"Prophets often choose to live in the wilderness."

Finnegan gave Doubleday a skeptical glance. "Did those prophets of old bring their women and a collection of children into the wilderness with them?"

"Not that I am aware of." Doubleday scratched his chin. "Although, some attributes of seclusion may not be included in ancient writings."

"Mr. Wilson has quite the brood, as you will see soon enough." Finnegan gave his mount a kick. "Come, gentlemen. I will introduce you." Finnegan guided his horse into the village and made for the stables that had been set up in an area the denizens of the village kept clear of snow, for the most part. As they rounded the corner to see the inside of the stable, Wilson could be seen currying a horse.

Wilson gave a wide smile. "Hello, brothers."

Finnegan stopped his horse and folded his gloved hands on the saddle horn. "Good day, Mr. Wilson. I have brought a few men who wish to have words with you."

Wilson nodded, still smiling. "More followers of Mr. Smith. I will be happy to chat with them. It is a pity Mr.

Smith did not make it to the West. I would have liked to chat with him, as well. I believe he would have enjoyed himself here."

"Perhaps you can have a chin wag next time you are communing with the dead." Finnegan swung down from the saddle and brought his horse into the stable.

"That is surely something to consider, Finnegan." Wilson sighed and dropped the handful of straw he had been making use of. "I am fond of talking with Mormons. They are all very polite." He gave a small wave to the Doubleday family. "But it will have to wait, unless they prefer to come with us."

"Come with us? You have an outing planned, Jack?"

"Yes, we are going hunting. I have been informed that you will have luck with your shotgun today and we could surely use a rabbit or two for the pot." Wilson patted the gunman on the shoulder. "I am occasionally mistaken, but never when it comes to filling the pot. God dotes on me in that respect."

Finnegan rubbed his face. "It is not so much that you are mistaken, Jack, but more like you are running late. I have already had luck with my shotgun today, and the game collected would make very poor table fare."

Wilson stared into Finnegan's eyes and then shook his head. "I am sorry, my friend. Take comfort in knowing you had no choice." He cocked his head to one side. "Or perhaps you should take comfort knowing it was their choice."

Finnegan rubbed his eyes. "They were the type that reminds a fellow such devices are referred to as booby traps. I do not require comfort in the matter, one way or other. Do you truly wish to go out hunting for rabbits?"

"Rabbits or other game." Wilson walked to the edge of the stable and produced a very well-used looking shotgun of the percussion type. "We welcome all meat in our pot."

Finnegan eyed the blunderbuss. "Are you ever given any news of your own chances for success hunting, Jack?"

The prophet shook his head. "No, the Almighty prefers to keep that sporting."

"Naturally, he would." Finnegan sighed. "Very well, we can try our luck at finding you dinner. Might I speak with Miss Meagher before we go tromping out into the cold and barren wilderness?"

"Miss Meagher is not likely to be in the village today. She intends to stay at the Wilson place until she has finished with the letters we were working on yesterday." Wilson smiled at the Doubleday clan again. "One is for your church father. You will take it back to him." He stepped out of the stable and addressed the family. "Do you men have guns?" All three nodded, staring at the odd fellow. "Wonderful, you can assist in the rabbit hunt. Do not be overly picky. A stew pot can digest anything eventually."

WHAT WILSON HAD in mind was something along the lines of an aboriginal hunt, the kind of rabbit and small game collection operation he had participated in as a child. The Piute would assemble as many people as possible and then herd all the game in the area into improvised fences they would build from brush. As Wilson explained it to Finnegan, two or three of the big hunts, in conjunction with the collection of pine nuts from the surrounding forest, comprised the brunt of the Piute diet for the year.

Lacking a full tribe, Wilson had merely guided Finnegan, the Doubleday clan, and Jock Bull Bear to the place the hunts had once begun. Wilson appeared somewhat melancholy, recalling better days, but Finnegan's scowl showed considerably more consternation.

"Do you not enjoy hunting, Finnegan?" Wilson hefted his ancient shotgun.

"Under most circumstances I take great enjoyment in the sporting life, Jack. I am in a bit of a mood this morning, though, and I am somewhat pained when I walk."

"I noticed you favoring your side. What happened?"

Finnegan gave Wilson a surprised look. "You do not know? God has not informed you of my recent difficulties?"

"The Almighty is too busy to discuss every varied matter with me, Finnegan. Some things are bound to go unmentioned. You are not the only soul he has under his care." Wilson began checking over his shotgun as though they were discussing nothing more incredible than the preparation of breakfast.

"It is not much worth discussing, but, as it happens, I was shot in the ribs by a youth, not hardly old enough to help his mother with the chores." Finnegan gave a small press to the wound to check its condition. "I have been in the fray most of my life. I could not tell you how many times I have been fired upon and the ball has occasionally been driven home on my extremities. Many more have kicked dirt in my face or hit rocks, nearly blinding me. I daresay, that boy got closer to ending my days than any man who came before him. Another goodly dollop of powder and I would not be here with you now. The world is a strange place, full of surprises."

"It would be odd for a man such as yourself to be killed by a child."

Finnegan looked over the assembled hunters. None of them appeared overly familiar with their weaponry. "Or a Mormon or an overly enthusiastic Indian fellow. If it is all the same to you, I believe I will keep clear of the rest of the troop while we wander about in search of these rabbits you crave."

Wilson nodded and turned to the others who lingered some twenty yards off. "Jock, you can show the nice men from Zion the route down the ridge that leads to the old briar fences. Spread out and do your best. Finnegan and I will take this other side of the ridge and turn to meet you at the bottom."

"Yes, sir, Jack." Bull Bear gave a wave and began seeing to the disposition of the Mormons.

"He is an eager sort," Finnegan said, checking his shotgun over.

"Jock is a fine young man. Let's have a look down in that thicket."

Finnegan held up one hand. "A moment, Jack. Why should we split off? Just the other day you assured me I will not be departing this earth for some time yet. Are not many more happy years guaranteed to me?"

Wilson squinted with one eye. "I have been told you will not die here, Finnegan. That does not mean Jock will not trip and maim you in some unspeakable way with his old shotgun. The young man has little experience hunting and is eager to please. Best to stand clear regardless of my predictions."

Finnegan nodded. "Quite right, quite right."

Wilson led the way, and the two men began weaving through the various stands of brush and briar that led down toward the valley floor. Thanks to the depth of the snow, it was not difficult to see where the game had been making its rounds. They tramped along on their snowshoes and made certain to each take a side as they approached any likely looking spot. They had traveled the better part of a mile when a turkey came meandering out of a stand of low pines. Finnegan brought the pump-gun up, thumbed back the hammer and fired. The load of shot knocked the bird flat.

Finnegan approached the still creature. "Ah, that is a fine, big one. It will make a passable good meal."

"Oh, yes, very fine." Wilson gazed somewhat adoringly down at the turkey. His smile faded when he looked up. Finnegan's head pivoted up as well. Two Indian men were approaching on snowshoes. Both held rifles. Wilson rubbed his face. "Strange, this has not been mentioned to me."

Finnegan pulled back the pump on the shotgun, kicking the spent casing out into the snow. He brought the action closed, chambering a fresh round. "And who might these be?"

"That is Tom Mitchell and his son."

"Who?"

"The one they call Hummingbird."

"Saints preserve us, the fellow who wishes to steal your magic beans?"

"He may attempt to take my booha from me. I have no beans, Finnegan."

"Pay it no mind, Jack." The two men neared them. "Best for you to introduce us, I think."

Wilson did not appear too happy to make introductions, but did with formality. "Hummingbird, Jonas, this is my friend Finnegan Gilhooley. He has come here to visit Miss Meagher, the one who writes the letters. He has killed a fine turkey just now. Would you care for some of it?"

The younger man sneered. "We will damn well take all of it, Wilson. We have been following that turkey all day and your damned white fool here has killed it just as we were about to."

"That is a fine tale." Finnegan shook his head and slowly pulled a cigar from his pocket. "Might you wish to lay claim to every turkey, rabbit or gopher on this mountain?"

The young Jonas, clad in furs with only an angry face exposed, took a step forward. "Yes, white man, I claim them all. They were mine before you came, and they will be mine after you are gone."

Finnegan struck a match and just got his cigar lit before the wind extinguished it. He puffed out smoke and smiled at the boy. "Well, you are a forthright little prat. It is good to see one of your race who still has some hackles to raise." He held the shotgun in one hand and knocked ash down to the snow with the other. "Admittedly, I have been rather missing brave braves. Thank you, son." He glanced from Wilson to the two new arrivals and back again. "Having passed from the passion of youth into what could be termed maturity, allow me to give you some advice: if being Irish has taught me anything, young fellow, it is that land is only yours if you can first seize it, then spill enough blood to hold it. If you are not capable of those two actions, endless ranting regarding ownership only tends to make a man sound bitter or, at a minimum, inept. It would be better for you to show some restraint and admit that the turkey laying before us is neither yours nor mine by right, but will reside with which ever man can claim it." The boy made a small move with his rifle and Finnegan brought his shotgun up to his shoulder, his cigar clamped between his teeth. "Do not attempt it, dear boy."

"Finnegan, there is no purpose to that." Wilson sounded quite unconcerned.

The gunman puffed out smoke. "Jack, I am merely trying to show the young man that it would be foolish to die here over a matter so small as the possession of a turkey." He did his best to sound stern. "I believe we can both agree that it would be best if our friends here simply went their own way."

"No, Finnegan, that is not what I meant. I have already told you that you are not the man who kills Tom Mitchell.

You are not the man who kills his son. You will not kill these men today. It is impossible. It cannot be."

Jonas Mitchell straightened up a bit. "He cannot kill me?" Wilson shook his head in answer. Jonas turned to his father. "Is that true?"

The elder Mitchell grimaced. "Wavoka should not take his medicine from the white man's book, but it does not change that his booha is strong and he never lies."

Jonas assumed a very superior look. "Well, if he cannot kill me." He began to chuckle.

"Boy, do not do that..." As the young man brought up his rifle, Finnegan depressed the trigger of the shotgun. The hammer fell with a dull thud. All the men appeared quite shocked, with the exception of Wilson. "Bloody hell."

"I told you it would not happen." Wilson shrugged.

Finnegan jerked back the pump, casting out the misfire, and drove home another shell. He pulled the trigger and got another thud. The second misfire made Jonas's eyes fairly bug out of his head. The young fellow began to raise his rifle once again. The action was cut short when Finnegan swung his shotgun around and bashed the youth on the side of the jaw with it. That done, he swung the weapon over the other way and smacked Tom Mitchell's rifle down into the snow. "Be gone, damn you, or I will bash both your brains in with this gun or a damn rock if needs be." Finnegan partially got a hold of his temper. "I doubt this damn soothsayer's prophecy can affect the function of a stone."

The elder Mitchell helped his son to his feet and looked at the young man's face. "This is not the end of this, Wovoka."

"Be gone." Finnegan kicked snow at the medicine man. "Or, so help me, I will go over on the other side of the ridge and find some men who might be fated to murder you." The elder Mitchell moved to pick up his rifle. "Leave it. I will not steal it from you, but I will not have you at my back all damn day with it, either. Come back for it tomorrow."

Jonas Mitchell clutched his jaw. "How can we hunt with no guns?"

"For the love of Pete." Finnegan hung his head. "Take the damn turkey."

Jonas slowly reached down and grabbed hold of the bird's neck. "That is decent of you, for a white man."

"After I twice try and twice fail to kill a man, I often send him home with a small gift to recall our association. Good day." Finnegan watched the two fellows disappear over the edge of the ridgeline and then turned back to Wilson. "Jack, I do not mean to be rude, and far be it from me to suggest in what manner you ought to dole out the gossip the good Lord sees fit to pass on to you, but might I ask a favor?"

Wilson nodded. "I am always happy to help, Finnegan."

"In the future, might you refrain from telling people whether or not it is my fate to kill them? Your time as a hired hand and prophet of the Lord has obviously not acquainted you with the finer points of violence. As a man well acquainted with violence, I feel it is my duty to inform you that the threat of danger, the bluster if you will, is often a key component in avoiding bloodshed. I would be much obliged if you would proceed as I have asked."

"Oh, I see..." Wilson rubbed his chin with one mittened hand. "You believe that the Mitchells would have been less bold if they thought you could shoot them?"

"Yes, Jack, I bloody well do."

"But you could not."

"They did not...Jack, I could have shot them. Your divination only encouraged them along with poor luck and rotten coincidence."

"It is not coincidence, Finnegan. It is what is meant to be."

"It is moisture finding its way into priming compound." Finnegan bit back a sterner comment. "Let us continue to look for game, Jack. Standing here, discussing fate's inclinations will not put supper on your table."

"STILL, sir, you must admit, it is somewhat fantastic." The elder Doubleday ladled gravy onto his potatoes at the boarding house dinner table. His sons and he had collected no less than four rabbits and a turkey for the Wilson family pot, but had not received an invitation to dinner. Doubleday had made mention of the fact that dinner would be a preferable time for them to conduct something of an interview, but Wilson had demurred and pointed out that they had all the time in the world, up to and including the rapture, so there was no need to rush. Somewhat put out, the entire Mormon legation had made the trip back to town just in time to find sustenance at Mrs. Culbertson's table. Naturally, they were all enthralled to hear the tale of Hummingbird and his son.

"I assure you there is nothing of the fantastic or incredible in it, Mr. Doubleday." Finnegan sipped his coffee while attempting to explain matters without resorting to revelation. "The truth of the tale lies in the simple fact that the arm I made use of this day is of recent and untested design, and so is prone to malfunction. I would also make mention of the fact that I have only recently begun to shoot the new shotgun shells with hulls made from waxed paper. With a more vetted firearm and the more trustworthy brass cartridges of old, I am certain both Mitchell men would have been sent to meet their great spirit in person this day."

James chuckled and shook his head. "That shotgun seemed to work quite well this morning, directly after breakfast."

Finnegan rolled his eyes. "That is the nature of malfunction, James. If the apparatus never performed properly, one would have no way of knowing when it was broken."

"But it is not broken." The comment came from Doubleday's oldest son Johnathan. It was the first time Finnegan had heard the boy speak up. "You collected two rabbits with the arm farther down the ridgeline, sir."

The gunman smiled at the overly enthusiastic young man. The youth was rather obviously excited to be privy to the details of what might be a miracle. Finnegan waggled a finger at the impetuous Mormon. "Careful, my friend. Two defective shells does not a prophet make. I have seen many an arm misfire and have never heard it attributed to the will of God. Many a man has cursed Sam Colt or Oliver Winchester, but the Almighty is rarely blamed." Finnegan turned to the elder Doubleday. "Now that I consider the matter, I might have to lay the blame at the feet of one of your brethren."

Doubleday arched an eyebrow. "How is that?"

"The shotgun in question is the product of one of your fellow faithful. The arm was built by a man named Browning. A gentleman of no small repute who is said to be inventing the most astounding weapons. The fellow I obtained it from claimed to have stolen the piece from the smith's own workshop in Utah, while the blackguard was passing through. The fellow offered it to me in exchange for his freedom after I had placed him in custody for the robbing of a mail coach in Arkansas."

James chuckled. "From your current possession of the arm, should we assume you accepted the bribe?"

Finnegan shook his head reproachfully. "Not every man is as mercurial in terms of morality as you, Alexander. I did not accept the proposition."

James grinned. "And yet you possess the shotgun."

Finnegan arched an eyebrow. "I delivered the man to the federal court at Fort Smith, where he was hung by a judge in good standing. The shotgun was amongst his effects at that time. You would suggest I should throw it into the river?"

James pursed his lips. "Oh, certainly not, Finnegan. It is a long-standing tradition in the great state of Missouri that a man is entitled to the belongings of his victims. I am sure Arkansas holds to a similar policy."

"You are hardly one to lecture me regarding victims or property, Mr. James." Finnegan sneered. "What would you suggest I do with the item?"

"Well, Mr. Deputy Marshal, did returning it to the rightful owner ever cross your mind?" James grinned as wide as the cat who had swallowed the canary.

Finnegan rubbed his eyes. "The next occasion I find myself in Utah I will be sure to drop it off."

"Very decent of you, Finnegan." James motioned across the table. "Perhaps you should simply place the shotgun in the capable custody of Mr. Doubleday. He and his brood are headed that direction. I am certain it would not be an imposition."

Doubleday assumed a very serious look. "Oh, I do not know if it would be correct for me to accept such a duty. I am not acquainted personally with Mr. Browning. I do not know if it would be proper for me to transport his property."

James groaned. "Ah, what a pity. If you were, you could have assisted me in placing Mr. Gilhooley in a very awkward position."

Finnegan stared sardonically at his old nemesis. "Alexander, being snowbound does not agree with you. I fear you are becoming bored and quite starved for entertainment."

"On that score, you are correct. Not every man can find the sort of amusement you do in the course of his day. Honestly, what was the first thought that went through your mind when that shotgun failed to fire? I imagine it came as quite a shock."

"Alexander, you know as well as I do that it is always a shock to have a weapon malfunction. You also full-well know that they only tend to betray a man at the most inopportune of moments. For pity's sake, if I did not know better, I would say you are beginning to become a disciple of this Wilson. Before long, you will don a loincloth and beget to dancing."

James shrugged. "There is little else to do when one is snowbound." The aged outlaw turned toward the dining room door. A thumping noise, readily associated with someone entering the house, could be heard out by the front door. James moved uncomfortably in his chair and let out a small groan. "A new boarder comes to thrill us, perhaps."

Finnegan let out a groan of his own before drawing his Remington and placing it within easy reach under his napkin in front of him. "Every day here presents a new thrill."

Doubleday pursed his lips. "Mr. Gilhooley, it is regretful that you so often find yourself... that your hand is often forced. I would ask you, however, to show as much restraint as possible while my boys are in the same small room."

Finnegan offered a resigned shrug. "I do as best I can, sir." All parties in the room waited and listened while a man's voice was heard chatting with Mrs. Culbertson. Finnegan's hand remained near his napkin until the dining room door opened and his face lit up with a strange sort of recognition. "Hello, Townsend. How have you been?"

The man who stood in the doorway was of average height

and build with a mop of blond hair. His only truly noticeable feature was a set of odd grey eyes that he had inherited from his father. Women often commented on them, and Finnegan recognized the attribute straight away. After a moment of glaring, realization dawned on the fellow's face, and he smiled. "Finnegan, what on earth are you doing here?" He crossed the dining room and gave Finnegan's hand a firm shake. He glanced down to the napkin. "You appear to be as cautious as ever."

"Indeed, I am, Major Duran."

Finnegan motioned to an empty chair. "You should sit and try the fare. It is...adequate." As the newcomer took his seat, Finnegan removed his pistol from the table and placed it back in the holster. "Gentlemen, this is Major Townsend Duran of the War Department. I take it you are still a government man, Townsend?"

The fellow began slopping potatoes onto his plate. "I remain in government employ, Finnegan." He speared a hunk of pork and began arranging his silverware. "I was told you had somewhat joined the fold yourself. Someone, I do not recall whom, said you had left the Pinkertons and were dragging in hides for that hanging judge in Arkansas. It was all very fantastic stuff."

Finnegan took a moment to consider how to explain. "It might be best to say that I was employed by Judge Parker in conjunction with the Pinkerton firm."

Duran grinned and nodded. "Conjunction is probably a fine word for it. You have always been quite creative when it comes to finance, Finnegan." He shook his head, looking amazed. "How very strange that you should be in this tiny, snowbound town. Are you stuck here?"

"It might be difficult to conceive of, but this place was truly my destination. How is it you find yourself here?"

Duran shrugged and dug into his food. "I was involved in a rather doomed attempt to cross the Sierras and review some matters at the presidio in San Francisco. This bleak place is the extent of my progress." He shrugged again. "It does not worry me much. The engineer assured me that the pass will be open in short order and trains will be passing through soon."

James chuckled. "That is precisely what he told me several days ago." He thought on it for a moment. "Although, I was coming from your desired destination, so it may have been a different scoundrel who issued your information. I must say, it is a bit perturbing to see you here, sir. If I had known there was a train from the east that had made it this far, I would have boarded it for the return trip."

Duran laughed. "You would be considerably more perturbed if you had seen how quickly those fellows displaced me from the train and began retracing their steps. I believe they were considerably more worried than I regarding being marooned here. If I had the opportunity to chat with you first, I might have made a different choice." He smiled at the old outlaw. "A pleasure to meet you, sir. As Finnegan mentioned, I am Major Townsend Duran."

"Alexander James."

"Alexander Franklin James." Finnegan corrected.

Duran gave the old outlaw an inscrutable look before turning to Finnegan. "Pardon my inquiry, but have you two gentlemen met previously?"

"Mr. James and I have met previously, yes."

Duran turned back to the old outlaw. "So, then you are... *the* Frank James?"

James let a small grimace play over his face. "It is more like I am what is left of him."

Doubleday leaned forward in his chair. "Excuse me, Mr.

James, did you say that you sometimes go by the name of Frank James?"

"Yes."

"So then, the deceased Jesse James was your brother?" Doubleday seemed rather awed.

"Yes, and mother's favorite."

Johnathan Doubleday looked from the outlaw to his father. "Who is Jesse James, father?"

"We can discuss it some other time, boy." Doubleday stood up from his emptied plate and set his napkin down. "I believe it is time for us to retire." The boys rather grudgingly got up and followed their father out of the room after wishing the other guests a good evening. It was clear they were irritated at being removed from what promised to be an interesting evening.

When the remaining diners were alone, Duran let out a laugh and looked between his two dinner mates. "By God, now here is something I never would have thought to see in all my born days. Frank James at the table with Finnegan Gilhooley, and the both of you sipping coffee and chatting like old friends. This is...well, it is quite incredible." He glanced back and forth between the two older men. "Do the two of you no longer have an interest in murdering each other?"

"Posh." James waved one hand. "I never did have an interest in murdering him. If the fool would have left off and settled into farming, instead of chasing me all over creation, I would have not minded a bit."

"No interest in murdering me?" Finnegan let out an astounded guffaw. "You shot me in the hip and left me to die in the Minnesota wilderness."

James shrugged and resumed sipping his coffee. "I do not recall inviting you to Minnesota. If you had not pressed the issue so aggressively, there would have been no need for such silliness." He carefully set his coffee cup down on a saucer. "I might also add that you have no proof of my ever having been to the state of Minnesota, so it is something of a moot point."

Duran chuckled. "By God, you are a pip, sir." He continued laughing, seemingly unable to help himself. "The two of you must be having quite a time, stuck here together, reminiscing and whatnot."

"The whatnot occupies most of our time, thus far." Finnegan produced a cigar from his pocket and drew his coffee saucer over to him to use as an ashtray. "It is good to see you are still with the Army, Townsend. Perhaps you will be a general before you are done."

The soldier wolfed down his meal as though he had not eaten in days. "Oh, at the rate I am going I shall be lucky to not be demoted or cast aside. Every year it seems our numbers grow smaller. All the talk in Washington is about the Navy. It grows larger and we shrink. Those sailors are all in a dither regarding the wonders of steam and how it will allow America to conquer the world."

"Steam belongs in a tea kettle." James brought out a cigar of his own. "How is it you gentlemen know each other?"

Finnegan lit his cigar. "Major Duran's father, Colonel Duran, was an aide to General McClellan. While Mr. Pinkerton was in McClellan's service, the two developed a liking for each other and became quite the pair at the poker table. Perhaps feeling obliged, due to the amount of money removed from the Colonel's pockets, Mr. Pinkerton took an interest in the rearing of this young man after his father passed." Finnegan knocked ash into the saucer. "As Mr. Pinkerton's preeminent troubleshooter, I was occasionally tasked with keeping the young man in good order."

James lit his cigar, wearing a scowl. "General McClellan

and Allan Pinkerton are not gentleman I can offer many kind words regarding, but I will not hold such associations against you." The old outlaw grinned. "I will not even chide you for joining the Union Army, what with it being the only army still extant."

"Thank you, sir." Duran slugged down a full cup of coffee. "Very generous. It is also quite impressive that you and Finnegan have been able to offer one another some civility." Duran turned to the gunman. "Finnegan is rather well known for holding a grudge."

The gunman sneered. "I offer forgiveness as easily as I expel breath. No man can accuse me of hardheartedness."

"If they did, they might place themselves in danger of a thrashing." Duran grinned. "I recall you being rather slow to offer forgiveness to myself and a slightly older boy who absconded from West Point." Duran turned to James. "The older fellow, Bartleby by name, as I recall, had formed a very solid theory regarding the location of Captain Kidd's lost treasure. He had determined the site of the cache through peerless research, mind you. Naturally, we young fellows felt it would be best if we were to cast off the yolk of education and seek our fortunes elsewhere. Mr. Pinkerton took umbrage with our plans."

Finnegan shook his head. "I was forced to follow this scamp all the way to Florida before I could lay hands on him and return him to his studies."

Duran aimed a finger at Finnegan. "Yes, but I also recall you leaving poor, dumb, Bartleby standing on a beach with outturned pockets and a sore nose."

"He was the older of the two of you and should have known better than to involve you in such a ridiculous scheme. I would also point out that the young man's disposition was none of my business. I was charged with returning *you* to school, nothing more." Finnegan seemed quite satisfied with the explanation.

"I find it a bit surprising to hear what an interest Mr. Pinkerton took in you, and how long he continued it." James puffed his cigar.

"Such are the bonds that form between soldiers." Finnegan stared at the outlaw across the table.

"I rarely have much to do with any man I knew in the war." James knocked ash into his saucer.

"Soldiers, Alexander, not marauders." Finnegan smiled around his cigar.

"Gentlemen, let us not reenact a war that was before my time." Duran finished cleaning his plate and sat back. "Might one of you have an extra cigar? I believe mine reside in my luggage."

James took one from his pocket and handed it across the table. "I will supply you with a smoke, since Finnegan took the time to bring you back from Florida. Now we are both invested in you."

"I still believe it would be worth a fellow's time to go and look under a few more rocks in the area Bartleby suspected." Duran lit his free cigar.

Finnegan shrugged. "When you are a general, and allowed to issue your own leave papers, I would be happy to join you on the outing." He wore a look of contentment. "By God, it is good to see you, Townsend. I can hardly credit that you are here. Just as I begin to think this recent journey of mine can become no more strange, you walk through the door. It has been a week of wonders."

James chuckled. "Yes, just the other day he was shot by a child and had his miserable life saved by no less a personage than Frank James."

"Saved my life? Now that is going a bit too far, Alexander." Finnegan winced, moving his ribs the wrong way accidentally. "If you wish to be credited with keeping my mortal coil set in place, I must insist that you offer me credit in turn. I did no less for you only an hour previous to my unfortunate incident." Finnegan smiled at Duran. "Mr. James was reacquainted with a few former residents of Lawrence, Kansas, a town where he is not held in the highest esteem. Now, there was a fellow who was adept at holding a grudge. The man who recognized Mr. James had been nurturing it for many a long year and was impressively keen on resolving the matter. Very impressive."

James shook his head. "It is hardly a comparable circumstance. I trust I could have extricated myself from the situation without assistance. It is not as if I was badly wounded, as you were by that child. Oh, I might also point out, for Mr. Duran's benefit, if nothing else, that I was forced, by you, to go wandering about, being introduced to the citizens of this godawful place. So then, it follows, that even if you were responsible for my salvation from those unchristian, unforgiving souls, you were also the cause of my troubles. As such, it would be the acme of foolishness to credit you with saving me, when you were the original cause of my peril."

Finnegan sneered. "If you wish to equivocate in such a ridiculous manner, I might argue that if you had not taken to robbing banks, I would not have been charged with chasing you. If I had not chased you, I would not have assumed you hired an assassin to shoot me while I was minding my own business the other day. If I had not been forced into that assumption, I would not have pressganged you into accompanying me and none of the whole ugly business would have occurred. Yap all you like, Alexander, you are to blame for your troubles and always have been."

Duran gave Finnegan a confused look. "What is this about an assassin?"

"Your godfather here is so beloved he can barely travel without tripping over one." James chuckled. "The blackguard was hit in the ham. It is his own good luck he carries a spare on occasion."

Finnegan shot the old outlaw an icy stare. "I suppose it is of little import, now that the fellow is no longer with us, but I was fallen upon by a man with a rifle just the other day. I came away from the incident uninjured, although that was only from sheer luck." Finnegan could see that his old ward was intrigued. "I had spent the first part of the day out hunting with a local dry goods merchant. We had collected a fine elk and were about the business of transporting the better cuts out of the mountains by means of a device known as a pack board. Are you familiar with those clever contraptions?" Duran nodded. "Yes, well, I had the better part of the beast strapped to my poor back and was slowly descending a hill, when a fellow placed a bullet in the already dead elk that resided atop me. Fellow got me twice, actually. The impact sent myself and the dry goods man tumbling down the hill, and it was only through luck we survived that, as well."

Duran stared unbelievingly. "And after all that you still managed to get the better of the fellow?"

Finnegan raised his eyebrows, obviously rather proud of himself. "I employed an old trick from the war that has served many a slightly damaged soul well. I laid still, and had no small bit of trouble convincing the dry goods man to do the same, until the bushwhacking villain came to inspect his work. When he stepped within range, I struck, and gave him his just reward."

Duran let out a shocked laugh. "Yes, well, it would seem it is not intelligent to approach Finnegan Gilhooley until the priest has said his bit and the hole is filled." He tapped more ash. "Did you determine the fellow's identity?"

"Chap's name was Albert Larson. He formerly labored at one of the mines in the vicinity. Gaining further knowledge of the man and his motives was the reason for the outing Mr. James and I undertook. In hindsight, it may have been a fool's errand, and I am currently of the opinion that further knowledge may not be worth the effort required for the two of us to traipse about this country." Finnegan shrugged and winced again. "Mr. James and I are strangely well known in these parts and have encountered great difficulty involving introductions."

Duran glanced back and forth between the two aged characters. "It certainly sounds as though you two have been getting a time of it. I would like to accompany you both on your next outing, but I would prefer to observe from a distance, if you don't mind."

"You may find it difficult to gain proper distance, young man." James motioned to Finnegan with his cigar. "Only this very morning, I sat in the parlor of this house and observed your guardian angel kill two men. Nevada is a disturbing land. A fellow is not safe anywhere."

Duran showed some pity on his face. "Were they former Confederates, Finnegan? I know many of that sort still hold out hope of seeing you put down."

"Ha, hardly." James fielded the question, clearly pleased. "The two that perished this morning were upset about Finnegan murdering some kin of theirs in the northern wastes of Montana. It would seem, at some point, he felt the need to travel all the way up there and convince the residents of that unknown place to howl for his blood. Your old overseer has a difficult time when it comes to endearing himself to folk."

"I shall try not to recall your unkind words the morning those nice gentlemen from Lawrence come by to chat with you, Alexander." Finnegan grinned. "I am not the only man who forms a lasting impression."

Duran shook his head, a look of pure glee on his face. "I must admit, I was somewhat dreading being marooned in this backwater sort of snow cave. I had visions of passing the winter with nothing but a borrowed Bible or merciful squaw for entertainment. Now that I see who my company will be for the duration of this visit, I am rather looking forward to it. Just imagine, someday I may be able to tell my grandchildren that I saw both Frank James and Finnegan Gilhooley involved in a shootout. Even more shocking, I will be able to say you two were not shooting at one another."

"Oh, do not discount that as an option just yet, Townsend." Finnegan smiled across the table at both men. "It is always difficult to say when two fellows may have a falling out."

Chapter 10

GREENFIELD, NEVADA

January 10th, 1890

Having visited Wilson's village just the previous day, and being somewhat skilled in the art of winter travel, the Doubleday family had secured their mounts from Dyer and gotten moving. The elder Doubleday nurtured the hope that arriving early would serve to keep the absentminded prophet on task.

Being second in line to receive mounts, Finnegan watched the Mormon emissaries ride off while Townsend Duran brought two more horses into the stable from the back pasture. He patted the neck of the well-cared-for creature. "How is that man Dyer keeping these beasts so well fed in this climate? Any hope of them finding grass out there is long since passed."

"Some of the railroad men have a partial interest in the ownership of the stock." Finnegan set a saddle on the back of the first animal. "They are prompt about grain shipments, and laid in an impressive store when..." Finnegan shook his head and tightened down the cinch strap. "They laid in extra in the fall in preparation for the great debacle Mr. Wilson was expected to conjure."

Duran chuckled. "They truly laid in additional stores on the word of this... loinclothed dervish?"

"The fellow does not wear a loincloth and many of the residents of this town place great store in his predictions. At least in matters regarding the weather." Finnegan looked his associate up and down. "Speaking of clothing, you are quite well prepared for the circumstances you find yourself in."

"Am I?" Duran set a saddle on his mount.

"You have heavy boots, a fine hat, and wool mittens." Finnegan scratched the horse between its ears.

"Only a fool trusts the railroad to carry him all the way through in winter, Finnegan." The soldier smiled. "I packed my luggage with the expectancy to walk to California, if needs be."

"I also notice you have acquired a fine Remington-Keene rifle at some point." Finnegan picked up the rifle from where Duran had set it and slipped the weapon into a saddle scabbard.

"Purloined from West Point. The Ordinance Board chose not to make use of them. I saw no reason to let such an impressive bit of engineering simply molder in a closet."

"Very practical of you." Finnegan looked across the saddle at the man he had known since he was just a boy. "Townsend, I find it difficult to believe that you just happen to have that fine rifle and an ample supply of winter clothing with you purely by accident. You have never been one to be well prepared, but you are always well outfitted for the task at hand."

The soldier appeared confused. "I am afraid I may not understand the distinction. What on earth are you suggesting, Finnegan?"

The gunman glanced down, appearing rather saddened. "I do not believe you are marooned here. I believe this strange place is in fact your destination. I would also point out that the work you do for the War Department has never involved the inspection of forts. I doubt the brigade at San Francisco awaits instruction in polishing their boots with bated breath. Tell me you were not sent here for the low deed that is my best suspicion?"

"Low deed? What do you take me for, Finnegan?"

"I take you for a man who does as he is told and usually accepts the best offer. There is no shame in it, Townsend. That method is how most of us travel through life, and I can claim no different."

"What have you got in your head, Finnegan?"

"I suspect that some mediocre mind in that fetid swamp they call the capital has come to the conclusion Mr. Jack Wilson is readying a rebellion, here, in this frozen waste. In keeping with that level of wisdom, you have been dispatched to shoot the poor fool down before he can raise too much Cain."

Duran lifted both eyebrows. "Finnegan, that is a serious accusation."

"Wilson would hardly be the first Indian the War Department shot based on hazy suspicion and hoped-for efficiency."

Duran shook his head. "I think you have been working on commission for too long, my old friend. The War Department is not the Pinkerton Agency. We are not a gang of assassins. I was not sent to gun anyone down in the street."

"Then please explain the presence of those mittens, Townsend. I am not a fool, and you are not the first man I have encountered who is not as smart and he believes he is."

"Very well." The young man shrugged with the resignation youth makes easier. "Fine, you may as well know; if *you* cannot be trusted in such matter, who possibly could? As you suspect, I am not waylaid on my way to San Francisco and the War Department does have an interest in Mr. Wilson. How can it not, Finnegan? The man has been writing letters predicting perdition and has sent them to the better part of those in Washington charged with administering the west. He has caused something of a stir."

"So, he is to be killed?"

"As I said, we are not a gang of assassins. I have been dispatched here to assess the situation. If it appears as though Mr. Wilson has a realistic chance of whipping these savages into an uprising, I have been given the duty of dissuading him from that action."

"Dissuading him by depositing the fellow in a snowy grave?"

"My profession is not the same as yours, Finnegan."

"My profession involves doing the bidding of my betters to preserve what they consider to be the status quo." Finnegan smiled. "On occasion, I have heard the truly pompous among them refer to it as the public good. Your masters in Washington are no better."

"My masters are not masters, but commanding officers, Finnegan, and they do not send me about murdering citizens." Duran seemed quite pleased with the distinction.

Finnegan rubbed one side of his face, looking skeptical. "Mr. Wilson is not a citizen, Townsend. Jack Wilson, along with his family and tribe, are enemy combatants. They cannot vote and are nothing more than wards of the government, their status as prophets notwithstanding. Men such as you are, from time to time, charged with locating and sorting out foreign agents; why should Wilson not receive similar treatment?"

Duran stared, unbelievingly. "A prophet? Finnegan, you have been trapped in this ice field too long." He laughed. "I cannot conceive that we are even engaging in this conversation. Why should you care whether or not some unwashed savage meets his demise in the best interest of the U.S. government? Is it not rather hypocritical of you to even suggest such a thing?"

"Townsend, I find myself in this ice field by the request of my oldest and dearest friend. She requested my presence here for the specific purpose of protecting Mr. Wilson from harm. To put it bluntly, Townsend, if you have been commissioned to engage in anything as lowly as assassination..." Finnegan shrugged. "You and I may find ourselves at cross purposes."

Duran stared over the saddle. "Your oldest and dearest friend? Who might that be?"

"The fine lady we are traveling to visit this very day."

"After all the time we have known each other, after you have been charged with my safety by the dearly departed Mr. Pinkerton himself, you would cast all that aside for a woman and a savage?"

Finnegan chuckled. The young man was doing a fine job of appearing offended. "Townsend, there is no need for such dramatic declarations. There is also no need to force me into choosing allegiances. The solution is very simple: do not attempt the assassination of Mr. Wilson, and we will have no trouble between us."

Duran threw his hands in the air. "I am not here to kill the man."

"Then there shall be no trouble." Finnegan motioned to the young man's horse. "Do up that cinch properly or you will end up in a snowdrift."

Finnegan sat sipping coffee in the parlor of the Wilson family farmhouse. Molly sat to his right, sorting through Wilson's correspondence. The two men had made it to the house just in time for the mid-day meal. Duran had gone from the dining room into the kitchen to make use of himself and to give Finnegan and Molly some time to themselves. Both the soldier and the members of the Wilson family exchanged meaningful glances as they departed.

"Am I incorrect, or does it seem as though our acquaintances are continually attempting to foment romance between us?" Molly smiled as she shoved papers into an envelope.

"Your parents certainly never attempted it."

"Mothers and fathers seldom know what is best."

Finnegan chuckled. "Do not tell such things to your students. You will find yourself without work in short order." The gunman glanced toward the kitchen and lowered his voice a bit. "Molly, how many letters have you written to government officials for Wilson?"

She paused in her filing. "Oh, I...do you require a precise number?"

"A rough estimate should do."

"A few dozen, at least."

"A few dozen?" Finnegan sipped his coffee and shook his head. "I believe it would be best if you were to cease that particular practice."

"Cease contacting government officials?" The schoolteacher scowled. "Wilson will not like the sound of that, and I do not understand the logic behind the request. If we do not communicate with the government, how will they ever be brought to the negotiating table?"

Finnegan groaned. "My logic is the product of my dear friend Major Duran visiting this quaint hamlet."

Molly motioned to the kitchen. "The man is marooned, Finnegan. Just as Mr. James is."

"Mr. James is, in fact, marooned, and, after careful vetting, I have no reason to believe otherwise. Major Duran has been ordered to tell people he is marooned. In actuality, he has been dispatched here."

"By whom?"

"The War Department potentates of Washington. The men you have apparently been haranguing with your vast correspondence."

"But why?"

"I would imagine it is largely the result of you sending them letters and nothing more. In my experience, the valiant men of the War Department are blissfully unaware of most occurrences in the world unless someone supplies them with carefully worded reports. Above all, they dislike pots being stirred, boats being rocked, and feathers being ruffled. You and Wilson are attempting all three."

"Finnegan, why does the man feel he must sink to subterfuge? Jack has been requesting a representative of the government for some time now. Your old friend should do nicely."

The gunman groaned. "Molly, Townsend Duran has not been sent here to discuss prophecy or stipends with Jack Wilson. I daresay, the man likely has little understanding of either subject. His only interest is to determine whether or not Wilson poses a danger to the basic peace and security of the nation. Duran wishes to know if Wilson is bringing about some sort of uprising among the Indians."

"He is not." Molly made it all sound so very innocent.

"Can you or Wilson offer any compelling proof that is true?"

"How can a man prove he does not possess an intention? It is ridiculous to even suggest such a thing. Jack would never stoop to something resembling insurrection, at any rate. There is no reason for us to bend and scrape to the wishes of some silly fellow from Washington. What is he to do if he is not satisfied? Will he scurry back to the capital and file a grievance?" Molly grinned. "I see no reason why a man such as Jack Wilson should be forced to explain himself to anyone."

"He may take it upon himself to shoot Wilson in the back and then scurry on his way." Finnegan watched as her grin disappeared. "Such are the expedient methods which are sometimes employed, Molly. There may be no reason for Jack to explain himself, but reason rarely enters into political matters."

Molly slowly looked from Finnegan, to the kitchen, and then back again. "I would not claim to be well versed in such matters, Mr. Gilhooley, but I doubt that young upstart currently enjoying milk and cookies would be so bold as to attempt any action if you instructed him otherwise. He certainly appears to consider you a mentor, of sorts."

Finnegan sighed. "My previous association with the young man may prove more of a difficulty than an asset. He has already jested that it would be unjust of me to negate our long friendship for a woman's affections and a lowly Indian." He rubbed his chin. "I believe he was jesting, at any rate."

"Finnegan, you cannot truly think that placid-faced young soldier has traveled all this way to kill a man he has never met. A man who is no danger to anyone whatsoever."

The gunman chuckled. "That placid young soldier may have done much worse in his time. Whether he is here with dire intentions or not, he is most assuredly a harbinger, and we should take the omen to heart."

"You speak of harbingers. You are beginning to sound not a bit unlike Jack. What is it you believe the arrival of Mr. Duran foretells?"

"I believe his arrival should signal our departure. Where one squirming Washington-reared creature slithers, more are sure to follow."

Molly emitted a small laugh. "You cannot be in earnest. We cannot leave. You have only just arrived and my work with Wilson has only begun. He will need me to..."

"He will need you to make his situation even more dire." Finnegan pointed to the kitchen door. "Molly, that young man was not sent here by chance. Wilson has caused enough of a stir that he has been noticed by men whose notice is not to be appreciated. That young man in the kitchen is not the last of his kind who will be dispatched to this place if you and Wilson continue to stir the pot. The irregular former Confederate or discontented kin of a rustler is the sort of difficulty I can overcome. An endless, consistent flow of men such as Townsend will prove too much for my petty skills quite quickly. I cannot fight the tide for you, lass, and an army is just as much a force of nature."

"I am more than a little surprised to hear you speak so, Finnegan. How many government functionaries can they send?"

"A company, a battalion, a regiment." Finnegan scowled. "The man comes from the Army, dear Molly. They can readily send an army if they wish. I consider myself a man of some prowess, but I still have not learned the proper method for dealing with an army single-handed." He shrugged and withdrew a cigar from his vest pocket. "As I recall from that old Roman history you once suggested to me, Mark Anthony wisely observed that only six cur dogs are required to kill a lion. The lion is by far the more noble beast, but outnumbered, such things do not matter."

Molly shook her head. "No, Finnegan, it is not time to begin considering matters like that. We are jumping at shadows. So far, the only agent of the government to appear is that young man, who you know to be a good man. There is nothing to fear. From what the youthful Major tells you, he is no more dangerous than a census collector and empowered to do no more than shake Jack's hand and ask a few questions."

"Molly, I said I knew the boy, I never said I knew him to be a good man. I know little of his behavior after reaching his majority. I would like to believe he has gained moral certitude -- more than his father ever possessed, preferably -- but I cannot say. I do know that the War Department is not in the habit of employing men based on their ability to sing in the Sunday choir. I am also certain the young man has a fine rifle with him."

"You are in the habit of traveling without arms?" Molly gave him her most sardonic look. "I would be far more shocked to hear he arrived without a firearm."

"Is there no method I can employ to convince you that trouble is brewing, dear lass?"

The schoolteacher sat forward and took Finnegan's hand. "Dear Finnegan, this sort of difficulty is precisely why I asked you to come here. Major Duran's arrival does not signal our need to depart, it signals our need to harden our resolve. Jack Wilson needs our help more than ever, my friend."

Finnegan sighed again and rubbed his eyes with his free hand. "Molly, I am aware how long you have been waiting for a...a figure in the manner of Jack Wilson to appear. I can also appreciate your inclination to help the strange sot. What I am having difficulty keening is what, precisely, we are supposed to be aiding him with."

"Aiding him with? Finnegan, this man could unite all the tribes of Indians as one."

"Yes, lass, and that would greatly aid the U.S. Army when they come to shoot them all down. As I recall, the greatest stumbling block they ever encountered when it came to shooting Indians, was locating the buggers previous to the massacre." He could see her eyes growing angry. "I do not know what else to tell you, Molly. It would not be right for me to lie to you, not even to preserve your illusions."

"Illusions? You of all men know Wilson is not filling my head with illusions. He told me what occurred with Mitchell. You know now that he truly is... what he claims to be."

"What does the man claim, Molly? If you have wrung a straight answer out of the fellow regarding any topic, I would be eager to know of it. He had the good luck to predict the malfunction of a shotgun that has, likely, not as yet been offered for sale to the general public due to a tendency to malfunction. All I have witnessed so far are coincidences and unfortunate circumstances, nothing more."

"You find yourself sharing a boarding house with Frank James and you will tell me it is mere coincidence? Wilson told you in no uncertain terms that the man would appear, and he is here. What more proof is required?"

"Sharing a roof with Alexander Franklin James is proof of nothing more than God's intention to begin punishing me for my sins in this world previous to the punishments that await in the next." Finnegan rolled his eyes. "I should also add that Wilson has not, as yet, specifically predicted anything. The fellow's vague prophecies relating to me encountering obstacles or men who hold vendettas against me is hardly the work of Merlin guiding kings to stones and swords. Most days I can barely cross a city street without encountering someone with an old grudge and a shoddy pistol. I do not know why this sabbatical to the wilderness should be any different."

"Whether the man can predict the future or not..." Molly threw her hands in the air. "Is not the possibility of his uniting the tribes alone worth this minor effort? Just imagine what the next ten years may hold if the Indians could be brought together to act in their own interests."

Finnegan rubbed one temple. "Molly, for more years than I can count I have heard the same philosophy purported by union leaders regarding their cause. I have heard it spouted in taverns and meeting halls and even the Haymarket, just before the bomb exploded. I have even seen the rabblerousers' mad visions come to fruition. Working men form up, and march, and strike, and when the smoke clears, and the cataclysm ends, they find themselves in a situation not unlike the one they were in at the beginning. The working men go back to their shacks and the union bosses retire to their clubhouses. If Jack Wilson could unite all the tribes of this country, I believe the only noticeable end result would be a collection of very fat, very corrupted Indian chiefs sitting in a circle. Wishes rarely come true in the form they were originally phrased, my dear."

"Any fate would be better than what the Indians currently face. They die of disease in droves on dozens of reservations. Whiskey and worldliness corrupt them in the white man's saloons. Their women are ruined, their children are abused in the schools..."

"A conquered people are bound to suffer greatly." Finnegan said the words quite matter-of-factly.

"How can you speak in such a way, Finnegan?"

"I come from a conquered people. It has made me practical."

"So, what do you suggest? Would you have me run off and leave Jack to his fate?"

"It would ease my suffering, at the very least." Finnegan grinned. "I have known you far too long to think you would abandon a man such as Wilson only halfway to his revolution. I know you will not leave, dear Molly. I only broached the subject so that the discussion would not be left unsaid at the end of our adventure here. You will not feel the disappointment of discovering Townsend is not a sweet young man and I will not consider myself remiss for not informing you of all the facts." Finnegan glanced around the farmhouse. "Are you certain you would not prefer a room in town where I could better keep an eye on you?"

"In the boarding house where you regularly shoot people?"

"It is hardly a regular occurrence." He shrugged and tapped ash from his cigar.

"That knowledge would be a great comfort as I attempted to fall asleep at night. No, I think I shall remain here where murders never take place and none of the residence are considered notorious."

"Well, if you do not believe the boredom will overcome you." Finnegan shook his head. "Molly, as I am here, might I make one more minor inquiry?"

"Certainly."

"Are we to remain here until such time as Mr. Wilson has congealed all the savage tribes into a formal lump and they begin practicing a republican form of government?"

Molly smiled. "Naturally. I shudder to imagine what sort of legislature they would put together without our assistance."

"Yes, well, I am certain it will rival the Roman Senate. At all events, what I would ask you now, dear lass, is what it is you envision the two of us doing when Wilson's miracles and wonders come to pass?"

The schoolteacher shrugged, smiling slyly. "What do you envision, dear Finnegan? Are you to return to Arkansas and resume hunting railroad bounties?"

"The days of wild Indian Territory are coming to an end. Judge Parker and his court will soon be no more. I doubt there would be anything recognizable to return to in a year's time."

"Chicago, perhaps? Would you leave me here and return to the Pinkerton Agency as you have done so many times before?"

The gunman chuckled. "Would you send me back to the agency without offering an alternative? Perhaps I recall incorrectly; I have a vague remembrance of you wishing to cherish your self-same sovereignty when I made suit the last time."

Molly blushed. "Well, perhaps you will have to make suit yet again, Mr. Gilhooley. Are you the sort of man who is only willing to make a single attempt before declaring defeat?"

Finnegan rubbed the back of his neck. "If I am bloodied in the first attempt, I generally wait to make another attempt until such time as I have a better chance of victory. Does that day approach?"

"As surely as sunrise approaches. I would suggest you act as you suggested. The day Mr. Wilson is formally elected governor of the great state of Nevada might make a fine moment."

"Oh, I believe he wishes to be governor of the entire west, lass."

"Once he is governor of one state, it cannot be too difficult to get him ensconced in a few more, and he could likely do without my instruction at that point." Molly grinned and stood. "Faithful Finnegan, would you truly still wish to wed me, after all these years?"

"After all these years, Molly, it warms my heart to simply have you near. As for the rest, I will gladly accept whatever you are willing to offer and be pleased with the bargain." He gave her his warmest smile and walked into the kitchen. As he entered, Townsend Duran was still sitting at the table and the two smallest Wilson children were removing their milk glasses and working to corral cookie crumbs. Finnegan sat down opposite Duran just as the children left, the smaller one chasing after the larger. The gunman picked up a molasses cookie and eyed it. "Do these satisfy?"

"They serve their purpose." Duran assumed a stern countenance. "I must warn you, Finnegan, having been raised in boarding schools, I consider the possession of sweets to be a serious matter. I have swelled many a lip in protection of my treasure."

"Then this shall teach you that we are far past boarding school." He took a bite of the cookie and nodded. "The lady knows her trade." He reached out and took up Duran's milk glass. "It is not a long journey from here to Wilson's camp, or village, or whatever it is he fancies it as. Would you care to meet the man today? Get it over with, as we once said in the Army."

"That would be fine. I suppose I should speak with the fellow at some juncture, if I am to be drawing conclusions regarding him. Although, such measures are hardly a strict requirement when it comes to filing government reports. Will he not be busy convincing those Mormons to let him run their church in the desert? I must say, the irony of that would tickle me."

"I have spent some time in the land of Utah, Townsend."

Finnegan dunked his cookie in the milk. "It is not so much a matter of Wilson convincing the Mormons to give him that place, but more a case of them casting about to find someone to accept the offer." He finished the cookie and swallowed the milk. "Ah, that is fine." He set the glass to the side. "Is it a fine thing to be an officer? It always seemed to be when I was a lowly enlisted man."

"It has its privileges. Although, in many ways, it is no different from your experience. There is always a man above you barking orders and, as time passes, those orders are composed of more foolishness and less wisdom." He chuckled. "I continually tell myself that if I were placed in command matters would change for the better, but would I be as silly and vain as the last man? Who can say? Were you ever raised above private while you wore the uniform?"

Finnegan groaned. "I should begin by explaining that I never did possess a full uniform. The chaps at the docks were nice enough to give me a pretty blue, albeit worn, blue jacket. At the time, I considered it quite the boon and never paused to consider what accepting it might entail. I suppose I was a private in rank the day I entered, and remained in that station when Mr. Pinkerton plucked me from the ranks and, most likely, perdition. As I recall, when you came of age Mr. Pinkerton offered you employment, his sons would likely extend the same offer. If you dislike your current work, I am certain the offer would stand."

"Foolishness is foolishness, Finnegan. It does not much matter which master you serve while perpetrating it. Consider the case of you and Mr. James. He fought for the grand Confederacy, you for the grand Union. Now, you both find yourselves residing in the same boarding house, trying to stay alive in turn and arguing the validity of an Indian messiah. Allegiances are fluid in nature, my friend. I rarely trouble myself with contemplating them." He grinned. "If nothing else, the Army offers more security. You Pinkerton employees are subject to the ebb and flow of those bastards on Wall Street in New York. If the workingmen do not take it upon themselves to lynch all of you one fine day, the robber barons may simply discharge all of you from service. I daresay, the U.S. Government will not be going out of business any time soon."

"Eventually all walls fall, all idols tarnish, all men die." Finnegan stood from the table. "Let's be on our way. Oh, just so you are aware, I have informed Miss Meagher of your orders."

Duran gave him a confused look. "Finnegan, as I have explained, I am not here to do the man harm. If I were to wish the man ill, I fail to see what Miss Meagher would do to prevent it. Is the lady in the habit of thwarting assassins?"

"The lady is in the habit of corresponding with newspapers. Just so you are aware, if anything untoward occurs with Mr. Wilson, there will be a respectable, white, Christian schoolteacher raising Cain in regard to it."

"That is an interesting angle from which to guard Mr. Wilson, I suppose, but hardly useful. I would not think an assassin would much care what a newspaper had to say regarding his character."

Finnegan placed his milk glass next to the rest of the dirty crockery. "I can assure you, from experience, assassins rarely pause to worry over the opinions of newspaper writers. That being said, the foolish masters they serve, whether in the government or in private employ, do little other than worry over the scribblings of newspaper writers. So much so that the newspaper writers often dictate the behavior of the assassins. A miraculous circle of stupidity, is it not? Just so you are aware, dear Townsend."

"Oh, Finnegan, do you truly have so little trust in your country that you would suspect I have been sent here with bad intentions?"

The gunman shrugged. "Townsend, it is not my country, and the men you serve are the same men who gave me that damn bottle blue jacket. I have been given little reason to trust anyone."

Entering the Indian village by way of one of the beaten in paths, the first sight that greeted the two wayward killers was one of the Doubleday sons chopping firewood. Finnegan nodded to the young man as they rode past and then leaned over toward Duran. "One thing you will find here is that Wilson has the most wonderful way of bringing these visitors closer to God. Much of his method involves them doing chores for him. I would assume Moses employed much the same methods for the general beatification of the promised land."

Duran stifled a laugh. "Yes, well, I seem to recall that if you teach a fellow to fish, he can be easily tricked into bringing you fish every day, or something like that." They rode to the stable and began removing their saddles. After the trip up the mountain and crossing the snowfields, the horses were sweating in spite of the chilled weather. "Mr. Wilson receives a great deal of free labor, I take it?"

Finnegan nodded. "I traveled here the better part of the way from Arkansas with a young Cherokee boy..." Finnegan paused. "Or is he Arapaho?"

Duran shook his head. "I cannot see how it would matter."

"Yes, quite. At any rate, the young man was sent here by

his elders to discuss matters involving the end times, or recent revelation, or some such rot. He has been here a good many days now and is charged with both hunting for Wilson and handling quite a bit of his correspondence to the other tribes. What is more, the young man considers it no small adventure and welcomes his chores with something akin to glee." Finnegan glanced about to make certain no one was within earshot. "There is a tradition among the savages, as Miss Meagher explained matters to me, wherein the emissaries sent to a man like Wilson are to bring gifts. Now, bear in mind, much of what I have seen the man receive would be considered small coin, claptrap, or table scraps by men such as us, but to Wilson it represents a great windfall."

Duran pulled his saddle free and placed it on a pole. "Finnegan, are you attempting to convince me that this man is nothing but a charlatan?"

"I am merely relating facts." The gunman shook his head. "As for his credibility, I honestly cannot say. The more time I spend around the fellow, the less I know for certain what he is or even might be. It is complicated further by his unwillingness to make formal declarations. It is difficult to discredit a man who claims nothing."

Duran placed a few trimmed branches across the opening of the impromptu horse stall. "If you have no idea whether this man is a prophet or a fraud, why remain here?"

"I remain here because Miss Meagher remains here." He eyed Duran as if he had gone mad. "Why on earth would I wish to seek out a prophet for my own sake?"

"Finnegan, I am not certain which is the stranger fellow, you or Wilson." They stepped out of the stable. "Have you seen anything from this Wilson that would lead you to believe he is any more than an Indian who has learned a few charming traits and tricks?"

"The townsfolk credit him with the amount of snow this place is receiving."

Duran gave the gunman a surprised look. "Snow?"

"Yes."

"Finnegan, the entire railroad west of here is covered in snowsheds, long buildings that guard the tracks from being overcome with snow. It does nothing but snow in high country like this. Can the fellow do anything else, aside from claiming responsibility for winter?"

"He does seem to possess some aptitude for predicting events." Finnegan held up one hand to stop the inevitable response. "Yes, Townsend, I too have met many an old gypsy woman scattering entrails and howling up at the spirits. I am aware of the methods employed. The more vague their predictions are, the greater chance there is the prediction will come to pass. I will tell you now that Wilson is fond of just that sort of prattle. Even so, he does appear to know more than a man should. Just when I come to the conclusion that he is nothing more than smoke and mirrors, he does something to give me pause. I have had a strange time of it in this place, I tell you that."

Duran paused and gave a confused stare. "Finnegan, I do not think I quite follow. What is the purpose of this conversation, precisely?" He let out a short laugh. "Certainly, there is no way on heaven or earth that I will ever come to believe this fellow is anything more than a clever trickster, more adept than some of his brethren. I must also remind you that my opinion in the matter has little weight. Even if Mr. Wilson chooses to raise Lazarus while I am visiting today, my elders and betters in Washington would never credit it. If they did... well, I assume you know that there is only one purpose for messiahs or martyrs. If the man does indeed possess magical powers, it would not be much of a stretch for some sharp intellect in Washington to decide the man needs to be nailed to a cross." Duran shook his head. "Honestly, Finnegan, you have been in these mountains too long. What can it matter whether the man is the second coming or not? My only concern is the fellow's chances of stirring other savages to the war path. If it appears as though he will not do that, well, he may sit here in the snow and raise Lazarus all he likes, just so he is quiet about it. That is all I would ask."

Finnegan groaned as he led the government agent toward the hut normally occupied by Wilson. "Yes, Townsend. I gave much the same advice to Miss Meagher earlier. If Mr. Wilson would simply diminish his daily correspondence, he would stand a much better chance of living to old age."

Duran stopped walking and Finnegan ceased, as well. "Might I make an inquiry, Finnegan?"

"You surely may."

"Have you seen any breed of Sioux around this place? As you may well know, they come in several varieties and even they seem to have a difficult time keeping track of allegiances."

Finnegan nodded with a bored visage. "There is hardly a tribe that has not had some type of emissary pass through this place. Some are undoubtedly Sioux. The rapidity with which Wilson's name has spread is hard to credit. It seems to outpace both the telegraph and the mail."

"It is primarily the disposition of the Sioux quartered in the Dakotas that concerns the men in Washington. They are a quarrelsome lot and their own chiefs have had very little success keeping the braves on the reservations. They wander into areas they no longer rightfully possess and cause no end of trouble. It is the opinion of the War Department that the invective of a man like Wilson could easily whip them into a frenzy. Who can say what the result might be?"

Finnegan squeezed the bridge of his nose. "I can easily say. The result will be a field of dead Indians, just as it always is." He shook his head. "In all these years of fighting the red man the army lost just the one regiment, am I correct?"

Duran smiled. "Yes, Custer's unfortunate 7th."

"And how many legions of red men have fallen? The Dakotas are home to many a regiment, Townsend. If, for some reason I cannot fathom, Wilson did choose to whip a tribe currently quartered in those barren wastes into a frenzy, it would not be more than a matter of days before a few companies of horse soldiers located them and ended the fracas. I have seen my fair share of Indians in the past few years, my friend. These braves are warriors no longer, not in any functional capacity. They are starving, they are diseased, they are broken. I fail to see the purpose in dithering over any of them much, currently."

Duran shrugged. "Finnegan, the day I receive a sensible order I may faint dead away. It is not for men like us to look to the purpose."

The gunman groaned. "As you like it, Townsend. Let us have a visit with the man so that you may file your report." Finnegan began plodding through the snow toward the hut once again. "With any luck, Wilson will have died of old age before some simpleton in Washington has a chance to peruse your scribblings." Finnegan gave the makeshift door to the small lodge a couple of soft thumps with his gloved hand. "Jack Wilson, are you within?"

There was the sound of something creaking and then the prophet came to the door. "Ah, Finnegan, very good." He put out his hand to Duran. "You must be the man from the Army."

"Major Townsend Duran." The soldier shook the proffered hand. "A pleasure to make your acquaintance, Mr. Wilson." He grinned. "Did the spirits tell you of my arrival?"

"My friend Ed Dyer mentioned it. He gossips like an old squaw." Wilson held open the door and motioned to the inside. "Come in out of the cold. Have you been to see Molly today, Finnegan? She looks forward to your visits."

The two men stepped inside. The small hovels were always cleaner and comfier than Finnegan expected. "We come from Molly and the Wilson Ranch."

"She is well?" Wilson waved to a log more or less carved to serve as a bench.

"She is quite well and full of vinegar, as always." Finnegan and Duran sat. The gunman nodded toward the soldier. "Major Duran has come to inquire as to a few matters, Jack. Would you mind chatting for a bit?"

"Any friend of yours is a friend of mine, Finnegan." Wilson looked to Duran. "It must have been a fine thing to have a fellow such as Finnegan to teach you the ways of being a man when you were young."

Duran's eyes narrowed. "Mr. Dyer surely did not tell you that. He would not know such a thing to tell. How do you come to know Finnegan and I are old friends?"

"Some things I am told, some things are obvious. You look to Finnegan as a son might look to a father. You are at ease with him. Did he teach you to be a man?"

Duran lifted one eyebrow. "In some respects. He once taught me a firm lesson regarding my responsibilities, along with a scattering of other instruction."

Wilson smiled and nodded. "You can forgive a man much if he is your teacher and guardian. Is that not so?"

"I suppose that is true." The soldier glanced over at the gunman. "Although, no grudge against Finnegan comes to mind." He turned back to Wilson. "You seem to be a very knowledgeable man. I believe it may be best if we are direct with one another, Mr. Wilson."

Wilson nodded. "That is usually for the best."

"Very well, then." Duran cleared his throat. "Mr. Wilson, have you been telling people -- white people, Indians from other tribes -- have you been telling them that the world is to be turned upside down by floods and other calamities and that the Indians will be left in control of this land again?"

Wilson rubbed his chin and wore a look similar to that of a professor about to explain something to a very dull-witted student. "Major Duran, you are a soldier, yes?"

"Yes."

"Then you know much regarding duty. There are some things you simply must do. You have no choice. It does not matter that you might rather not perform the act, you are compelled to act by your duty." Wilson smiled warmly.

"Most assuredly. I can understand that very well."

"So, then, you can understand that when I went into the hills by the river, I was given a vision. I was shown what you speak of. There was a great cataclysm. The earth was turned over and rivers flowed backwards. The skies were dark and torn by lightning. The white men were all flung back to where they came from and the red men, like me, were left here to live." Wilson grew very serious. "Major Duran, I do not know if this vision will come to pass. I do not know if these things will happen or not. What I do know is that I was not given the vision so that I would keep the knowledge of it to myself. If a man is given a vision, he is meant to tell people of it. I have not told any one of my vision who did not ask me of it."

Duran nodded very slowly. "You make an interesting observation, sir." He rubbed the back of his neck. "Mr.

Wilson, I come from Washington. Do you know of the city of Washington?"

"It is the town where the great white father keeps his lodge."

Finnegan groaned. "Enough of that bosh, Jack. Words such as great white father and cataclysm hardly belong in the same head."

"I speak to Major Duran as I do so that he will understand. He does the same." Wilson reached to the side and brought up a gourd with a cork stuck in the top of it. "Would you care for milk?" He held up a plate of meat. "Or food?"

Finnegan grimaced. "No, thank you, Jack. I would hesitate to take from your supplies." He shrugged. "I would also hesitate to imagine where that milk was procured. I have not seen a cow anywhere in the vicinity."

"Nature provides, Finnegan."

"Yes, I have many fond memories of our last hunt together."

"Gentlemen?" Duran fidgeted on the bench a little. "I would greatly enjoy the chance to discuss the local game populations, at some point. For the moment, though, I would appreciate staying on the topic of Mr. Wilson's prophecies." The soldier rubbed his face. "As you said, sir, you received a vision of events you... believe may occur. I take it, you have told many of the other Indians who have come to visit you about your vision."

"That is why they have come." Wilson sipped the milk gourd.

"What else do you tell them, Mr. Wilson?"

The prophet appeared confused. "I tell them many things, Major."

"Do you tell them to rise up against the government? Do you tell them to disobey the soldiers on the reservations?"

Wilson shook his head. "Do soldiers tell the people on the reservations what they can or cannot do?"

Finnegan chuckled. "I tried to explain matters to you, Townsend. Mr. Wilson does not have an understanding of matters pertaining to the reservations. He has never lived on a reservation. His tribe has not been provided with one. At least not in the strictest sense."

Duran licked his lips. "So, then, you do not tell the other Indians to disobey the soldiers or the great white father?"

"No." Wilson carefully set his gourd down and took up the plate of meat. "You must try to understand, Major. I am not the first man in my family to be given a vision. My father had many visions and saw many things. When he was a boy, he thought the visions were pictures of what would come to pass. He thought that what he had been witness to must come to pass. As he grew older, he came to see that many of the visions were warnings. If men tried to help each other, the visions did not need to come to pass." Wilson smiled at the soldier. "I tell the other Indians that we should live in peace with the whites. I tell them that they should work, that work is salvation. I tell them to earn wages and build houses. I tell the white men in Washington, the men we write letters to, that they should be kind to the Indians. I tell them that we can all live in peace together."

Finnegan chuckled again. "Be sure to inform Major Duran as to your aspirations toward the governor's chair."

"Oh, yes." Wilson smiled and set his plate down. "I have asked the great white father to allow me to be the governor of the west." He glanced between his two visitors. "So that I may help everyone live together happily."

Finnegan choked back his laughter. "A very noble goal, would you not say so, Townsend?"

The soldier shook his head. "It is fascinating to me that you always discover a way to amuse yourself, Finnegan."

"Lacking more grave pursuits, I must confess to an interest in enjoyment. Especially when it comes at the expense of our betters in the great city of Washington." The gunman slowly stood. "Do any other questions for Mr. Wilson spring to mind, Townsend?"

The major let out a long sigh and stood to join Finnegan. "I suppose I have learned enough. More than enough to send off a report." He extended a hand. "It was pleasant chatting with you, Mr. Wilson. Thank you for seeing me."

"I enjoyed visiting with you as well, Major Duran." Wilson grinned. "If I am made governor, would you be available to assist me? You have been to Washington; I am sure you would be of great help."

"Uh, well," Duran shrugged. "I imagine there could be worse postings for a fellow. In that event, Mr. Wilson, I shall give serious consideration to turning in my commission and accepting your offer." He smiled somewhat somberly to Finnegan. "Perhaps better a lieutenant governor than a major destined to never be a colonel."

Finnegan nodded to Wilson. "Regretfully, I cannot accept a post in your administration, Jack." He threw his hands up. "Shall we begin making our way back toward Greenfield, Townsend, so that we may arrive in time for another of Mrs. Culbertson's questionable culinary creations?"

"Yes, that would probably be best." Duran nodded to Wilson and followed Finnegan out the hut door and into the snow. As they walked toward the stable, Duran put a hand on Finnegan's shoulder. "You might have explained matters to me before we arrived, old friend."

The gunman withdrew a cigar from his pocket. "Would

you have given the tale any credence without viewing matters for yourself, Townsend? The stories related regarding Wilson hardly give the fellow due credit. The only method to truly make you understand that the man is no more dangerous than a wagon-bound snake oil salesman is to see the chap in person." Finnegan grinned. "Now, at a minimum, you have been offered steady employment in the new government of this great land. What an exciting adventure lies before you. For my own part, I look forward to being a personal acquaintance of two such powerful men. My retirement should be very comfortable, indeed."

"Has that man honestly penned such rubbish to the President?"

"If he has, he would hardly be the first, I imagine. What difference does any of it make? You were sent on a fool's errand by the War Department, not for the first time, and you and I have had the chance for a lovely visit. Both our duties have been seen to. Yours to your country and mine to my lass. Come, dear Townsend, let us get our dinner."

The major stared skeptically over his coffee cup. "Please excuse my ignorance, Mrs. Culbertson; I am not familiar with the men you are referring to. I do not know a Stuart and I have never had cause to strangle anyone." He set down his cup and grinned across the table. "What have you been getting up to in your idle time, Finnegan?"

The Pinkerton shook his head. Mrs. Culbertson had inquired of Major Duran whether or not he had the honor of having served with Finnegan in the company of Stuart's Stranglers. The question had caught Duran quite off guard. "It is nothing more than that most human adoration for alliteration rearing its ugly head, Townsend." Finnegan looked to his landlady. "Major Townsend is with the Army, ma'am. He does not typically concern himself with cattle rustlers."

Mrs. Culbertson set a platter of chicken on the table. "Well, if you have never heard of the bold men of Stuart's Stranglers, you are at a loss, young man. I am proud to say this man Finnegan Gilhooley put down no less than two of those rustler scum right here in the hall of this very house. Never been prouder in my life to have a banister broken. I'll hand the carpenter a dollar with my chin held high when he comes to repair that bit." She frowned. "Pity about the rug, but it is a small price to pay to make bad men face justice."

Duran leaned to look out the dining room doors and view the broken railing on the second floor above the hall. "Two men, Finnegan?" He leaned back. "Old friend, I know it is not my place to keep track of such matters, and it may not make for quite proper dinner conversation, but you seem to be doing a brisk business in this apparently empty place."

"Nothing more than a confluence of ill fortune, I assure you." The gunman took up the chicken platter.

"Ill fortune?" The soldier chuckled. "Precisely how many instances of ill fortune have occurred while you have been domiciled in this quaint hamlet?"

"Well, there the two on the stairs." Frank James motioned to the hall Duran had been peeking at. "And, of course, that fellow who attempted to drygulch you out hunting." The outlaw took the chicken from Finnegan. "I suppose any other incidents could be better said to be attempts rather than actual killings."

"Attempts?" Duran snorted.

"He did his best to shoot two Indians the other day, but the powder was fouled." James laughed.

"That is not quite the proper way to frame the incident."

The elder Doubleday felt the need to weigh in. "Mr. Gilhooley had little choice in the matter. The action he attempted was in defense of his person."

James passed the Mormon the chicken. "I cannot say how such a thing should be made out to be, all I said was that it occurred."

"What's this now?" Duran found the whole tale intriguing. "You only *attempted* to kill two Indians? Are you growing soft of conscience, Finnegan, or slow of hand?"

The gunman groaned and took up the potato platter. "As Mr. James referenced, my weapon malfunctioned, or was possibly the victim of a curse from Mr. Wilson. It is difficult to trace the source of the problem."

Duran laughed out loud. "I must say, for a small town this place does not lack for entertainment."

Elsmere Doubleday took the potatoes. "Mr. Wilson does not, to my knowledge, level curses upon people. As he explained the matter to me, he should be held in no way responsible for your shotgun not operating properly. He did not...magically postpone Mr. Mitchell's death. The man merely prophesied that you would not kill Mr. Mitchell and, as it happens, you did not."

"Ah, now that is a fine talent, indeed." Duran wore an impressed look. "We shall have to bring the fellow along for the next war. It would be rather nice to know if one should bother to rise early for a battle or sleep the day away. I could inquire as to whether or not my enemy is fated to die, and if he is not, well, I could simply skip over the whole ugly business."

Doubleday gave the soldier an irritated shrug. "Take it as you will, sir. I only pointed out that the man does not level curses."

Finnegan sipped his coffee. "Have you come to any

conclusions regarding Jack Wilson's position in relation to the Almighty, Mr. Doubleday? I notice you have spent considerable time with him or his people the last few days."

Doubleday thoughtfully chewed a hunk of chicken. "I cannot say as I have drawn any conclusions as yet, but the fellow does give one pause, does he not?"

Duran raised both eyebrows. "Mr. Doubleday, I cannot say as I have had much acquaintance with followers of Mormonism, but I certainly credited you folks with a bit more sense than the average Indian living in a hut on the plains. Are you truly giving consideration to the idea that the man up there in his crude shelter, drinking milk from an old gourd, no less, might truly be in some sort of communication with the Lord our God?" Duran stared at the emissary from Zion. "I chatted with the man only this afternoon and he seemed more interested in obtaining political office than leading his people out of this desert. He struck me more like Jubal Early than Moses."

Doubleday sighed and shrugged. "I would freely admit that Mr. Wilson is one of the stranger fellows I have ever encountered. Everything about the man appears to be at cross purposes. He is surely of two worlds, neither of which fit together very well. But, honestly, who can say what manner a prophet should conduct himself in? Mr. Gilhooley and I discussed this same matter before I made Mr. Wilson's acquaintance. I did not have an answer then, and I still do not. How does one test a fellow's ability to communicate with angels or the Almighty? Where does proof end and faith begin?"

Duran rubbed his chin. "Mr. Doubleday, I can see that you are somewhat fascinated by Mr. Wilson, and no doubt he *is* fascinating. You have spoken with him and his friends at great length. How much influence would you say Mr. Wilson exercises over the actions of other Indian tribes?"

"Ah..." The old emissary gave a knowing smile. "I think perhaps you are not so stranded here as you might have us believe, Major. Mayhaps, neither you nor Wilson wishes to leave the desert?"

Duran let out a guffaw. "Why is it that everyone in this place assumes I am on some sort of mission for the government? Cannot a man simply be left off of a train through poor luck?"

Doubleday shook his head. "I find it somewhat saddening that while I have been here Mr. Gilhooley has had cause to kill several men. Of course, his reputation for bloodshed precedes him wherever he goes, or should." The old man sipped his coffee and looked to Finnegan. "That having been stated, the man who kills miners in the foyer is the only white man who has been honest with me since I have set foot in this place. Mr. James felt the need to obfuscate his true identity. Now you, Major, are somewhat incapable of admitting your true intentions here. Do you truly think any one of us will go on believing you are here by chance and only wish to skulk about Mr. Wilson from idle curiosity?"

Duran only stared blank-faced. "Mr. Doubleday, I have no idea what you are referring to."

The emissary was obviously disappointed, but continued. "At all events, I can see no harm in answering your question. Put simply, Mr. Wilson does not appear to have a great deal of influence with the other tribes. For the most part, he does not seem to possess much knowledge of how they live or their conditions. The Paiutes of this area are not reservation Indians, and they have great difficulty understanding how other Indians have been corralled. Mr. Wilson has not traveled much from this place and, even if he did wish to attempt influencing some other tribe, I do not know if he would fairly know what to suggest to them. So far, all I have heard him give by way of suggestions, to fellows such as Mr. Bull Bear, is the advice to work hard and attempt peaceful existence with the white man."

"Just as Wilson himself told you today, Townsend." Finnegan smiled at the major. "Even as a child, you always needed to be told twice."

James cleared his throat. "Mr. Doubleday?"

The emissary scowled. "Yes."

"As many unkind words have been said regarding my character over the years, I can understand your angst upon hearing my...professional name. I would like to say, though, that I in no way obfuscated anything. My Christian name is Alexander and I believe a man has the right to go by his own name if he wishes. Would you not agree?"

Finnegan shook his head. "Alexander, you indulge in the oddest tendencies. I should think by now you would be inured to having other men impugn your character or ask you to leave their presence."

Doubleday held up a hand. "I did not impugn the man's character or suggest he should leave. I was only...shocked to discover a well-known personage where I had thought a mere traveler sat." He frowned. "I have encountered many surprises in the last few days and, given the number of them, I am having difficulty greeting them all with grace."

James wore a satisfied smile. "There you have it, Finnegan. Mr. Doubleday bears me no ill will. You may apologize for suggesting otherwise whenever you wish."

Finnegan wiped his face with his napkin. "I only wish I had been a better marksman back in '76."

Chapter 11

GREENFIELD, NEVADA

January 11th, 1890

Finnegan had awoken in his cold room and washed up with cold water in preparation to meet the day. After donning his pistols and frock coat, he had removed the strings from the shotguns that guarded his room. Hungry for breakfast, he was just reaching for the doorknob when he heard a clatter down in the foyer of the house. Still having a fair amount of trust in the general reliability of the weapon, Finnegan snatched up the Winchester shotgun and opened his door a small crack. Peeking out, he began to hear Molly's voice drifting up toward him. It sounded as though the schoolteacher was arguing with the landlady. Finnegan let out a sigh and set the shotgun to one side of the door. In all likelihood, it was going to be an arduous day.

Descending the stairs, Finnegan found his old friend in heated debate with Mrs. Culbertson. "Is there something I can be of assistance with, ladies?"

Mrs. Culbertson turned to him, red-faced with shock. "Mr. Gilhooley, I apologize, but I cannot allow a single woman to visit a man who is not her husband in one of my rooms. I do not care what woman or what man. It is unacceptable in any Christian home."

Finnegan gave a tired nod. "Yes, well, I am here now, so perhaps it would be best if Miss Meagher and I spoke in the parlor." He felt his stomach rumble. "That way you will be free to see to breakfast for the house."

"I do have the reputation of my house to consider." She cast a rebuffed glare toward Molly and stalked off to the kitchen.

"Finnegan, that woman is an anachronistic old..."

The gunman held up a hand to stop her. "I doubt you traveled here so early to have a row with my landlady." He motioned to the parlor. "What troubles you, Molly?"

"Oh, yes, of course." She began moving toward the parlor and pulling her fur-lined hat off at the same time. "That woman made such a pest of herself I nearly forgot my purpose here." She pulled her mittens off. "You must come to the Wilson Ranch and help Jack. He was fallen upon by Tom Mitchell."

"Fallen upon?" He sat next to her on a sedan. "Is Wilson gravely injured?"

"Injured, no. Well, not in the usual sense."

Finnegan licked his lips and proceeded carefully. "If there is anything that transpires in this place in the usual way, I should be quite shocked to learn of it. Very well, in what manner was Mr. Wilson assaulted?"

"Tom Mitchell secreted himself by one of the close corners among the rocks leading to the river. When Jack came around the corner of the trail, Mitchell fairly pounced on him and blew river sand into his face."

"The man is blinded?"

"The man is hobbled by fear and sorrow."

Finnegan paused once more to collect himself. "His condition is the result of the sand, lass?"

"It may seem strange to you or I, Finnegan, but with the act of blowing sand into Jack's face, Mitchell has essentially placed a curse on the poor man. As with all curses, the degree to which the cursed is affected hinges on how much stock is placed in the curse. The Paiutes place great stock in such things."

"Ah, well, yes. I can understand how they might." Finnegan rubbed his eyes and then patted Molly's hand. "Well, so long as there is nothing pressing, come have a spot of breakfast with me. Mrs. Culbertson improves greatly after some acquaintance with coffee. By a strange coincidence, she is fond of any man who rode with Granville Stuart during our raiding days when you were teaching at Maiden. I am certain she would find any tales you have of old Granville interesting."

"Finnegan, there is no time for that. We have to get back to the village so that you can assist Jack."

"Molly, I cannot claim any great experience washing other people's eyes. I am certain that with a dish of clean water and some initiative Jack will be in proper condition again in no time." His stomach grumbled again. "It can surely wait until after breakfast has been served. Even if the fellow temporarily lacks sight, it is my understanding that most of a prophet's work takes place in his mind's eye. If he remains in his hut until it clears up, he should be all right." He paused and let a small smile play over his lips. "Although, I must remember to mention to him that I warned he might be ensorcelled."

Molly cocked her head to one side. "Ensorcelled?"

"Yes, the act practiced by a sorcerer. Why is it..."

"Finnegan, we do not have time for you to practice your vocabulary lesson this morning. It is not a physical injury that troubles Jack. Having been attacked as he was, Mitchell has stolen part of Jack's medicine."

"I see." Finnegan hung his head and wished to God that Mrs. Culbertson would announce breakfast so he could at least be assured of that before delving into the mysteries of aboriginal assault and mystical robbery. "And by medicine, you do not mean a bottle of laudanum or some such?"

"No. Jack is what we refer to as a medicine man among his tribe. His medicine describes his ability to...well, do what he does. His medicine allows him to speak with the dead, cure illness, see the future, even change the weather." Molly rattled off the list, taking no note of Finnegan's expression.

"Yes, it would be a pity if Mr. Wilson was forced to take a day off from all that."

"This is no matter for jesting, Finnegan. You or I may find the whole affair absurd, but Jack certainly does not, and neither do the other Paiutes. There is already talk among the men sent from the other tribes. Some are saying that if Jack has lost his medicine there is no reason for them to remain here. They are saying they might as well return to their reservations and announce that Jack is a false prophet, or a failed one, at least."

"That may be the most fortunate outcome Jack can hope for, Molly. If those other Indians disperse back to their homes and make Jack out to be a lost cause, then he will cease to be of interest to those who would do more than blow sand in his face."

"Finnegan, you have to help him. It is for a possibility just such as this that I requested your presence here."

"And here I thought you simply could not live without

me near any longer." The schoolteacher only stared with an irritated grimace. "As always, I am willing to do all I can, but what do I know of mysticism, Molly? Would you have me gut some beast and read the entrails? I do not possess a deck of tarot cards. What can I do to get a man... un-ensorcelled?"

Molly's irritated look worsened. "Repeating that does not make it any more of a word. There is no need for you to practice any mysticism, at any rate. What is required is more in keeping with the skills you do possess. Jack has informed me that you must locate Mitchell so that a ritual of sorts can be conducted and Mitchell can return what has been taken."

The gunman groaned. "I did not much enjoy my last visit with Mr. Mitchell, and would prefer to avoid another."

"Be that as it may, you are Jack's only hope."

"Jack seems willing to embrace many faiths, Molly. Might not we tell him that I am a special sort of priest? I could read some Latin to him from one of these old books you have given me, Seneca, or some such. We could tell him that the white man's medicine has lifted the curse, and he would be none the wiser. Would that not be preferable to dashing off in search of some savage who is not overly amenable to company, in my experience?" The schoolteacher continued to give an angry scowl. "You will not even consider it?"

"Finnegan, you will go find Tom Mitchell. If you will not perform an act like this, what is your purpose here?"

The gunman groaned and rubbed his eyes again. "I had hoped to contribute something of a calm and considered quality to this mad place. Since I cannot, very well, I shall go and find your damned Indian. It will not be an easy task to get the blackguard to come with me, though. My usual methods may fall short, seeing as..." Finnegan smiled. "I believe I shall bring Major Duran and Mr. James along for this merry little chase."

Molly gave him a pensive glance. "I would not think you would require much assistance to procure one man."

"It would behoove me to have some assistance in this case. Tom Mitchell is under the impression I cannot kill him, so threats from me will not carry much weight. Wilson has assured the man I am not fated to shoot him; he did not, however, mention anything regarding either Duran or James. They should do nicely as traveling companions." He rubbed his chin. "I take it this occurred at first light, or close to."

"Yes."

"Is it snowing this morning?"

"Not as yet."

"Then I stand a good chance of finding your Indian. Although, it would be far easier to simply yammer at Wilson in some dead tongue and be done with it. I swear, you insist on being impractical at the strangest times, Molly."

The three men deposited Molly at the Wilson Ranch and made their way toward Jack Wilson's village. As was always the case, Finnegan had eventually resigned himself to laboring at a cause he little understood or possessed an interest in, but resolved to look on matters in the best possible light. Major Duran rather welcomed the outing as an opportunity to investigate more strange goings on involving the local Indian population, and was quite cheerful as the horses slowly crunched their way along. Frank James was the sole despondent member of the expedition and was not interested in the least in keeping quiet about it.

"I truly thought that we had come to something of an understanding, Finnegan. You had finally cured yourself of your silly suspicions and imaginings of malice on my part, and we had agreed that you would no longer be pressganging me into these ridiculous outings of yours. First, you force me to accompany you on a search for more men who wish to kill you when the original assassin proved inept, and now, this. I am not even capable of conceiving our purpose here. Are we truly out to locate one Indian who has played a prank upon another? Are we to spank the ornery one and make him apologize? I am not a conceited man, but does this not appear somewhat below our station?"

Finnegan, in the lead of the little party, hung his head as his horse plodded along through the snow. When James found himself in the mood to rant, he could do so seemingly without end. "Alexander, you are accompanying us today because I find it vexing that I am forced out into these snowy wastes to sort out the horseplay of these savages while you may wile away your days safely ensconced at the boarding house. It seems somehow wrong that I should be the one to suffer since you have spent your life flouting the law and wreaking mayhem, while I have spent my life upholding the law and attempting to create some sort of order. I consider your being drafted to join me on this outing a small bit of justice being meted out. It is important, especially given the fact that no one else seems much interested in levying punishment upon you for all your various misdeeds and sins."

"Oh, Finnegan, where to begin listing the umbrage I take with your sanctimonious outbursts. I might begin by pointing out that you have never been in the service of that old whore Justice. You labor in the interests of the railroad barons, the bankers, those damn carpetbaggers, and all your other damn Yankee brethren."

"I am not a Yankee, Alexander. We have been over this ground before. If you wish to bombast a Yankee, I would direct you to Major Duran. His family goes back several generations in Massachusetts. They are quite proud of their Yankee heritage."

James turned back in the saddle. "I am not one to judge a man by who his father was, even if the bugger was from Massachusetts." He grinned at the Major.

Duran grinned back. "Oh, I would hardly disagree, Mr. James. I spent most of my youth in the company of Yankees and I would eagerly testify they are an awful bunch. Drive them into the sea at your earliest convenience, I say." He raised his voice. "Although, Finnegan, if it is not out of order, I would like to ask you a question similar to that of Mr. James. I am a bit confused as to why our presence here is required, as well. Cannot the terrible Finnegan Gilhooley be counted on to collect one scraggly savage, dead or alive? Especially given that the savage in question is accused of nothing more than having ensorcelled one of his brethren."

The gunman brought his horse to a stop and turned to look back at the soldier. "Townsend, did I hear you say ensorcelled?"

"Yes, that is what a sorcerer does, is it not?"

Finnegan nodded, as though the answer mattered little and got his horse moving again. "Yes, of course that is what a sorcerer does. As for the offending sorcerer's death, that is specifically what concerns me."

James gave his horse a small kick and came up next to Finnegan. "Yes, about that. Now, you say that Indian Jesus of yours has prophesied that you cannot kill this man Mitchell?"

"Correct."

"So, then, you have come to believe in the fellow's predictions?"

"No, of course not."

"But, then why have you dragged myself and the Major along?"

Finnegan rubbed his eyes. "It does not matter if *I* believe Wilson's prattling; Mitchell believes it."

James gave a confused stare. "Would it not be simpler to just shoot Mitchell and put the whole matter to rest?"

"Damn it, Alexander, I am not going to shoot someone to settle the petty squabbling of two fools who dwell in huts and claim to commune with the spirits."

James rubbed his chin. "Did you not already attempt to murder Mitchell once?"

"I did not try to murder him, I attempted to shoot in my own defense and... it is pointless trying to explain such matters to you." Finnegan shook his head. "I would think that you would rather be hoping for a diversion, at any rate. What can you possibly have to do all day at the boarding house? You must be half mad with boredom by now."

"Oh, I have plenty to keep me busy." The old outlaw shrugged. "Several periodicals depend on me for commentary."

Finnegan raised one eyebrow. "Commentary? What would a periodical want with comments from the likes of you?"

Duran could be heard laughing in the rear. "The admission may not be timely, Finnegan, but I have read several of Mr. James' articles and have spent more than a small amount of time contemplating what your reaction to them might be." The major tipped his hat to the outlaw. "For an insurrectionist and brigand, you are a surprisingly articulate fellow. I have especially enjoyed the few pieces of yours I have seen regarding capital and labor."

Finnegan shook his head. "What is this world coming to? How is it that a bank robber can write regarding capital or labor? What would you know of either? One you could never manage, the other you would never stoop to."

"You always were a pretentious one, Gilhooley." James pulled a cigar from his pocket. "How is it that you can so consistently find methods to consider yourself the better man, morally speaking? You would chide me for doing as I pleased in the wake of a great war, but you never pause to consider your own actions? Who appointed you as the arbiter of right and wrong, just or unjust? Is all your authority derived from your former association with that old charlatan Pinkerton? He would hardly be the one I would select to determine the blessed from the damned."

Finnegan sighed. "If it would improve your opinion of the world in general, Alexander, I would be more than happy to show you the badge presented to me so that I may serve as a deputy marshal. Although, having been acquainted with more than a few judges by this time, you may not place as much stock in such items as a less experienced man might. I suppose any proclamation I might make is nothing more than wasted breath, at all events. You, of all men, know what I derive my authority from."

"I am thrilled that the two of you are so well informed. I wish you would inform me regarding that particular mystery." Duran seemed to be enjoying the whole outing greatly. "I have often wondered what supposedly gives Finnegan the right to do as he pleases."

James turned in the saddle, looking grave. "Like all men, he derives his authority from his ability to do violence, and his willingness. Mr. Gilhooley has never lacked ability or willingness, hence, he possesses authority."

Finnegan laughed. "That may be the finest compliment I have ever received, Alexander."

Finnegan ducked into Wilson's hut and was promptly followed by James and Duran. The gunman was more than a bit irked at how much glee his two associates appeared to take in the absurdity of his errand. He had suggested that they wait in the stable, but both had insisted on seeing Wilson. As they entered the hut, James brushed past Finnegan and plopped down on the wooden bench Wilson occupied.

"Hello, Mr. Wilson." The outlaw spoke in a serious tone. "I understand one of your fellow Indians has unmanned you...in a spiritual sense, that is."

Wilson slowly turned, looking quite forlorn with an old blanket wrapped around his shoulders. "I did not think Mitchell would truly do such a thing. I did not believe he could be so...we are of the same people."

Duran leaned against one wall of the hut for a moment before feeling it begin to give. He righted himself and issued a small chuckle. "Did the fellow not attempt to shoot you just the other day, Mr. Wilson? I would think relieving you of your mystical abilities would be a small matter in comparison."

"The only one with proper claim to be despondent is myself." Finnegan removed his hat and rubbed his temple. "If I am forced to listen to this rot much longer, I believe I may become truly cantankerous. Now, then, what would you have us do, Mr. Wilson?"

The prophet appeared to be choosing his words very carefully. "I do not know if there is anything to be done, Finnegan. Hummingbird has taken my booha. It can only be restored to me if Hummingbird chooses to return it."

"What's this about a hummingbird?" James glanced between Finnegan and Wilson.

Wilson turned to the outlaw again. "I was fallen upon by a man named Tom Mitchell, but my people know him as Hummingbird."

James frowned. "Mr. Wilson, it is not my place to go around telling other men their business, but I got to say, in this life the way other men view you, the esteem they hold you in, is mighty damned important. If I was you, I think I would call the fella that jumped you by his Christian name. It don't look good to go around telling folks you took a whipping from some old boy named Hummingbird."

"Alexander, you may have managed to convince a few twit newspaper editors that you have something of use to say, but that does not give you license to go about bothering the rest of society with your nonsense." Finnegan rubbed his other temple. "Now, then, Jack, you wish for us to go and collect Mitchell?"

"I cannot say if it will do any good, Finnegan. Even if you bring him here, he will have no reason to return my booha." Wilson hung his head.

"Oh, I am certain one among us will conjure a method to make him amenable to the suggestion." Finnegan patted the prophet on the back. "Where did you last see the scoundrel?"

Duran looked over the holes in the deep snow leading away from the well-worn trail the people of Wilson's village used to travel back and forth from the river. He no longer appeared in a humorous mood. "This fellow seems to have scampered off into these snowdrifts, Finnegan."

Finnegan gave a somber nod and dismounted his horse. "Yes, these Indians do so adore larking about in the damned snow." He led his horse to where the footprints departed the trail. "We will all be wishing for a set of Mr. Dyer's fine Chicago made snowshoes before this hunt is over."

"Now, hell and perdition, Finnegan." James whined. "It is one thing to drag me out of the house to cuff about a truculent Indian who ain't afraid of you, it is quite another to make me suffer a death by slow freezing. Even you cannot be so mad as to want to follow this savage out into the damned wilderness."

Duran dismounted to begin leading his horse. "The bulk of the land between Denver and the Pacific is wilderness, Mr. James. What difference does it make which part you are currently mired in?"

James stood in his stirrups and looked over the ground in front of them. "Major, I am aware of the unsettled nature of much of this country. That does not mean I do not have preferences. I would prefer a spot without snow. I would prefer country that is not full of hostile savages. I would prefer a bit of land where every armed man had long since forgotten my name. Thus far, Nevada does not seem to fit any of those strictures."

Finnegan looked up at the old outlaw, smiling. "Why should any man hold ill will against you, Alexander? Are you not a harmless newspaper contributor?"

"You, my friend, are nothing more than a wet nurse for a false prophet, and yet, you find yourself constantly entangled in difficulties. The world around us does not change simply because we wish it to change, Finnegan." James swung down out of the saddle. "However, after a bit further contemplation, it occurs to me that a well-known assassin and a federal army major might be held in considerably lower esteem by savage Indians than I could ever expect to be. As long as I keep a little distance between myself and you two, I should be able to witness the death of Finnegan Gilhooley and remain safe at the same time. I had hoped to witness the final act the other day from the comfort of the parlor, but this will do."

Finnegan began to plod through the snow, following the tracks before him. "You are a remarkably cheerful fellow, Alexander. If fate determines that I must die today, I am glad you will be present to gain some amusement from it, at any rate. I will go to the next world believing my life had purpose."

"Always thinking of others, Finnegan." James motioned off toward the mountains. "Lead on."

As the party stalked forward, it began to appear as though Mitchell had no particular place to be after assaulting Wilson. The medicine man's trail would meander one way and then another, slowly gaining elevation and moving off steadily away from both Wilson's village and the town of Greenfield. While Mitchell did not seem to have much purpose in where he wished to be, it did seem he knew where he did not want to be. After roughly ten miles of wandering and staring down at the pot marks in the snow, Finnegan called a halt and stood staring up into an outcropping of rocks that loomed in front of them.

Duran came up next to Finnegan. "This damned Indian is in fine condition, my friend." The soldier let out a long breath and sucked in another. "Do you have the foggiest notion of where he might be headed? I begin to suspect he may run all the way to the ocean before turning right or left to a great degree. If he turns to the right, I fear the snow will deepen."

"You have developed a unique wit in your manhood, Townsend. It is good to see you can retain your humor on such a journey."

From where they stood, the men could clearly see that

the tracks progressed into a large mass of boulders that led up to a near-vertical collection of rock walls with small crevasses creasing the cliffs. It was a formidable formation, to say the least. Duran pulled his hat from his head and wiped sweat. "I would say our quarry has gone to ground in there."

Finnegan nodded. "Or it is the shortest path to whatever lays on the other side of the escarpment."

"Well, regardless of the fellow's motive, we cannot take the horses in there, unless they are more spry than the rest of their breed." Duran turned to look at the area to the south, where it appeared the escarpment ended, some half mile off. "Being the youngest, I suppose it is my place to offer to take the horses around."

James came up to join them. "Being the youngest, you may go with this fool Irishman. I do not know if I am too old for such journeys as this, but I am damn well certain I am too old for climbing around in boulders and scaling walls. I will leave such things to detectives and soldiers. I am, as you pointed out, Finnegan, only a mere newspaper contributor."

The gunman looked to the escarpment and then back to James. "You will meet us on the other side?"

"What other task could possibly warrant my time?" James reached over and took the reins of Finnegan's horse. "You wish to chase Indians among those rocks, have at it. If neither of you appear on the other side of these boulders before nightfall, I shall assume you have been murdered and will return to the boarding house. It should go without saying that the remainder of my sojourn here will be spent in deepest grief."

Finnegan reached over and withdrew his Winchester shotgun from the scabbard. "I would assume my remains will not be found for many years. In the interim, if you would not mind too much, please affix a small plaque to that boulder over there noting how two heroes sallied forth against impossible odds to reclaim a common charlatan's snake oil recipe."

James nodded and took the reins of Duran's horse. "It shall be my first priority. Enjoy the rocks, gentlemen."

Duran removed his Remington-Keene from the scabbard. "Are you attempting to prove some point by continually bringing that shotgun to bear on Mr. Mitchell?"

"I rarely know what I am doing these days, Townsend." Finnegan checked the chamber on his Winchester. "Do not shoot the fellow unless absolutely necessary. "Wilson, daft bugger that he is, insists Mitchell must be returned alive so that the proper concoction of pixy dust can be sprinkled about."

Duran nodded, looking a bit bored. "I have had much to do with Indians, Finnegan. I doubt I shall lose my senses and shoot this fellow without cause."

"I only mention it in jest, Townsend." He looked back to see James beginning to take the long way around. "You have obviously grown into the sort of man that is capable. I did not relish my time in the Army, but different men react to such things in differing ways. I am glad to see you have found something of a home in the service of your country." He peered up at the rocks. "I have been meaning to ask how your mother fares."

"She passed away this last year."

Finnegan frowned. "I am sorry to hear that. She was a fine, sturdy woman. Did she ever remarry?"

"She did not. Many people in our set back in Boston marry for reasons of practicality. The old men pick and choose alliances based on shipping company manifests. I always felt my parents were wed out of genuine affection. Mother held father's memory in high regard and spoke of him well, right unto her passing."

"It is unfortunate that well-matched people cannot remain together longer."

"Fortune does not dictate how long a man lives when he is shot down, Finnegan. The man who shoots the fellow down makes that determination."

"He surely does." Finnegan began picking his way toward the first collection of boulders that blocked their path. "Did I ever mention to you that my father was killed in the war, as well?"

Duran paused in following. "You did not."

Finnegan looked back at the young soldier. "Lost in a skirmish preceding a battle. Nothing more than a fluke of fortune. If we had not met with an enemy patrol, if the ball had not landed so high in his chest..." The gunman shrugged. "Such is fate. We all hang by a delicate thread." Finnegan passed between two large boulders and began to climb. In places where the rocks were too sheer to hold snow, Mitchell's trail could be discerned by the wet marks and scuffs the fellow had left behind. Finnegan kept a wary eye out in front of him as he ascended. Mitchell had not appeared overly clever at their last encounter, but genius was not required to roll a landslide of rocks down onto the men following you. After several hundred yards of vertical and horizontal travel, the two pursuers came to a crevasse roughly three feet wide that appeared to lead all the way through to the other side of the escarpment. Finnegan was about to proceed when he heard the faint sound of a voice and froze. Additional voices began to drift through the crevasse. Obviously, there was more than one fellow on the other side of the rocks.

Finnegan leaned toward Duran's ear. "We have stumbled upon the church social."

"I hold out hope for pie." Duran motioned to the side of

the crevasse. A chimney in the rocks led up to the top of the escarpment. He whispered to the gunman. "If I scale to that opening, I can obtain the high ground, or should be able to. If there are a number of them over there, you may find it accommodating to have me looking down on you with my rifle."

Finnegan nodded approvingly. "Can you clamber up that?"

"Barracks life has not made me as soft as all that, Finnegan." He slung his rifle over one shoulder and approached the chimney. "Give me a few moments and then proceed."

Finnegan sat down on a nearby boulder. "Well, be quick about it then, I have not got all day." He grinned as he watched the soldier climb the cliff and disappear over the top. He considered having a cigar, but did not want to sacrifice the element of surprise. When he reckoned that Duran must be in a position to be of some use, he checked his guns and began to move slowly through the crevasse. From the look of the beaten gravel floor of the small cutting, it appeared as though it was a popular path for all sorts of men and animals who wished to avoid walking all the way around the escarpment. He eased into the opening on the far side and managed to conceal most of himself behind a nearby rock. Below him and ahead some twenty-five yards, Mitchell sat by a group of six other Indians. They were all gathered around a spot that had been kicked clean of snow and one man was attempting to get a fire going with a flint and tinder. All the members of the circle held rifles and, from their general appearance Finnegan assumed they also possessed pistols, although he could not say for certain thanks to their layered winter clothing and furs.

Assessing the situation, Finnegan's first inclination was to shoot one or two of Mitchell's associates. Doing so would likely chase off the rest, but that plan did not allow a method for obtaining Mitchell. If the Indians decided to shoot back, instead of running, Duran would surely open fire above. Duran had no way of knowing which man was Mitchell. If he killed the wrong fellow, there would be hell to pay from Molly. Finnegan felt the strong urge to holler out a few curses, but stifled the impulse so as not to betray his position.

Unable to conjure a superior plan, Finnegan took a deep breath and settled on attempting palaver. Molly had been clear that she would prefer Mitchell to be found, returned, and reprimanded without bloodshed. Finnegan had given his word that he would, at a minimum, make the attempt. With his shotgun held in one hand by the comb, he came out from behind the rock and began walking slowly toward the group making camp. He held up his free hand. "Hello, gentlemen. Have you begun looking to supper yet?"

The collection of men around the as-yet nonexistent fire all snapped to attention. The man standing closest to Mitchell moved to raise his rifle and said something Finnegan did not understand. Finnegan paused and raised his empty hand. "There is no need for that." He raised the shotgun slightly. "If you push the issue, I shall retaliate and, I daresay, we will all be a bit regretful at the finish. Now then..." He pointed to Mitchell. "My only purpose here is to have a word with that gentleman. We find ourselves at cross purposes and a brief discussion may be all that is required to sort the matter out."

Mitchell rolled his eyes and shook his head. "There is little purpose in speaking to them in your language, Mr. Gilhooley. They are Utes running from their reservation. They know more Spanish than English."

Finnegan nodded and took a few more steps forward, smiling at his new acquaintances. "Unfortunately, I know very little Spanish. It is lovely to meet you, gentlemen." Finnegan hoped a comforting smile might bridge the language barrier. "You have business with these fellows, Mr. Mitchell?"

The medicine man shrugged, looking somewhat resigned. "They wish to return to their reservation and cast out the soldiers so that they may live as they please. We are..." He grew puzzled. "I am not certain...we are bartering as to the price of my helping them."

"Negotiating?"

"Yes, that is it." Mitchell smiled, pleased with the assistance.

"Mr. Mitchell, you seem to be a man of many talents, not the least of which is negotiation, but, I must ask, precisely how do you intend to help these men rid themselves of occupying soldiers? You are quite cunning, but hardly capable of fighting off an army, I should think. Will they not be a bit disappointed in the service you render?"

"I will trade with them for Wavoka's booha. With Wavoka's medicine they will be rid of the soldiers easily." Mitchell gave the Utes a reassuring smile.

Finnegan could only stare at the medicine man for a long moment. "These men intend to pay you for the use of the... magic you stole from Jack Wilson?"

"I did not steal his booha, I took it. That is not the same thing. A white man cannot understand such things."

"That is quite true, sir. I cannot understand any of this." Finnegan sighed. "What does the fellow here offer?"

Mitchell scowled. "I do not know yet. I told him to steal from the miners. We shall see how well he has done."

"The miners?" Finnegan could not conceal his surprise. "This man will pay you for magic in gold?"

"Or silver. I do not care which."

"That is, well -- to be truthful, that is very impressive, Mr. Mitchell. This is a fine bit of capitalism you have stumbled into, and I commend you for it. By all means, do not let me interrupt such inspired dealing." Finnegan chuckled. "Negotiate a price with this fellow, gain your bounty and we can be on our way. I will give you my personal guarantee that your remuneration will not be tampered with. As a matter of fact, I will add to it if you play your role properly, of course."

Mitchell appeared confused. "You will let me trade with the Utes for Wavoka's booha?"

"Certainly."

"But then you wish for me to go with you?"

"Would you not prefer to have an armed escort out of these mountains? I also offer a fine gratuity for nothing more than returning to Wilson's village and making amends with him."

Mitchell shook his head, looking sour. "No, that I cannot do."

"I assure you that no harm will come to you, sir. You will be under my personal protection."

"I...I am not concerned that Wavoka will hurt me." Mitchell cocked his head to one side. "I cannot go with you to him. If I go to him, he will wish to have his booha returned, but if I trade with the Utes for it, I cannot return the booha."

Finnegan raised one eyebrow. "What are you about? Mr. Mitchell? We are practical men. Jump about, shake your backside at these Ute people and tell them they have received Jack Wilson's boohoo. When you are done with that, let us be off so that you can do the same in Wilson's hut. If you cooperate, I may yet get my dinner in a timely fashion."

Mitchell shook his head again. "I cannot give the booha to the Utes and to Wavoka. Such things are of one spirit and can only be held by one spirit."

Finnegan made a concerted effort to keep his voice from sounding overly harsh. "Mr. Mitchell, I believe I have been quite reasonable in this matter, but I will not stand about in the freezing snow discussing the minutia of your pagan superstitions. All I ask is that you go through one ridiculous show with these fellows and then give a repeat performance with Wilson."

Mitchell threw his hands in the air. "I cannot."

"Sir, there is no need for subterfuge. As you said, these men do not speak the king's English. Would it not be preferable to gain extra funds and end the day both richer and wiser than when you began? Give this man his magic in return for thirty pieces of silver, I will compensate you in kind. Agree to these terms and no one need be shot or killed. Is this not the best possible solution, Mr. Mitchell?"

The medicine man stared at Finnegan as though he were an especially dull-witted child. "But I cannot give the booha to two men."

"Damn you, Mitchell, continue with that idiocy and I swear by all that is holy..." Finnegan glanced to the Utes who were growing uneasy as he lost his temper. He paused and licked his lips. "Mr. Mitchell, tell this man he has obtained Wilson's...magnetism or mysticism and let us be on our way."

"If I give it to the Utes, how do I return it to Wilson?"

"Bloody hell, enough of this." Finnegan made two large, leaping steps forward before grabbing Mitchell and shoving him between himself and the Utes. He jammed the Winchester into Mitchell's back and did his best to somewhat hide behind the smaller man. "Now, then, gentlemen. I am taking this fellow with me and, if you know what is good for you, no attempt will be made to stop me." The Utes had their guns up but did not seem to know quite how to take the odd turn of events.

"I have already told you that they do not understand your language." Mitchell slowly shook his head. "Why is that so confusing to you?"

"Mr. Mitchell, I do not know if you possess magical powers, but you are, by God, aggravating. That I will attest to." One of the younger Ute braves stepped forward and leveled a few, seemingly choice, and surely aggressive phrases toward Mitchell and Finnegan. "Now what in hell is he going on about?"

"He..." Mitchell turned to look back at Finnegan. "He is like you. He does not believe in the medicine and thinks it best that we should both be shot."

"Under differing circumstances, I would buy the man a cigar and suggest he become the leader of his tribe." Finnegan chuckled to put off fomenting worry. "Sadly, it is a poor moment to be meeting a practical savage. Tell him that I am not alone here. Tell him he will be fired upon if he is stupid enough to try an assault."

Mitchell raised an eyebrow. "He is not a fool, Mr. Gilhooley. He will not believe that."

"He bloody well should." Finnegan yelled back toward the escarpment. "Townsend! Townsend, fire a warning shot over these savage's heads so that they will know our intentions." Only silence answered him. "Townsend!" The young brave laughed and said something to the other Utes. "What was all that?"

"He said, it is very funny that you talk to your God and expect an answer. He says you are crazy and that we should be shot." Mitchell frowned. "It would have been better if you had not followed me."

"I very well might agree, Mr. Mitchell." Finnegan glanced between the Utes, who were growing bolder by the moment, and the top of the escarpment, where he still did not see Duran. Various members of the Utes were now yelling and brandishing their guns. "My friend, it would appear as though my arrival here has somewhat queered your business proposal to these men. Would you agree it is now in your best interest to accompany me while I flee?"

Mitchell looked from the Utes to Finnegan. "I do not see as I have much choice in the matter, now. It may not matter; I think they will surely kill us before we get to the rocks."

"They stand a much better chance if we stand here like so many sheep." He tried to estimate the distance to the crevasse. It looked to be about thirty yards, which was farther than he would have preferred. "On my word, begin to run." He looked to the escarpment one last time, but Duran could not be seen. "Damn it, go now." Mitchell took off at a surprisingly brisk pace, never once pausing to look back. Finnegan attempted to follow by running backwards for a moment so as to see what the reaction of the Utes might be. Unfortunately for the gunman, he could not watch the Utes and find his footing among the rocks at the same time. His feet became tangled, and he fell to the ground. One of the Utes fired a round that hit in the snow near Finnegan. In response, he snapped off a round from his shotgun. Only part of the load struck the brave, who dropped his rifle and then called out to rally his comrades. Finnegan worked the slide action on the gun and was aiming for another brave when a bullet whined off a rock near the lead Ute. For a split-second, Finnegan thought Duran had joined the fray, but the bullet had come from the wrong direction. Looking to the left, Finnegan saw James. The old outlaw was several hundred yards away and shooting mounted. More bullets hit the rocks around the Indians and their leader chose the better part of valor. In the name of caution, Finnegan took the opportunity to roll behind the closest rock, but the departing Indians never gave him so much as a second thought.

James saw Finnegan come out from the small collection of stones as he rode up. "It is not all that far around from the other side." James grinned, still holding a '73 Winchester. "In case you ever pass this way again."

"I shall keep it in mind." Finnegan began knocking the snow off his clothes.

"Did any of my rounds make contact with those fellows?"

"No, I do not believe so." Finnegan looked over the rifle. "How long has it been since you fired a shot from a distance?"

"Oh, many years. I was somewhat of a mediocre marksman in my youth and have never much cared for hunting."

"So, how is it you knew you would not hit me when you fired?"

"I did not. In all earnestness, it seemed a perfect excuse to fire off a few rounds in your direction. Regardless of where they landed, I would be better off." He placed the Winchester back in its scabbard. "As it happens, I accidentally saved your life once again. If it would not be too much trouble, I would appreciate a written letter of thanks so that I might include it in a future newspaper piece." James brought his gaze over to the crevasse behind Finnegan. "Ah, young Major Duran has your Indian, I believe."

Finnegan turned to look at the approaching pair. "Pleasant to see he is good for something. I presumed he had found a harlot to run off with after we parted ways." As the soldier approached with Mitchell, Finnegan called out to him. "I am dreadfully sorry if all my hollering disturbed your mid-day nap up in those rocks. It was terribly rude of me to make such a fuss over the minor matter of my continued survival."

Duran gave Mitchell a small push forward and all four men were together. "Such difficulties are bound to arise from time to time, Finnegan. There is no proper vantage point up there. I would agree that from here it appears quite useful. From the top it is noticeably different. Some time was wasted in search of a route to the edge, then, I was forced to retrace my steps." He motioned to Mitchell. "It might be considered a stroke of luck. If I had not gone back, I would not have bumped into this fellow and the whole outing might have been a wash."

"Yes, we at least have this to show for our efforts." Finnegan stuck a finger in Mitchell's face. "Now, sir, you are to return with us to Wilson's village and return to him...whatever the hell it is you have supposedly stolen."

Mitchell did his best to appear intractable, which is difficult after one has been captured and relieved of his rifle. "I will not."

Finnegan licked his lips. "You will, sir, or I will be forced to make use of methods to convince you."

Mitchell grunted. "Wavoka has said you cannot hurt me. You cannot do anything to me."

"Mr. Wilson has proclaimed that I am not the man fated to kill you, sir. He has made no predictions pertaining to my torturing you, and if greater ends are required, these men are more than willing and able to assist where hexes have barred my path." Finnegan motioned to Duran and James.

Mitchell laughed. "Wavoka has told me that I am to live many years, and I do not think these men will kill me only because you say so. It is not their woman who makes them do this."

James chuckled. "This fellow has an excellent handle on your domestic situation, Finnegan."

"It is lovely to know he is so well-informed." Finnegan

thought on the matter for a moment. "Mr. Mitchell, you may be correct in assuming I will not murder you for stealing another man's magic wand. You are also correct in assuming that these men will not kill you solely on my command. What you fail to take into account is that this fellow..." Finnegan pointed to Duran. "Is with the War Department. That is the portion of the government which currently possesses custody of Indians, the great white father. Major Duran, what sort of Indian do we have before us here, do you think?"

Catching on, Duran did his best to sound serious. "I believe this savage to be a Seminole, escaped off the reservation. Probably best to ship him back to Indian Territory with all due haste. It should not take more than a week or two, riding in a filthy pig car, to get you back to the vicinity of Oklahoma or Arkansas, friend."

Mitchell glanced between Finnegan and Duran, wearing an angry scowl. "That is where the Indians who come to see Wavoka live?"

"Yes." Finnegan nodded. "It is not a pleasant place, let me assure you."

"Where the soldiers tell them how they may live and where they may go?"

"Yes." Finnegan pulled a cigar from his coat and looked it over to see if the snow had soddened it. "While this place is not necessarily heaven, it is a far cry better than Indian Territory, Mr. Mitchell."

Mitchell hung his head. "I will go to Wavoka."

"Ah, yes, now there's a good fellow." Finnegan placed his cigar between his lips and began attempting to remove the snow from his shotgun. "If we make haste, my dinner can yet be had." He slid the shotgun in the scabbard and swung up onto the horse.

Mitchell looked around. "There is not a horse for me."

Finnegan leaned over. "Ride with me for a time. In most instances, I would tell a captured man such as yourself that if he could walk up here, he could bloody well walk home, but I cannot have you dawdling and keeping me from my meals."

FINNEGAN WATCHED as Mitchell emerged from Wilson's hut. The rather bedraggled medicine man walked to the Pinkerton and stood waiting. Finnegan puffed his cigar and assessed the man. The detective had seen the medicine man's look a time or two before. It was the visage of a thief who has been forced to hand over the stolen property. "You have made all your proper amends, Mr. Mitchell?"

"I have." Mitchell kicked the snow. "You have any more tobacco?"

"I do." Finnegan handed the defeated shaman a cigar.

Mitchell bit the cigar in half and began chewing it. "Why does your woman care if Wavoka has his booha or not? She is white; what does it matter to her?"

"Miss Meagher has a history of strange notions which I occasionally endeavor to fathom, but never fully understand."

"She is your woman?"

"Not in the sense that you likely mean."

"Nothing you white men do is sensible." He shook his head. "Will you give me my rifle back?"

"Certainly." Finnegan withdrew a dollar from his vest pocket and handed it to the medicine man. "And you may take that as a gratuity, as well. I know you were expecting better from the Utes, but you cannot lay the blame for that situation at my feet. I explained a fine method wherein you could have increased your profit considerably. You chose not to follow my advice."

Mitchell slipped the dollar in his pants pocket without a second thought. "You do not believe in Wovoka's medicine?"

"I have never manifested much belief in much of anything, Mr. Mitchell. The tangible world presents enough tribulation without the addition of ghosts, goblins, and seances."

"Your woman believes."

"She does appear to."

Mitchell motioned toward the many visitors in the village, Jock Bull Bear among them. "They all believe."

"They appear to, as well."

"But you do not believe."

"It does not much matter what I think one way or the other, Mr. Mitchell. I am truly only an observer in a situation such as this, at any rate." Finnegan puffed his cigar. "Now then, I would hope that I should not be expecting any further trouble from you?"

"I will not bother Wovoka so long as you are here."

Finnegan smiled at the medicine man. "That is all I would ask."

Mitchell looked back toward Wilson's hut. "I go now. I do not like to be here. Wovoka should not bring so many of these others together. His father could speak to the dead, as well. He was not so stupid as to bring so many here. Wovoka will regret this someday."

"I have told him as much myself, Mr. Mitchell." The gunman shook his head. "It would appear Mr. Wilson is not of a mind to consider our council."

The medicine man grunted and began walking off in the snow. "Goodbye, white man."

Finnegan watched the medicine man disappear into the trees at the edge of the camp. The gunman was nearly done with his cigar when Duran came plodding over. The soldier was obviously displeased with something. "What has you looking so sour, Townsend? Please do not punish your conscience too much regarding your failure to assist me earlier. A man of my experience is often left wanting when it comes to receiving assistance from inexperienced young men such as yourself. Take heart -- perhaps you will do better the next time."

Duran shook his head. "I may never forgive myself for failing you, Finnegan." He rolled his eyes. "Although, I am currently bedeviled by more pressing business. These red men have invited us to dine with them."

"Ah, yes, damn it." Finnegan pulled his watch from a pocket. "It is far too late to make it to Mrs. Culbertson's table. The woman's use of a stove is mediocre at best, but considerably more refined than what we should likely expect from these people."

"What do they tend to eat?"

"Hares and nuts from pinecones. How they ever managed to survive before Dyer brought canned goods to this valley, I cannot tell you."

"I eagerly await our proffered meal." He motioned toward one of the huts. "Mr. James was being ushered inside when last I saw him."

Finnegan groaned. "Ah, Townsend, I must confess: I am not much distressed that you failed to come to my aid today. What will surely grieve me in the future is that James came to my aid."

Duran nodded. "Yes, I suppose I do owe you an apology for that."

It was late at night when the three men neared the town of Greenfield. It had been a very long day for all of them, and while the accommodations at Mrs. Culbertson's boarding house were not precisely decadent, all the boarders were looking forward to their beds. The road leading to the town had been trodden down rather wide, so the three rode next to one another.

Finnegan grimaced. "That gruel those people construct from pine nuts does not agree with me. Perhaps if one is reared on such food, it is easier to digest."

Duran shrugged as he jostled in the saddle. "I have spent more than a few years among the red men. The army saw fit to exile me to several forts where there was little to do other than drink whiskey and watch Indians starve. I was always impressed by their ability to make the most of what victuals passed their way. They were not above eating beavers, dogs, old horses, or injured horses. There were many tales of them even eating each other in the winters, though I cannot speak to the veracity of that rumor."

"I have dined on horse." James pulled his collar tight around him. "Many a mighty steed ended as a simple repast during the war. I did not find the meat wholly different from that of beef or sheep. Well, perhaps a bit more chewy, due to the animals' age and hard use. I cannot say as I have ever been hard enough pressed to eat dog, but it cannot be too far afield from other flesh."

"If that is how you view the matter, I dearly hope we are not truly marooned here for the entirety of winter." Finnegan smiled at the old outlaw and looked back to Duran. "I have passed through a few forts on the frontier. Life in them was rarely enjoyable for the soldiers or the officers. Many of the difficulties arose from men taking liberties with the Indian women. I would suspect you are too intelligent for that sort of thing, Townsend."

"Oh..." The soldier took a moment to gaze up at the night sky. "The thought is bound to pass a man's mind when he finds himself so far from civilization without diversion of any kind. I would like to tell you my virtue was preserved by remembering the admonishments of my sainted mother, but the truth of the matter is that most of the squaws were either spoken for by older officers or clearly infected with some form of communicable diseases."

James chuckled. "That will tend to keep a man honorable."

"It surely will." Duran pointed to Finnegan. "It certainly saved me from the type of entanglement that presently tortures this poor buffoon."

"Buffoon?" Finnegan arched his eyebrows. "That is bold talk for a man who becomes lost on his way to gunfights. In what way am I buffoonish, young Townsend?"

"Well, I quite shamefully overheard some of your conversation with Mr. Mitchell, and I must admit, I have asked myself some of the same questions he posed."

"Such as?"

"If this fair damsel Miss Meagher is not your wife and you do not entertain any intentions of taking her as a wife, why in the name of all that is holy did we spend the day chasing Indians and nearly becoming maimed in rocks?"

Finnegan laughed. "Townsend, you spent the day engaged in those activities because I am your elder and it would have been poor form on your part to shirk. I might also remind you that there is absolutely nothing else of even blushing interest to do in this frozen tomb other than chase Indians."

"I will cede you that point." Duran looked to James for

confirmation and the outlaw nodded. "All right then, aside from boredom, why do you find yourself here doing some woman's bidding at the drop of a hat? I, myself, am accustomed to taking orders, Finnegan. You have never struck me as the type to blindly accept instruction."

Finnegan smiled and slowly shook his head. "Ah, Townsend, perhaps as you age you will come to understand. It is not that I am in thrall to the woman or some such romantic notion; it is more that she is the sole person still remaining that is in need of me." The gunman shrugged. "As you said, your mother passed recently. As you age you will lose more and more of those you love, those who depend on you, those slim few who give your daily chores meaning. My mother passed years ago. I corresponded with my brother for some time after, but have not sent post to him in some years. I might not know the man any longer if I met him on the street. For a time, there were agents among the Pinkertons that I mentored and watched over. Those that are still living have little need for the guidance of an old man whose time has passed. Even my work in the Indian territories has come to a close. If Molly had not sent her telegram, I do not know what I would be doing with myself presently."

Duran gave the gunman a truly quizzical stare. "Finnegan, are you telling me that this Molly Meagher is all you have left?"

"Travel far enough down life's path and you may find yourself in much the same position, Townsend."

James grunted. "I must say, Finnegan, becoming acquainted with you, beyond assuming the cloud of dust to the rear signals your approach, has been intriguing. I always knew you were dogged, but I would not have thought you loyal. It is good of you to come to a friend's aid. Many men claim willingness for such pursuits; few make good on the offer."

"Well, I cannot say my motives were purely..." Finnegan brought his horse to a stop. They were approaching the few lights that still burned in Greenfield. The moonlight reflecting off the snow made for excellent night vision. A collection of half a dozen mounted riders had just come out of a short alley across from the church. All three men stopped and squinted to assess the new development.

"Do you think a new group has been marooned?" James asked, leaning forward.

Finnegan groaned. "This may prove vexing. I would say there is a good likelihood those are the Utes Mr. Mitchell was attempting to bargain with earlier."

"Damnation." James scowled. "Do you believe a bunch like that would chance coming into a town?"

"Why should they not?" Finnegan reached inside his coat and found his Remington revolver. "Only an army patrol out of their wits with boredom would give them trouble. Most of the world could care less if Indians decamp their reservations."

"From the way that one is favoring his arm, I might think you are correct." Duran motioned toward one man off to the side. "You wounded one with your shotgun, did you not?"

James rubbed his chin. "Gentlemen, I did not get a close review of those Utes, and cannot say as I would have cared to, but I have seen a few Indians during my time here, and I would say that one of those shadows is not an Indian."

Finnegan sat forward, squinting. "To which do you refer?"

James offered a glance that said the answer ought to be obvious. "The big fat one. I do not imagine a fellow could get like that from eating pinecones and bunnies."

"Now that you make mention of it, those Utes were quite slim." Finnegan scratched his face. He was about to suggest that they take the horses around to the back of the town stable, thus avoiding contact with the Utes, but the Indians made such a detour a moot issue. The plump shadow fell from the saddle, raising a cloud of snow. The other riders began letting out great, whooping laughs. One man tossed something down toward the fallen rider and the rest begat to exiting the town in the direction opposite Finnegan and his two compatriots. "It would appear as though the party has ended, gentlemen."

"Good grief." Duran shook his head. "If that is not just what I have come to expect from the red man. They likely came into town to procure firewater from that man Dyer. Now, with a gut full of the evil stuff, they will get up to no good and have left one of their own to perish in a snowbank. It is sad to view the way savages treat their own."

James chuckled. "As I said, son, I don't think that's an Indian laying down there. Regardless of the poor devil's coloring, we ought to go drag him under a roof next to a stove."

"Yes." Finnegan gave his horse a small kick. "It will not do to have a corpse in the street."

"Hey..." James got up next to him. "You ever discover where they're going with the bodies you keep dropping around here?"

Finnegan glared at the outlaw. "A local man keeps an icehouse. Thus, the bodies will be kept somewhat preserved until the ground is completely thawed. What is it to you?"

"I only mention it in case this fellow in the snow is dead. If he has passed on it would only be proper to lump him in with the rest."

"You are an intriguing man, Mr. James." Duran brought

his horse to a stop and stared down into a snowbank on the very edge of the town. "Ah, damn the luck, this does appear to be a white man." He leaned over farther in the saddle, holding himself by only one stirrup. "You there! Hey, you there! Are you among the living?"

The snow slowly began to heave and part to reveal the fleshy form of Vincent Heth. He struggled to roll over and make it to his knees in the snow, where he sunk yet again. He wiped the crust of snow from his eyes. "By God, this is a strange place. I swear, only moments ago I was imbibing a strange liquid with red savages, and now I am being accosted by one of them Yankees that talk through their nose. I should not have gone into the pay of Mormons; nothing good ever comes of it."

Finnegan rode up and stared down at the disheveled guide. "Mr. Heth, I had rather begun to wonder what had become of you. We have not had the pleasure of your company at dinner for some time."

From the snowbank, Heth shook his head and jowls. "Couldn't hardly take being with them teetotaler bible thumpers no more. It always strikes me as a simple enough method for making a dollar in the beginning, but to live with them kind..." He shook his head again. "It gets to a man more and more, day by day, no women, no whiskey, no song...damn it..." He slumped into the snowdrift. "What I can't reckon is what in hell's bells a man would want with a dollar if he's one of them kind that's got nothing to spend it on."

James arrived just in time to hear the statement. "As a younger man I had that same wonder regarding Baptists. Later on, I discovered that most of them will find a use for a dollar, given the opportunity. "You would not happen to be a Baptist, would you, sir?"

Heth chuckled and began making a rather half-hearted

attempt at extricating himself from the snowdrift. "I was always of a temperament to join up with whichever congregation was offering pie at the picnic, back in my youth." He made it nearly to a standing position before losing his balance and tumbling back into the snow. "Now, I find myself with only one possible choice and I cannot say as they are too damned generous with their pie." He heaved himself onto his side and rolled out of the bank and into the beaten down road. "Hell and perdition, would any of you have a refreshment handy? I grow quite chilled playing in this damned snow."

"I do not believe a man among us carries a flask, Mr. Heth." Finnegan pointed down the road. "There is more sour news. Unless you had borrowed a mount from your companions, it would appear those Indians made off with your horse."

Heth staggered and took hold of Finnegan's leg. "Oh, that will not sit well with Mr. Dyer. The animal was rented, and I do not believe it was meant to be given over to savages."

"Likely not." Finnegan dismounted. "Since you broach the matter, we should get our animals back to that dry goods man, as well. I will see to these beasts, Townsend, if you and Mr. James would be so kind as to guide Mr. Heth back to the boarding house. I fear that without proper assistance he will surely perish. It would be a shame for him to depart the earth before he has a chance to explain himself to Mr. Dyer."

Duran swung down from the saddle and put his hand out to the snow dweller. "Major Townsend Duran. Pleased to make you acquaintance."

Heth took the proffered hand, more for support than anything else. "Vincent Heth. I was once Private Vincent Heth, but it did not suit me nor the other men in the barracks. I was under the impression we parted ways by mutual consent when I let out of there. You ain't by any chance here to return me, are you?"

Duran patted the man's shoulder. "Desertion is a serious offense, sir, but it would seem the army of these United States continues to function without your services. I believe we can consider you honorably discharged and leave matters at that."

"That is damn decent of you, sir." Heth stumbled as he let Duran's hand drop. Fortunately, James had dismounted and was able to take the man by one arm. The drunk smiled at his new friend. "Oh, hello there, Mr. James. Hey, you know that Doubleday fella didn't even know you was famous when you told him your name?"

"Probably because I do not possess much in the way of fame." James began tugging the sodden man toward the boarding house along with Duran, while Finnegan split off to see to the horses. Heth swooned and was caught on the opposite side by Duran. "Ah, Mr. James, me and the Major here was just discussing our time in the army. Was you ever in the cavalry?"

"After a fashion, yes."

"Yup, well, I never did sit in the saddle one damn day while they had a hold of me. Never was in one damn battle against these red skins, neither. I suppose I wasn't much good at soldiering, but I could peel potatoes and sweep out the barracks like no other man. Was damn good at shoveling horse apples, as well."

"A pity you did not choose to make a life-long pursuit of it, Mr. Heth." Duran grinned at James. "A man who can muck out horse stalls consistently has a very real chance of becoming president. The two occupations are surprisingly similar."

"Ah, well..." Heth hiccupped and stumbled forward a few steps along with his guardians. "I did consider making a go of it for a time, but I got to thinking that I never did much care for the thought of being a hero and it would be better to let younger men have the glory."

"How very humble of you, Mr. Heth." James struggled under the man's weight as they fought to get him up the front steps of the boarding house. "I am sure Mr. Dyer will take your service to your country and your history of good deeds into account when you inform him of the disposition of his horse."

Chapter 12

GREENFIELD, NEVADA

January 12th, 1890

FINNEGAN ENTERED MRS. CULBERTSON'S DINING ROOM to find only young Major Duran sitting at the table. After surveying the room, he sat down and frowned. "No coffee as of yet?"

The major shook his head. "None as yet." He removed a cigar from his jacket pocket and tossed a spare across the table to Finnegan. "If you care for one before your breakfast."

The gunman picked up the proffered smoke and rolled it between his fingers. "Traditionally, I abstain until after my coffee, but as Mrs. Culbertson does not care for the smell, perhaps it will quicken the pace by which our breakfast is delivered." He lit the cigar and puffed out smoke. "Mr. James and Mr. Heth have not seen fit to join us?"

"Mr. Heth may sleep for the remainder of the winter and Mr. James was worn quite thoroughly by yesterday's adventure. I expect he has earned sleeping in for one morning." Duran lit his cigar. "How is it you have risen so early?"

"I find I sleep much better now that there is a large hole in my bedroom door. I have affixed a covering to it in the form of an old pair of long johns. However, the garment is left free to flap about and lets in a good deal of warm air from the house below. Now that the quality of my napping is enhanced, I find I require less of it."

"Grand. You shall have to shoot a hole in the door wherever you stay from now on."

"Oh, I shall insist on it." Finnegan puffed out more smoke. "Are you truly to be quartered in San Francisco when you are finished here, Townsend? I am told it can be a fine city if one is so inclined toward it."

"Oh, who can say what foolishness awaits a man when his fate is at the mercy of generals and politicians." Duran spit a small bit of tobacco down onto Mrs. Culbertson's floor. "Did you know that I have never once killed an Indian?"

Finnegan was a bit taken aback by the statement, so early and so off subject. He chuckled. "I suppose not every fellow is apt to." He tapped ash into a saucer that was wanting a coffee cup. "Although, given your long service and the army's fixation with the savages, I suppose that would be something for a man such as yourself to ponder. Have you ever found yourself engaged with the red men?"

Duran rubbed his chin. "By hook or by crook, it has never come to pass. It always seemed that if the troop were at the fort to refit, the Indians would attack a homestead. If we were on patrol, the silly buggers would attack the fort. I came to wonder if perhaps my luck was fouled in some manner." He puffed his cigar. "Of course, those incidents all occurred during my shining youth as a bold lieutenant. My first year in the west we all thought we would be fighting the red savages for the next hundred years. They would never surrender, and we would all be bathed in glory before it was over. In what seemed an eye blink, they were beaten and begging for scraps at the fort gate they once assailed."

"It often wears on a man more to lose his dignity than his life." Finnegan shrugged. "The loss of dignity is inevitably more drawn out."

"Yes, quite." Duran eyed the Pinkerton. "Have you had cause to kill an Indian?"

Finnegan licked his lips and nodded. "Yes. Although, fighting the red men was not my intention when I began."

"Was it during your time in Montana? I have been told the Indians there were rather rambunctious in their day."

Finnegan smiled. "No. Oddly enough, my only difficulties in that territory came from interactions with my fellow white men." He tapped more ash. "Before arriving in this sleepy hamlet, my one and only donnybrook with the natives occurred near the border with Mexico. I had the honor and privilege of trading shots with the great Geronimo."

Duran let out a laugh and sat forward. "Geronimo, the Apache war chief?"

"Do you know of another man making use of that moniker?"

"How do you find your way into these situations, Finnegan?" The soldier grinned. "Although, it should not shock one to be informed that you found yourself tasked with shooting the last great Indian leader. You have been this nation's premier shootist for some time. I can think of no one better qualified to the task."

Finnegan shrugged again. "In the end, I proved unequal to the chore. As far as I know, the gentleman currently resides on a reservation. Painted into a corner like all the other red men. The Mexicans would not tolerate him any longer and the Americans would not tolerate him being free to roam. Left with no alternative, he took to behaving." The gunman offered a sad smile. "Perhaps it is the choice we all will face, someday."

Duran rolled his cigar back and forth in his fingers, watching the smoke rise. "I must confess, dear Finnegan, as a boy reading of your exploits, even as a grown man suffering in anonymity in louse-ridden frontier forts, I often woolgathered speculating what it must be like to be a man such as yourself."

Finnegan arched one eyebrow. "Of course, you refer to my handsome visage. I know the likes of it is rarely seen, but it is a burden one learns to live with."

Duran chuckled. "I was referring to your fame, Finnegan. I suppose every man who is not well known is apt to wonder what renown offers. You and Mr. James have been personages of celebrity most of your lives. Does it warp a fellow's thinking as time goes by?"

Finnegan blew out more smoke. "How do you mean, Townsend?"

"Well, as an example: you are the most famed assassin to have been produced by the Pinkerton firm. As such, do you feel compelled to continue in that vein permanently?"

"Townsend..." Finnegan rubbed his eyes. "I do not currently, nor have I ever, considered myself an assassin. The late Mr. Pinkerton never assigned that particular label to my work." He paused to consider the matter. "I greatly doubt Mr. Pinkerton's sons would choose that term to describe my labors, either. It is my understanding that the profession is viewed in more of a dim light with each passing year."

"Who can say?" Duran grinned. "The day may arrive when the noble practice of assassination is considered wholly unscrupulous."

"We can only pray we pass before that sad day arrives." Finnegan rubbed his chin. "What was the purpose of your inquiry, Townsend? I am afraid I have quite misplaced it."

The soldier laughed. "Yes, well, that will happen. I inquired regarding your current status. From what you have told me, this new generation of Pinkerton men were no longer able to provide you with steady labor, so you drifted into the unsettled Indian nations to collect railroad bounties. You chose that work over..." he threw his hands in the air. "Over all other available options. You are a man of no little knowledge and experience. I would imagine there are any number of endeavors you might prosper in. Why resort to more of the same? I would think that after so many years in what is essentially the same trade, you might welcome a change."

Finnegan rubbed his ribs where he had been recently struck. The wound had improved considerably. "Yes, well, I might ask you why you continue on with the army when a world of other options present themselves. Why does any man do what he does, Townsend? It is not as though I have not dabbled with other trades or endeavors over the years. I once attempted to enter into the cattle industry in Montana and made a fine bargain with some gentlemen who were already established. A cruel winter nearly wiped the herds from the earth and now I find myself waiting in abeyance with all the other investors. A similar fate has awaited other schemes that have come and gone. Railroad stocks, mining claims, the list is not small." The gunman waved one hand. "When these conflagrations assault a man, he tends to fall back on the familiar. He returns to what has consistently nurtured him. I have always earned my keep with a gun in my hand. Perhaps I always will."

"So, then, it is habit, and nothing more?"

"Well, a fellow does somewhat scorn the notion of clerking in a grocery store after he had spent a lifetime striking fear into the hearts of bandits far and wide." Finnegan laughed. "Would you care to be broken to the ranks, mucking out horse stalls and fetching for sergeants?"

"Ah, you have come across a fine point there, sir." Duran nodded. "A man is loath to lose a ladder rung, once ascended." The soldier pondered further. "Truly, though, what is it like to have your name so well known, to see it in print in periodicals?"

The gunman stubbed out what remained of his breakfast cigar. "As a younger man, I did take the occasional bit of... I do not think pride would be the proper term...perhaps astonishment might be more fitting. What must be understood, Townsend, is that when it comes to so-called public personages such as Mr. James and myself, what few pause to appreciate is the simple fact that most of our public persona is nothing more than unabashed fiction."

The soldier shook his head. "Certainly, the dates and circumstances might be adulterated, but..."

"Bosh, pure bosh. Alexander Dumas has penned more truth regarding musketeers than any newspaper man has ever penned regarding myself or Alexander Franklin James. To hear those fools expound, one might come to the conclusion that there is nary a man on the continent who does not carry a scar from my revolver. If Alexander has truly made off with the amount of loot they credit to him, the old bugger would be rich as Midas and would hardly bother contributing to those same fish wrappers." Finnegan dropped his cigar butt to the saucer. "Men of our class are little more than drivel contrived to sell papers. In truth, there is little that separates any of us from any fellow who labors at the same profession but goes unnoticed his entire career." Finnegan laughed. "In all earnestness, it could easily be argued that a skilled detective should strive for and easily achieve anonymity. Since I was unable to achieve it, I am obviously not a skilled detective."

"Your lack of skill in that arena may explain why the term

assassin was so often bandied about." Duran stubbed out his cigar. "In some respect, I suppose we are all at the mercy of other mens' opinions." The soldier gazed thoughtfully over at the man he had known so very long. "What is next for you, Finnegan? Will you return to Arkansas to finish off the last of the bandits, or is it to the chapel for you and the lovely Miss Meagher?"

The gunman leaned back in his chair. "It is strange to admit that I would readily welcome Miss Meagher's acceptance. Regardless of whether my cattle futures prosper, I have managed to put a fair sum by. It would be sufficient to get us set in some sort of venture. The very prospect of domesticity would have once made me bridle. Now, the notion gains favor with every passing day. A small house, a decent woman, perhaps a child scurrying about, harassing the aforementioned dame."

Duran chuckled. "Are not you and Miss Meagher a bit... ripened for such as that?"

Finnegan scratched his head. "I had not paused to consider that aspect of the thing. It seems to me that I have met a few women of Miss Meagher's age still toting about brats."

Duran held up one hand. "I would certainly not be the one to say what is possible in that particular area. Thank the Almighty, it has never been forced to my attention." He laughed, but grew serious. "Finnegan, might I inquire as to one more personal issue?"

"We have known each other for many years, Townsend. I cannot imagine what subject would be barred to you."

"Did you kill the man that shot down your father?"

Finnegan only stared at the soldier for a long moment. "Townsend, I do not know what man shot down my father." The gunman thought back. "I can say with some certainty that he did not fall due to an accident by another Union man. Make no mistake, many a fine young man was killed by his own in that miserable war. As I recall, we sighted grey troops. We witnessed the smoke from their rifles. One man in the troop was wounded and my father fell dead." Finnegan's lip curled slightly. "We were expected to keep in line of march to another position. There was no time for mourning while the firing continued. I returned that night and buried him."

"How old were you?"

"Thirteen, but big for my age. I could more or less heft a musket in my own defense, given warning, of course."

"Young, to lose so much."

"You were far younger when your father passed." Finnegan drummed his fingers on the table.

"Yes, but...well I hardly recall the man and I did not see him fall as you did."

"I do not think on the incident much. Truthfully, I had not thought on it in a long time before you brought the matter up just now. What caused you to contemplate the matter?"

"It is difficult to say what makes a notion flit into a fellow's mind, especially when he has not yet received his breakfast." Duran squirmed in his chair and looked to the kitchen door. "Perhaps I should remove myself and seek victuals at Mr. Dyer's store. I am not certain if the fellow was in earnest, but Mr. Heth requested that I accompany him to see the dry goods man this morning so that he might have a witness present to explain the loss of the horse."

Finnegan laughed. "Yes, I am certain your recitation of the encounter will sooth Mr. Dyer a great deal."

"What do you have planned for the day, Finnegan?"

"Oh, if I am ever given my repast, it would likely serve me best to repair to Wilson's village and confirm that his magical, mystical prophecy factory is properly in operation. Who can

say how many knaves may have secreted into his hut while he slept and helped themselves to the revelations the man undoubtedly leaves lying about?"

"You are a salty one, Finnegan." Duran got up out of his chair. "I must say, I have always had difficulty determining who is in your favor and who is not."

"You are in my favor, Townsend. Many thanks for not leaping to assumptions concerning Mr. Wilson."

The soldier shrugged. "When you are told by Finnegan Gilhooley to move cautiously, a wise man takes it under advisement."

Finnegan groaned. "Ah, if only the brunt of men were as wise as you, Townsend."

As Finnegan rode into the small village, he could see Wilson toward the center of the place. The as-of-yet-unvetted prophet had a collection of followers assembled around him. The onlookers sat on logs and stumps, while Wilson stood in the center, extolling some portion of his philosophy. Finnegan could pick out the Mormon contingent along with Jock Bull Bear and a few clusters of other Indians, either recent arrivals or long-time disciples.

Not having an overwhelming desire to hear Jack speak on any given topic, Finnegan moved toward the huts and was surprised to discover Molly larking about in the snow with a few of the village's smaller children.

The gunman smiled. "Ah, Molly, it is good to see you in such fine feather."

The schoolteacher stood and planted her hands on her hips. "And why should I not be, Mr. Gilhooley? It is a fine sunny day. A grave injustice has been corrected. Above all else, my heroic knight has come for a visit. What more could a lady possibly ask?"

"If you had witnessed the quest in totality, you might have cause to question my knighthood."

"I am certain you were as valiant as ever. Regardless, you vanquished the windmills and returned that rather shabby dragon to make his amends with Jack. So long as the destination is reached, the route matters little."

"Well, so long as you are content with the results." Finnegan smiled and kicked at the snow by his feet.

"My contentment is of primary concern to you, Mr. Gilhooley?"

"It does weigh on my mind quite often." Finnegan looked up from the snow. "In point of fact, I contemplated that very matter the whole way to this camp. The trail has become well-worn, and a fellow can now allow his mind to wander a bit while the horse plods along. Due to the length of the journey, I believe I was able to reach what might be considered a conclusion."

She took his hand and began leading him down one of the paths in the snow that was wide enough for them to promenade side by side. "Ah, that is fine to hear, Finnegan. Please, share your conclusion with me, as it pertains to my contentment. I have never succeeded much when it came to delving into that particular question."

Finnegan nodded. "Yes, it does present something of a puzzle, does it not? I must confess a deficiency in the area myself. Perhaps that is why I was so surprised today to discover that I had what the philosophers would refer to as an epiphany."

"Well, how lovely, indeed."

"It did brighten my mood considerably."

"Oh, do not keep me in suspense, Finnegan."

"It became quite clear to me as that old nag I borrowed from Dyer plodded to this place that you and I are most certainly a pair of pitiable fools."

"Hmm." Molly nodded once more. "Finnegan, I realize that you rarely practice the fine art of courting, but I feel compelled to offer some advice. If a gentleman wishes to gain a lady's favor, it is most often considered best to avoid labeling her either foolish or pitiful. At the least, it should be avoided within earshot of the lady."

Finnegan chuckled. "Yes, well, I never claimed to be descended from Lothario. What I meant, dearest Molly, is that we have both acted quite foolishly."

"In what manner?"

"Have we not both crossed the length and breadth of this continent, casting about to arrive at some place we are content? This endless wandering never seems to profit either of us much. I would go so far as to say that the last few years, I engaged in it more from habit than from any other motive. I might venture that you felt a similar way. We search for contentment apart, and never once pause to consider that we may be most content together. Could it be that I do not truly need an infinite string of ne'er-do-well outlaws, chicken rustlers, and shoddy replicas of old adversaries to keep me amused? Could it be that you do not truly require a new messiah to be happily settled?"

"Finnegan, what precisely are you working at?" She grinned.

"Molly, you know perfectly well what I suggest." He stopped and took up her hands. "I would have us wed. When our work here is complete, I would have us light away to the nearest chapel so that we may begin our life together. We have approached this moment many times. I daresay, we have each found reasons to procrastinate in the past. I believe it is time we cease such measures. I can foresee no future without you by my side. If you can foresee no other, please give me your pledge. I can offer little more than unflinching dedication and affection, but perhaps that is enough."

Molly kissed his hands. "Very well, my Finnegan. Perhaps you are right. I can think of no practical reason to put matters off any longer. If you cannot, either, I suppose we are finally caught." She leapt up and put her arms around his neck. "I will marry you, and happily, at that."

Finnegan hugged her as well as he thought propriety would allow and then set her back in the snow. "Ah, yes, well, this is very fine." He took her hand and they continued to walk down the path. The gunman stopped and looked over at his newly-minted fiancée. "Molly, does your father still live?"

She giggled once. "Well, yes. Last I received correspondence from him, he was quite well, and I have no reason to believe his condition has changed."

He nodded. "Excellent. In that case, I shall post a letter to him and see that it makes it onto the next train."

"Traditionally, it is the gentleman's family who announces the engagement, Finnegan. Although, I believe, in our case, everyone would agree we are a bit aged for all that foolishness."

"I mean to announce nothing, my dear. I intend to write so that I may ask the man's permission."

Molly assumed a surprised look. "I apologize if I appear shocked. I have never known you to ask another man's permission with regard to...well to anything, truly."

"I have never intended to wed before." Finnegan drew his brow together and appeared quite serious. "Molly, I may have committed many a scurrilous act in my time. I daresay, I have, on occasion, sunk near-to as low as some of the men I have chased. That being admitted, I would never so much as consider marrying a woman without the express permission of her father. A man does have to have some standards for his behavior that cannot be deviated from."

Molly slowly nodded and they returned to walking. "You never fail to surprise, Finnegan. I can only hope our marriage will be as entertaining as our courtship has been. Although, a somewhat restful honeymoon may be preferable."

The moon was high when Finnegan stepped onto the front porch of the boarding house. He and Molly had made their announcement to the various members of Jack Wilson's circle who might have an interest, and enjoyed something of a small celebration with those present. When they had been properly feted, Finnegan had escorted Molly down to the Wilson Ranch so that they might make another announcement. Naturally, the Wilsons had been kind enough to invite the new couple to dinner, and smoking a few celebratory cigars with the Caucasian Mr. Wilson had taken up more time than Finnegan had expected it would.

Back at the boardinghouse, the gunman was doing his best to move across the porch and through the door without rousing the house, but when he was halfway to the door his name was called out in a muffled tone. "Finnegan?"

He slowly turned, with his hand moving in the direction of his pistol, as it always did, but relaxed when he saw that it was only Duran standing in the snow by the far edge of the porch. "Good evening, Townsend." Finnegan glanced around. "What has you still roused at this late hour?"

The soldier shook his head and moved over to Finnegan. "You would hardly credit the day I have experienced, my friend. My chores ran far longer than I could have imagined.

My initial mistake was in taking pity on Mr. Heth. I spent the first part of the day explaining matters to Mr. Dyer and attempting to relate the events that transpired involving the Utes. After that, Heth managed to convince the dry goods man that his horse might still be retrieved." Duran shook his head once more. "I could hardly argue the matter one way or the other, and as such had no choice but to venture out with the fool."

Finnegan chuckled. "Did you locate the Utes?"

"You stood a better chance of finding the new messiah at Wilson's camp today. We ranged quite far and wide, but saw nary a trace of them. Heth did manage to allow his second rented horse to step wrong and damage its leg. Dyer had a merry time haranguing him about that, I assure you. I do not believe the man stands much of a chance of turning a profit during his engagement with the Doubleday clan. He burns through horse flesh far too quickly."

"That can become an expensive habit. I have always found it best to avoid confrontation with stable keepers who have become incensed. The most sensible solution is to leave town on the last of the rented stock and never return. Of course, it is assumed that one is bright enough to initially rent stock under an alias. In the case of Mr. Heth, he has already made a misstep and fouled the entire plan. There is likely no remedy."

"Likely not." Duran turned up his collar. "And what required your attention for so very long at Wilson's camp? It cannot have taken too awfully long to determine whether or not the man was still capable of performing miracles. It should only take a moment for the fellow to make water into wine, if he is capable."

"He transmogrified water into coffee before my very eyes. Does that impress?"

"I suppose it is better than nothing."

Finnegan reached out and clapped Duran on the shoulder. "It was not strange Jack Wilson that performed a miracle today, young man, but Finnegan Xavier Gilhooley. You may find my tale hard to credit, as well. This very morning, I made a supreme effort and convinced the fetching Miss Meagher to enter into an engagement with me."

Duran raised his slightly frosted eyebrows. "Truly? Well, that is very fine, Finnegan. Bully, just bully." He patted the gunman on the shoulder and reached into his coat, withdrawing two cigars. "Congratulations are definitely in order." He handed Finnegan one of the cigars and fumbled with his rather chilled fingers to find a match. He got one going and held it out for Finnegan. "You left your betrothed in Wilson's village? I would think you would secure her lodging here until you are formally wed." He chuckled. "A honeymoon would be a fine excuse to board the train and go...well, anywhere but here."

Finnegan puffed his cigar and groaned. "Yes, well, I assure you I would like nothing better. My betrothed, on the other hand, is quite insistent on remaining in this lovely hamlet until such time as we can get Mr. Wilson properly fit out for his coming role as ruler of the west, or sultan, or whatever it is the man aspires to." He shrugged. "I suppose it does not matter much. I left dear Molly at the Wilson Ranch, where she resides most nights. I suspect those huts are comfortable enough if one is reared in them, but Molly makes no secret of preferring a feather bed and a proper roof."

"Yes, well, charity only extends so far, I imagine. Personally, I would draw the line in the area of losing limbs to freezing, just as your Molly has done." Duran patted Finnegan on the shoulder. "Ah, Finnegan Gilhooley is finally to settle down." He motioned over one shoulder. "Will you be making

Dyer an offer on the dry goods store? He seems to do a tidy business, and you will have to find something to occupy your time, being as you are somewhat mired here."

"Oh, very droll, Townsend."

"I only mention the notion, as it would appear a detective in private employ may not do much of a brisk business in this spot."

Finnegan rubbed his chin. "I do not know if I would dismiss it out of hand. I have been fairly busy since making landfall here. All I lack is someone to pay me for my trouble. Perhaps I could get the remaining miners to take up a collection. They may rather appreciate the removal of so much scum from their midst."

Duran puffed his cigar and smiled. "Well, Finnegan, I honestly do not know if you will make a good husband, but you will certainly be an interesting one."

Chapter 13

GREENFIELD, NEVADA

January 13th, 1890

It was not Finnegan's habit to sleep late, but the previous night's festivities had kept him up well past his normal bedtime. For once, the gunman had piled enough blankets and quilts over him to fend off the cold in his rented room and had remained unconscious until nearly nine in the morning. Feeling quite well rested, he dressed and made his way down to the dining room to investigate whether or not any chance remained for receiving breakfast.

Entering the dining room, he found Mr. James nursing a cup of coffee and flipping through a newspaper. "Good morning, Alexander. How does the day find you?"

The outlaw shrugged. "I suppose matters could be worse. I helped myself to the lion's share of breakfast. With only the Doubleday clan to contend with, the pickings were quite good. I have also received a newspaper here..." He held up the smudged sheets. "That originated in San Francisco and is only a little over a week old. It was passed from an engineer, to Dyer, to Doubleday, but is still something of a jewel in this empty spot."

Finnegan took up the coffee pot and was delighted to discover some brew still remained. He filled a spare cup and sat at the table. "You may have burst without Heth to contend with."

James shrugged again. "No sign of the fellow, nor your friend Duran." James motioned toward the street. "They may have overslept, as you did, and run to the café in shame."

Finnegan rubbed his chin. "I suppose there is very little likelihood of Mrs. Culbertson preparing a late repast for me."

"I do not think you murdered nearly enough cattle rustlers to warrant that type of treatment."

"No, likely not." Finnegan sipped his coffee and smiled.

"For a man who is not to partake of breakfast, you are in a fine mood. Have you gotten word that the pay for shooting strikers has doubled, or some such thing?"

"Not all windfalls are of a financial nature, Alexander. Some agreements augment a man's happiness as opposed to his pocketbook." Finnegan grinned. "I have made a proposal to Miss Meagher, and she has accepted. We are to be joined as soon as the formalities have been seen to."

"Ah..." James nodded approvingly. "That is wonderful news, Finnegan. I daresay, you two should have arrived at this decision long ago. It might have kept you from trailing around after me. You could have saved us both much discomfort."

"I can only assume Miss Meagher was selfish and failed to take your comfort into consideration these many years."

"I am far too gregarious to hold it against her." James sipped his coffee. "Does this town contain some form of clergy? You will be requiring some fellow who claims to be sanctified if you wish to properly wed the lady before the thaw comes."

"I am certain that Mr. Wilson will suffice if no other holy

man is available. God's own begotten ought to trump the run of the mill, whiskey sodden priest, I should think."

James rubbed his beard stubble. "There may be a few who would call that plan blasphemous, or even suggest you run the hazard of damnation by implementing it. Although, as a man who has spent more than some years bound in matrimony, I will freely tell you that the best course for you, from this point forward, will always be to ask the lady her inclination, and promptly adopt it. If she wishes to be wed by Wilson or Dyer, or one of the horses in the livery, you are to merely smile and tell her you believe that to be a most darling notion. Follow that precept and you may yet die a happy man, Finnegan."

The gunman slowly nodded. "And now that I have received marriage advice from Frank James, I may also consider it a full and varied life." Finnegan drummed his fingers on the dining room table. "Would you consider standing up with me, Alexander?"

The outlaw coughed around his coffee cup and set the vessel down in its saucer with a clatter. "What's that, now?"

"Would you consider functioning as my groomsman? I shall be requiring at least two for the ceremony. I know no one but yourself and Townsend in this place." He grinned. "If Wilson is to be the preacher, you are my only alternative."

James shook his head in wonderment. "By God, it is a strange and awesome world we linger in. Of all the oddities I thought I might encounter before passing on, I certainly never considered I might participate in the nuptials of Finnegan Gilhooley."

"This should not come as quite such a shock, Alexander. It is only fitting that you ought to be present when we are joined. If not for you, Molly and I would never have been acquainted. To think, if you were a slightly better, or slightly worse, marksman, I would never have met my one true love."

"Just lucky for you I always embraced the time-honored practice of mediocrity in my shooting." James laughed. "I would be proud to stand with you while some savage chants in his pagan tongue and you marry the gal who dug my bullet out of your hip." James raised his coffee cup. "May God himself smile on you both." He shrugged. "If nothing else, perhaps being wed to that winsome beauty will tend to keep you around home so that you are not roaming about harassing innocent men such as myself while they attempt to make a living."

"I am certain Miss Meagher's only intent in becoming my wife is to see to it that you and your ilk are no longer bothered, Alexander."

"I would doubt no less from that sweet lass."

GIVING up hope of receiving breakfast from Mrs. Culbertson, an item that was meant to be provided as the cost was included in his rent, Finnegan moved on. His first stop was the Dyer mercantile. He came through the door, shook the snow from his person, and plucked a coffee cup from a hook above the near-glowing stove. With the aid of a rag, he was able to lift the coffee pot from the cooktop and pour himself a cup of the odd brew Dyer favored.

He was just taking his first sip when Dyer came in to investigate who had arrived. "Ah, Finnegan." The shop owner shook his head. "If you had not gone to the trouble of... forcing old Tom Mitchell to return whatever in the hell he purloined from Jack, do you think it might have ceased snowing?"

"I think this place is well above sea level and given to receiving snow in the winter months. Beyond that, I offer no conclusions." He smiled around his coffee cup. "I have news and was hoping I might find young Townsend Duran here to share it with him."

"Haven't seen that pup, though I wish I had. He's with the army, ain't he?"

"He is."

"Well, I'm missing some horses, and I sure as hell can't figure who could have made off with them other than those damn Utes that been hanging around here looking for trouble and anything else they can lay their sticky fingers on. Army's supposed to be keeping them in line -- I say Duran ought to do it."

Finnegan shrugged. "I can conjure no other chore that requires my time this day. Once I locate Duran, the two of us will see about your stock."

"You ain't with the Army. If you want to stay in town and keep your feet warm, I won't hold it against you."

"As I said, I have nothing in particular to do this fine day. I might as well chase a few Indians, even if they are Indians I have already chased. A bored man cannot afford to be finicky."

"All right then. Good hunting, I guess."

"If Duran is not here, I suppose he must be at the café. I am not certain there is another option in this quaint little hamlet." Finnegan flexed his cold fingers and gripped his coffee cup. "Oh, that brings something else to mind. Is there a man of the cloth in this town?"

"Even if there was, I don't know what the hell he'd want to speak over Utes for." Dyer got himself a cup of coffee. "Though, killing them seems a might harsh. Could you maybe manage to just put the fear of God in 'em without actually sending 'em to meet the Almighty? I know horse theft is a serious matter, but they were some ragged old sway-backs and might not have lived out the winter at any rate."

Finnegan let out a small sigh. "I did not kill any of those Indians the last time I encountered them, and will likely not need to the next time. I inquired regarding the preacher because I have made a proposal to Miss Meagher, and she has accepted."

Dyer nodded approvingly. "Ah, well, that's right nice, Finnegan. You two will make a mighty fetching couple. Good to hear you finally got around to staking your claim on that gal. Better you than any of the other candidates."

Finnegan chuckled. "To whom do you refer?"

"Uh, Doubleday, for one. Wasn't here too long and he asked if Miss Meagher was in any way attached. Reckon he thought she might make a good addition to his harem. You know them Mormons keep more than one woman at a time?"

Finnegan contemplated the matter. "Yes, I have heard that."

"Yup." Dyer refilled his cup. "Now, I've known more than a few bucks who keep a few squaws at any given time, but that's a different matter entirely. Living with a squaw is a right nice way to go through life. As for the notion of keeping more than one white woman in your house, well, that just seems like something that would drive a fella to the bottle or the end of his own pistol."

"I suppose that could become...vexing. I have noted that Molly is in the habit of holding a man to account for his actions. Receiving that treatment from a number of women at once could be a true hardship for a fellow." Finnegan drained his coffee cup. "I shall repair to the café in search of Townsend. Once I locate the young man, we will be needing the two best horses that still remain in your possession. If we are better mounted, it should be a small matter to find the less desirable creatures."

Dyer shrugged, looking glum. "I'll see what I can do for you, but don't expect too much in the way of bangtails. Hell, that chubby Heth got drunk and more or less gave my best horse to them Utes the other night, to hear him and Duran tell it."

"Yes, Mr. Heth does have an aptitude for finding trouble."

"He'll likely have an aptitude for having my boot up his rump if he tries to skitter out of this town without paying for the animal, assuming you can't locate it." Dyer spit down onto the floor. "Hey, if you do come across the horse Heth lost, just tie it up out on the outskirts by that old sluice box. It would tickle me to make that plump sod sweat some."

Finnegan rolled his eyes and replaced his coffee cup where he had found it. "If we are able to recover any of your stock, it would likely be best for you to count it a boon and not attempt to gain more than breaking even." The gunman waved. "I am off to the café."

The café was only a short trudge up the street and across. When Finnegan entered, he once again shook the snow from himself and was somewhat surprised to see that nearly an inch of the stuff had piled on his shoulders. Inside the small building, it only took a moment for him to survey the place and see that his missing Army major was not within. The cook stuck his head out from the kitchen. "You want food?" the burly former miner inquired.

Finnegan nodded and pulled out a chair. "I would, sir."

"It will not be quick. I have not got the cook stove going yet."

"You have had no other customers today?"

The man rubbed one side of his stubbly face. "Town's

dying, friend. If Wilson and his...hell, I don't know what to call 'em, maybe followers?" Finnegan nodded again. "If they don't come in here to eat, who the hell else would?"

"I was looking for Major Duran."

"Can't say as I've met that fella. He one of them stuck here from the snow on the main line?"

"He is." Finnegan lowered himself into his chair. "Well, whatever you might have about will do. I am quite hungry and willing to consider most any sustenance."

The cook smiled at the declaration. "Ah, most excellent. The last Indian that came in here took umbrage with my selling goat meat, but I'd like to know what else I am meant to offer these days. If we don't get a few beeves in here soon, we will all be making damn hard choices."

Finnegan rubbed his eyes. "Goat meat? Truly?" He groaned. "I must find the time to go elk hunting again, presently."

The cook began stoking his cook stove. "That would be damn decent of you, sir. I have always preferred elk to goat."

With what had turned out to be a relatively satisfying repast of goat in his stomach, Finnegan made his way back to the boarding house and once again attempted knocking on Duran's door. When there was no answer, the gunman stared at the beaten brass knob for a long moment. While Finnegan had never considered himself a practiced detective, he had learned the subtle ways of deductive reasoning over the years. If Duran was not to be found at any of the locations in the town where a fellow might be, and there was no way to escape the town, then it reasoned that he very well might still be within his room at the boarding house. If he was within, and not answering his door, it stood to reason the man might have died in the night. Duran was neither old nor sickly, but stranger things had happened, and someone must check into the matter at some point.

Finnegan took the knob in his hand. He would prefer to not see the corpse of a man he had watched grow up, but someone must check on the fellow. He turned the knob and let the door swing open. On the other side, Finnegan saw nothing other than an empty room, an empty bed, and a small empty table. All of Duran's things were gone, along with the Major himself.

Leaving the room, Finnegan made his way down to the boarding house kitchen. He found Mrs. Culbertson there, sitting on a stool and reading a periodical. There were a few cans of Mr. Dyer's stock lying about on the table and counter, but she did not appear to have much interest in preparing them for the midday meal. The gunman cleared his throat to get her attention. "Mrs. Culbertson, might I have a word with you?"

The landlady sighed and closed her tattered magazine. "What is it, Mr. Gilhooley?"

"I am in search of Major Duran. Have you seen him?"

"I have not. Did you see if he is in the parlor?"

"He is not."

"Did you knock on his door?"

"I also took the liberty of opening his door and discovered that his belongings have been removed. I take it he did not declare to you that he would no longer require lodgings?"

"You opened his door!" The landlady turned a whiter shade of pale and wore a truly astounded look. "Mr. Gilhooley, how could you? Such behavior is beyond all propriety."

"I suppose my actions might violate some of the norms in place for a polite society." Finnegan raised one eyebrow.

"Madam, might I also assume that Major Duran neglected to pay you for this past week's lodgings?"

The lady's visage turned from deeply offended to obviously angry in an instant. "Well, no, as you mention it, he did not." She glanced furtively toward the rented rooms. "His belonging are truly gone?"

"Yes, madam. I find it quite odd that the young man has left without saying a word to anyone. Even if he discovered the trains were in full operation, I would have thought Townsend would at least take the time to bid me farewell. I have known the lad many years."

Culbertson grew hopeful. "Ah, so then you will be covering his due expenses."

Finnegan gave her a cold stare. "I did not stipulate to that, madam. He tipped his hat to her. "Good day." He left the kitchen and was walking past the parlor when he spied James in repose in one of the chairs. He still had his nose in the more or less recent newspaper he had obtained. "Alexander, have you seen Major Duran about anywhere this day?"

James shook his head. "I have not. Thinking on it, I cannot say as I saw much of him yesterday, either. You did not locate him at Dyer's store?"

"Nor at the café. His room is empty. His things are gone. Did you hear or see him departing last evening?"

"I cannot say as I did." James folded his paper. "It is odd, don't you think, that the young man would leave without so much as a by your leave? I thought he and I got on rather well."

Finnegan rubbed his eyes. "Yes, the fact that the fellow has disappeared without first bidding you adieu is by far the most puzzling aspect of all this." The gunman motioned to the other rooms above. "Have you seen anything of that Heth chap? I have not seen hide nor hair of him, and Dyer was joking that he might be inclined to run off without first paying his bills."

"I have not noticed Mr. Heth about. Although, the man is hardly regular in his habits. Perhaps the fellow has crawled off on another lark with a bottle and a few Indians. Despite his protestations, he seemed rather fond of the company offered by that last bunch."

"Ah, bloody hell." Finnegan cupped his forehead. "Do you imagine it is possible that bloated sod Heth managed to convince poor Townsend into joining him for a spree?"

James gave the gunman a quizzical look. "I would say there is some small chance your friend Duran is off deep in his cups with that vagabond Heth, but if Duran agreed to such behavior I doubt the blame can fully lie with Heth. Perhaps you have difficulty noticing that the boy you knew has grown considerably. Grown into an Army Major, no less."

"Ah, posh. That sort of thing does not necessarily imbue a man with good sense. Townsend has always been susceptible to the suggestions of Heth's type. A bad seed such as that can have a very poor effect on a fellow. Especially when boredom is at play."

James laughed. "Yes, well, I may not be able to fully enjoy my nap worrying over them. You speak of Duran as though he could not keep his own council."

"Well, he was so very easily taken in by that school chum years ago."

"He was only a boy, Finnegan."

"Hardly. I had already killed several men by the time I was of that age."

Now it was time for James to groan. "Good grief, man. Is there no other means by which you measure any milestone?

You do apprehend there is more to life than murdering your fellow man?"

"I occasionally find mirth in maiming a fellow and a good cup of coffee soothes the soul. Will you accompany me to search for Duran and Heth, or will you be spending another day of your oh-so-precious time stewing in this parlor flipping through newspapers?"

"By God, the choices for diversion in this place are less than satisfactory." He rubbed his by-then bearded face. "Very well, I will accompany you. Know that I go under protest and am only grudgingly joining you so that I may witness the dressing down of a drunken Army Major by a man who surely never climbed above Private."

Finnegan stared at the outlaw for a long moment. "How can any of you damn rebels possibly dither about rank? Your regular army was a fabrication made from whole cloth, and I find it difficult to believe the officers guiding you Missouri bushwhackers from massacre to massacre attended a proper military academy."

James raised up out of his parlor chair and ambled toward the front hall of the boarding house where he kept his hat and various coats. "Well, you certainly are high and mighty for a man who comes from a race of rebels. I had no idea you put so much stock in the petty permissions meted out by the aristocracy. Soon enough, you will be telling me the only true officers in an army are those that hold the queen's commission."

Finnegan squeezed the bridge of his nose. "This promises to be an arduous journey. Perhaps I was wrong to ask for company."

The gunman and the outlaw had followed the barely visible set of tracks that led away from the north end of Greenfield. They had no way of knowing who had created the track or what their intentions had been. The trail might have been the product of Dyer's horse thieves. It may have been left by Duran and Heth. There was nothing else to pursue, so the men followed the tracks. After the first few miles, the trail disappeared, covered in the fresh snow, so the men were forced to simply continue in the basic direction the trail had pointed.

Finnegan brought his horse to a stop. Peering through the descending flakes, he stood in the stirrups. "I thought I saw something moving ahead."

James came up next to him. "I do not know how you might spy anything in this. We will only know we have reached California when we tumble into the ocean."

Finnegan knocked the snow from the small brim of his fur hat. "It is not as bad as all that. I believe we are in the vicinity of the Wilson Ranch."

"That Indian has a ranch to go along with his village? He is quite well to do for a messiah. Although, I can think of no reason a vow of poverty would be required to converse with the Almighty."

"Ah, damn the luck." Finnegan reached down and began removing the leather tong that held his shotgun in the scabbard. "There is someone approaching."

James peered forward, but made no move to gain a weapon. The traveler was far too close before they could make him out. Just as Finnegan had the shotgun clear of the leather, the visitor raised a hand. "Hello, Finnegan. Hello, Mr. James. I am glad to see you have become so fond of one another. I always tell the people who come to speak with me that if we all work hard, we will all get along and be happy."

Finnegan sighed and began replacing his shotgun. "Hello, Jack."

James looked over the new arrival, who rode a fine black stallion and led a bay. The animal had only a bridle and a blanket thrown over its back. "Well, Mr. Wilson. That is a fine mount you have there."

"Both were a gift from the Lakota."

The outlaw grinned. "And did you give a gift in return?"

"Of course. I gave them instruction so that they might dance and see those separated by death."

"A very fair trade for something as commonplace as a horse." Finnegan shook his head. "Jack, we are in search of some men who have absconded with some of Mr. Dyer's horses. We are also in search of Major Duran and that chubby rascal Heth. Have you seen them?"

He nodded and pulled his furs tighter. "Yes, I have seen them."

James let out a chuckle. "The horse thieves or Duran, Mr. Wilson?"

"Both. All of them. Mr. Heth, as well." Wilson smiled.

"Ah, marvelous." Finnegan glanced between James and Wilson, appearing quite satisfied. "We should be able to mark off a few small accomplishments for the day, then. In what direction was Major Duran headed when last you saw him, Jack? We ought to collect him first so that he might assist us in subduing our thieves."

"Major Duran was not headed anywhere, Finnegan." Wilson reached down and gave his horse a pat on the flank. "He was standing about in close palaver with Mr. Heth and the Utes that wish to possess my booha."

James cleared his throat. "Mr. Wilson, are you saying that you saw Major Duran in some sort of cahoots with them Indians I was shooting at the other day?"

"Yes, sir. As clear as I see you right now."

Finnegan rubbed his somewhat bearded face. He had ceased shaving upon the discovery that a bit of fur greatly assisted in keeping out the cold. "They were simply chatting? That is a damn puzzlement." He looked to James. "We had best look into this matter." He turned back to Wilson. "Where did you see them, Jack?"

"They are below the yellow cliff at the great bend in the river. They are camped there."

"Camped?" James could not hide his surprise. "What the hell are Duran and Heth doing camped with a bunch of horse thief Indians?"

"They are speaking of my booha." Wilson offered the explanation as if it were a perfectly natural topic for renegade Indians and an Army Major to discuss.

Finnegan sighed. "Never mind about that, Jack. How far is it to this cliff? Is it difficult to locate?"

"It is quite a good distance from here, Finnegan. We will not reach it until the sun is low." Wilson patted the horse again.

James appeared confused. "Mr. Wilson, if this place is so damn far from here, how the hell did you manage to get over there and back to talk with us so early? Sun has only been up an hour or so. You been running around in the dark or something?"

Finnegan sighed again and rubbed his tired eyes. "Jack, did you see Major Duran in a vision, or...please simply tell me whether or not you saw the Major in a damn vision?"

Wilson cocked his head to one side and spoke as though Finnegan were an exceptionally dull-witted child. "My friend, you continue to ask me questions with answers that are not of consequence. Whether I saw the boy you taught in a vision or as a man, flesh and blood, we are going to the yellow cliff by the great bend. We will travel by way of the ranch and then continue on to reach the cliffs at sunset. I have seen it. It will come to pass."

Finnegan groaned. "You are correct in imagining we are to visit the Wilson family ranch."

"You are damn well correct in that assumption." James sounded more than a bit perturbed. "I certainly have no intention of riding ten or twelve miles in this insufferable blizzard for no other purpose than certifying one of your damned hallucinations. You are a very affable man, Mr. Wilson, but I must draw the line somewhere and I believe this to be a reasonable point. Admittedly, it would be intriguing to know if Major Duran is truly in league with horse thieves, but I am surely not curious enough to not consider waiting back at Greenfield so that I might ask him about the matter upon his return."

"I could not agree more." Finnegan gave his horse a small kick to get it moving. "We will take our midday meal with the Wilsons, check in on Molly, and be on our way. My apologies, Alexander. In hindsight, it was rather silly to go traipsing about in search of horse thieves in this weather. Wherever Major Duran has gotten off to...well, he is a grown man and quite capable of seeing to his own business."

"Wonderful to hear you have come to your senses." James got his horse moving and the two men passed Wilson, who turned his horse to follow.

"It would be very good if Mrs. Wilson has a pie around. I would very much enjoy some pie before we move on to the yellow cliffs."

Finnegan craned his neck to speak over one shoulder. "We are not traveling to any bloody cliff."

Wilson hung his head a bit. "I feel sadness that there must always be blood where you travel, Finnegan."

"That is not the meaning of that particular phrase, Jack," James laughed. "Although, now that I ponder on the matter, your way of taking it is rather more fitting."

THE THREE MEN were still a quarter mile from the ranch house when one of the older Wilson boys appeared from out of the front door and began running toward them through the knee-deep snow. Instinctually, Finnegan urged his horse on quicker while his two companions matched his pace. By the time they met the boy, he was out of breath and frost already shown on his hair where it peeked out from his cap.

"Mr. Gilhooley..." The boy grabbed at one stirrup. "My ma said it was you. I hurried much as I could to make sure you didn't pass us by."

"We travel to your home, boy. We had no intention of passing. What has you so agitated?" Finnegan stared down at the clearly frightened child.

"Father says we can walk into Greenfield, but he might just be claiming that to keep mother from being scared. I ain't so sure I could make it, though." The boy wiped his nose. "That's why I come a running when I saw you folks. I got to make sure we don't get left out here. One of the girls could get sick and then what kind of pickle would we be in?"

Finnegan leaned over to better hear the boy. "What are you on about, child? Why would you have need to walk into Greenfield? You possess several horses."

"Not no more we don't, mister. They all been taken, along with Miss Meagher." The boy snapped his mouth shut and widened his eyes. "I most likely should have told you about Miss Meagher before whining about the horses, eh, mister?"

"Young man, are you attempting to tell me that someone has come to this ranch and departed with Miss Meagher?" Finnegan glanced to James and Wilson, smiling. "That is absurd, child. Who would possibly do such a thing in this ghastly weather, no less?"

"They was injuns, sir."

James let out a laugh and grinned at Wilson. "Well, now, you do not hear that much anymore, do you Jack? I would have thought red men making off with white women was a thing of the past." The outlaw shook his head. "Boy, you just said, your own self, that your Ma and sisters are still here. I can't say as I have heard of too many raiding parties that only take one woman out of several available. Renegade Indians ain't the kind to only borrow their share."

The boy straightened up and glared at James. Apparently, he did not enjoy being joshed in the cold and snow. "All them injuns wanted was Miss Meagher and the horses. The white men with them said not to touch nothing else and held them right to it. The one even leveled his pistol on them and told them right out. I saw him do it myself."

Wilson came up beside Finnegan and leaned down to give the reins of the horse he led to the boy. "I brought you this horse, Edgar. You need not worry over getting to town if you must. Take her and put her in the stable. She is saddle broke and sweet enough."

The boy snatched up the reins and grinned at the shaman. "Oh, thanks much, Wavoka." He began tugging the animal forward. "Damn nice of you. Sure more help than telling me I don't know what I saw with my own damn eyes."

Finnegan knocked the snow from his arms and the mane of his horse. "We best get to the house and learn what has transpired here." He got his horse moving. "Likely Miss Meagher has gone off to visit your village, Jack, and the boy's father is off on some errand with the horses. Young men are often given to flights of fancy." Jack remained silent as they rode toward the ranch house. When they came to the door, the shaman made no move to dismount his horse. Finnegan swung down out of the saddle. "You do not wish to come inside and take your leisure, Jack?"

Wilson shook his head and produced a small bit of jerky. "We will be leaving presently, Finnegan. I will wait here."

The gunman stepped up on the porch and shook the snow from his hat and stamped his boots. "Very well. When you are cold, come inside." He knocked on the door and let himself in when he heard someone inside yell out for him to enter. Before he had a chance to get his coat off in the hall, the eldest Mr. Wilson came in from the parlor, looking haggard. "Good day, sir." Finnegan smiled at the man. "Your son has told me quite a fantastic tale."

"If it sounds like the act of madmen, then you ought to have been here to see it." Wilson spit out the words with genuine anger. "May hell be my heaven, Finnegan, I would have tried to stop them if only I had known. Molly...hell, she invited them two in here and then them Utes was all over the place and they all had their guns out before any one of us could even note what the hell was going on. My rifle was in the house and it ain't like I could fisticuff the whole bunch -- or even one, at my age."

"Mr. Wilson..." Finnegan took a long moment to assess whether or not the man was jesting. "Are you telling me that someone has actually...made off with Molly?"

"Somebody, hell. It was that damn eastern Major. That Duran fella and that fat scoundrel Heth came in here like we'd invited them over for a picnic before taking out their pistols and grabbing your lady. They lit out of here to the north with all my horses to make certain I wouldn't follow or try nothing. They got six Utes with them and Molly and..." Wilson hung his head. "I swear to God Almighty, Finnegan, if there was anything I could have done...with my wife and children...I just couldn't raise too much fuss for fear of them doing something to the little ones."

Finnegan held up one hand to stop the man. "Mr. Wilson, you were fallen upon by superior numbers. You did what was best to keep your family from harm." He wiped the snowmelt from his face. "You are certain it was Major Duran who took Molly?"

"As I live and breathe."

Finnegan shook his head, hoping it would make matters clearer, but it did not. "But why would Duran do such a thing?"

"He did not pause to properly explain himself, Finnegan."

"You are certain this is not simply a misunderstanding? Could it be that Molly has departed with Townsend of her own volition on some errand related to the Indians?"

"Finnegan, I know that, being one of them Pinkerton detectives your whole life, you probably seen some damned strange occurrences, but I can't rightly understand how a fella can have all his horses and the schoolteacher stolen at gunpoint and come to a conclusion other than that a fella's been robbed. From what Molly said, you and that Major Duran have known each other a long time, but that don't cut no slack with me. I see that bastard again, I'll be shooting him down and not bothering to give notice."

"I simply cannot fathom why Townsend would perpetrate an act such as this."

"That tub of guts Heth gave me a good indication before lighting out of here with all my stock. He told me that I was to send you and Jack to the yellow cliffs by the big bend and the Utes would trade the schoolteacher for Jack's..." The rancher rubbed one side of his face. "I can't never recall what he calls it."

Finnegan hung his head. "I believe the word you search for is booha."

"That would be it." He shook his head. "If it is any comfort, I don't believe Duran or Heth would let anything untoward occur with Molly. They kept a close eye on her and surely were riding herd on them Utes."

Finnegan set his hat back on his head. "They only requested myself and Jack? Ransom or some such payment was not mentioned?"

"Lousy scum already made off with just about every decent animal in the territory. I don't know what else there'd be to ransom off anyone around here anymore, anyhow."

Finnegan sighed. "How far is it to these cliffs?"

"Round about ten miles." Duran tossed his hands in the air. "In this weather, if you push hard, you'll likely make it around sundown."

"Yes, well, that seems to be the consensus." Finnegan turned to see the door open and James come inside.

The outlaw stamped his feet and shrugged off the snow he had missed on the porch. "Good Lord, Finnegan, what's keeping you in here? Are we going or staying? I would prefer to not freeze to death malingering with that Indian."

Finnegan closed his eyes for a moment. "We will be on our way shortly, Alexander. The young man's assessment of the situation appears to be more factual than we credited." The gunman motioned toward the stables outside. "Jack had the forethought to bring you a mount, sir."

The rancher nodded and smiled. "Bully. In that case, I'll be coming with you boys."

Finnegan shook his head. "Use the animal if you have

need of it. Living far off as you do, you people should not be without a horse. We will collect the beast on our return. With luck, we will be in possession of your stock by then, as well."

Wilson grew serious. "You gonna shoot them Indians and Duran and Heth?"

"I will shoot no man who does not by his own actions make it necessary." Finnegan buttoned up his coat. "This is a damn unfortunate errand I find myself faced with. Good day, Mr. Wilson." He trudged to the front door and motioned for James to exit once again.

When they were outside, James began tugging his gloves back on. He leaned toward Finnegan. "So, then, your associate has, in fact, abducted your fiancé?" Finnegan nodded. "Yes, well, a yellow haired gal stolen by a villain employing renegade Indians..." He chuckled. "This is all a might bit like one of them books your old boss wrote."

"Thankfully you are familiar with the subject matter. Let us be on our way. There is no joy in this next endeavor for me."

James finished putting his various overcoats back together. "Do you have any notion at all as to why Duran would do a thing like this? He appeared affable enough."

Finnegan simply shook his head and mounted his horse.

WITH JACK WILSON leading the way, the three men began the slow business of traveling toward the yellow cliffs in the big bend of the river that so many had made reference to. As the journey dragged on, Finnegan eventually felt the need to speak up as to James's previous question.

The gunman cleared his throat and glanced over at the outlaw who rode beside him. "Now that I ponder on the matter some, Duran may have somewhat of a motive for his behavior."

James laughed, letting out a plume of breath in the cold air. "He may have reason to go completely mad and steal your woman? I would be damned curious as to how a man can be friendly to you one day and commit a low deed such as kidnapping the next. Even at the height of our... well, I suppose you could call it revelry after the war, no one in our outfit ever made off with a woman for ransom. Hell, I don't even recall the idea being broached. This sort of business is beneath even bank robbers."

"Yes, I would agree that Major Duran has committed a despicable act. He may feel he is somewhat entitled to lash out at me and this is the less-than-honorable method he has chosen."

"Why in Hell's bells would Duran think he's got a right to do something like this to you or Miss Meagher?"

Finnegan rubbed one side of his beard. "I would assume that some person, for reasons that are obscure to me, has put Major Duran under the impression that I shot his father."

James shrugged. "Given your predilections, I suppose you could be accused of shooting just about anyone. Even so, that is no reason for the young man to credit such a tale." The outlaw looked over at the Pinkerton. Finnegan was a bit too stone-faced for his liking. "Is there a reason the young man might credit such a tale?"

Finnegan licked his lips. "Alexander, having devoted your life to idle acts of self-indulgence and base behavior, you can hardly conceive that some men must see to their duty, regardless of what distasteful consequences may result."

"Pardon me, Irishman, I do believe I have spent a far greater time in the service of a genuine cause than you ever did, and..." James only stared and blinked for a moment. "Are you telling me that you did, in fact, kill that young man's father?"

Finnegan shrugged. "The blackguard was beyond redemption. He was in the employ of the Confederates, accepting money for information regarding troop movements. When we finally put an end to his dastardly behavior, he was laboring at slipping Rose Greenhow through the blockade so that she might resume her machinations." Finnegan shrugged again. "The more senior agent I accompanied gave the man every opportunity to turn himself over to the auspices of the law. The fool would have none of it."

James rode on, stunned, for the better part of a hundred yards. "Finnegan, I do not find it surprising to hear you shot a man by order of your mad employer, likely based on nothing more than one of the fellow's many fantastic theories; what I find difficult to fathom is why you would in any way associate with the orphaned son of the deceased. Even a man as dull as you must have known it could only lead to trouble." The outlaw scowled. "I would not go so far as to say that the Major is justified in this cowardly act he had perpetrated in regard to Miss Meagher, but he surely would have been justified in taking action against you."

Finnegan shook his head. "There is something deeply amiss in the way you southern men are educated. You constantly revive these ridiculous notions centered on such ribaldry as justification. As though a man were given some endless stream of choices and allowed to select that which is most to his liking. You certainly never presided over a manor house where such foolishness is possible -- why do you suggest that it should be?"

"Chatter on all you like, Finnegan. It is you who have been ridiculous in this instance." James chuckled, unbelievingly. "I can conceive of how your sanctimonious old employer might have felt guilt in the widow and orphan his idiocy left behind. I can readily understand why he felt the need to soothe his blackened soul by gifting the boy protection and schooling. What mystifies is what his motive could have possibly been for assigning you to the task. I have lived a long and strange life, Finnegan. Still, I have never been forced to associate with the sons or daughters of those I have shuffled off. I do not believe I would be capable of the hardness of heart required."

The gunman rubbed his eyes. "What are you blathering on about, Alexander?"

"You took the boy's father from him, then sat down to dinner as though nothing had passed between you."

Finnegan sighed. "I took the boy's father because the man was a sodden, whoremongering spy who refused a lesser fate. I was only a boy myself when I shot the fellow, and he left me with no other alternative. The elder agent with me had already been wounded when the drunken ape opened fire on us, and..." He glanced over to James. "There, now, that is the trouble with you Confederates. We talk for a few minutes, and I am already drawn into the ill behavior of justification." He gave the outlaw a confused stare. "And what in blue blazes are you alluding to when you suggest I took the boy's father from him? It is not as if the imp were left destitute in the streets begging for change or selling newspapers. When they applied the shovel to the elder Duran's grave, the boy became heir to an estimable estate and had nary a care in the world."

"That is hardly the point, Finnegan."

"Then what might be the point, Alexander?" Finnegan sighed again. "During the brief time I knew the man, Townsend's father did not appear the type to read the child a bedtime story and tuck him in. Like most fellows of that class, the man would have likely seldom seen the boy. I will grant you, Townsend's mother did apparently feel some affection for the sot, but she is hardly the first woman to mourn a man she was better off rid of." Finnegan dug around in his coat in search of a cigar. "I would never claim to be without sin, Alexander. What man can? Even the prophet who leads us on today might admit to a fair bit of it. My actions over the years have not been perfect. That admitted, I fail to see the great sin I committed in regard to Townsend Duran. I have done worse to better men and been no less than lauded for it."

"I would surmise most of the angst young Major Duran feels toward you is the result of you omitting the fact that you shot his father. An omission you had ample time and opportunity to correct." James let out a small laugh. "Obviously, the young fellow feels you attempted to conceal your role in the man's assassination."

"I neither concealed nor omitted anything." Finnegan began to search for a match. "It is damned odd to receive a lecture on forthrightness from Frank James." He shook his head. "Might you inform me as to what good it might have done to give the young fellow all the scandalous details of his father's demise? Your father was no less than a preacher, as I recall?"

James nodded. "For a time."

"He was well thought of by friends and neighbors?"

"Yes, well enough."

"And you would prefer to go on considering him a good man who lived a good life." Finnegan sparked his cigar. "You would surely prefer your current conception of the man to hearing that he was a lair, a philanderer, and traitor to his country." He tossed the match down into the snow. "Townsend's father, thanks to the story Mr. Pinkerton concocted, received full honors and a funeral complete with some boots backwards in the stirrups, or whatever the silly notion is with soldiers." He pulled the cigar from his mouth and motioned to James with it. "I buried my own father where he fell with far less pomp and circumstance, I assure you. No, I fail to see what great wrong has been done to the boy."

James let out a groan and wrenched his reins to keep his horse on the trail. "Yes, well, let us forgo examining that particular ground for a moment. I still do not understand why your idiot employer felt the need to remain connected to the boy. As you said, he was left well off and had no need of a nursemaid. Fatherless or not, the child was hardly in need of Pinkerton agents for playmates."

Finnegan puffed his cigar. "I suppose Mr. Pinkerton took an interest in the boy for the same reason he took me on, or any of a handful of other young fellows. When Allen Pinkerton gazed out on the world, he found much evil, many conspiracies, plots, schemes, robbers, and charlatans. Perhaps offering what kindness he could to men such as Townsend and I was simply his attempt at improving his view."

"It seems an ill-conceived notion for a man so given to his own plotting. Old Pinkerton had to imagine that someday the boy would learn what had transpired with his father." James let a shiver run through him.

Finnegan sounded almost offended. "There was no credible reason to expect Townsend would ever become privy to the details of his father's demise. How could he? The only men who knew the specifics of what had come to pass were myself, an older agent by the name of Sampson Stolypin, and, necessarily, Mr. Pinkerton. Mr. Pinkerton was given to keeping secrets. He might have placed the information somewhere in the bowels of his files, but, considering the size and scope of that collection, I can hardly imagine how Townsend might have come across the information. Even a diligent search with purpose would likely prove fruitless."

James motioned toward Finnegan's coat. "If you can locate one, I would appreciate a cigar. Mine are buried somewhere in the depths of these damn saddlebags." The outlaw nodded thanks as Finnegan passed him the smoke. "Yes, well, I think it is safe to assume that Major Duran did not gain knowledge of his father's demise from the spirit realm, as Mr. Wilson does. That leaves only a few possibilities. It might be that your employer informed the boy before he passed, although he hardly seemed the type for last hour confessions. The agent you were paired with could have felt the need to unburden himself. Although, given the character of you Pinkerton men, I find that unlikely, as well. Last..." James grinned over at the gunman. "And this theory I find most poetic: the young Major may have been informed of your past actions by the offspring of your very own mentor."

Finnegan slowly swiveled his head over to James. "You would suggest I have been betrayed by the remaining Pinkertons?"

James smiled. "Given their lineage, I would say they are no less than born and bred for such a stratagem. Those two heirs, not unlike twin Mephistopheles to Lucifer, would have complete access to any paper the old man left. Pinkerton the elder would have surely left a written record so that he might brag in one of his books someday, if the tide flowed toward making such an act appear heroic."

Finnegan licked his lips. "Alexander, truly, what possible reason would either of the Pinkerton sons have for betraying me? Lay aside the fact that I was practically raised by their side by their very own father, what good can it do them to make known the more distasteful details of former assignments?"

"Such disclosures are only harmful if they are made generally known, Finnegan. Is it really so difficult to believe that one of those loathsome derivatives was pawing through his father's things and discovered a tidbit relating to the assassination of a colonel? Such an item would naturally be laid away for future use, and what better use than to rid themselves of a nagging stain from a previous era that refuses to disappear."

"Did you truly just refer to me as a nagging stain?"

"You do not keep yourself well-enough informed, Finnegan. The agency you labored so long for has assumed a quite different visage in recent times. The days of you riffraff chasing train robbers and the like has gone by the wayside. The new Pinkerton Agency is primarily in the business of supplying thugs to beat honest workingmen into submission. The politicians of this country have declared such things a necessary evil and are proud to have an agency with so spotless a reputation as the Pinkerton firm to draw on." James lit his cigar and tossed the match aside. "Now, then, given the large sums your dear William and Robert Pinkerton intend to receive for providing this service, I suppose even a dullard such as yourself might be able to understand why it simply won't do to have an assassin wandering about. You, Finnegan, are a lingering symbol of the company's wild youth and you need to be done away with."

"You always were given to flights of fancy, Alexander." Finnegan shook his head and knocked ash down into the snow. "Duran's knowledge could be nothing more than the product of the other agent indulging in liquor and bragging in some Boston saloon. The elder Duran was a well-known personage in the east. Idle gossip flows quickly. While it would surely please you to possesses solid proof that Pinkertons turn on their own, I doubt you will receive your good news this day."

"Time will tell, Finnegan."

A SMALL GAP in the rocks allowed Finnegan to view the enemy camp with his binoculars. Below, he could see a scattering of the Utes wandering about and a few U.S. Cavalry-issue tents that either Duran or Heth had purloined at some point. Several small fires burned and someone in the group had set to cooking the evening meal over an iron spit. The horses were picketed under a copse of trees. By all appearances, the marauders were settled in to pass the night.

Finnegan passed his binoculars over to James. "They do not seem to be overly wary of reprisals."

The outlaw fussed with the small brass focal knob and had a look. "For men fleeing justice, they do look rather prosaic." He pulled his eyes back and assessed the binoculars. These are a quite fine optical instrument, somewhat finer than I would have given a man of your means credit for."

Finnegan nodded and placed the glasses back in their carrying case. "They were a gift from a client of the agency. I watched over the fellow while he collected specimens during a wilderness outing. When the trip ended, he was kind enough to gift me both these glasses and the rifle I carry."

James rubbed his face. "I know of a New Orleans prostitute who amassed a considerable fortune in much the same way. The baubles she was given as additional gratuity added up impressively over the years."

"We whores learn to save our pennies." Finnegan grinned. "It is a trick you bank robbers should have picked up. If you had been less of a spendthrift, you would not be penning drivel to make ends meet today."

"Always said there was much to learn from whores." James moved back from the rocks. "Best we return to the horses and include Jack in our plotting. He has as much interest in this as any man among us."

"Agreed."

Finnegan and James rejoined Wilson at the horses and Finnegan lit a cigar after testing the wind to make certain it was headed away from the camp. He groaned and rubbed his chin. "I am somewhat ambivalent as to how to proceed. I am tempted to wait until both Townsend and Mr. Heth present themselves. After they are dead, I should think we would need to only knock over a few of those Utes before they depart in a panic. Their kind is given to bolting when things do not go as planned."

James rubbed his eyes. "Finnegan, have you ever attempted to solve a problem you are faced with in a manner other than committing murder?"

The gunman puffed his cigar and arched an eyebrow. "Alexander, in my time I have offered much mercy." He held up one hand to cut off the coming rebuke. "You may find it difficult to credit, but it is true. There are many men still drawing breath only due to my clemency. I have even been known to go so far as to allow men to live when they have stolen horses or purloined women." He slowly removed the cigar from his lips. "I am not without pity for those who deserve it, but I believe, in this instance, dear Townsend has more than earned what I intend to proffer him. The leader of those miscreants on the other side of that ridge not only injures me, but insults me. Never in all my born days have I met a man with the gall, the outright audacity, to offer a personal affront to me in the manner that bastard Duran blithely has. Townsend bloody well knows what my response to this sort of activity is bound to be, and yet he persists." Finnegan shook his head disdainfully. "No, I swear by all that is holy, Alexander: that man will be shot down before this day is over."

James gave the gunman a critical look. "You would truly shoot down the boy you helped to raise?"

"Once upon a time I retrieved the idiot from a fetid swamp he had scampered off to in an attempt to discover pirate treasure. That one action, for which I was paid, mind you, hardly places me in the position of being the fool's godfather. I have as much right to kill the bastard as any other man."

"Perhaps more." James gestured with one hand to calm the gunman. "I would not claim otherwise. The fellow has made off with your woman in an unabashed attempt to draw your ire. It is quite natural of you to want vengeance. I would only make mention of the fact that so far, there has been no violence. No one has been shot. The Wilson family was only relieved of their stock, and we have no reason to believe Miss Meagher has suffered any more than inconvenience." He offered a smile. "You truly cannot see that it would be a bit absurd if we were the party to open fire?"

"For a man who spent the better part of his life avoiding constables and sheriffs, you are strangely concerned with the nuances of the law, Alexander." Finnegan sneered. "What, pray tell, would you suggest as a plan of action?"

"I would suggest we follow the course of action that Duran has requested. Let us enter the camp. Jack can exchange...his conjuring abilities or what have you, and we will retrieve Miss Meagher. At some juncture, both Duran and Heth simply must come to understand that this is an absurdity. Who can say? They may have already sobered up and realized the desperate mistake they have made." Wilson shrugged as if in agreement. James chuckled and shook his head. "I have been given to my fair share of lunacy, but I have yet to willfully abscond with the fiancée of the most renowned assassin extant. Could you even offer an estimate as to how many men you have killed?"

Finnegan sighed. "It is likely the total will include at least a few more very soon. Might we please..."

"Hey, you there!" The voice came down from the rocks above.

Finnegan tossed down his cigar and turned to the boulders. "Mr. Heth, is that you?"

"I been coming over here every hour on the orders of your friend the Major." The rocks and falling snow obscured the man from vision. "I come to give you our terms. May I approach?"

Finnegan glanced to James and Wilson. Both men seemed willing to leave the decision to him. "Very well, come down and offer your terms. I have no more interest in lingering in this damn snow than you do." All watched as Heth slowly descended from among the piled boulders. When he made it to the bottom, steam was rising off the man's ample body. Finnegan stared up into the rocks. "You come alone?"

The chubby fellow moved his weight nervously from one foot to the other. "Them Indians figure you'd be less likely to shoot a white man, and Duran...well..." He tried chuckling, but it only made him sound more frightened. "I ain't too certain that man is quite right in the head no more, boys. He brought all this up whilst I was damn deep in my cups and, what with me owing that damn dry goods man for the one horse, I sorta figured in for a penny, in for a pound, eh?" He looked from Finnegan to James and back again, but they only stared in wonderment. "But, that Duran, he has a powerful hatred for you, Mr. Gilhooley. Claims you killed his father. Claims you're the devil incarnate. Claims you got all this and more coming to you..."

"Mr. Heth..." Finnegan cut the man off with one stern finger pointed. "You, sir, have participated in the theft of horses and my betrothed. If I were you, I would not elongate this particular conversation. Every moment we stand here I am more apt to dangle you from that tree or make use of you for target practice. Out with the terms, damn you."

Heth swallowed and his jowls bounced. "Uh, yes, sir. Um, I'm to take you and that Indian over there..." He motioned to Wilson. "Over on the trail and more or less swap you two for the schoolteacher."

Finnegan appeared nonplussed. "Swap us?"

"You and the Indian for the woman. 'Course, I'm to make sure you ain't armed, and Wilson there is gonna have to give them Utes his..." Heth scratched the side of his head. "I don't rightly know just what the hell they want him to give over, but he's got to do it."

Finnegan licked his lips. "Mr. Heth, I am never certain if the behavior of men such as yourself is the result of simple intemperance, or if you are dull-witted from birth, but I must say it is vexing."

Heth sneered. "Hey, now, there ain't no reason to get uncouth. I come over here to deliver our terms in an honorable fashion. If you two ain't amenable to them terms, I will return to our camp with the message so's Duran can chew on it."

James slowly shook his head. "Mr. Heth, I must agree with my esteemed associate; it is hard to say how you came to be so obtuse. Are you honestly unaware of the trick Major Duran has visited upon you by sending you here to parlay?"

"I don't rightly see a trick at work here." The fat man rubbed his chilled face.

Finnegan turned up his collar. "Mr. Heth, in all likelihood Major Duran does not expect you to return from this minor errand. I would expect he waits as we speak to hear the shot that will end your miserable life." The gunman frowned. "It is a cruel sort of use he has made of you, sir. Mercifully, for you, the young officer has not been properly acquainted with the more realistic aspects of the type of poor behavior he is currently engaged in. I am not going to kill you, Mr. Heth."

The fat man cleared his throat. "I knowed you wouldn't, what with you being a gentleman and all."

Finnegan shook his head. "I am no gentleman, sir, and damn you for suggesting such a thing. No, the only reason you will continue to draw breath for the moment is because you are a man of no small girth and I estimate the amount of blubber and meat that has been assembled to form you will stop no small number of bullets."

"Say what now?" Heth looked to James for an explanation.

"The gentleman intends to use you as a shield as he approaches the camp, Mr. Heth." James did his best to stifle a smile. It seemed needlessly harsh under the circumstances.

"Uh, well..." Heth stood up as tall as he could and puffed out his chest. "I will not be a part of such a cowardly action, sirs. Do what you may, I will not collaborate."

Without the chubby messenger noticing his hand had moved, Finnegan brought his Remington up and placed the muzzle under Heth's ample chin. "If you do not find yourself amenable to being cooperative, then I see no reason to suffer your presence any longer. Perhaps you were meant to stay here in the snow forever more, Mr. Heth. I suppose a man is, at least, entitled to choose the place he is to die."

Heth angled his eyes down to view the revolver. "Upon further consideration, I mean since I intended to amble on back to camp anyhow, I might as well walk over with you fellas. I guess it don't much matter which of us goes first or which goes second."

James chuckled. "You might be brighter than I gave you credit for, Mr. Heth."

Wilson walked to Heth and set one hand on the chubby fellow's shoulder. "Do not despair, Mr. Heth. This world is full of disappointment and temptation. There is none of that in the next world."

Heth spit out a long stream of brown tobacco juice. "Now just what in the hell is that supposed to mean?"

Finnegan groaned. "Do not fret over it, Mr. Heth. Jack is overly fond of dispensing prophecy at inopportune moments." The gunman shook his head. "Jack, I would suggest you wait here or possibly on the lower side of that small escarpment there. We will undoubtedly require your assistance driving the stolen stock back to Greenfield, but until we are firmly in possession of all we have come here for, you may wish to remain out of sight and out of the line of fire."

Wilson let out a small laugh and stared at Finnegan. "Mr. Gilhooley, I will go with you into the camp. I am in no danger from those men. They cannot shoot me. If I die, my booha dies with me. I have seen my death, and it is not today."

James let out a laugh in return. "Hey, Mr. Heth, are you and Major Duran aware of all that?"

"I don't know what in hell he's talking about, and I'm standing right here listening to him say it. I got no notion of why Duran would know any better."

James smiled at the prophet. "Could be you are not as safe as you assume, Jack."

"We all walk the path God has chosen for us." Wilson pointed to James. "You are quite safe, as well, sir. You will die in a place called Missouri."

James nodded. "That knowledge hardly makes you the second coming, Jack. Every fool that ever met me knows I intend to die in Missouri. That is where I have lived, and I do not intend to let the bastards drive me out."

"This is all very interesting, but hardly a proper use of our time." Finnegan motioned to one of the horses. "Jack, if you would be so kind, please get the thongs off that bedroll for me. Mr. Heth, I intend to make certain you are properly dressed before we return you to your business partner."

Molly held her hands out to warm them from the heat of the small, collapsible camp stove inside the tent. Bits of wood little better than kindling were all that could be placed in the firebox, but what heat the contraption did offer was well appreciated. The cold seemed considerably worse when one was not in motion.

Major Duran sat on the opposite side of the small tent. He had a foot tall pile of sticks one of the Utes had supplied him with. He wore a dismal look on his face as he fed more fuel into the stove. With his other hand, he pressed his temple. "I must admit, it is difficult to believe I have finally let matters develop to this point." His bleary eyes moved from the stove to Molly. "Since arriving in this place I have questioned whether or not I ever would."

Molly gave the officer a quizzical stare. "Major, I am more than a bit confused as to what purpose you believe you are approaching by your actions. When you first arrived at the Wilson Ranch, I rather jumped to the conclusion that you and the others were quite drunk and would come to your senses after some exposure to the cold and some time had passed. By now, the effects of whatever you imbibed must have diminished, but you still persist in this ridiculous folly. Have you all gone mad, or is there some aspect to all this I fail to appreciate?"

"Oh, there is much to this you could not appreciate." Duran placed another piece of wood in the stove and massaged his temples. "There is a devil in liquor that never fails to attack my head," he groaned. "I have been told my father suffered from the same difficulties. We are both prone to extreme overindulgence and are given to...poor judgement during a spree."

"I should certainly say so." Molly shook her head. "Of course, you realize that Finnegan will not be amused by your antics, and he is not a pleasant man when not amused."

Duran paused to assess the woman across from him. "It is intriguing to me to hear you make such a statement, ma'am. I have often wondered since arriving here, what sort of woman you might be to be the object of Finnegan Gilhooley's affection. I have often wondered what sort you must be to return the affection."

She sighed. "Major Duran, I do not think you are as well acquainted with Finnegan as you purport to be. He is as loyal and dependable as any man who walks the earth and is as fine a prospect for marriage as there might be." She chuckled. "Though, I would think you might be at least well enough acquainted with him to know the theft of his fiancée is a poor notion."

"Yes, yes, that aspect of it is what I would refer to, ma'am." Duran moved a bit closer to his side of the stove.

"What aspect of it, sir?"

"You are wholly aware of what sort of man he is. You

realize that he will likely arrive here soon to visit a terrible punishment upon me for abducting you from that ranch house. You are likely familiar with some of his other acts, and yet you have agreed to marry him. You are obviously quite well educated. You are hardly in need of support, as you seem more than capable of proving that for yourself. Why marry a man who is...well, who is nothing less than an infamous murderer and hired assassin? I cannot comprehend why a woman such as yourself would do such a thing."

Molly sighed again. "You are still quite young, Major. There is much you cannot understand. To begin -- the Finnegan Gilhooley conjured by tawdry journalism is not the man I am betrothed to. I intend to marry the real man, not the somewhat silly character of dime novels. Next -- to me, Finnegan Gilhooley is not an assassin or Pinkerton spy; he is my oldest and truest friend, who has more than proven his loyalty to me on several occasions." She laughed across the stove. "You would have me believe he is some sort of monster stalking the country's downtrodden, but I have yet to witness him kidnap a schoolteacher, which you are certainly guilty of. The notorious outlaw Frank James has shown me more courtesy than you, Major Duran. What do you have to say to that?"

"Gilhooley shot down my father in cold blood from ambush. He committed the act with no more regard than a man might show a deer or other animal that has stumbled into a shooting lane." Duran gave the schoolmarm a rather truculent look. "I doubt the man would even deny it if confronted."

Molly pursed her lips. Duran was not the first frightened man weaving a tale to his own preferences that she had encountered. "Major Duran, I would never claim to understand the various petty squabbles and vendettas you men appear to be constantly consumed by..."

"You would label my father's murder petty?"

"I would say absconding with a man's fiancée several decades after the fact is somewhat petty, yes." She crossed her arms. "Major, I do not believe you have given this tale you have so ardently embraced the scrutiny such a thing requires."

He shook his head. "It is none of your affair to know where or how I have gleaned the information, but I assure you, it comes by way of a very reliable source."

"Does it now?" She raised her eyebrows. "Let us examine matters as they stand, Major. You were but a small child when your father died, is that correct?"

"Yes."

"So then, you did not witness the act? All your information is, by necessity, secondhand in this matter?"

"By necessity, yes. I would rather do without this foolish questioning, Miss Meagher. I am not quite the fool you think me to be. I have given the matter great consideration and have not come to my conclusions lightly."

"Major..." She adopted the tone she used with particularly dull students, "you do not seem to have properly assessed the facts presented to you."

"Facts!" He let out a laugh. "Given the number of men your betrothed has killed, he would make a fine suspect for murder even if no known connection existed between him and my father."

Molly nodded. "I would not deny that Finnegan did, in all likelihood, kill your father. He has known little other than violence in his life. What I would take umbrage with is your assessment of his motives and your obvious obsession with placing all the blame for the act on his shoulders."

"The man who pulls the trigger is responsible for what the ball does, Miss Meagher. To claim otherwise is ridiculous."

"Is it truly? I assume your father died during the war?"

"He did."

"And you have been told that Finnegan shot him?"

"Yes, by a reliable source."

"You are aware, of course, that Finnegan was little more than a boy himself during the war between the states. He could not have been more than a day over fifteen when Lee signed at Appomattox."

"I am aware, yes."

"So, you have come to believe that a boy, likely not yet making use of his father's razor, conceived of a plan to assassinate a superior officer, then executed that plan solely of his own volition? What reason might have Finnegan had for this dastardly act, Major? Did your father offend him in some way?"

"Very well," Duran offered a snide smile. "I would cede to you the fact that Finnegan was likely not the progenitor of the plot. He was quite obviously assigned the task by his mentor, Allan Pinkerton." Duran shrugged. "That damnable fellow lies moldering in his grave. I can hardly take vengeance upon a dead man, so I have decided to take vengeance upon his hireling."

"A rather elegant solution, I suppose, but it does not really examine the heart of the issue, does it, Major?"

"The heart of the issue, ma'am?"

"You show a great deal of bluster and a claim a great wrong has been perpetrated, but you have not yet spoken to motive."

"Motive?"

"You have not once made mention of the reason a fellow

such as Mr. Pinkerton would take the time and resources to have your father assassinated. Were they in a whirl over a mistress? Did Pinkerton owe your father a great deal of money from cards?" She pouted to show she was being facetious.

Duran scowled. "The likely explanation is that General McClellan wished for my father's removal to further his ends within the army."

Molly let out a small giggle and placed her hand over her mouth. "My apologies, Major. On occasion, it is difficult for me to fathom some of the fairy tales you men are capable of putting faith in."

"Fairy tales?" The Major did not see the humor.

"It is quite fantastic, is it not? Tell me, Major, how many other officers did General McClellan have murdered during the war? Was this a common practice, or did only your father manage to raise his ire to the point where hired mercenaries were required?" She shook her head slowly. "The Pinkerton agency was tasked with ferreting out spies during the war, Major. When a country splits in twain, many loyalties split with it. You truly cannot imagine a more realistic motive for Allan Pinkerton's plot against your father?"

"Oh, how easy it is to besmirch a man when he is not present to defend himself," Duran sneered again.

"Is that not precisely what you have been doing to Finnegan? He is not present, and yet you accuse him of terrible deeds." She smiled. "Although, I cannot help but notice your bluster is only manifested when Finnegan is not present. When you find him close at hand, you do little but put on a façade of friendship. Tell me, Major Duran, if you are acting out of nothing more than a righteous defense of your family honor, why did you not simply challenge Finnegan to a duel when you first laid eyes on him? This subterfuge and chicanery is hardly the practice of a man wronged, seeking justice."

"I would not expect a woman to understand the strategies and tactics required to deal with a man such as Finnegan Gilhooley. Subterfuge and chicanery have served him very well over the years, I see no disgrace in making use of them to mete out what he richly deserves."

"You are quite correct that I know little of strategy and tactics, sir, but I know much regarding cowardice. I see it frequently in the great majority of men and can recognize it readily."

"Cowardice?" Duran spit out the word.

"I can only assume the man who attempted to ambush Finnegan while he was out hunting was in your employ. Who else would have cause to plot such a low act?"

Duran gritted his teeth. "I did not so much employ the fellow as encourage and equip him. It does not take much prodding to get any number of men to attempt the murder of your fiancé."

"Then the man who accosted Finnegan at his boarding house were also sent by you?"

"I merely informed them of Finnegan's location. The rest they took upon themselves. My only regret is the manner the various attempts all ended in." Duran licked his lips. "That man manifests luck as no other."

"Perhaps your luck would improve if you ceased making use of drunkards and fools. Sending men like that to Finnegan is little better than sending sheep to slaughter. Frankly, you ought to be ashamed of yourself."

"Well..." Duran sneered. "I am not certain if any man travels through this world without a bit of shame to bother him."

"I could surely name one, and I believe he rapidly approaches." Molly smiled at her kidnapper.

"I suppose the quality or quantity of heroism Finnegan chooses to exhibit is of little import, ma'am. I have dispatched Heth to inform old Finnegan of how things will be. I have that which he holds most dear. He will present himself here, unarmed, as a proper savior ought to, and I will dispose of him in the same uncivilized manner in which he disposed of my father."

"I would think the onset of sobriety would have revealed the incredible nature of that plan, Major." Molly frowned. "Belief in an obvious falsehood can often give a man courage, but I would not suggest placing all hope in it. Finnegan is not about to surrender himself to you and that gaggle of liquor-soured Indians. As I said, I have little experience with such matters, but one hardly requires a profound understanding to know you will all most likely die here."

Duran swallowed and turned a bit pale. "He will surrender himself. He has no other choice to guarantee your safety."

"Major, you have consistently demonstrated your inability to confront Finnegan in a manly fashion. Do you honestly believe he will seriously consider you capable of harming me? Even if you possessed the blunt stupidity for such an act, at the very least you must understand it will only function to increase Finnegan's anger with you. Are you intent on being skinned or burned instead of simply shot? As you said, I am what he holds most dear. What do you believe the proper penalty might be for the man who has separated us on the eve of our wedding?"

Duran swallowed and grew more pale. "You cannot divert me with idle threats, Miss Meagher. I do not frighten so easy."

"Major Duran, it is not me you should be frightened of."

FINNEGAN WAS NOT OVERLY kind in his treatment of Mr. Heth. He had pulled the length of rawhide quite tight when he had affixed the shotgun to the back of the chubby guide's head. Heth seemed knowledgeable enough regarding firearms that he was most uncomfortable with the chambered and cocked shotgun so perilously attached to him.

Admittedly, Finnegan was also a bit rough with the man as he prodded him toward the camp, the shotgun in one hand and his Remington revolver in the other. The group, including both James and Wilson, stopped on the edge of the camp just inside the trees. James leaned toward Finnegan and whispered, "Are you certain you do not want that shotgun easier to wield?"

"If I have need of it, I will simply decapitate this loathsome fool and it will tug free quite nicely." The gunman shrugged. It will only be a momentary annoyance once his head is out of the way."

"Damn you both, I don't deserve this." Heth had sweat standing out on his skin, despite the cold.

"I have seen far worse visited upon horse thieves. You should know better than to keep company with them, Mr. Heth." Finnegan motioned to the camp in front of them. "I will enter and announce myself. When we discover which tent conceals Molly...well, once we learn her disposition so that we might avoid her with our fire, I see little reason to leave any of them breathing. If you would be so kind as to offer assistance from this tree line, I would greatly appreciate it, Alexander."

"Might we not, at least, attempt negotiating a settlement?

From what I have witnessed, those Ute Indians appear to have little better than a passing understanding of events. I cannot say as they should be shot simply because they found themselves momentarily drunk enough to follow a fellow idiot such as Major Duran."

"Oh, very well then." Finnegan let out a long sigh. "I will give them the opportunity to surrender or flee, does that suit you?"

The outlaw held up one hand. "That is all I would ask. I do not know how many Ute Indians walk the earth, but I had never heard of one until I arrived here, and it seems a terrible shame to shoot too many men of a breed one never knew existed."

"Well, I..." Finnegan shook his head and jerked Heth over into line to walk toward the camp. "I cannot truly say as spending time with you has made your actions or inclinations any easier to comprehend, Alexander. We can discuss the matter further in a few minutes." He pushed Heth out from the tree line and the two men slowly slogged through the nearly knee-deep snow toward the collection of tents. Only two Utes still lingered by the fire, while the rest had opted to crawl inside the army bivouacs. When they were only about thirty yards from the campfire, Finnegan gave the shotgun a tug and brought Heth's forward progress to a halt. The tired Utes had still not taken notice of them. "Townsend Duran!" The two Utes leapt up, holding their rifles, but seemed fairly stumped as to what they ought to do next. A handful of other Utes began to slowly emerge from the tents. Some were armed, others appeared to have lost interest in conflict. "Townsend! You bade me to follow, and now I am here. Come out and face up to what you have wrought." Finnegan ducked behind Heth just a bit.

Instead of the burly form of Major Duran, a far more

slender shape passed between the tent flaps. Molly stretched out her back and offered a small wave to Finnegan. "Ah, I see you have gained possession of that reprobate, though what use for him you might have I cannot imagine. He would make a very poor pet."

Finnegan turned with Heth so as to better cover the tent. "Molly, move away from there. Go to the right and then walk to the trees. You will find Mr. James there."

"You have brought Mr. James to assist in my rescue." She nodded and grinned. "If a woman lives long enough, she will eventually see all manner of things, I suppose."

"Molly, move away from there." Finnegan's voice had a quite aggressive edge to it.

"Oh, you need not bother about flinging bullets into the tent, Finnegan. Major Duran no longer resides within." She turned to the side of the tent and pulled one support rope free while kicking the center support out with her foot. The canvas structure collapsed into the snow and lay flat. "As you can see."

Finnegan stood to his full height and jerked back on the shotgun hard enough to break the rawhide tethered around Heth's neck. "No longer resides? Where the hell has he gotten off to?"

Heth rubbed the red mark forming around his throat. "Hey, that smarted."

"Hush, you jackass." Finnegan turned back to Molly. "He has fled?"

The schoolmarm threw her hands in the air. "We were discussing the various sad fates that awaited him upon your arrival and it would seem his sober mind chose discretion as the better part of valor." She let her hands drop. "He rather unceremoniously crawled under the back flap of the tent and begged me not to alert the others as to his departure." She began walking forward to Finnegan as the Utes watched. "I suppose if you had not arrived by morning, I would have explained matters to these gentlemen and taken a horse to return with." Molly patted the gunman on one shoulder when she stood next to him. "Difficult trip?"

"Little more than an inconvenience, lass." Finnegan motioned to the picketed herd of horses. "Townsend truly crawled off and left the rest of these to fend for themselves?"

"As I live and breathe, Finnegan. It was a somewhat less-than-sterling display of manhood." She grinned.

"Well, now, what in bloody hell..." Finnegan paused, seeing that Jack Wilson now stood beside him. "Jack, why are you not back with Mr. James?"

"I grew restive waiting. It is lovely to see you again, Molly. Are you quite alright?" Wilson smiled at her.

"Is she quite alright?" Finnegan holstered his Remington and rubbed his eyes. "Do you not know her condition? Did the good Lord Almighty not take the time to inform you as to her health and disposition?"

Molly put her hands on her hips. "Well, you are in a mood. Jack only means to be polite. What has you so very aggravated?"

"Aggravated indeed, dear Molly. First you are kidnapped by a man I held to be a friend. Next, I am forced to follow the fool through many a weary mile of snow and cold, only to discover that the coward has fled yet again. Lastly, I cannot pursue the imp further as I must see to these stolen horses and the rest of this varied trash. I say, if a man was in need of an excuse to be aggravated, this day I could offer up more than a few fine specimens."

One of the Utes wandered over to Heth and they exchanged a few words. Wilson walked to the two men, and they exchanged a few more. Wilson turned to Molly and

Finnegan. "Mr. Gilhooley, this man wishes to know if I am still willing to exchange my booha for Miss Meagher."

Finnegan groaned. "Explain to the gentleman that he is no longer in possession of Miss Meagher. Given the current arrangement, I am willing to grant him the opportunity to get the hell out of here in due haste and nothing more. If he remains, I will likely kill him and his associates out of simple meanness." The look on Finnegan's face transcended the Ute man's ability to understand English. He grunted a few words toward Finnegan and began turning to leave. "Yes, well, and lovely meeting you, sir."

As the Ute was turning, Heth made a surprisingly quick move and pulled the pistol from the man's belt. At the same moment, he slipped an arm around Wilson's neck and pressed the Colt up to the shaman's temple. "You'll not be taking me to hang today, Pinkerton." He began pulling Wilson back toward the tents and the fire. "I have heard all Mrs. Culbertson's clucking about your time with Stuart's Stranglers. I'll not add to your tally, bastard."

Finnegan cupped his forehead in one hand. "Mr. Heth, if there was ever a man more deserving of a bullet and yet not nearly worth the price of a cartridge, I have not had the misfortune to meet him." Finnegan brought his head back up and watched as the guide slowly dragged the prophet back. "Mr. Heth, there is no need for this stupidity. Release Wilson and be on your damn way. I could not care less."

"You lie. All you damn Pinkertons lie. Just like Duran and any damn officer I ever met lied. You wish to shoot me in the back as I attempt to depart."

Finnegan sighed. "Mr. Heth, do not vex me. It has been a long and wearing day, and I am not of a mind to suffer fools."

"You will not do a damn thing so long as I have got your messiah here. Now, listen..." Heth was not able to finish his thought. As he spoke, Finnegan drew his Remington revolver and shot the man near directly between the eyes. Heth went instantly limp and collapsed down into the snow. Wilson stood, dumbfounded, a strange, far-off look on his face.

"Finnegan!" Molly smacked him in one arm. "Are you mad? You might have hit Jack. You may have killed him!"

"Molly, there is not a chance in all creation that I could have killed Mr. Wilson. He has told me on several occasions that the Lord our God Himself has guaranteed the man's continued existence many a long year into the future." Finnegan holstered the Remington. "Although, I must say, your damned prophet appears awfully shocked." Finnegan grinned. "Jack, dear boy, did that ball come near you?"

Wilson cleared his throat and came back to his senses somewhat. "My apologies, Finnegan. I have never witnessed a gun firing from that particular angle. It was unsettling enough that even I momentarily forgot the good Lord's proclamation."

"As you well might." Finnegan turned to the assembled Utes, who were all, more or less, staring at the scene in amazement. "Jack, tell these daft buggers to be gone, and on their own damn stock while they're about it. If I have to shoot one more man over Mr. Dyer's miserable assortment of glue bags, I swear I will renounce my vocation join the priesthood."

"This is not the time for that sort of jocularity." Molly gave him a very judgmental look.

"My apologies, my dear. I sometimes forget that this sort of behavior is not common to one and all."

In an unusually coarse tone, Wilson passed the message on to the Utes. As they made their dejected way to their own obviously malnourished animals, Wilson nodded his approval. "This is very fine, Finnegan. Now you and Molly can be wed, and I may continue to pass my visions on to those who seek my council."

"Yes, the loss of your magic beans to those renegades was always my primary concern." Finnegan looked behind him and saw James approaching. The outlaw had an inscrutable look on his face. "What has you so puzzled, Alexander?"

James stopped and put his Winchester over one shoulder. "I am more than a bit befuddled, Finnegan. I see the Indians have departed, you killed poor, dumb Heth, and I never did see Duran. What in hell has transpired here?" He looked to Molly. "Oh, very fine to see you in safety and good health, ma'am."

"Marvelous to see you as well, Mr. James." She offered a small curtsy.

Finnegan flung one hand out toward the tents and abandoned fires. "Duran fled before we arrived, the Utes proved spineless, and poor, dumb Heth simply pressed the matter too far. I offered him every opportunity to turn tail and run."

James scratched one side of his face. "I couldn't see too well from the trees, but it looked like Wilson was a might close to the fat man when you fired."

"What is the use in enjoying the protection of God if He will not consistently deflect revolver balls?" Finnegan motioned to Dyer's herd of misappropriated horses. "Come now. We have a long evening ahead of us driving these nags back to..."

James sighed. "I would suppose the Wilson Ranch is the best we can hope for. We cannot get them to Greenfield in the dark and the snow." He glanced around the country they found themselves in. "Are you of the opinion that Major Duran has taken flight and left the vicinity? He was in possession of that rather fine rifle when last we saw him, Finnegan."

The gunman sighed. "It may be that he has taken to concealing himself in some of these damned rocks and he may attempt to remove me from the saddle as we make our way." He shrugged. "Or there may be any of a hundred other damned fools lingering about wishing to murder you or I. I do believe Major Duran has fled in earnest, but that does not mean he took all our other foes with him. I suppose men such as us must run the hazard every day. As much as we would have the past be forgotten, it is difficult to get others to join in."

James shivered and drew his coat collar closer. "Yes, well, now that you mention it, I suppose I have been a bit too cavalier roaming these hills, as well. Probably best we get back to civilization so that I might resume hiding in the hotel."

Chapter 14

GREENFIELD, NEVADA

February 1st, 1890

DYER MARCHED INTO MRS. CULBERTSON'S DINING ROOM and quite unceremoniously slapped down a yellow telegram sheet. He grinned at Finnegan and flicked the snow from the shoulders of his coat. "Well, I was beginning to think that those damn railroad men would never get that telegraph line working again, but wonders never cease. When it started spittin' again this morning, that message came through."

Finnegan slowly picked up the paper and read the short missive. He turned to Frank James, smiling. "Molly's father sends word that I do, in fact, have his permission to marry his daughter, on the condition that we honeymoon in the environs of Minnesota so that he may once again lay eyes on the wayward lass." Finnegan chuckled. "All things considered, it was far more labor winning over the affections of that gentleman than it was the woman."

James shrugged. "It oftentimes is, my friend."

Finnegan sipped his coffee. "All I lack now is to locate a proper ring for the young maiden. Wedding bands are not among Mr. Dyer's inventory."

The dry goods man shook a finger at Finnegan. "Them damn things are as dangerous as pistols, and I would venture the same dire warning applies to both. If you keep one on hand, you will be tempted to use it."

James chuckled and slowly pushed back his chair. "An intriguing sentiment, Mr. Dyer. Please excuse me for a moment. I believe I can remedy your difficulty, Finnegan." The outlaw disappeared for a few minutes and then returned holding a small gold band. "I doubt it is correctly sized, but it should suffice in the short term."

Finnegan took the small band from him and held it up to the light of the kerosene lamp. "For what reason would you possibly be in possession of such an item, Alexander?"

"I purchased it -- legitimately, I might add -- from Cole Younger when he was shy of funds part way through one of our tours." James shook his head. "Some men never learn to manage their money."

"Cole Younger?" Finnegan arched an eyebrow. "You expect me to wed my true beloved with Cole Younger's wedding ring? The blackguard nearly shot me once."

"I doubt it was the man's own property. Given Cole's various predilections, he likely filched it from some tart, which would explain why he was short of funds."

"So, then, this would be a whore's stolen wedding ring?"

James clapped the gunman on the shoulder. "Finnegan, it is a gold band, and the only you are likely to find in this damned wilderness. Accept it as my wedding gift to you. Do not concern yourself with its history. A man makes his own luck." James resumed his seat at the table and sipped his coffee. "What I have been puzzling over is your lack of a priest. I am under the impression that you papists cannot do much of anything without one of your black clad snake oil salesmen close at hand."

"I have conjured a suitable solution to that problem, Alexander. Do not worry yourself about it." Finnegan tossed his napkin down onto the breakfast table and pushed his chair back. "Very well then -- with permission granted, I go to collect my fair lady." He turned to Dyer. "Would it be possible to have the cobwebs cleaned out of the church and a fire kindled within by the afternoon?"

"Oh, that ought to be possible." The dry goods man shook Finnegan's hand. "Go collect your bride."

As Mrs. Culbertson wiped tears from her eyes, the various residents of Greenfield, both those who lived there and those who were merely passing through, assembled in the town's small church. Jack Wilson came forward, holding the Bible he had been gifted years earlier. Thanks to Molly, he had only recently become able to read it for himself. He smiled at the couple. "Thank you for allowing me to join the two of you." He looked almost as if he might cry. "It is very kind of you, Finnegan."

"Yes, well, I have not been presented with an abundance of alternatives." The gunman smiled back. "You will, of course, require a minor adjustment before the ceremony." Finnegan glanced toward James. "Surely, Alexander, you must be familiar with the tradition that allows ship captains to marry those of various faiths?"

"I am. Do you propose to wait to be wed until the Navy sees fit to give Jack here his own vessel?"

"I would submit that a captain is a captain, and to otherwise split hairs is a waste of time." Finnegan turned back to Wilson. "Raise your right hand, Jack." The prophet complied. "Jack Wilson, by the power invested in me by

Allan Pinkerton, I hereby bestow on you the rank and position of Captain in the Pinkerton Agency, along with all the duties and privileges that accompany it." Finnegan grinned. "You may lower your hand, Captain Wilson."

"Captain Wilson." The prophet's voice was full of wonderment. "I will do my best to be a good Captain, Finnegan." He cocked his head to one side. "Are you a captain?"

"Now that you mention it, I am not fully certain what position I currently hold, although I have been a captain here and there over the years. I suppose I never gave much wight to such things." He looked to his patiently waiting bride. "Yes, at all events, now that you are properly fit out to link various parties in matrimony, I suppose we best begin."

Wilson opened his Bible to the sheet of paper he had prepared the night before. "Dearly beloved, we are gathered here before Almighty God...

Chapter 15

SEATTLE, WASHINGTON

March 18th, 1890

MAJOR TOWNSEND DURAN EMERGED FROM THE STEAM room of the Imperial Baths and found a towel on a nearby rack. He pressed the dry cloth to his face and could feel it pulling the moisture from his skin. The towel he wore around his midsection was doused with water from the steam bath, and he could feel the cold creeping into it on the outside of the sauna. He would miss such civilized contraptions as steam baths in the north. The Yukon and surrounding environs were a wild unsettled land, full of promise and opportunity. Still, there is much to be said for the trappings of civilizations and the Major would lament their absence.

He brought the towel away from his face and turned to the small room where the lockers were located. Each locker featured a small inset area where a curtain could be drawn, allowing a fellow a modicum of privacy as he changed back into his clothes. Duran found the cubby he had made use of and pulled back the curtain to find the tiny space empty. His clothes, wallet, and Colt's revolver were all missing. He simply stared at the bare bit of bench for a moment, before sighing and slowly turning to face the steam bath.

"Hello, Finnegan. It would seem I have been lingering in this fine town too long."

The gunman shrugged. "Barring the incessant stink of fish, I can easily understand how a man might settle in here. Although, the varied comforts offered here are the cause of my having found you."

The Major did his best to appear poised, which is difficult for a man caught in nothing but a towel. "The draws on the family fortune?"

"The railroads may be more infested with Pinkerton men than the banks, but only slightly. Your family accounts are somewhat of an open book to the agency, and it was not difficult to determine you were likely in the vicinity of the bank the funds were being transferred to. You might have saved yourself a great deal of trouble by simply switching hotels from time to time, young Townsend."

The soldier curled one side of his mouth into a smile. "You cannot be assured of a seat in the restaurant if you are not a guest of the hotel. They have a French chef who is beyond compare, Finnegan. It is always difficult to say what thread a man's life may hang by, but after all those years of salt pork in Army forts, I am somewhat willing to die for a decent meal."

Finnegan nodded and withdrew a cigar. He sparked the match off his belt buckle, never once taking his eyes off Duran. "If you would not mind, I have a few questions before we see to the conclusion of this."

Duran sighed. "Nothing else requires my attention, presently."

"My various assailants in and around Greenfield, they were all in your employ?"

Duran nodded. "Yes, although to say they accosted you for the money would be a gross exaggeration. Oh, I had nothing to do with that boy shooting you. That was purely happenstance of your own making."

Finnegan puffed. "And the negros who attempted to lynch Mr. James?"

Duran laughed. "Again, only a humorous coincidence. Honestly, Finnegan, how could a man contrive such a thing?"

"I rather assumed as much, but it cannot hurt to confirm such things. I thought there was a small chance you were more cunning than I gave you credit for." He knocked ash down to the tiled floor. Now, on to matters of more importance. Who informed you of my involvement regarding your father's demise?"

"Ah, yes, now we come to that." Duran lowered himself onto a nearby bench. "You are truly a creature of habit, Finnegan. All that has transpired, and you can think only of your own vengeance. You will have yours, and I shall never have mine. I suppose that is the way events were meant to be."

Finnegan removed his hat and hung it on a hook near him on the wall. With that done, he scratched his head. "You are a damned odd fellow, Townsend. Why in hell are you so very set on revenging yourself on me, at any rate? If you so wished to visit vengeance upon a responsible party, why not Allan Pinkerton, or even the elder agent who accompanied me on the assignment? I was barely more than a child myself when I shot your father down, while he was damn well desperately trying to shoot me, I might add. The man was a drunk and a traitor to his country. Aside from your mother, I never met a person who claimed differently. Why did you choose me for your vendetta?"

Duran shrugged again. "Allan Pinkerton is dead. The

elder agent who accompanied you is dead. I was only recently informed of your deed. I suppose I became somewhat fixated on the matter." He cocked his head to one side. "You, of all men, must be able to sympathize."

Finnegan puffed again. "I do have some experience with such matters. Who informed you?"

"I received a letter. The document informed me of your role in my father's death and little else. I cannot say who penned the missive, but the list of suspects is surely a short one. Who could have knowledge of such things, Finnegan? I would say, by all appearances, your employers have determined you are no longer in keeping with the image the firm wishes to present to the public. They are currently the defenders of private property far and wide. The old crew of assassins and bushwhackers will have to go."

Finnegan chuckled. "If you were more familiar with the Pinkerton offspring, you might find yourself less shocked by this betrayal. I am certain whichever one of them is responsible considered it little more than an intelligent business necessity."

"I have been betrayed by generals often enough to appreciate such things, Finnegan. As a man who has been in your boots, I sympathize." He rubbed his face. "I should also take a moment to apologize for the hirelings I sent after you. It was a cowardly act. I can only say that I made many decisions while inebriated. My career in the Army has not panned out as I might have hoped, and I have been finding greater solace in drink than a man ought to." He sighed. "You are a better man than I ever gave you credit for being, Finnegan." The soldier took in a deep breath and stood. "Very well, then. You have learned what you wished to know, and I have made what passes for amends. Let us finish matters." He closed his eyes. "When you are ready, sir."

Finnegan groaned and knocked more ash from his cigar. "Open your eyes, you daft bastard. I am not about to shoot an unarmed fool in a towel."

Duran swallowed and slowly opened his eyes. "You do not intend to kill me?"

"I have given my word to my wife that I will not, unless circumstances require it, of course." Finnegan shook his head. "She assures me that you are nothing more than a blithering idiot hell bent on his own misfortune."

"She is a fine lady. Please thank her for me."

"She is no less than your saving grace this day, Townsend." The gunman rolled his cigar between his fingers. "What is your intention coming to this harbor town? You surely did not arrive here with only a series of square meals in mind."

"I..." Duran slowly sat down on the bench once more. "My intention is to wait until the thaw and travel north. Alaska or one of the British possessions. I have heard wonderous stories about the country and the possibilities."

"This would make for a fine starting point." Finnegan plucked his hat from the hook. "I suppose I may assume you no longer bear a grudge against me? You will not get into your cups and resume this foolishness this evening?"

Duran shook his head. "I have been cured of that fixation, Finnegan. I am not of your kind, I suppose. I...well, it would seem I simply do not possess the wherewithal for murder."

"It is a singular skill." Finnegan gave the young officer a sad smile. "I think it best if we do not see each other again, Townsend. I wish you luck in the frozen north, I truly do."

Duran cleared his throat. "Thank you, Finnegan. You have been better to me than I was to you."

"All men err, Townsend. It is how we correct those errors

that makes us either good or bad men. As I said, I wish you luck."

A Look at: Trample Over the Dead (Finnegan Gilhooley 5)

He thought the fighting was behind him. Then the Pinkertons came calling.

It's 1892, and former Pinkerton agent Finnegan Gilhooley is ready to settle down. With a new wife and plans for a quieter life, he's chasing down old debts to secure his pension—and his future. But peace is short-lived. When William Pinkerton demands one final assignment in exchange for that pension, Finnegan finds himself back in the fray.

Tasked with guarding industrialist Henry Clay Frick during a rising wave of labor unrest, Finnegan is thrust into the heart of a storm. As tensions boil over in Homestead, Pennsylvania, he faces not only the fury of striking workers but the darkest moment in the Pinkerton Agency's violent legacy.

In a war between capital and labor, where does a gunman stand?

AVAILABLE APRIL 2026

Thank You

Thank you for taking the time to read *As the Crucible Closed.* If you enjoyed it, please consider telling your friends or posting a short review. Word of mouth is an author's best friend and much appreciated.

Thank you.
R.F. Ryan

About the Author

R.F. Ryan lives in Montana with his beautiful wife and comparatively ugly gun collection. When he is not writing, he can usually be found out in the woods hunting. He's currently retired from a variety of odd jobs that have interfered with his free time, including (but not limited to): ranch hand, green chain operator, bounty hunter, private investigator, and process server. Robert has written over twenty books in multiple genres, both fiction and non-fiction, and has penned hundreds of outdoors-focused articles for websites and print magazines.

About the Author

[illegible]

www.ingramcontent.com/pod-product-compliance
Lightning Source LLC
LaVergne TN
LVHW040215110826
845146LV00005B/1291

* 9 7 9 8 8 9 5 6 7 5 8 6 1 *